HEARTBEAT

A COURAGEOUS LOVE NOVEL

TERREECE M. CLARKE

LIFESLICE MEDIA

Heartbeat Chapter by Chapter playlist on
Apple Music or Spotify and Review Trigger
Warnings

This is dedicated to everyone with enough optimism to dream and enough courage to love.
While cynics assert both are for the naïve and foolish, the wise know they are the key to life and longevity.

Dream wide awake, love courageously and read voraciously.

CONTENTS

"In all the world, there is no heart for me like yours. In all the world, there is no love for you like mine."

— MAYA ANGELOU

HEARTBEAT CHAPTER PLAYLIST

1. DON'T LET THE BEARS EAT ME

1. Ave Maria by P!nk

2. Crazy by Cabu

2. CONVENTIONAL LITTLE DICK METHODS

1. Bohemian Rhapsody by Queen

3. GOT HER

1. Way Down We Go by Kaleo

2. Creep by The Voice Kimberly Nichole

4. APPLES. ORANGES

1. Nuvole Bianche by Ludovico Einaudi

5. NO CRINKLES

1. Beautiful by Meshell Ndegeocello

6. I'VE BEEN WRONG BEFORE

1. Question of U by Prince

7. THIS MAYA WOMAN

1. Crush by Yuna

2. You're the One I Want by Alex and Sierra

8. I BET THEY LIVE FOR THAT FACE

1. Dirt off Your Shoulder by Jay Z

2. Bag Lady by Erykah Badu

9. WHAT THE HELL WAS THAT?

1. Refuse by Kevin Garret

2. Wicked Game by James Vincent

10. LOOKS LIKE WE'RE HAVING BREAKFAST TOGETHER

1. Butterflies by Michael Jackson

11. TESTOSTERONE ALL UP

1. Thieves in the Temple (Remix) Prince | The Purple Medley by Prince can only be found online - YouTube specifically and for purchase through the Prince Estate.

12. HELLUVA HUSTLE

1. A Song for You by Donny Hathaway

13. BEARS. THEY'RE ASSES

1. Lay Me Down (feat. John Legend) by Sam Smith

2. Nothing Else Matters by Lauryn Hill

14. DO YOU TRUST ME?

1. Sweetest Taboo by Sade

2. Whenever, Wherever, Whatever by Maxwell

3. Thank You by Dido

4. Your Hands by Marsha Ambrosius

15. CUTENESS IS INSURMOUNTABLE

1. Leave the Door Open by Bruno Mars, Anderson .Paak, Silk Sonic

2. Lose Control by Ledisi

16. HIS TENDER CARE

1. Red Dust by James Vincent McMorrow

17. GIVE ME PEACE

1. Hard by Rihanna

18. NO!

1. Crawling by Linkin Park

19. THIS IS A COURTESY

1. Desperado by Rihanna

20. PEACHY KEEN

1. Golden by Jill Scott

21. STAY WITH ME A LITTLE LONGER

1. Heathens by Twenty One Pilots

22. YOU FORCED MY HAND

1. Bitch Better Have My Money by Rihanna

23. OBELISKS

1. Crazy by Aerosmith

24. WHAT ARE YOU ASKING ME

1. Those Sweet Words by Norah Jones

2. The Point of It All by Anthony Hamilton

3. Scandalous by Prince

25. IT MEANS YOU'RE MINE

1. I Belong to You by Lenny Kravitz

26. EVERYTHING YOU ARE

1. Issac Albeniz, Opus 165, Prelude

61. LOSS

1. Romeo and Juliet Theme by Hirotaka Izumi

63. SUNSHINE

1. Hold Back the River by James Bay

I

DON'T LET THE BEARS EAT ME

MAYA

"Nationwide coverage my ass."

Maya checked her brand-new smartphone one more time. Siri was still "thinking" about her location. After watching the maps app churn for a few seconds more, she threw the phone back onto the passenger seat of her deep blue pickup truck. She watched as it ricocheted off the door and bounced to the floor.

Good thing I splurged on the all-weather, super-tough phone case.

She looked at the multi-colored, squiggly lines on the map she'd spread out on the hood of her pickup before looking up and down the lonely, dark mountain road. It was after midnight; she could only see just past the lights of the truck before darkness pressed in on all sides. Pine, spruce, and other trees she barely remembered the names of grew thick on each side of the road. With each twig crack and branch creak, her panic grew.[1]

Maya bit her lip nervously and shifted from one foot to the other to stay warm. She also hoped she would appear to be a moving, less appealing target for whatever monsters lurked in the darkness beyond the tree line. The wind increased, making her wish she'd bought a heavier coat.

An Ohio girl by birth, she was used to the cold. This thin air, closer-to-God-therefore-closer-to-his-weather-position on the side of a mountain, threw her for a loop. Flat open plains ... the city ... hell, the French countryside was more familiar. And although it was mid-April here, snow stubbornly dusted the ground. She hoped she would make it to her destination before more arrived.

Why she found herself on the side of a Colorado mountain this late was too painful to think about, but soon she would be safe. Money couldn't buy her more time, but it bought a little protection, a new name; and a decent new start in a place where no one would think to look for her.

Only her best friend, Shay, knew how to reach her. And with cell signals spotty in this area, it could be days or weeks before she had reliable cell service and internet access. She figured it worked out because, if confronted, Shay could honestly say she hadn't heard from her.

Maya glanced at the wrinkled map again, then looked up the road. The view and her lack of navigational skill hadn't changed. She shivered. There was nighttime in the city, then there was this wild, mountain night. It felt... alive. Like it wanted to overtake her.

"Shit. I'm going to die of hunger and get eaten by a mountain lion on the back roads of Colo-freaking-rado," she muttered, rubbing her mittened hands together.

"Maya Angel Wal—, no Maya Anderson." She corrected herself. "Get it together. You will not die on this stupid mountain. You have a lot to live for now." Placing her hand over her stomach, she deliberated her next move.

Climbing back into the truck, she threw on the flashers. She'd wait for a couple of hours and if no help came, she'd go modern survivalist —getting snow to melt for water 'n such. Maya watched a ton of survival and prepper TV shows in the past, usually after work, while waiting for Griffin to get home from whatever the hell he did all day and half the night.

Naked and Afraid was her favorite, and she spent hours in front of the TV watching people waste away while she ate junk food. The blurred private parts and triumphant animal eating combined with personal sniping made for great TV. The shows also taught valuable life lessons like: bug bites on your cooch could happen (a level of hell she never wanted to experience); and it is important to balance your energy output with your available resources.

"Eventually someone will come along who is not a bear or an ax murderer and tell me where the hell to go."

Ten minutes later, a matte black Range Rover rolled by and pulled in front of her. She tensed as the door opened. Out unfolded one of the biggest men she'd ever seen in real life. At least six feet six inches tall, with massively broad shoulders and chest, close-cropped hair, and a stride that showed he was completely comfortable with his body and knew how to use it. He wore jeans, work boots, a white long-sleeved tee, and one of those puffy vests everyone west of the Mississippi seemed to own.

"Welp. I'm dead." She slid her hand underneath the passenger seat and flicked open the small black box partially hidden under it.

Just in case.

As he walked into the brightness of her headlights, something oddly familiar struck her. The man was handsome, but more surprisingly, he was Black. Maya didn't think there were many Black people in the Colorado mountains doing mountain-type shit, but here he was. A giant Black man on the side of a mountain, presumably on his way to do mountain-type shit. Lighter-skinned, he looked racially mixed, and she couldn't shake the thought she'd seen him somewhere. She braced as he entered her space.

When he bent slightly to see into her high truck window, she could see his light brown eyes clearer and took note of his runway-ready face.

"Need help?" he asked with a deep, rumbly voice. It was all bass, all man, and most women, including her friend Shay, would have been already naked by now.

"Um ... yeah. I'm headed to a town called Rough Ridge, but I'm not sure where I am. I passed the last gas station a while back and I didn't want to keep going the wrong way deeper into mountain-land," she said, waving her hand toward the road, "and run out."

He stared at her for a moment.

"Follow me." And he turned to walk away.

Okaaay ... brotha' doing a caveman thing. She lowered the window a scooch more and raised her voice.

"Yeeaah ... not following a strange man into the woods brotha'. No offense. Can you tell me how to get there and I'll be on my way? I mean ..." She shrugged.

He stopped and turned to her, chuckling a bit, and gave her a half-smile. He had an arresting smile, too. The passenger side of his Range Rover opened and out hopped a pregnant woman in three-inch heels. She smiled big and hustled her way over to the truck. Maya checked his left hand.

Dang, Shay would be so disappointed and would plot to steal this woman's husband, she thought with a smile. Wearing that smile, she greeted the giant man's pretty wife.

"Hey there! Are you okay? I saw Caine laughing, and I had to come and see what was so funny." She smiled brightly.

Hmmm.

Either "Caine" laughing was a big deal, or she wanted to see who was amusing her husband. *She must get that a lot.*

She had nothing to worry about. Maya wasn't interested in the mountain man-god before her or any men. Maybe ever. She'd already stocked up on a lifetime supply of batteries for her vibrator. Her smile, however, made Maya relax. The bling on her finger, sleek hair, and heels screamed high-maintenance chick. She didn't always get along with that type of woman, or most women, so being friendly was a good start.

"I'm headed to Rough Ridge and neither the GPS nor the map has been successful in getting me there and—Caine?" He nodded. "Caine told me to follow him, but ... " She trailed off.

"You're not in the habit of following random men to destinations unknown." The woman finished with a laugh and nod. "Well, most women would follow Caine anywhere, but I see your point."

It was Maya's turn to laugh until they heard a small call of "momma" from the backseat of the couple's SUV.

"Shoot that's Gabriella. Listen, we can show you the way. It's where we live. Where are you staying?"

"The Rough Ridge Hotel, I hope," Maya said with a shrug. "I was supposed to check-in hours ago."

"Oh, Ms. Shirley is already in bed by now."

Shit. Ms. Shirley? This is like an old-timey TV show around here. "Okay, so where is there a motel or hostel?"

Caine shook his head and said, "None."

Shit again.

She threw her head back in frustration and blurted at the car roof, "Is there anywhere on this damn mountain where I can avoid bears and mountain lions for the night?"

"Yes," the woman said, cutting into Maya's lament. "With us." She smiled bigger and leaned into her husband as he instinctively put his arm around her.

Maya wondered if the woman wasn't just friendly, but crazy as hell. Apparently, her husband Caine thought so too, because he said in a voice low with concern, "Babe."

"Listen—" Maya started.

"Tori."

Of course, she'd have a cute name to match the bubbly personality.

"Tori," Maya started again, "that's real sweet, but it's late, you have no idea who I am and while you both are super attractive, except for that one time in college, I'm not interested in swinging or a ménage à trois."

As soon as she said it, she regretted her loose lips. It was one reason she didn't have many girlfriends and why she fit in with her male contemporaries better.

Tori blinked twice while Caine barked out a loud booming laugh through the quiet night. He had a great laugh and Maya liked it, but not in the way she suspected most women did ... she found it comforting. Tori quickly joined in with a genuine belly laugh and relief washed over Maya. They got her.

She wasn't joking about the college tryst and still had concerns. Maya didn't want to have to fend off a horny couple from the mountains, but at least she hadn't offended them. Watching them laugh together for a few seconds, she decided she liked them. Colorado might be thousands of miles from her old life, but so far, the people were all right.

"What's your name?" Tori asked.

"Maya Anderson," she offered.

"Maya, you're cute, but the only thing we are sharing is our home, where we have a guest room that's perfect for you. There's no place in town open this late, but the bar. We've got plenty of room."

Another cry from Caine and Tori's Range Rover.

"Babe," Caine said.

Tori smiled at her husband, gave Maya a wave, mouthed "you're coming," and sashayed to the SUV. Obviously pregnant, with snow on the ground, she walked in heels like she was born in them.

"Girlfriend is working those heels," Maya said out loud to herself.

"Yeah, she is," Caine said.

Maya turned her head to him in surprise. He had spoken three whole words.

He stopped watching his wife's ass long enough to stare at Maya again.

A chill moved through her like he could see into her soul. It freaked her out.

Defensive, she matched his gaze and said, with a hint of snark, "A picture would last longer."

Grimacing, Maya wondered why she was a perpetual dork. Surely, she could've picked a better comeback. She rolled her eyes slowly and looked back to the SUV ahead of her, thinking her next step through. She had to be careful.

"Okay, I—," she started. But she never finished her thought because flashing lights slid in behind her truck.

Maya weighed the sudden increase in options and issues - Colorado police in the back, polite possible swingers in the front. She reached over and grabbed her brown leather purse. Quickly snapping it closed, she slid the small black box further under the passenger seat. She was so focused on the cops she didn't think to hide her movements from Caine.

Clutching her slim, black wallet tightly in her hand, she prepared herself to sweet-talk her way out of any trouble. She couldn't appear in any system if she wanted to stay under the radar forever, or at least until God himself saw fit to smite those overdue for serious, biblical level, pillar-of-salt-type smiting. While certain her new I.D. would pass scrutiny, the idea of testing it left her stomach in knots. Maybe she was over-reacting.

Maya looked back at Caine, and his posture was alert and ready.

Shit. Maya heard gossip from a few towns back - cops here were heavily involved in messed up stuff. They got caught framing a man for murder, torturing his wife, and ... wait.

That's where Maya knew him from! She'd driven into Colorado and ran straight into Caine Walters, one of the most famous police corruption and abuse cases in the last few years. It had to be about six years ago or so ...so deep in her work she hadn't focused on it much, other than the typical horror, disgust, and resignation.

Clicking back through her mind's eye, she saw the headlines again. He had spent years in jail for a crime he didn't commit. The chief of police and mayor committed the murder and others hid a host of other crimes. Money laundering, strong-arming residents, drugs, if Maya remembered correctly. Caine found evidence against them, and they paid him back by incarcerating him. When their scheme had all come undone, they took Caine's wife and tortured her. The same wife Maya had watched sashay happily to the car ...

Oh, man. It was ill-advised, especially given her current predicament, but she had to give him an out at her expense.

"Um, hey listen. If you want to cut on out, I can deal with the police."

"I'm fine."

Oh man, if it goes down on the side of the mountain, it's going to be all my fault. Maya rubbed her hands together nervously.

Suddenly, Cain relaxed, and she turned to see why.

"Hey Caine," another deep voice rumbled.

Goodness. What is it about the mountains and these vocal cords? Is it the air? She wondered. Low with a smooth tone, the voice made her heartbeat quicken.

Ok, that's weird. Maya forced herself to shrug it off. She obviously was jumpy and tired.

"Lost," Caine said, gesturing in her direction.

Another mountain of a man came up to her door. He didn't wear a uniform. She observed the navy-blue Henley with a white thermal shirt underneath, well-broken in jeans, and one of those police necklaces with the badge like you see on TV. He bent his head to her window and her breath stopped.

[2]*Wow.*

It sounded juvenile, but he had to be the most beautiful man she had ever seen. And he was currently looking back at her.

WTF, Colorado?

The first thing she appreciated was his wild, long hair. It fell past his shoulders. Thick, dark strands with light brown, almost blonde highlights rippled, dipped, and tumbled around his head. Some strands worked together to form waves and others worked against their brethren, striking out in their own dance. It looked like he'd ridden a tornado to their side of the road. No product, no effort, just wild, and that shit *worked* for him.

His straight nose had a minor bump on top, like he had broken it before. It only made his face more handsome... rugged. He had dark brows and a dark goatee rimmed an awesome pair of lips. She could see a hint of a beard shadow, and he had to be as tall and as broad as Caine. His waist didn't taper as dramatically, but it didn't make him any less spectacular.

His best feature were his eyes. Gorgeous green eyes, brilliant even in the dark, and rimmed with dark, straight lashes. Those eyes stared right at her while she had many naughty, wild thoughts.

Jeez, instead of a "Welcome to Colorado" sign, they should have photos of these men with "Welcome to Giant Gorgeous Man Land." Women would come in droves.

All the thoughts went through her head as she stared into the deep green eyes of Officer Hunk. His new name. 'Cause damn.

"Where are you headed?" he asked and drew her attention back to his wonderful mouth.

She took in those white teeth, the goatee, and winced at the pull deep inside her. Instinctively, it clutched her between her ribs, almost suffocating her. She shook her head to lessen the pain and undo the connection from his eyes.

"Huh?"

Brilliant, Maya.

The eyes focused on hers hardened and the friendliness left. He took a sniff. "Have you been drinking?"

She burst out laughing.

She thought he was joking, like she was so much of a dork she must be drunk. Instead of smiling, he said, "Step out of the car please, ma'am."

"Wait, what? No, I haven't been drinking! I don't drink!" she protested. "It's late, I'm tired, lost ... I haven't had a drink since my twenty-first birthday ages ago. I may be a dork, but I'm no drunk."

"Ma'am. I'm going to need you to step out of the car."

Motherfucker.

"Mike, chill," Caine said, stepping in front of the car door.

Well, that was nice.

"Caine, you know I respect you and your family. I'm doing my job," the cop said.

Maya blew past irritated to angry. Normally she could handle a crisis very well, but this was too much. Too much drama right after escaping the hell that waited for her in Ohio. Tightly wound and terrified, she craved a bath and M&M's and so ... she snapped.

"Then go find bears to shoot or rescue a kitten from a tree instead of harassing me! I heard cops here were on the take, but DAMN."

Aaannd ... Too far.

The officer's eyes narrowed as he quickly dialed his phone. "I got a ten-fifty-five at Bears Road mile marker thirty-six. Send backup with a breathalyzer."

Panic set in. They'd arrest her, find the gun, run her prints and realize she wasn't who she said she was. Not only would they incarcerate her, *he'd* find her. With his money, it wouldn't take much to get someone in jail to do what he promised two weeks ago. How many commissary cupcakes would it take to convince someone to "ice" her with a shank made from a bar of soap and a toothbrush?

Normally calm and collected Maya went from zero to eleven as panicked, terrified Maya. She started hearing snatches of his voice, as flashbacks of how his face twisted when enraged streaked across her brain. Then she recalled how serene and detached his face became when the gun fired so close to her head. The stink of gunpowder filled the truck's cab.

His cologne.

His breath.

Suddenly, she was right back at a small bathroom window, praying as she crawled out. She could smell it, smell him, and her body shook. Her chest tightened.

Maya was a lifelong asthmatic and normally kept it under control. After her escape, the panic attacks started. Those triggered her asthma and, of course, she hadn't been in the position to buy a new inhaler before she left town.

Her shoulders drew tight to her ears as she struggled to take air in. She shook so hard each breath in or out came jagged and shallow.

The cop dipped his head again and must have noticed her eyes wide and panicked as she shook uncontrollably.

"Can't breathe," she gasped. "Can't. Breathe." Each word more painful than the last.

Caine and the officer moved with such speed if she hadn't been struggling for breath, she would've had time to register shock. Caine snatched open the door, and the officer reached in to undo Maya's seatbelt.

He turned her to him and placed his hands over hers.

"Ma'am, are you all right?" he asked, his eyes full of worry and checking her vitals at the same time. "Talk to me, Sunshine."

Sunshine? Now I'm Sunshine.

"Panic. *Wheeze*. ... Panic ... *wheeze* ... Asthma ... asth ... *wheeze*."

The officer called back into dispatch requesting an ambulance for an asthma attack victim and looked Maya in the eyes, placing her hand over his heart. He gently commanded her to relax and breathe with him.

"Feel my heartbeat, Sunshine," he whispered. "Breathe with me slowly." He took a slow breath in and let it out.

Maya tried to relax, but her mind raced with thoughts of arrest, her monster finding her, the bears who could get her while her body lay on the side of the road if she died right there, and what a dick the officer had been until the 'Sunshine' part of the encounter. The officer's voice faded, and she saw spots in front of her eyes. Her right hand still under his, she used her left to grab his shirt, and as she leaned her head on her arm, she whispered,

"Don't let the bears. ... *wheeze* ... eat me ... *wheeze* ... asshole."

And the world went dark.

---

1. Av Maria by P!nk
2. Crazy by Cabu

2

CONVENTIONAL LITTLE DICK METHODS

MAYA

You know when you wake from a nightmare and you're glad it's over? Yeah, that didn't happen.[1]

Maya woke in a freaking hospital room wearing an oxygen mask. Office Hunk sat to her right, a second guy with a badge and a gun standing at the foot of her bed, and, for a reason only God knows, a pissed Caine on her left. The sitting men looked comically too large for the standard hospital chairs, and while amusing, Maya's primary focus was getting her eyes to adjust to the intense sunlight of a new day.

The Colorado sun shone, no... streamed, no... *earnestly blared* through the hospital windows to her left. Her skin chafed against standard issue white hospital linens and when she moved there was the odd plastic foam squish of the hospital bed mattress. The sterile white walls could have been in any hospital in any town - the smells chemical-laced and off-putting.

She hated hospitals.

She'd been a worse asthmatic as a kid and spent a considerable amount of time staring at those same types of walls. The smell and little kids crying always got to her.

She could deal with the IV pokes and the unlimited supply of odd tasting, but addictive orange Jell-O. But the other kids were almost always worse off than her. Asthma never hurt, not like a broken arm or burns. She always felt guilty sitting there with her hidden disease.

The familiar scent of albuterol combined with the cool, damp breeze of the medicine flowed into the mask over her face. Funny, two things she always associated with childhood were the taste and smell of albuterol and M&Ms.

She wore a hospital gown—a weird greyish white with random patterns designed to hide blood and other bodily fluids. Along with the mask, an IV made her ensemble complete - fetching.

She tried to sit up, and that's when she realized they had handcuffed her to the hospital bed.

"You have got to be fucking kidding me," she said through the oxygen mask. The noise of the machine and the mask muffled her voice.

"Ma'am?" the plain-clothes officer at the foot of her bed said.

Maya sighed, used her free hand to pull off her mask, and looked him in his eyes.

"You. Have. Got. To. Be. Fucking. Kidding. Me." She held up her chained wrist.

The officer looked uncomfortable, which was good, but it wasn't helping. Caine radiated a dangerous level of anger next to her and she refused to even glance in Officer Asshole's - his new name - direction once she saw he'd cuffed her to the bed like an Old West outlaw.

"So. Am I under arrest officially?" Maya asked, barely holding on to the last piece of civility she had left in her. "I already told you I don't drink."

"She's right," a voice said as the curtain around Maya's bed moved and a petite, blond doctor strolled in with her eyes on what Maya assumed was her chart on the iPad in hand. "There is no evidence of alcohol or drugs in Ms. Anderson's results."

"You ran blood tests on me?" Maya growled. Her heart rate galloped as she progressed from pissed to beyond pissed. "What kind of shit show is this?! Take the cuffs off me. Give me my clothes. I'm getting the hell out of this state. You people are crazy."

She threw off the covers and began eyeballing the area around her bed for her clothing.

"Ms. Anderson, please calm down. I need you to finish your breathing treatment, okay? I'm Dr. Megan Kent and the tests are standard procedure with a suspected DUI."

Maya paused for a moment, put the breathing mask back on, and glared at the doctor and the plain-clothes officer, but still wouldn't look at Officer Asshole.

"Detective Sheppard was being cautious," the blonde detective, who identified himself as Detective Paul Cabot, said. "These roads can be dangerous to navigate even when you're not impaired," he added.

Detective Cabot nodded to him, and Officer Asshole rose to take the cuffs off her wrist. His size nearly blocked out the overhead lights as he released her.

His big hand was gentle as he held her wrist and brought the keys to the lock. He slowly, gently removed the cuff and ran his thumb once over the place where it had made a small indentation. It was a thoughtful, almost absent-minded gesture. Maya stared at the path his thumb took. The heat of his touch zipped up from her wrist to buzz at the base of her spine. The clink of the cuffs broke the spell, and she snatched her wrist back from him.

She looked into his eyes.

"Asshole."

Even with the mask around her face, there was no mistaking what she said. His eyes flashed something - was it pain? Whatever it was, all business quickly replaced it. His cop's mask.

Whatever.

"Where are my clothes?"

Dr. Kent cleared her throat nervously. "I'm sorry Maya, we cut your clothing off when you arrived in the ER."

Maya completely snatched the mask off her face and turned her steely eyes to Officer Asshole. She had found that tee in a thrift shop somewhere in nowhere Missouri. The kid at the register didn't know what it was worth, and she didn't have the heart to cheat him, so she paid through the nose for it. It wasn't mint, but it was awesome and a piece of wearable history. She washed it by hand in the sink of whatever no-tell-motel-by-the-bushes she stopped in after every wear.

"That t-shirt was amazing," she said to him.

"Ma'am, I'm sorry. We were trying to save your life," he said quietly. "I can replace your property."

"You can go back in time, to 82, get to the UK for the Hot Space tour and snag a genuine Queen concert tee? While you're there, can you get it autographed by Freddie Mercury?" she asked sarcastically. "Or better yet, use that time machine and NOT arrest me in the first damn place."

She snapped the mask back on. It hurt a little. She played it off.

The officer at the foot of the bed cleared his throat. "We're sorry for the misunderstanding, ma'am. We'll be going," Detective Cabot said, as he conveyed a small sense of sympathy with his intense blue eyes. He gave Caine a nod. Maya glared at him and crossed her arms.

"Ma'am," Officer Asshole said, nodding his head to her.

She flipped him the bird as a reply.

She heard a small chuckle come from Caine and saw maybe amusement briefly in the eyes of Officer Asshole.

"You throw a lot of sass," Caine said.

Sass? What year is this? She figured a small town in the mountains was ten years behind the modern world, but now she wondered if it was more like fifty.

The doctor stood there, looking at Maya expectantly.

"Ms. Anderson, I'd like to discuss your condition further ... privately," she said, eyeing Caine.

Caine looked at Maya again for a long moment and, apparently satisfied with what he saw, rumbled, "I'll be outside." He unfolded himself from the hospital chair, tapping into his phone as he moved.

The doctor looked from him to Maya with curiosity.

"Do you know Caine well?"

"Nope. I met him and his wife on the side of the road last night. I pulled over, lost. They stopped, and so did Officer Asshole. I had a panic/asthma attack and landed here. They seem nice, even if he doesn't say much." She waved her hand toward the door where Caine had disappeared.

Dr. Kent searched Maya's face. She seemed to change her mind about something.

"Ms. Anderson ... "

"Maya."

"Maya ... when you came in, you were unconscious. And during our examination, we found serious recent injuries ... "

Maya closed her eyes.

Shit.

No matter how far I run, he is still fucking up my life.

Maya adopted the armor and demeanor that served her well before she left Ohio. Leaning her head from left to right, she cracked her neck to release tension. She lifted the mask and spoke in a cool and low voice as she looked into Dr. Kent's blue eyes.

"My partner and I disagreed on a key point in our relationship. I tried to leave, he tried to make me stay by using conventional little dick methods," Maya said slowly and clearly. "As soon as it was humanly possible, I ran."

"Did you press charges?" Dr. Kent asked quietly.

"No, though not for lack of trying," she said, shaking her head. "He and his family are powerful, with long money. I learned quickly and brutally you don't fight them. You get the hell away and pray they don't come looking for you."

Dr. Kent nodded; her eyes filled with deep concern. She sat at the foot of Maya's, weighing her next words.

"Maya, you're pregnant."

Maya looked at her hands and her professional facade slipped.

"I know. That's why we disagreed." She shook her head. "And there is no way he will ever lay eyes or a hand on my child."

Dr. Kent reached out and placed her hand over Maya's. "I'm so sorry."

"I'm not," Maya said, jutting out her chin. "It wasn't planned, of course, but the reality of my pregnancy and his reaction opened my eyes to a lot of things, including, instead of falling in love with a normal person, I was involved with a soulless monster." Her face clouded with pain. She paused and hit Dr. Kent directly.

"And now I need to ask you something, Dr. Kent. How secure are your patient files and what will it cost to make them disappear?"

Besides promising Maya that she would have her records placed on the restricted records server, Dr. Kent also got a little more of Maya's medical history, including info about her pregnancy, checked the medications she was currently on for her asthma, and wrote a few prescriptions for her medications and for prenatal vitamins with iron.

"These are like the drugstore brand you already have, but the iron will help with your anemia, which is pretty common in pregnancy," she said. "Although I am concerned about you being dehydrated. You need to be careful, Maya. Take it easy and get plenty to eat and drink. Where are you staying?"

"The Rough Ridge Hotel for now, if I can ever make it there," Maya replied ruefully. "I thought I'd start there and get my bearings, but two minutes into town, I was basically arrested. Not the welcome I hoped for."

"It's a wonderful town," Dr. Kent said, laughing. "Some crazy stuff has happened over the years, but the people here are good people. Give them a chance."

She stood and smiled. "Now let's get you scheduled for a prenatal check-up in the next couple of weeks and get you on your way."

MIKE

"Mike. You wanna explain?" Paul said evenly, his intense blue eyes hidden behind his mirrored aviator glasses. He was several inches shorter than Mike and leaner, but he was one of the best hand-to-hand fighters in the county. He didn't fight the underground circuits anymore, for obvious reasons, but that didn't mean he ever stopped training or adding new skills.

Mike looked over at Paul as they stood outside the hospital. He turned to watch a set of visitors walk past with balloons and flowers.

"Strike a balance, man," Paul continued.

Mike worked the toothpick in his mouth. He was pissed - at himself. He had overreacted. Her lack of focus and bloodshot eyes had made him overly cautious. He also thought he'd detected alcohol. But it was what she said that shook him. *I heard you cops here were on the take, but damn.* After that, Mike reached straight to the rule book, including cuffing her to the bed. It was a shit move, and he knew it.

"You're a good cop, an honest cop. As honest as they come, but you can't be so black and white—"

"The law *is* black and white," Mike bit. "When cops get to thinking there are gray areas, they lose their way."

"The *law* allows for discretion and discernment," Paul replied evenly.

Paul was right, and Mike knew it. The idea she might have risked her life or anyone else's by driving drunk ... The eyes, the sass ... He was wrong. He had to right another wrong.

"I fucked up," Mike retorted. "I'll take care of it. Won't happen again."

Paul watched him closely. And Mike knew what he thought. It had almost been a year since Mike first reached out to come back to town and join the force. Everyone thought he was crazy then and still wondered about him now. If they only knew.

Mike and Paul saw Caine coming out of the hospital on his phone. He ended his call and looked directly at Mike.

"Keys."

It wasn't a request.

"Caine, I have to sign them over to the owner," Mike said.

"Keys."

Mike and Caine were on decent ground since Mike returned to Rough Ridge eleven months ago. Mike gave Caine's family a wide berth and Caine respected Mike for it. Even so, no one interfered with Mike doing his job and he was no one's bitch. Mike stared Caine directly in his eyes and waited.

"I'm driving her home," Caine offered, keeping a thin grip on his patience.

"Where's she staying?" Paul asked, hoping to disarm the two big men in their face-off.

Caine's eyes slid to Paul's.

Mike knew Paul worked undercover to keep Caine's family safe while accumulating evidence on Mike's father. Caine returned the favor, single-handedly saving Paul's 100-year-old family home from a devastating arson attempt. The two shared a history. The jury was obviously still out on Mike despite his respectful overtures.

"Tori wants her at our house," Caine rumbled.

"You sure?" Mike asked. "Didn't she just meet you guys?"

Caine's eyes zeroed back in on Mike's.

"Keys, man."

Paul intervened before the men became even more agitated. "It's all right. Note it in the report."

Mike worked the toothpick in his mouth more, reached in his pocket, and tossed the keys to Caine.

Dr. Kent, an orderly, and Maya in a wheelchair, descended the short wheelchair ramp as Mike watched.

She looks worn out ... and gorgeous. Smooth brown skin that was completely flawless. High cheekbones, full lips, a dimple in her right cheek, and a cute, round nose. She also had a freakin' ton of hair in two-strand twists.

His eyes settled on the hospital logo t-shirt and sweatpants she wore, and he felt ten times worse. Caine took off in a jog across the parking lot to retrieve Maya's truck from a spot where a uniformed officer had parked it at Mike's request.

Mike watched the sun settle on Maya's hair, revealing a pretty mix of auburn and lighter brown natural highlights that sparkled and swirled throughout the twists hanging down her back. He itched to bury his hands in her hair and imagined how it would look fanned out across his pillow.

Caine brought Maya's pickup truck around, stopping in front of them and dragging Mike out of his fantasy.

What the hell is wrong with me?

Maya and the hospital crew arrived next to the officers. Mike spoke first, trying to make it right.

"Ma'am, I am sorry for the trouble this caused you. Is there anything I can do?" Mike said in the low, quiet voice he seemed to prefer to use when speaking to her.

Maya considered him for a moment, then reached out her hand for him to help her out of the wheelchair. He took it instantly, and the sun caught her eyes as she stood. They morphed into a beautiful amber, reminding him of sweet tea in the summer—the kind his mother would steep in the window for hours. His eyes dropped to those luscious, damn near illegal lips as she parted them and spoke.

"You can kiss my ass," she said with a smile that didn't meet her eyes.

Paul choked back a laugh while Mike was both stunned and upset, mainly because it wasn't a genuine request.

Maya put her second hand out for Caine to help her into the passenger side of the truck.

Caine nodded to the group and walked around the front of the truck and drove off.

"Detective Cabot, may I speak with you a moment?" Dr. Kent called.

The orderly wheeled the chair back into the hospital. Dr. Kent and Paul walked out of earshot to talk and Mike stood there a long time watching until the truck drove out of sight.

---

1. Bohemian Rhapsody by Queen

3

GOT HER

ELEVEN MONTHS EARLIER IN ROUGH RIDGE, COLORADO...

MIKE

Mike pulled his Jeep into the lot of the precinct, cut the engine, and stared at the building. Long and single-storied, it had the pale, cement brick build most official buildings did. Fresh flowers in pots dotted the front of the building, neatly lining the manicured lawn. It was an attempt to appear friendly. The town council must have added them as a part of the rebranding effort to restore trust. Outside of a few cosmetic touches, not much had changed in the last twenty years—except his father had nearly destroyed the whole place.

His father, Stan, was dead. Getting mowed down by his own cruiser was poetic and now Mike was back to pick up the pieces.[1]

The darkness in the men of his family had a long reach in Rough Ridge, but that reach ended with his father's death almost six years ago.

He never thought he'd move back, but with his father gone and his sister taking a turn for the worse, he needed to be close to her—and this town kept calling to him. Rough Ridge was a small place full of so much beauty. It had an eclectic vibe which combined a bunch of bikers, mountain people, former service members, a fair number of artists, and now, during a few months of the year, a gentle wave of tourists. Being an hour outside of Denver Metro also gave the town a special appeal. It was far enough to be "rural" without the hassle of not having a mall or airport nearby. Rough Ridge also avoided the drama of development and most of the big city crime spillover other towns experienced.

It was a decent town filled with solid folks who needed public servants they could trust. So, here he was, getting ready to join the same force his father had single-handedly ruined.

"I'm dumb as shit," he said as he gripped the steering wheel, feeling the hard plastic and steel beneath it give a bit under his strength.

Fuck it.

He unsnapped his seatbelt and unfolded his six-foot-six-inch frame out of the dusty, battered, green Jeep. He took a deep breath and strode into the precinct.

"I'm here to see Detective Paul Cabot," Mike said roughly to the first officer he encountered. He worked the toothpick in his mouth and observed her. The woman looked to be in her late twenties, tall, and severe. She wore her dark hair pulled tightly back into a bun with a straight side part that looked like she had meted it out with a ruler.

Instead of a traditional police uniform, she wore what seemed to be Rough Ridge's new standard: a khaki button-down shirt with jeans. The look aimed to relax a leery public, but on her, it screamed control freak. She wore everything starched to perfection. He suspected she was former military, and right now, she stood at her desk, deep into paperwork while sipping her coffee, her travel mug emblazoned with a colorful, hand-drawn design.

She looked up, way up, took him all in, appearing slightly alarmed. Her eyes reached his wild hair, then dropped back to his holster, narrowed. He was used to it. Normally he would have flashed his badge, but he turned it in when he resigned from the Los Angeles Police Department two weeks before.

"One moment." Her voice clipped.

She lifted the black phone to her right, smoothly maneuvering around her coffee cup where others would have knocked it over.

She tapped buttons and waited. "Cabot, there's a—"

"Detective Sheppard."

She stilled at full alert; body ready.

"It's Detective Sheppard," she clipped, "Do you ... "

She listened, never taking her eyes off him or his lips, set in a grim line. Finally, she said tightly, "Go on back, second door on the right."

Her eyes burned a hole through his back as he strode away. He'd have to get used to it. In L.A. people, women, had very specific reactions to him, something more than friendly.

Then again, he was more relaxed there, his smile usually put people at ease. It was harder to smile here, and his name would never put people at ease ... but he'd made the decision and as always, he would stick with it. Mike was home and come hell or deeper hell, he was here to stay.

PAUL CABOT TOOK in the man standing before him. Mike Sheppard had returned after twenty years looking like a wild man.

Paul stood reaching out his hand, slightly apprehensive. Mike took off his mirrored glasses and grasped his hand while his face offered a small smile. Paul relaxed clapping his long-distance friend on the shoulder.

"Have a seat Mike," he said, backing up and sitting at the table. He moved papers off to the side, clearing the space in front of him. Mike registered several large piles of paperwork in front of Paul. Enough to keep the single detective on the Rough Ridge police force more than busy.

"I'm going to level with you," Paul started. "It's good to see you, but are you sure about this?"

Mike sat across from Paul and simply said, "Yep."

"The way they worked this town over," Paul continued as he rolled up the sleeves on his blue plaid shirt, revealing bands of black tattoos on his forearms. "The stuff that happened since,"—he shook his head — "it's not going to be easy," he said, looking Mike in the eye. "Still, you were long gone before it got bad. Folks that can remember that far back know you weren't anything like him."

Paul was the one to tell Mike his father was dead. The first thing Mike said was, "I'm sorry he fucked up your life and I hope the bastard rots in hell." Paul liked him right away. They'd kept in touch ever since, but it floored Paul when Mike called with the news he wanted to come back home and take up a post on the force.

"How's Tammy and Trent?" Mike asked.

Paul broke into a big grin, his eyes lighting up, years easing off his face, and Mike watched a peace come over him.

"They're good, man. Trent is getting bigger every day and that boy can eat," he said with a laugh.

Mike nodded, his eyes smiling. "I'm glad you're good. That your family is good." Mike looked at Paul seriously.

"Mike—" Paul started.

"I have to get used to the carnage Stan left behind." He called his father by his first name. "It's everywhere, on everyone."

"You're not responsible."

"I left everyone behind and gave that monster free rein for years," Mike replied.

"You graduated early to get shot of him, Mike. Two years early. You were a kid."

"I haven't been a kid for a long time. I knew what was happening back here and didn't come back."

"Mike—"

"He destroyed my sister," Mike growled.

Paul looked at Mike for a long time. "How is Rose doing?"

Mike shook his head and looked out the window of Paul's office, not seeing anything. "They gave her six months."

"Jesus man. I ... have you been to see her?

"On my way here. I stayed in Denver for two weeks to be with her and see to shit. She's on so many drugs to keep her mind straight. She's a zombie half the time. The other half, she's lonely as fuck and misses her friends. She doesn't even know dad's dead. Doesn't know she's dying; she's trapped in the past." He shook his head. "Trying to figure out why her hair's falling out and doesn't understand it's the chemo." He looked back at Paul. "I'm here. There's nothing left for me anywhere else. Let's go see your captain."

ELEVEN MONTHS AGO, COLUMBUS, OHIO...

GRIFFIN

"Father. I appreciate your efforts to," —he paused— "pull me into the company fold," Griffin said, using air quotes. "I'm not interested in another Levy building project for the unwashed masses."

"This project is your grandfather's idea, and you WILL be on hand dealing with it. Like it or not, you are a Levy and it's time you pulled your weight and stopped making messes for your mother and me to clean up," Marion Levy said. "This is the type of project you need. It's an opportunity to learn more about real people, take the lead, and grow up. I myself was wild, nothing like you and your friends these days, mind you, but when the time came, I manned up, worked from the bottom in dad's business, met Sharon, and took my place at the helm of the company."

Marion took his place at the long, unconventional conference table of M.A. Wall Designs. The table appeared to be reclaimed wood, bound with woven aluminum and bamboo brackets, and topped with glass. It was a novel design.

Griffin snorted. "Father, I hardly think entering the company as a Senior Vice President with no prior experience; and a Harvard Business degree bought and paid for well before you were born counts as a boot-strapping rags to riches story."

Marion Levy took a hard look at his son, his jaw twitching. His father was doing what he did best - taking inventory of the project before him. In this case, it was him. He could practically hear the calculations of his $300 haircut, $3600 bespoke suit, the $100,000 tan he received chillin' in Dubai for the weekend ... As his father sighed, Griffin discerned he was factoring in a few of the incidentals from the past couple of months. The 250K for a bitch in London, 50k for a bottle girl here, the small incident in Dubai... But in his defense, she OD'd before he'd sunk his dick in. Well, he got a bit of a taste, but it wasn't what he had planned for her.

Griffin broke eye contact with his father and took in the rest of the office. This position, as his father's right hand, bored him. He noticed while the office appeared to have the standard accoutrements; they were anything but when you paid attention.

Instead of beautiful photographs of buildings they had designed, the firm displayed photos of the number of trees saved on the project or the smog-choked skyline of a city with the words— "Our inspiration."

Ugh. Inspirational, eco-friendly bullshit. Who cares about carbon footprints? Those who mattered would weather whatever storm, making bank off those who didn't.

As the Levy party settled in around him, studiously avoiding the father/son conflict, a tall woman with long, coily hair approached.[2]

She wore an impeccably cut suit. The navy pencil skirt, cream silk blouse, and matching navy blazer nipped in at her tiny waist emphasizing her generous curves. They reminded Griffin of a classic Coke bottle.

She dressed conservatively at first glance until you took in the spiked silver bracelets on one arm, the diamond ear bar piercing in her right ear, and her shoes - fire engine red booties with metallic heels. She looked to be young, but when she opened her mouth, she sounded mature... in control.

Griffin had his new muse.

"Good afternoon, everyone, Mr. Levy," she said in a smooth, low voice. "Welcome to our offices."

She nodded to everyone at the table. Griffin noticed they all leaned in as she spoke. Instead of barking out words like some female execs were prone to do to establish dominance, her quiet voice commanded attention without being abrasive. It was soft, but not docile, and he knew there was more to this woman. He was keenly interested in bringing it out—and bringing her to heel.

She turned to address the senior Levy. "Have you reviewed the information my assistant sent over?" She sat at the head of the table, expectant.

The room shifted uncomfortably.

"I was under the impression Wall would be at this meeting," Levy said straight out. Griffin noticed a hint of irritation briefly flash across her beautiful face before being replaced by quiet, professional smoothness once again.

"I assure you, Mr. Levy, I am thoroughly prepared to finish this out for the company," the woman said with a slight smile.

"I know, Angel, honey, but I like to at least meet the man I'm doing business with," Levy said with more than a trace of irritation.

"Of course, Mr. Levy." She demurred. The woman named Angel—who did not like being called honey, not that Marion Levy noticed anything—reached over to the phone next to her. "Selene, please ping Mark and connect him to the conference monitor."

"Conference monitor? You mean he's not here?" Mr. Levy sputtered.

Now was Griffin's chance. Her hand moved from lightly holding her pen to a death grip. It was a brief involuntary reflex, but when combined with the rapidly ticking pulse in her neck, told him all he needed to know. She'd exposed a bit of smooth underbelly and he'd attach himself there vowing to work until he was so intertwined with her, she wouldn't know where she ended, and he began. Father said he needed a good woman, right? Seizing his chance, Griffin spoke.

"Father, I think we need to relax a bit. Ms. Angel is obviously extremely capable. If this Wall person is the genius you say he is, he must have left us in expert hands."

Maya Angel looked at the younger Levy. His vote of confidence got her attention. Griffin smiled at her. And she briefly, cautiously, gave a small smile back.

Got her.

ELEVEN MONTHS AGO, ROUGH RIDGE

MIKE

Mike walked up and took in Paul, leaning his long frame against his SUV as he talked on the phone.

"Where's your car?" Paul asked.

"I'm staying at the Rough Ridge Hotel, no sense in driving," Mike replied.

"You're not staying—"

"No." Mike cut him off quickly.

Paul nodded. "Well, let's go get that drink."

"You expecting trouble detective?" Mike asked mildly.

"Just thought I'd wait for a friend."

"Outside?" Mike skewered him with a look. Shaking his head, he muttered, "Let's go get this shit over with." Striding past Paul, he yanked open the door.

Jake Matthews stood behind the bar in his usual black tee and jeans, talking with a pretty redhead when they walked in. The after work and no work crowd filled the bar. A short, sturdy man with a close-cropped beard and bald head did a double take, sizing him up, before he noticed Paul standing next to him.

"Hey Mac."

Mac took his eyes off the wild man in front of him.

"Paul. How's Tammy?"

"Good, she said you all are coming through for girls' night this week. Don't tear up my shit." He teased.

Mike looked mildly interested at the mention of girl's night but said nothing. Paul led the way to the bar. "Jake, Leslie, this is Mike," he started. "Mike, you remember Jake? This is Leslie, his wife."

Mike gave Jake a nod, reached out his hand. "I remember."

The men shook, each assessing the other carefully. Leslie looked from each man to the other, noticing the tension. As the men let go, Mike's eyes skated to Leslie.

"I'm Mike. Mike Sheppard."

Leslie's eyes flew wide for a moment, but she quickly recovered.

"Hi Mike, I'm Leslie," she said in a warm voice, and with a warmer smile, reached out her hand. Mike looked at Jake, Jake nodded, and only after, did Mike take Leslie's hand. It was the briefest of moments - the men's exchange - but Jake took a relaxed position and Mike sat on the stool next to Paul.

Regina, bar regular and resident busybody, peered down bar at them, her eyes wide with surprise.

"I'm so sorry for your loss," Leslie whispered.

"I appreciate that Leslie," he said with a small smile, "but it's no loss. My father was a piece of shit. I thank God every day he's rotting in hell. Can I get a beer? Anything cold is fine."

While a stunned Leslie blinked, Jake uncapped a cold one, tossed a coaster in front of Mike, and set the beer on it.

"Thanks." Mike held Jake's gaze. Jake nodded and leaned against the back wall.

"So, what brings you back Mike?" he asked, eyes watchful.

"I joined the force."

Regina choked on her beer. She swiveled on the stool that seemed molded to her butt and looked at Mike full on.

"Are you crazy?!"

"Maybe," Mike said with the first hint of a smile.

"No maybe about it," Regina declared.

"Mike was a detective in Los Angeles up 'til two weeks ago, comes highly recommended," Paul said to the bar, his eyes on Regina.

Mike took a swig of beer; he wished Paul hadn't said a word. He didn't need anybody explaining him. His actions would speak for themselves. Maybe.

"What happened two weeks ago?"

"Regina," Jake growled in a warning.

Mike looked at Jake. "I got word Rosey is dying."

Jake's eye widened in surprise while grief flashed over his face.

"Damn, suga', I'm sorry as hell to hear that," Regina said.

"I am too, Mike," Jake said. "I—"

The door opened and in blew Tori all smiles and glitz. "Hey y'all!"

"Hey Tori," everyone greeted back.

Mike turned to wood hearing her name, and the guilt washing over him threatened to take him to a dark place. His beer sat like a rock in his gut. Jake looked from Tori to Mike, finally meeting eyes with Paul.

"I wanted to know if you needed us to bring anything tonight?" Tori asked brightly, pushing her sunglasses up on her head while tossing her long, dark hair over her shoulder.

"Uh," Leslie said, glancing at Mike, "no, we're good to go."

"Ok, and wait until you see the cute outfits I got for Liv today. She starts ballet soon. I went for leotards and tights, but I saw so many other cute dance outfits I got carried away."

"Girl, you know you can shop," Regina said from the end of the bar.

Tori giggled at Regina. "Caine says the same thing. That and I can walk my ass off in heels - both are true."

Mike sensed Paul's eyes on him as he continued to study his bottle, listening to every word. He finally reacted when Paul moved to put his money on the bar.

"This round is mine," he said.

Paul paused, nodded, and slipped the bill back in his pocket. Mike placed money for two beers and a generous tip on the bar.

"Thanks for the drink." He rose, using every fiber in his being to will his body to move. Jake nodded, his eyes studying Mike with interest and concern.

Paul also stood, as Tori noticed Mike. She looked up at him with a dazzling smile, surprised by his height and wild look. "Tori, this is Mike."

"Hi Mike!" Tori waved.

Mike nodded his head in her direction, forcing sound past the large, dry lump in his throat.

"Ma'am."

He paused for the briefest of moments to stare at the long, thin scar along her cheek. The only imperfection on her beautiful face, he also noticed the small tip of her ring finger missing. He clenched his jaw tightly, getting sick to his stomach. He nodded again and strode out the door, hearing the chatter behind him.

"That was one wild-looking man," Tori said, laughing. "And that's saying something in a biker bar."

"Tori," Jake said quietly, "that was Mike Sheppard, Stan Sheppard's son."

"Oh shit!"

"You got that right, chickadee," Regina confirmed with a head shake.

Mike let the door slam behind him.

His stomach hadn't unclenched since he heard her name. Tori. The woman his father almost murdered. The woman who had to do what no civilian should ever think about walked into the bar and he hadn't been in town for a whole six hours.

Everywhere he turned, he saw how his father had inflicted pain.

Stan Sheppard was a cancer that had metastasized through the town. Before he got too far, Paul caught up with him in the parking lot.

"Listen, Tammy told me to tell you when you, get settled, come over for dinner."

"Thanks man, and tell Tammy thanks, too."

"I mean it, and so does she."

Mike paused and locked eyes with Paul. "I'll take you up on that someday." He threw up a hand and started walking toward the hotel with legs full of lead and stomach acid eating a hole straight through to his lungs.

⸻

THE NEXT MORNING, Mike drove his Jeep to the garage at the other end of town, pulling into a parking space. He took the Jeep's door off. It was one of those perfect, clear Colorado summer mornings. He had spent the last twenty years in California with its nearly perfect weather, but there was nothing like Colorado mountain air.

It was officially his first day on the job, and there was one thing he had to do before taking up his post to protect his hometown.

He squared his shoulders, muttering, "Still cleaning up Stan's shit."

As he walked across the forecourt, a man he recognized came out of the office.

"Mike? Mike Sheppard?" Doc said, smiling.

"Hey Doc." Mike smiled back, happy to see a friendly face.

Doc looked almost the same as he had when Mike was a kid. A little grayer and softer, reflecting good years, but he still held all the energy of a man half his age.

"How long you stayin', son?"

"Long term, Doc." Mike held Doc's eyes when they widened in surprise.

"Is Caine Walters here?"

Doc's eyes grew wider as his mouth dropped open.

Two men walked out of the huge bay doors and began moving toward him. One was tall with a swimmer's build—an unmistakable younger version of Doc. With salt and pepper in his hair and a full mountain man beard, he wore a white t-shirt and jeans. Jake and Blake both had tried to get his sister off drugs, both failed to slay the demons Stan planted in her from the day she was born.

The second man needed no intro. He'd seen Caine Walters on the wall-to-wall news coverage after Stan's crimes against Caine came to light. It was rare for a small town like theirs to make national news, but a police chief framing an innocent man for murder was big time news. They'd made the news again after Stan kidnapped and tortured Tori. Mike clapped Doc on the arm and met the men.

Caine wore a set of coveralls open to the waist with a crisp white tee underneath. He had an inch or two on Mike in height, but pound for pound, they were evenly matched. Mike hoped it didn't come to that. He noticed Caine sizing him up as Mike took off his sunglasses, slipping the earpiece in the collar of his deep green t-shirt.

Mike reached out his hand. "I'm Detective Mike Sheppard, and I'm here to apologize."

Whatever Caine was expecting Mike to say, it clearly wasn't that as his eyebrows shot to the top of his face and his head jerked back in surprise. Recovering, Caine carefully considered him for a moment. Finally, with a bit of a side-eye, shook Mike's hand firmly. As they shook, Mike looked Caine in the eye and continued, his voice a little rougher.

"My father was a son-of-a-bitch and I'm sorry as fuck for what he did to you and the pain he caused your family. Nothing I can say will give you the time back." He shook his head. "Or take away what your wife endured." Mike paused, his jaw clenching and unclenching. His mind flashed to the pretty young woman he'd seen just a day earlier, the scars marking her face, her manicure minus her missing fingertip...

After a long swallow, he continued. "I've moved back to town, and I don't want to cause you or your family any more discomfort. I intend to stay away from you and yours and ensure you can live your life in peace."

Caine considered him again and nodded. Mike returned the nod.

Mike turned to Blake. "I never got a chance to say thanks for trying to get Rosey help, and I'm sorry to hear about your brother."

Blake nodded, jaw tight, and asked carefully, "How is Rose?"

Mike took a breath and shook his head. "She's ... she's dying man. Cervical cancer."

Blake's head snapped back; eyes wide. "Jesus man. How—how long do they give her?" Blake said, alarmed.

"Six months, maybe a little more," Mike replied, his voice thick.

"Does Jake know? Can she have visitors?"

Mike nodded. "She's in and out here." He pointed to his head. Mike cleared his throat. "Be prepared."

Blake nodded.

"I gotta get to the station. Mr. Walters," he added with a nod.

"Caine," he replied, indicating all was well.

Mike relaxed as he nodded.

"Tori said she saw you yesterday."

Mike paused. "I left as soon as I realized she was there. It won't happen again."

"Not a problem if it does," Caine replied.

Mike's stomach clenched with the guilt of forgiveness given he didn't deserve. He shook his head. "I can't look at her and not think about what he did ... and I don't want to remind her of what she had to do either. She seems like a real sweet person. She doesn't deserve that."

Mike gave a chin lift to the men, turned, and walked back toward his Jeep. He threw up a hand to Doc on his way past. As he slid in, he clenched and released his fingers to stave off the shaking in his hands. It didn't work.

---

1. Way Down We Go by Kaleo
2. Creep by The Voice Kimberly Nichole

4

APPLES. ORANGES.

ROUGH RIDGE, PRESENT DAY...

MAYA

Maya leaned her head back on the headrest. She was wiped. Lost, scared, almost arrested, and had an asthma/panic attack. *Shit ...* Being on the run sucked and being at the mercy of her new surroundings sucked even more. She was getting sick of being powerless. She had no trouble controlling boardrooms and her life until she fell in with Griffin. Slowly, in what seemed like small ways at the time, she lost herself.

She looked over at the giant man next to her, driving her truck well over the speed limit.

"Are you trying to get me arrested again?"

"Apples."

"Oranges," she answered back. "I'm not sure I know how to play this game."

He chuckled again. The sound was comforting to Maya.

"Your apple juice is bad. It smells like alcohol," Caine explained, looking over at her and smiling.

Maya lightly smacked herself on the forehead. She bought it at her first stop weeks ago and forgot it was even back there, never noticing the smell. Officer Asshole must be a freaking bloodhound.

"Fermented apples almost got me locked up." Maya leaned her head back and watched the scenery, eyes getting heavier until she drifted off.

She woke sometime later to the sound of a garage door opening. She got a glimpse of a massive house before entering the inside of a garage with a kick-ass black Ford Mustang, a chromed-up, midnight blue Harley Fat Boy, and the Range Rover she'd seen before. As sweet as the mini car lot was, it was not the hotel.

"This is not the hotel."

As soon as the words left her mouth Tori came out to the garage barefoot in cutoff short shorts and a tight, pale blue tank over her pregnant belly, with three gorgeous little girls in tow. The oldest girl was about five and wore a soft pink and purple sweater dress with matching Converse. The one on Tori's right was about four and currently in motion, a blur running out to meet them at the truck. She rocked leopard print and a sparkly top. Adorable. The last little one in Tori's arms sucked on two fingers and wore a unicorn onesie. She looked almost two.

These people were fertile.

"Daddieee," the middle girl screeched as she jumped into his arms. He caught her and swung her up onto his back with practiced ease. Maya swallowed a small bite of longing as she watched them.

Tori walked up to Maya before she got out of the car, a talking tsunami.

"You're staying here with us. The hotel is okay. It's more like a motel. Ms. Shirley is a hoot, and you'll love the pool and Saturday brunch service, but you need someone to look after you. We've got a ton of room and it doesn't have to be forever girl just until you feel better." She grinned.

Maya waited until Tori took a breath to refuse when the oldest, and seemingly shyest, girl spoke up.

"You need a nap."

Damn.

"You may be right, kid." Maya tapped the little girl on her nose. She smiled and grabbed Maya's hand. When Maya reached back to grab her bag, Caine had already beaten her to it. Maya marveled at how fast he was, even with a wild child climbing all over him.

"Leave the piece."

She froze. How did *he* know, and the cops didn't?

"I saw you move it last night. I took it before they took your truck. Put it back this morning. You don't have a lock, and I have kids."

"Understood."

Olivia informed Maya her nickname was Liv and prompted her to come into the house.

"One night," Maya called to the adults behind her, "and only because I'm still lost on a Colorado back road."

Tori and Caine chuckled as they followed her and Liv into the house.

Caine and Tori's house was a revelation. Maya was beat, but she was never too tired to check out a beautiful building. She loved the glass-filled gables that were iconic to the area's architecture, but made modern in their space. The way the designer brought in the natural wood and harnessed the big Colorado skies and bigger sunlight was beautiful.

Architecture had been Maya's passion since she was a little girl. One day, as she passed a bookstore, she fell in love with a book featuring mosques from around the world. Maya's mother Elise was a professor at The Ohio State University and showed early support for her academic interests. After watching Maya look for the book every time they passed by, her mother purchased the huge, expensive, coffee table volume with the glossy cover and crisp pages. It was a big deal because while Elise made a good salary; she was careful to save most of what she earned. As she filled out her checkbook, she would always say, "Good or bad, life can turn on a dime, Maya Angel, and while you can't predict it, you can prepare for it."

Maya treasured the book, and spent hours poring over the pages, reading the editor's notes and looking up words to understand what they meant.

On her eighth birthday, Maya's mother surprised her with a personal tour of a mosque right outside of Toledo.

They spent hours exploring while Maya happily chattered away. It was one of the best days of her life. From mosques, she moved on to Catholic cathedrals, which were abundant around Ohio. From there, another brief obsession with zeppelins, then the Titanic. Later she moved on to skyscrapers.

She excelled in math and the arts and joined the high school's architecture club when she was in seventh grade. It was her first love, and so far, her only genuine love. She got a pain in her chest as she realized that part of her life was over as long as she was on the run. It was something else Griffin had stolen.

During the tour, one small hand slipped into her left hand and a second one into her right. She stared at the two little faces looking up at her.

"Mommy says you are sleeping in grandma's room," Liv informed her.

"Oh, that sounds awesome, Liv."

"And daddy said we need to be quiet so you can get some sleep," Gabriella announced in the loudest whisper Maya had ever heard.

"That's a nice thought Gabriella, but right now I could sleep through a bomb, so please be as loud as you normally are."

Gabriella took off running, hair flying, yelling, "Follow me!"

Maya could barely contain her laugh as she watched the little maniac. Her sister looked at Maya and started walking. Obviously, Bri took after her outgoing mother and Liv was her father's child.

Maya's favorite room in the house was the second door on the right. Floor-to-ceiling windows opened to a gorgeous view of the valley below and featured a deck wrapped around three sides of the room. The bedding and curtains were muted, feminine shades of pale green and lavender.

Maya sat on the bed in grandma's room, stared out at the magnificent view, blinked twice, and drifted off to sleep.

CAINE

It was late. Caine walked through the house, checking the locks and the alarm. He couldn't sleep and even spending quality bedroom time with Tori didn't make him tired. Something was off, and it had to be their visitor. She was hiding something. He was drawn to her, but not like any other woman before. He still only had eyes for Tori, but Maya was something else. Beautiful and charismatic, yet something in her eyes said she was someone he needed to monitor. He checked the time ... it wasn't too late to call.

He only had to wait for the second ring. "Jake? Caine. We need to talk."

MAYA

Maya woke in a full sweat. She didn't know how long she slept, but someone put her bag in the room and tucked her into bed. The high thread count sheets smelled like lavender and were so soft, she could have buried herself in them forever if her heart wasn't racing. She looked at the mahogany nightstand and saw a glitter pen drawing and a cookie with a bite missing.

Ok, those kids are seriously cute. She slipped off her hospital sweatpants and wondered if there were pain meds in the bathroom for her eye-crossing, splitting headache. Suddenly, her dream came back to her — the same one she'd dreamed for weeks. She was running through a dense forest and his breath was hot on her neck. He tackled her from behind and started biting her. The bear.

"Shit Maya, you don't have to be a shrink to know what it means."

She squeezed her eyes closed to shut out the dream. And practiced what they taught her at the women's shelter. Deep breaths in and out. Find a focal point on the wall and recite the street names from her childhood home. [1]

"Pinewood. Inhale ... exhale ... Dorr Street. Inhale ... exhale ... Avondale... Inhale ... Exhale ... Belmont ... " she said slowly and quietly.

She started to calm when her brain stubbornly restarted the flash backs. Memories of Griffin's mouth on her thigh tearing at her flesh overwhelmed her. She screamed and vomit snaked its way up her throat. Jumping up, she ran to the bathroom, barely making it in time.

CAINE

A scream jolted Caine and Tori out of sleep, and they both leaped out of bed. It was Maya.

Caine checked the security panel on the wall. The alarm was still armed. As they moved down the hall, Caine barked "Kids." Tori peeled off to check on her babies.

His body taut, Caine quickly moved to the guest room. Checking Maya's door, he found it unlocked. He stepped in and heard her retching in the bathroom. Crossing the room with three strides of his long legs, he saw her on her knees, bent over the toilet, wearing only a t-shirt and underwear. As she retched again, he saw enormous bruises on her legs and thighs disappearing up under her t-shirt. *God, were those bite marks?*

Overwhelming anger surged through him.

Tori came in as Maya vomited again. She nodded wordlessly to him the kids were all right. He followed her eyes to Maya on the floor. Her hand flew to her mouth upon seeing the young woman's injuries. Caine wrapped his arm around her and pulled her back a couple of steps out of sight of the bathroom. He gave her a nod to reach out to the young woman.

"Maya?" Tori called.

MAYA

Shit.

Maya pulled down her t-shirt and quickly sat on the floor. She didn't need the entire world knowing the unbelievably stupid series of choices she'd made. The cool marble floor felt good against her bruises. Sweaty and trembling, she felt like shit — but at least she had nothing else left to vomit. Now she was thirsty. Like Sahara Desert dry.

"Maya?" Tori called again, a little more urgently.

"Just a minute," she called.

She got to her feet, flushed the toilet, and hoped she sounded normal. Maya walked to the sink, rinsed her mouth, and splashed water on her face. Willing herself to appear sunny, she took two steps into the bedroom on shaky legs as she pulled down her t-shirt.

"Sorry I woke you Tori, I ... "

And the lights went out.

CAINE

Relief mixed with worry when Caine managed to catch her before she hit the floor. Looping an arm under her legs and the other under her arms, Caine picked her up, surprised how light she was. He swiftly moved out of the room and down the hall, with Tori waddling quickly ahead of him to disarm the alarm. She jumped aside as he stepped through the door to the garage, grabbed the keys to the Mustang and hit the buttons to unlock the doors. He used the hand under Maya's legs to open the door and gently eased her into the car.

Tori chucked his phone to him before he folded himself into the driver's seat. Caine quickly maneuvered the car out of the garage, down the drive, and out of sight.

Flying down the road, through the development on the way to Rough Ridge County Hospital his phone rang. He hit the hands-free button without looking.

"How is she?" Tori asked, out of breath.

"Don't know. I'm trying to get her there as fast as I can."

"I called 911, Detective Sheppard is close — he'll meet you on the way. An ambulance is on the way too."

"Mmm ... " Maya moaned next to him.

Up ahead, Caine saw flashing lights and pulled alongside Mike.

"How is she?" he asked as he climbed out of his Jeep.

"She's starting to come to, but I'm not sure what's wrong. It's not her asthma," Caine replied hurriedly.

Mike opened the door to the Mustang and bent to check Maya's pulse. It was faint and fast. As Mike checked her pupils, Maya began convulsing.

"Shit, she's seizing," Mike growled.

Caine's heart sank. "What do you need?"

Mike already checked the area around her seat to ensure she wouldn't hurt herself and leaned the car seat as far back as it would go.

"Nothing, we just have to make sure she doesn't bang into anything and hurt herself," Mike replied as he grabbed his walkie. Caine was gone and back in an instant while Mike barked in his radio, "Where is that damn ambulance? I'm two miles out of Rough Ridge on West Ridge Road. The victim is an adult female, unresponsive, having a seizure, known asthmatic."

Maya finally stopped seizing and fell terribly still.

"Is she breathing?" Caine asked.

"Yes, but her pulse is still faint."

In the distance, Caine and Mike heard the sirens.

"Hurry," the men said at the same time.

---

1. Nuvole Bianche by Ludovico Einaudi

5

NO CRINKLES

MAYA

Maya's whole body was crazy heavy, and her tongue hurt.

"Ugh ... I feel like someone dropped an anvil on my head." She turned, blinked open one eye, then the other. Upon focusing, she saw brilliant green eyes with flecks of gold in them.

"Mmmm ... pretty, sad, sexy eyes," she mumbled.

The pretty, sexy eyes lost their sadness and widened in surprise.

"Shit. Did I say that out loud?"

"Ms. Anderson?"

Maya rolled her head to the voice calling her name and got hit by the hospital scent as all her senses woke up.

Yelk.

She blinked slowly again, as the world around her came into focus. She realized Dr. Kent stood at the foot of her bed with Detective Cabot. Caine was on her left, in a too little chair. Again. Officer Asshole sat on her right.

Again.

"Déjà vu. Folks, we have got to stop meeting like this," Maya said, as she rose slowly.

"You're right about that, Ms. Anderson. Mr. Walters tells me you didn't eat or drink since you left here the first time," Dr. Kent lectured.

"I don't remember anything after I left. I've been on the road for weeks, and think I fell asleep once I got a peek at those gables and panoramic view."

The room paused.

"What? I like good design," Maya said with a slight, self-conscious shrug.

"Well, as beautiful as Caine's home sounds, you moved from dehydrated to severely dehydrated, causing your electrolytes to go out of balance. You had a seizure, and it could have been far more serious if not for Caine and Detective Sheppard."

Maya sat straight up in bed. "A seizure?! Is my b—" she clenched her hand to stop it from going to her stomach and composed herself. "Is everything okay?"

Dr. Kent reached out and patted Maya's foot. "Everything is fine, but it won't be if you don't start taking better care of yourself."

Maya sat back in relief. She brushed away tears, swallowed, and asked the ceiling, "When can I blow this popsicle stand?"

"We are going to keep you for a few days. I want you to see a neurologist, just in case, and get some fluids in you. I've got to finish my rounds, but I'll be back to check on you."

Dr. Kent clicked her pen, and, with a smile and a nod to the room, she walked out.

"Maya," Paul called. She looked at him. "I'm glad you're going to be okay."

"Thank you," she whispered, completely overwhelmed at the whole situation. He nodded before leaving.

Maya was alone with Caine and Detective Sheppard.

"This is awkward," she whispered. "I have got to be the worst houseguest ever. I'm sorry to have caused so much trouble."

Embarrassed, she couldn't meet Caine's eyes.

"Don't worry," Caine said, his voice soft. His tone made her peek over at him and he did that soul search thing again.

"Thank you," she whispered. He reached out, squeezed her hand with his giant one, and stood.

"Gotta call Victoria," he said, and, after giving a quick nod to the man sitting on Maya's right, he strode out of the room.

More awkward silence.[1]

"So ... Officer Ass ... um ... " May started looking at her hands.

"Sheppard," he said from way too close to her right side.

"Detective Sheppard," she said, nodding. She plucked at the covers on her lap, doing anything to busy her hands. She couldn't think of a quip or sarcastic remark to ease the moment, so she opted for honesty.

"I owe you a thank you and an explanation."

"You don't—" he started, sounding even closer.

"I do," she said, interrupting him and turning to him. She locked eyes with him. Her heart skipped a beat and pounded louder in her ears. The way he looked at her made her momentarily lose her train of thought. His face was soft, and his eyes were intensely focused on her.

She inspected him again. He seemed like one of the good guys. Even though she'd made the mistake before, she wondered if this time she was right. She moved to shake off the pounding in her ears, took a deep breath and said, "Apples."

Did I say apples? Maya mentally kicked her own ass.

Detective Sheppard smiled, and this time, it reached his eyes. She wondered what it would be like to kiss the little crinkles around them. The rational part of her brain kicked in and urged her to pull it together.

No crinkles.

No crinkles.

No crinkles.

"What about apples?" he prompted, leaning in a little more, his head cocked.

"Right. The other night when you arrested me," she rushed on. "It was apples. Apple juice fermented, long forgotten in my junky truck. Caine found it. That's why you detected alcohol."

He looked pained and made her sorry she'd said anything.

"Maya, I'm sorry about all of that. I should have trusted my gut," he sighed. He looked so sad and humbled. In that moment, he looked years older and carrying the world on his shoulders.

"Hey, I didn't say that to cause you distress. You had a little cause ...

distant, razor thin ... Don't take it so hard. I'm fine, you're fine and you got to save my life twice. That's gotta be a cop record, right? Plus, now you're aware you have a nose like a bloodhound, so if the detective thing doesn't work out, you could always become a bomb-sniffing dog."

Mike blinked twice and roared with laughter. It was beautiful to see. His entire face lit up, his head fell back, and those marvelous locks of his tumbled back and over one shoulder. He looked ten years younger. Maya wanted to see him laugh like that again and again. As his laughter died out, it got low and gravelly, which gave her another reaction the hospital gown would give away.

Whoa there.

She crossed her arms over her chest in what she hoped was a nonchalant way and waited for a beat. "Listen, Sheppard, I recognize you've got work to do, and I'm supposed to be here for a few days. I appreciate you staying close to check on me, but you don't have to hang around."

His eyes were unreadable. He stood and again blotted out the lights. As he leaned in, he looked at Maya and softly said, "I'm glad you're okay." He tucked a fallen twist behind her ear. His fingers lingered over the lock of hair for a moment.

She leaned into the heat of his fingers and sighed.

"Soft," he whispered.

"Hot," she breathed, startling herself.

WTF Maya?!

A knock on the door broke the spell and plugged her verbal diarrhea. Detective Sheppard became professional again. He stood and faced the door, watching.

"Hey!" Tori called. "I was on the way over when Caine called!" Her belly led the way as she tipped in wearing a pair of killer camel-colored boots and a snug, dark purple sweater dress. She took one look at Detective Sheppard and froze. So did he.

Tori seemed to catch herself and said, "Hi Mike," cautiously.

"Ma'am." After a slight nod, he took two strides toward the door, grasped the handle, yanked it open, and walked out.

What the hell was that about?

Tori stared after him a moment and turned to Maya. "That could have gone better."

"What *was* that?"

"Honey, long story short, his daddy did this," she said, pointing to the scars along her cheek, neck and wiggling her hand where Maya noticed the tip of her ring finger missing.

"Shut. Up." Maya whispered.

And with a shiver, she said, "And *I* ran him over...three times."

Damn.

MIKE

Every time he saw Tori, it was a shock to his system. It was a rare occurrence because Mike worked to avoid Caine, Tori, and their growing family for almost a year. With Maya in town and forming an instant friendship with the Walters, Mike realized he'd now have to avoid another person in a town that seemed to get smaller by the minute.

Consumed by his thoughts, Mike realized he was halfway to the door of the hospital when he saw Dr. Kent. A petite redhead with large hazel eyes, she worked to look older by wearing her hair pulled back, with heavy, black-framed glasses covering most of the freckles on her face.

"Detective Sheppard, how is she doing?"

"She's much better now that she's shaken the cobwebs out. Tori is in with her now."

"Oh."

There it was, that pause everyone takes as they remember.

"Mike," Meg started.

"What's going on with Maya?" he interrupted. "I saw the bruising last night and there was something you both left unsaid in that room."

Meg looked around briefly and grabbed Mike, pulling him aside. "What you are asking for is protected by patient/doctor privilege."

"Meg," he growled, "it looks like someone beat the hell out of her and I'm no forensic guy, but I saw what looked like bite marks when she was seizing."

Meg shook her head. "I can't tell you anything Mike. If she wants to file a report, she will."

Right. Mike inhaled. *No one in this town would trust him with anything.*

"I know what you're thinking, Mike, and it's not that."

Mike glared at her, turned on his heel, and stalked out.

MAYA

"Maya, honey, I saw the bruises," Victoria whispered. "And when you're ready to talk," she rushed on before Maya could voice her protest, "I'm here. I've seen and lived through my share of shit, but even if you don't want to talk to me, talk to someone."

Maya held her eyes for a moment and nodded a bit. "I'll think about it."

Tori looked at her and changed the subject to inform Maya she'd invited a few friends to the hospital to bring her some proper food. Maya was apprehensive about Tori's friends visiting her hospital room, but she didn't have time to worry because, once they started, they never stopped. It was the town parade, and her room was Main Street. It was welcoming and weird.

The first knock at the door brought in a leggy redhead with a big smile. She was maybe in her forties and dressed in badass biker chic.

"Hey, I'm Leslie, you're Maya and you've had a heck of a time in our town already," she said with a smile.

"I am and I have," Maya said, returning her smile. "Tori said you'd be by ... "

"Oh honey, I'm a part of the first wave," Leslie said brightly.

First wave?

"I came with chocolate," Leslie started.

"Oh, thank God! Bless you to your toes," Maya yelped as she began making grabby hands for the treat.

Leslie and Tori laughed big at her response and only stopped when there was a muffled banging on the door and a deep voice barked out, "Red!"

Leslie rushed to open the door and in walked a dark god from mountain heavens and football hell.

Maya's mouth fell open. Beautiful blue eyes, dark hair, and built like sin. He was the third fantastic male specimen she'd seen in this weird-ass town, and she knew him well.

"Holy Buckeyes, you're Jake 'The Tank' Matthews."

Turning to Tori, she said, "He's Jake the Tank!" Turning back to Jake she yelled, "Do you know you're Jake the Tank?" Maya bounced in the bed excitedly, her tired face beaming.

Jake stopped with several gigantic bags in his arms and looked bemused.

"I have loved you ever since I was old enough to know the difference between boys and girls," Maya gushed, clapping her hands to her cheeks.

"Uh Maya—" Tori said.

"Which is counterbalanced by hating you since I could understand the difference between first and ten and a touchdown," she said, eyes twinkling in delight. "You two-time All-American University of Michigan butthole! You spoiled Ohio State's chances at the Rose Bowl two years in a row!" she groaned. "Then you went to play for the Steelers, for crying out loud, when you could have gone to play for the Browns! I don't know whether to kiss you or kick over your bike." She sat back, exhausted from the sudden burst of energy.

"Uh Maya, Leslie is Jake's wife," she whispered.

Maya pulled a face. "Right on, yikes. Sorry Leslie, I'm an ass and I talk too much. So ... I'll kick over his bike." She nodded, narrowing her eyes at Jake.

"You kick over my bike, darlin', and Imma have to eat this burger and tan your hide." His deep voice gave a warning few ignored.

She leveled a challenging look at him. "Yeah right, you're married. You aren't spanking anyone but her, so you only have the burger as leverage and if I don't eat actual food, I'll wither away."

She placed the back of her hand over her forehead and forced a weak sigh. "And you'll never know about the kid that is going to smash your junior year record his freshman year. AND he's not signed yet, but I know for a fact he's headed to OSU even if Michigan is sniffing around thinking they can turn him." She leveled him with an obstinate gaze and raised one eyebrow.

Jake looked at Maya for all of two seconds, gave a full-on belly laugh, and tossed the burger bag to her. Leaning a hip against the low hospital dresser behind him, he looked at her.

"Spill."

Maya glanced over to see Tori and Leslie stare at each other in complete shock.

Jake and Maya talked about Ohio State and Michigan's recruits and the prospects of national titles for both teams (they did not agree) for at least twenty minutes, during which they laughed, argued, and teased like they'd known each other forever.

When a nurse came in to check Maya's vitals, Jake and Leslie got ready to leave.

"You're a lucky duck," Maya said thoughtfully.

"I know," Leslie said, smiling.

"Not you, him." Looking at Jake next to Leslie, she said, "You don't look beaten by your pro-career. You looked cared for... nurtured. Few survive post-NFL and look as happy as you. She's a blessing to you." She nodded slowly.

Leslie's face went soft, and Jake leaned in, kissing the top of his wife's head softly. "She's right, Red, I am."

It was a sweet moment. Oddly, she thought about Detective Sheppard.

---

1. Beautiful by Meshell Ndegeocello

6

I'VE BEEN WRONG BEFORE

MAYA

AFTER A FULL DAY OF VISITORS, Maya was beat. She met the kind, older woman that owned the local hotel — who said she'd take great care of her. She met the goth proprietor of the local bakery, who left behind cookie bar thingies with dark chocolate, toffee, and marshmallows that were next-level good. The owner of one of-the-art galleries/coffee shops gave her a custom-made travel coffee mug that hilariously read "Middle Finger to the Law" in a kaleidoscope of colors.

Seemed like half the town visited and left food and drink, which was awesome and incredibly thoughtful, but it left Maya with enough to feed an army, but no refrigerator.

She invited the nurses on shift throughout the day to take whatever they wanted - except the cookie bar thingies. Still, a ton of food remained.

She also now owned an amazing blanket and comfy pajamas that didn't leave her butt catching a breeze like the hospital gowns. It was all Leslie and Tori's handiwork and she appreciated it so much she called to thank them one more time and ordered each an enormous bouquet of roses to arrive the next day. Finally, as the day moved to night, she clicked on her favorite show - *Naked and Afraid* - and settled in for the evening.

MIKE

A restless Mike sat in his room. It was after visiting hours, yet he couldn't shake the urge to see Maya again. He quickly convinced himself he was simply checking in on her like any self-respecting public servant would. Besides, according to the gossip Paul shared over lunch, half the town traipsed through the hospital to meet its newest visitor.

After making his way to the hospital, he walked onto the ward, flashed his badge, and strolled to her room. Recognizing the excitement building in him, he stopped before he knocked.

"What are you doing Mike?" he mumbled out loud.

"Visiting a friend by the looks of it," Dr. Kent said, coming up behind him with a slight smile.

"Don't you ever go home?"

"Not really," she said with a shrug. "Occupational hazard."

"We're not friends."

"You could be. Seems the whole town is friends with her now. If she hasn't hightailed it out of here after all that, she can handle you."

"Sounds like she doesn't need anymore."

"Mike, you weren't like this before —."

He cut her off. "Is she okay?"

"You mean in general. Not getting into her actual medical history that by law I can't share?" she asked pointedly as she crossed her arms.

Mike might have growled if she hadn't smiled.

"She's fine."

Mike let the tension release from his fingers and shrugged off the bite from his car keys.

"Go in, Mike. She was watching some show with naked people in the jungle and cracking up."

Mike smirked, knocked quietly, then turned the handle, and walked in. Peeking around the curtain, he saw Maya asleep with the TV watching her. She was curled on her side, her hair spread out like dark vines over the white pillow, a hand tucked under her cheek. Instead of a drab hospital gown, she wore soft lavender pajamas with a patchwork quilt pulled to her shoulders. He studied her a moment, making sure she was breathing, taking in how sweet she looked when she wasn't flipping him the bird.

An argument on the television made him look up. There were naked people, blurred out where it mattered, on an island. Despite himself, Mike got sucked into the show. As the narrator explained how the show rated contestants' survival skills, he settled into the chair next to Maya. During the commercials, Mike noticed a ton of food in the room.

"Jesus," he whispered, "it's like they're feeding an army." Snagging chips and a cookie bar, he settled back in.

In the middle of the second episode, she woke up.

"It's addictive, isn't it? Wait until you see what happens with the snake. It's hilarious and frustrating. Mister Supreme Alpha Male screws the pooch."

She watched him in the same position she slept, now with a slight smile on her face, her dimple barely noticeable in the dark. Something in his chest pulled.

"Didn't mean to wake you." He leaned closer to her in the dark.

"Hard to sleep in hospitals, especially with this thing squeezing me every hour." She nodded to the blood pressure machine near her head.

He suddenly was anxious. "Are you uncomfortable? Want me to get a nurse?"

"Heck no. They time their visits with my REM cycle. I get settled. They come and shake things up. We have a routine. Wouldn't want to put them off their game." She winked at him.

That center line in him tugged again.

"Have you eaten dinner?" she asked.

"I ate some of your shit."

"You need more than chips and cookies. There's lasagna over there, it's delicious ... I'm completely full."

Mike stood and rooted around in the different storage containers, pulling out the lasagna and a breadstick. "How did you get the town to feed you?" He tore off a piece of breadstick with his teeth and snagged a plastic fork.

"I didn't. Tori did."

Mike paused briefly, nodding as he sat down.

"She told me ... well ... I mean to say - are you mad at her?"

His eyes on his food, Mike answered right away. "No, of course not."

"I might have been."

"Some people deserve to die." He realized he shouldn't have been so frank once he saw her reaction.

Welp, too late now.

Her eyes were wide, the TV light reflecting on them. "Is that the law talking?"

"Law of nature often supersedes the law of man," he said, still focused on his food.

"Vengeance is mine, saith the Lord."

"He also works in mysterious ways. And that ... was divine justice."

"Reaping and sowing ... " Maya took it all in with a small shiver. "Hmm ... "

"What happened to you Maya? I saw the bruises and ... everything else."

Maya jerked back further into the bed as her eyes narrowed on him. "That's a messed-up way to change the subject."

"The person who did it. They doin' time?" He looked at her directly and softened his face and voice. "You can trust me."

Maya ignored him. "She wants to be your friend."

They both knew she was talking about Tori.

"Got enough friends," he said as he looked away.

A pause.

"Why are you here detective?"

Good question.

"Making sure you're good." He stared ahead, chewing. He swallowed and turned to look at her. She was studying him like she was memorizing him. Finally, she seemed to make up her mind about something.

"I'm good, Detective." She tried to stifle a yawn, and he saw her eyes getting heavy.

"Go to sleep, Sunshine," he murmured. And she did. He watched another episode before turning off the TV. After sliding his chair closer to her bed, he watched her sleep and crocheted for hours. As dawn arrived, Mike rose, stretched, wrapped up his project and went home.

MAYA

The next day Maya wasn't up for any more of Rough Ridge's friendly and talkative residents. She slept through most of the morning and fell asleep during Caine's visit in mid-story — or mid-sentence — as she told him about that one night in college that put her off drinking and group sex. At some point, Caine and Tori must have left, placing Maya's cell phone on the bed next to her. It was obvious Tori called off the next round of visitors because she woke alone, the room quiet.

She set her phone to her "Love Groove" playlist and sat in the chair closest to the window as Sam Smith, Adele, Prince, and Maxwell washed over her. With her feet tucked tightly to her butt in the chair and her chin on her knee, she watched the day move outside her window. Prince's "The Question of U" was playing when she sensed him behind her.[1]

"I'm all out of chips, Detective." Her voice sounded tired even to her. She kept her eyes focused on the window.

"Checking to see if you're good," he rumbled.

"Mmm ... " The best noncommittal reply she could muster.

She had no idea whether she was or wasn't. She felt so many things she didn't know what the priority was.

"Are you?" He prompted.

She shrugged. Mike came around to look at her. She must have looked as exhausted and worried as she felt because he squatted beside her and peered into her eyes.

"Sunshine?"

"Have you ever got the sense that your time was moving by too quickly? Like your plans for your life were slipping through your fingers?"

"Talk to me."

There was such a kindness in his eyes, and he looked at her like her words mattered, like he truly cared and wanted to know... but she'd said too much. No good could come of that...

She let herself stare at him, absorb his kindness and intense interest for a moment more before she forced herself to turn back to the window.

"This is a nice place to raise a family. Even the bikers are nice."

"Some of them are," he replied. His eyes were still on her.

"You're one of them."

"Maybe."

She nodded. "I've been wrong before." *Amazingly wrong. So wrong it stupefied her.*

"Maya ... "

"If you are going to stay, no talking." she demanded and waited for him to leave.

Instead, Mike stood, went over to the other chair in the room, and brought it next to hers. He sat in it, putting his motorcycle-booted feet on the windowsill, and stayed with her until she went to sleep.

---

1. Question of U by Prince

7

THIS MAYA WOMAN

FOUR DAYS LATER...

CAINE

Hey Caine, it's Jake. Listen brother, something's going on with this Maya woman."

"What?" Caine wiped his fingers off on a towel and stepped away from the engine he was working on. After she was discharged three days ago, Tori insisted Maya come back to their house. The kids loved her, Tori adored her, and she had a way of throwing sass that made him smile. She was special, but something was off. She was hiding something, and he couldn't let anyone with secrets be around his family — especially ones that came with the type of injuries she'd endured.

"Maya Anderson is completely clean. That's the good news," Jake started. "She's got no credit issues, no record, no actual employment history, nothing..."

"What?" Caine stopped wiping his hands and scowled at a blank spot on the ground in front of him. "How is that possible? She's what, 25? She's gotta have something."

"That's the thing. Maya Anderson didn't exist until six weeks ago, brother."

Shit. "She's playing us." The muscles in his neck tightened.

"I don't know about that man, but she isn't who she says she is. Whoever got her a new ID knows their shit. A total pro. It all looks legit until you look too deep. Real companies, but they mainly operate as a front, for the sole purpose of confirming the info on these IDs. What I do know is she paid cash for her truck and registered the title in Vegas."

Hearing Vegas, Caine's whole body tightened. His first thoughts flew to a time he usually refused to let himself think about. There were several low lifes from his past that made his life hell when he was on the inside. He'd been out for years, but that didn't mean there weren't people hoping for a chance to come after him.

"Someone from the inside?" Caine asked, holding his breath.

"I don't think so, man. Anybody important from your time in doesn't have that kind of pull anymore, especially since you got out."

"You met her. What do you think?"

"She's a sweet kid ... gorgeous, funny, and self-assured when she forgets about the wall she lugs around. She's as big a goof as your wife. Not exactly the makings of a hardened criminal."

"Right, but she's also wicked smart ... smart like Mace." Mace had a rumored IQ that put him in the genius circle and an off-the-book, post-rugby job they called "research and acquisitions." Both Mace and Jake's side professions sometimes took them out of legal lines. Brains like that could be dangerous, especially when hidden behind a bright smile and charming eyes.

"Whatever is going on, man," Jake continued, "you don't want that shit to blow back on you and the family."

Never again.

"Thanks man, keep looking."

"You know I will, man."

Caine stared at his phone for a moment and thought about the young woman he found making glitter pen drawings with his daughter this morning. He grew more uneasy. He would find out who Maya was tonight, or she had to go. No one would ever put his family in danger again.

LATER THAT DAY...

MAYA

Maya decided she would make herself less of a mooch by making a meal. She liked the Walters. Tori was a hoot. The kids were sweet, loud, and a ton of fun. She even liked Caine. Especially Caine. Lately he seemed antsy - in a quiet, broody dude kinda way - and she wanted to take his mind off whatever put him in that mood. She enjoyed seeing his tender side when he was with his family and how gentle and attentive he was with his girls. They knew they were the center of his world. It was a beautiful bond.

Before she died, Maya and her mom were close. They'd have all-night gab sessions and dance while cleaning the house on Saturday morning to old school R&B. Maya's mom was so proud when she graduated from high school and college early. It was as if she beat back cancer just long enough to see Maya cross the stage one last time.

Maya smiled to herself, thinking about the smile on her mother's face as she crossed the turf at THE Ohio State University, diploma in hand. Their eyes met and their dimpled grins matched. It had been a gorgeous, Midwestern, blue sky day. Distracted by her memories, Maya bumped right into a wall at the end of the grocery aisle. She quickly realized the wall was a man in a tight navy-blue t-shirt, wearing a badge on a silver chain like on TV. And she knew who it was before she looked up.

Detective Sheppard.

Maya was almost 5'10, wearing wedge sneakers, and still needed to tilt her head all the way back to see those gorgeous green eyes. She could feel his body heat and her brain flashed to a picture of what he would look like naked, all those muscles and that hair and those eyes. She bit her lip to keep those thoughts from escaping her unpredictable mouth.[1]

"I'm glad to see you're doing better Maya." His voice was low and deep as he searched her face.

God, she loved hearing her name on his lips. A tingle activated by his voice washed over her from head to foot.

I'd love for other things to be on his lips - like my nipples.
No!
Get it together Maya. It's pregnancy hormones. Get. It. Together.
Maya took a big step back. "Detective Sheppard, nice to run into you," she said politely.
Run into you after you literally ran into him? Dork.
"Wait ... I meant not actually running into you that would be assaulting an officer, right? But you know ... seeing you," she finished awkwardly.
Dork.
Dork.
Dork.
Why was it Maya had no trouble discussing contracts worth millions of dollars with titans of industry, but talking to one small town cop made her sound like a junior high kid? It was disturbing on several levels, but mainly because junior high sucked.
What didn't suck was the way he was looking at her right now.
"You changed your hair," he said, reaching out to touch it. Thinking better of it, he dropped his hand. He brought his eyes back to hers and waited.
"What? Oh. Yes. I just took the twists out. Though, as the day goes on, it gets bigger and, unfortunately, I can no longer fit it under my hat." She lifted her knit beanie from her little hand cart and twirled it.
That was cringe.
He stepped back into her space and took all the air with him. "I like it."
Maya swallowed hard, and it was a wonder she could manage that. He was ... overwhelming. His size, his presence, his pull on her ... Maya forced herself to take a step back. Losing her train of thought again, she heard herself whisper, "Oh, I do too."
He again stepped into her space. "You do what?" he whispered back as he reached back out to touch a curl, unable to resist.
"Like it," she whispered, not bothering to move her feet again because the blood had left her extremities and was traveling to other, more sensitive places. His lips came closer as he bent down. His hands

were traveling deeper into her hair and there was nothing Maya could do but watch, wait, and pray he kissed her.

Rational Maya was trying to make sense of all that was happening, trying to hit the panic button, but it was too late. The Maya standing in the middle of the frozen food aisle with melting ice cream had no time for rational thought because she could count the number of freckles on Detective Sheppard's nose. They were small, unnoticeable until he was close, and thank God, he was close.

So close she inhaled him to the back of her throat. She detected musk, sandalwood, fresh air and just ... man. He was so close, she wondered if he sensed her growing wetness. So close his lips moved in slow motion when he asked again, "What do you like, Maya?"

"You."

She'd done it again. She said the quiet part out loud, and the crinkles returned to the corners of his eyes as his lips parted into a smile. Her heart dropped to her feet - it was devastating, that smile. She didn't have time to gather her senses because out of nowhere, a high, shrill voice killed the mood.

"Mike Sheppard?! Mikey Sheppard, is that you?!"

An older woman with a big voice practically galloped to Mike situating herself closer to him while also slightly bumping Maya out of the way. Her skin-tight, sky blue velour track pants and fried, blonde extensions distracted Maya from the personal space invasion, so she just stared with curiosity. The different textures and otherworldly stiffness of the woman's hair mesmerized her. She wanted to poke it.

"I thought that was you! You remind me of your daddy, Mikey, and I swear you've grown a foot since I last saw you!"

Maya slyly slid her phone out to snap a picture for examination later, but at the mention of his father, both Mike and Maya froze. Mike stood ramrod straight as the patience drained from his eyes.

They were standing in the frozen foods section where it was already cold, yet Maya noticed the temperature drop another twenty degrees. The older woman didn't seem to notice. Probably because of all the hot air she pumped out. It somehow kept her cocooned from the large waves of deadly chill Mike radiated.

"Mrs. Snyder, nice to see you again, ma'am," Mike said politely as he took a step back and out of Mrs. Snyder's grip, causing her long French-tipped nails to click together. She was undeterred and kept yakking.

"Guess what, Sarah Beth is back in town as well!" she shrieked, stepping forward and gripping him again. "We were talking about you and first loves and how you two should reconnect." She sighed happily.

Mike glanced at Maya uncomfortably, and she got pain in her chest. It made her breath hitch in the back of her throat. Rational Maya used that opportunity to take over and remind all the Mayas arguing in her head that it would be a lot easier to keep to the "no men vow" with a "Sarah Beth" around.

While deep in inner monologue, Maya blurted, "It's always nice to reconnect with old friends."

Mike looked at her like she had two heads, and Mrs. Snyder pointedly ignored her.

Okaaay.

"You should call her," Mrs. Snyder tried again.

"I'm working a lot right now." Maya watched with growing amusement as he slid his arm away from Grabby Hands Snyder, yet again.

"You know what they say about all work and no play," the old woman teased as she reached in and pressed herself against Mike.

Mike cringed. Maya's eyes widened in shock, and she silently shook with laughter. It was good Cougar Snyder ignored Maya because she struggled to keep it in.

"Oh Mikey, you have grown up," the woman purred as she shivered in delight and her ass wobbled to and fro.

It. Was. Horrifying. And FREAKING HILARIOUS!

Maya lost it. A loud snort escaped, followed by Maya slapping her hand over her mouth. Her body was still shaking with laughter, a stitch threatening to form as she tried in vain to hold in her merriment. Maya almost forgot her wet panties and melting ice cream. She watched Mike with wide eyes, her eyebrows raised to her hairline. The woman suddenly turned and narrowed her own. The amount of venom coming from the woman shocked Maya. She swallowed the guffaws and moved cautiously back.

Yeah, it was time to go.

"I'm sorry, Detective Sheppard, I've got ice cream, so I should be going."

The older woman took the classic bitch stance with a hand on her hip and gave her the top-to-bottom glance. Heat rose from Maya's cheeks and headed for her scalp. She had about three seconds before this turned into a viral video and she could NOT get caught in any shit.

"Is she shoplifting?" Cougar Snyder whispered loudly. "Were you going to arrest her, Mikey?"

"Wait, what?" Maya's head jerked back.

Turning to Mike, Asshole Snyder leaned in and whispered loudly, "Some of us don't think your dear departed daddy was wrong."

To recap, I'm standing in the frozen food section with melting ice cream, an interrupted kiss I don't need, but unfortunately want so bad, I have wet panties; and fate adds a racist old bitch to the mix.

Beautiful.

Maya gave the woman a death stare and turned to leave when Mike placed his hand on her arm. He stepped out of the older woman's grip and stared at Snyder, hard.

"Those people better get over it," he growled. "The rest of the town is glad to be rid of the bastard." The anger coming off him was stifling, and the cougar's claws flew to her mouth. She looked as frozen as the pizzas behind her, much to Maya's inner glee.

Mike turned to Maya, his hand still gripping her arm. "I'll walk you to your car, Maya." Maya took one glimpse at his face and nodded. This was not a time to "throw sass" as Caine would say. They stood quietly in the checkout line, his anger palpable. She was still kinda pissed, but she'd dealt with people like Cheapy McCougar before. She wasn't numb to it, but she didn't need to call attention to herself. One well placed "I feel threatened" could end with Maya being exposed.

It was so awkward, yet it was also nice that he was pissed on her behalf. When they finally began checking out, she noticed the cashier stealing glances at Mike as she rang Maya's groceries. Finally, the cashier spoke. "Mike Sheppard, right?"

"Yes. Amy Gibson?"

"Yes! You remembered! How have you been, hon?"

"Good Amy, how's your family?" he replied, the heat from his anger slowly dissipating.

"They're good. Glad to have you back, Mike," she said with a smile and a pointed expression.

He nodded and Maya sensed him relax even more. The small act of kindness truly affected him. *It must be hard for him*, she realized. Every day was a reminder of who his father was and what he'd done. Amy announced the total. By the time she reached into her purse, Mike had his money ready.

"Oh, Detective Sheppard, that isn't necessary, I—" Maya started out.

"Sunshine."

Boy, he packed a lot in one word. It was a request, an order, and an apology. It wasn't his fault Snyder was the way she was. Why did he feel obligated? But she realized the gesture meant more to him than the 40 dollars for dinner fixings, so she gave in, nodded, and slid her wallet back in her purse.

He nodded once and Amy finished the transaction. "Amy, this is Maya. She's new to Rough Ridge. Maya, Amy and I attended school together."

"Nice to meet you, Maya. Welcome to Rough Ridge." She smiled big.

Maya took in the fresh-faced beauty and instantly liked her.

"Thanks, Amy, I appreciate that." Maya smiled back.

Mike lifted the bags of groceries and waited for Maya to walk ahead of him. They made their way out to Maya's truck in silence. Mike stopped by the smaller, second cab door of her truck and waited expectantly.

"Listen, Detective Sheppard, that was nice, but you didn't have to pay for my groceries," Maya said.[2]

"Open the door Maya," he said with his eyes locked on hers.

Maya shrugged and opened the door, and Mike put the groceries inside.

"You want to come to dinner?" she asked in a rush with a small smile. "You paid for it. I'm making dinner for the Walters' crew to say thank you and to be less of a mooch."

At the mention of the Walters family, Mike shut down. Maya had never seen anything like it. It was absolute. A gut punch.

She realized ... he lived with an overwhelming amount of guilt. He was always trying to right a wrong around her. It wasn't about her. Guilt was his cilice, a painful penance he submitted himself to everyday — and that broke her heart. No one should live with guilt like that. She should know. The weight from her own actions was almost unbearable. Imagine carrying around the weight of someone else's.

An overwhelming need to provide comfort to him destroyed her good sense. Maya stepped in close and put one hand on his chest. The rhythm of his heartbeat made her own rush in her ears. She braved his closed-off face, and, letting instinct guide her rather than sanity and basic social boundaries, she stroked his jaw, bringing her fingers through his goatee, and grazing his chin with her thumb. Her gaze shifted from his chin and lips to his eyes.

"You don't have to pay for the sins of others," she whispered. She saw his face go soft. "You're a good man and you've done nothing wrong. Tori and Caine understand, too." As soon as she mentioned their names, his face hardened. He grabbed her hands and pushed them away as he stepped back.

"You don't know anything about me," he growled.

"I know you sat inside my hospital room for two nights just to make sure I was okay. You stepped in with that woman in there when you didn't have to, and I know you're so arrow-straight you'd give Joe Friday a complex."

"Like I said ... you don't know shit about me," he growled as he stalked away.

"Right," she whispered to herself, nodding, and turning away. "From a monster to a martyr. Stop being so fucking gullible, Maya." She shook her head as she snatched open the driver's side door and threw her purse in.

---

1. Crush by Yuna
2. You're the One I Want by Alex and Sierra

8

I BET THEY LIVE FOR THAT FACE

MAYA

MAYA STARTED HER TRUCK, carefully pulled out of the parking spot, and gunned it down the street. Still fuming and chastising herself, she looked over at the auto shop Caine co-owned and saw Jake and Caine talking in front of the garage. It was spring, and even though there was still snow on the ground, people started bringing their bikes to the shop. She remembered she heard a belt start the squeak of death, so she zoomed into the forecourt of the garage, slipping a parking space.

"Hey Caine. Hey Skunk Weasel," she said to Jake. Maya started calling him that instead of kicking his bike over. Jake grinned, and Caine gave her a nod.

"Listen, I've got groceries in the back and I'm trying to beat Tori home so I can make dinner, but I remembered my belt is slipping, saw you guys, and stopped real quick," she said in a rush.

"Leave it here and I'll ... " Caine started.

"No need dude, I've got it," she said as she started over to the big, triple bay doors. She walked to Blake, grinned, flashing her dimple. "Big man, where's your serpentine belt remover?"

Blake paused, confused, and gestured over his shoulder. Maya ran over, picked it up, and ran back to the truck. She opened the driver-side door, popped the hood, and dove under it, taking care to be gentle with her still bruised and sore body. As she leaned all the way in, she struggled to get to the bolt she needed.

"I. Just. Need ... Damn, this is tight," she muttered.

She was in the middle of the forecourt of an auto shop, in a biker town, with her whole ass in the air, wiggling, as she worked the bolt.

Belatedly, she remembered she was wearing a pair of leggings that lifted and cupped each cheek. They were great for looking good in the gym, but on display in the middle of a busy auto shop? Oof.

The garage was full of men, so she had an attentive audience to her antics. It also didn't help that Maya was blessed with an ample ass.

Griffin would never allow ...

Wait. No.

She shook her head to rid it of his voice and focused on the task at hand.

Make small talk ...

"So, that Mrs. Snyder is a real bitch huh," she yelled from underneath the hood.

Jake looked at Caine with a grin. "What happened?"

"Captain Raymond Holt and I were talking in the grocery store."

"The cop from that TV show?" Jake asked, completely confused.

"Sheppard. Straight arrow, rule book dude, you know, like Joe Friday or Raymond Holt." She mimed a marching soldier.

Jake's grin got bigger while Caine shook his head. They watched as Maya walked past again, grabbed a wrench extender out of Blake's hand, and walked back.

"Anyway," she yelled while climbing back into the truck engine, "she's all in Joe Friday's face going on and on about how he looks like his dad, how her daughter is his lost soulmate, then she grinds on him purring about how he's all grown up."

"Ugh," Caine and Blake said together.

"Exactly." Maya worked with the extender a bit.

"Hey, Blake, can you slide me a roll under the car thingie?"

"Uh, darlin' we're not covered for that by insurance. It's already bad for business to have a lady fix her own car in our lot."

Maya climbed down and took him in. "Blake, I don't have time for chivalry and testosterone. I have ice cream in the back."

Blake hesitated for a second, and Maya put her hands on her hips. He sighed, got her a "roll thingie," and slid it to her. She stopped it with her foot, removed a ponytail holder off her wrist, and pulled her large mane of hair into a bun on top of her head. She carefully laid on the "rollie thing," and slid underneath the car.

"I kinda lost it when she ran full-court press on the poor man." She started laughing until she snorted again. "She copped a 'tude and looked at me like I was dirt under her shoe. THEN she loudly asked him if he was arresting me for shoplifting *and* tells him 'Some of us don't think your daddy was wrong.'"

The barks of indignation and expletives that sizzled through the air were instant and took Maya by surprise. She paused in her story, slid back out from under the truck, and looked at the entire crew standing there.

"Hey, no point in getting pissed now. I was/am plenty pissed enough," she said with a small smile and a shake of her head.

"What did Mike say?" Caine asked.

"Well, I wanted to kick her old ass in the kneecaps, but that's more trouble than she's worth. I opted for a death stare and tried to walked away."

She slid back underneath the car. "Mike was completely pissed!" she shouted. "He's quiet, but boy, don't get on the wrong side of him. I thought he'd shoot lasers out of his eyes and melt the velour jogging suit off her ass. He got right in her face and told her those people needed to get over it and that the rest of the town was essentially dancing a jig the man was dead. She almost choked on her tongue. It was brilliant. He paid for my groceries and walked me to my truck, which wasn't necessary."

Maya rolled back out and sat up. "She's gotta be knocking on late '60s early '70s and the way she sounds, she's sucking back a steady diet of cigs and booze, which means she's got one foot in the grave and a drunk one on a banana peel. She'll get her due soon enough." Maya shrugged. "I've been Black all my life, and it's exhausting to fight every asshole. You've gotta pick and choose who you bitch slap. Plus, I had ice cream melting," she said, grinning at them as she took her hair down and shook it out.

She fiddled with the "wheelie thingie," and thought for a hot second. In a burst of child-like energy, she launched herself across the forecourt on the car creeper, grinning the entire way, hair flying. She finally stopped right in front of Blake.

"That was awesome. Haven't done that in years."

"That's why it's not covered under our insurance," he said, unable to keep his smile hidden.

She slapped him on the back. "Lighten up, life is very short. And I need a new alternator for my truck. Can you order it? I'll stop by and pay for it tomorrow. I only brought enough to cover groceries."

Maya briskly walked over to where Jake and Caine stood and pulled the greasy rag out of Caine's hand, wiping her own hands on it.

"You fellas can close your mouths now. You've seen a girl change a belt before," she said.

"Girl, that ain't why they watchin'," Jake said with a laugh.

Maya shrugged, embarrassed, and handed the rag back to Caine. "Y'all have seen ass before too. See you at the house, Caine. I'm making you guys lasagna tonight and a bomb dessert." She did a little dance as she walked away and hopped back into the truck. When she started it, they heard Jay-Z's "Dirt Off Your Shoulder" blasting out of the windows as she backed out of the forecourt into the street. She beeped the horn and took off.[1]

CAINE

Cain and Jake watched as she drove away while everyone else got back to work.

"Definitely not a criminal mastermind," Jake said quietly to Caine.

"Something's up. The ID, and if you'd seen the bruises man ... whatever her shit is, I can't have it around my family."

"All right brother, we'll keep digging. I'll call in a few favors on it," Jake said.

MIKE

Mike followed a bit behind her after she left until she threw her truck into the garage's front forecourt. He pulled over, unable to keep his eyes off her. He still enjoyed the sensation of her hand on his face, chest. *"You don't have to pay for the sins of others."* Detected her perfume, *"You're a good man ... I know you sat inside my hospital room two nights to make sure I was okay."* And hear her admonish herself, *"From a monster to a martyr ... stop being so gullible."*

Mike took a deep breath and tried to clear his mind as he watched her climb into and under her truck and finally slide across the concrete on a wheeled scooter, her big, open smile on full display. He noticed how she held herself ... obviously still hurting from whoever beat the hell out of her, even though she tried to minimize it.

His concern for her injuries didn't make him feel good about noticing how her leggings hugged her hips, her ass, and her toned thighs and legs. Her little jacket emphasized her small waist and that smile when she flashed her dimple ... it was a losing battle. He shook his head as she peeled out of the garage and toward the Walters' home.

He didn't follow. Instead, he headed back to his room to take a swim and wash her out of his mind. A woman like her could easily become as important as oxygen. Shit, he already hated to watch her go.

LATER THAT DAY...

MAYA

Maya was in the kitchen cooking, listening to the Temptations blaring out of the speakers in the living room. Flour covered the oldest girls. The baby sat in her highchair, banging on a pot. Tori sang into a broom and shook her ass. Then Maya joined her with her own spoon mic, both being real extra.

"Daadeee!" Gabriella screeched.

The Walters girls ran to greet Caine while Maya hung back and watched. He lifted each of his little girls and kissed them, then leaned in for a long, passionate kiss from his wife. He was the quintessential Girl Dad.

Maya looked away wistfully and was a bit embarrassed. Touching her stomach, she thought about the family life she would have soon. It wouldn't be "traditional," but it could be a good life if they remained hidden.

She sensed Caine watching her and smiled slightly at him.

"Hey man, the food is almost ready, so if you two want to hop in the 'shower.'" She held up her fingers in air quotes. "I can handle the kids and clean up."

"Mommy's not dirty," Gabriella pipped in.

"Not yet," Caine growled and led his wife away to the bedroom.

"Rabbits," Maya muttered to herself with a laugh.

"Hey kids, let's vacuum the flour off."

"Yay!"

CAINE

The next thing Caine heard was the hand vacuum.

"Is she?"

"The kids love it, honey," Tori said, waving off his concern. "She vacuumed them yesterday. It was a big hit. She's great with them and it's been nice having her here."

Caine's eyes clouded over.

"What?" Tori brought her hand to his face and watched his eyes.

"Babe, we don't know who she is." He sighed, rubbing his hand down his face.

"What do you mean? She's a good person who's obviously been through a lot," Tori said incredulously. "She reminds me of me."

Tori began stripping off her clothes and slowly peeling off her husband's.

"Jake found some things that don't add up."

"Jake?!" Tori paused at her husband's zipper. "You had her investigated? Why don't you ask her yourself? She's a sweet girl. You two have a lot in common and you obviously like her. You guys laugh all the time."

"Let's take a shower."

Tori paused, looked him in his eyes, and nodded, letting her husband lead her to the shower to get a little dirty while getting clean.

CAINE SAT BACK from the table full as hell and dreading what came next. He glanced at Tori, and she gathered the girls for their baths.

"Hey Caine, I've got warm, salted caramel, chocolate chip turtle cookies, and ice cream with fresh whipped cream," Maya said. "I have a secret ingredient I add to the whipped cream for zip. I don't cook much, but the stuff I can cook is the booomb!"

She did a little dance.

Complete goofball.

"I've got a massive sweet tooth," she said as she hand-whipped the cream, "and I saw Tori sneak you a little something after the kids go to bed."

"Maya—"

"Can't stop, it's a process and if I stop, something will lose temperature," she said distractedly.

She moved to the freezer and took out a cold dessert plate. He watched her squirt a drizzle of caramel, drop three dots of chocolate sauce, and carefully scooped out rounded mounds of French vanilla bean ice cream. Then she opened the oven where cookies warmed, slid one off the plate and carefully sliced it in half. She placed the two halves across the top of the ice cream, gave the cream one last whip, swirled it on the side of the ice cream, and topped it off with a bit of caramel drizzle, a few shaves of dark chocolate, and a single perfect, caramelized pecan.

Caine watched her build the treat like she was building a bridge to the other side of the moon. She concentrated with her tongue out, and

Caine glimpsed how she must've looked as a little kid. She reminded him of his Gabriella when the kid settled long enough to focus.

Finally, she grabbed a fork and pushed both the fork and confection across the island over to Caine.

"Let that hit you," she said with a grin.

"Maya—"

"Man, if you wait too long, the temperatures are off. Warm cookie, cold ice cream, cool cream," Maya said, her eyes big and excited. "Eat it or I will."

He looked at her, shook his head, and dug in. She was right. It was the shit. The temperatures, flavors, and textures were an amazing combination. She watched him, and when he closed his eyes, she slapped her hand on the counter.

"That's it! The face. I'm not a chef, but I bet they live for that face."

She started making herself one.

"Yo, Maya, wait."

She glanced over, saw his expression, and put the plate on the counter.

"What's up? You've got a scary face going on, man. If I were a chicken, I'd have run by now." She laughed nervously.

He studied her for a moment and bluntly asked, "You fuckin' with my family?"

She blinked twice. "Wait. What? I noticed the lasagna noodles were dry on the sides, but I think dessert makes up for it."

He didn't laugh.

"Who are you?" When she didn't respond, he asked again. "Who?"

"My name is Maya," she mumbled, looking over his shoulder.

"Maya Anderson didn't exist a couple of weeks ago." He slapped his hand on the table and growled out, "Lie to me again."

"My real name *is* Maya. The rest doesn't matter. I am who you see in front of you. The rest is bullshit that needs to stay where I left it," her voice quivered, and a single tear escaped her eye. She brushed it away impatiently, crossed her arms in front of her, and stood, placing her feet wide apart, taking a defiant stance.[2]

Caine watched her. She looked like a trapped animal prepared to fight. He stood and walked to her side of the kitchen. Her eyes grew bigger as he approached, but she didn't back away. She stood rod straight and faced him, her hands coming to her sides and clenching.

"Maya, those bruises."

As soon as he said it, he regretted it. Her eyes lowered to the floor. She looked so ashamed. The fight just slid right out of her. She tugged at her shirt in jerky movements, as if she could cover them more, hiding them from his memory.

He reached out and lightly grabbed her hands to stop her from moving.

"Maya, who did this to you? What happened? Maybe I can help or get you help," he whispered.

She looked stunned at his gentle suggestion. He searched her face as he said, "I can't have whatever is happening with you hurt my family. Let me help."

Her eyes widened with horror.

"Oh God! I never thought of that."

She jerked her fingers out of his and ran them absentmindedly through her hair as her body became a ball of nervous energy.

"Oh God, the babies ... you and Victoria have been through enough ... No,"—she shook her head and switched to rapidly nodding — "you're right. No shit will come on you guys, I promise."

Her breathing became irregular, and a sob escaped her throat. She looked at Caine and whispered, "I gotta go. I gotta go now. I'm so sorry."

"Maya, wait, tell me—"

But she'd taken off, quickly walking toward her room.

He heard her close the door to her bedroom. In record time, she was back in the kitchen, grabbing her keys as they heard the kids running down the hallway. She looked at him, quickly wiped her eyes, blew out a breath, and turned to face them.

"Maya! Mommy said it's time to say goodnight!" Liv said.

"And thank you for the basagya and cookies," Gabriella interrupted.

Caine admired Maya for trying to put on a brave face.

"You're welcome, cool cat and wild child."

Liv looked at Maya and her bag. "You leaving?"

"Yes sweetie, I am," Maya said with a watery smile.

"Why?" Gabriella yelped.

"Because Sweets, all good slumber parties must come to an end." She lifted the two oldest girls and placed them on the counter.

Looking at Liv, she said, "Remember what I taught you today?"

"Next time my teef come out, ask for diamonds or bonds, both accum-mumate value over time," she whispered.

"Perfect," Maya whispered and kissed her on her nose. Then she turned to his wild one. "What about you, girlie? What did you learn today?"

"My inside voice is powerful; my outside voice is powerful. I am a warrior!" Gabriella screeched to the heavens.

"Yes love, you are," Maya brushed her hair back and kissed her on the nose too. "Bye chica," she said, hugging Tori tight. She tucked baby Simone under the chin until she giggled and bent to touch Tori's belly. "Bye baby boy," she whispered.

"Boy?" Victoria asked.

"I can feel it."

Maya straightened and looked at the big family, giving them a toothy fake smile.

"Bye Caine, take care of them."

Once Maya left the house, Liv ran to Maya's room and came back with a piece of paper.

"She forgot her picture Momma. She keeps it under her pillow."

And she held it up.

Tori saw it and tears filled her eyes. She looked at Caine as he realized it was an ultrasound.

"Damn."

----

1. Dirt off Your Shoulder by Jay Z
2. Bag Lady by Erykah Badu

9

WHAT THE HELL WAS THAT?

MAYA

IN A CRUEL CASE of Déjà vu, Maya found herself once again staring down a dark mountain road. By now, the lines and curves had a comforting familiarity. The next curve would take her past the deep gray home with black shutters and a long drive. She would often see a little girl bouncing away on the trampoline in the backyard. The next block would bring her past the expansive cabin home that reminded her of Christmas. Something about the evergreen trees, the logs, and the herd of fake deer posed in the front just screamed "Ho, Ho, Ho."

Maya focused on the road in front of her and willed the tears not to fall. The further she got away from the family, the more her heart ached. She finally pulled over for a moment and let it all out. After fifteen minutes of intense tears, Maya forced herself to get it together.[1]

"Maya, you can do this. You are a grown woman and you're about to be a mother. It's time to stop playing fairyland with other people's families."

She gripped the wheel tightly as she navigated the dark roads to the Rough Ridge Hotel. Her destination two weeks ago.

"Delayed but not denied," she whispered.

She pulled into a parking spot, hopped out of the truck, grabbed her bag, and the.38 she picked up in Texas (compliments of the same woman who gave her the new ID). She tucked it into her back waistband and pulled her shirt over it. There wouldn't be a Caine or an alarm system here. The hotel - more like a motel - was cozy and well cared for — but crazy shit had happened in Rough Ridge. Tori gave her all the gossip, and she wasn't interested in being the latest headline.

She opened the door to the office and went to the front desk, where Ms. Shirley's great big hound greeted her with a nuzzle to her tummy. Maya yelped and jumped into the nearest chair.

"Hey honey! Oh, I'm so glad you finally came to join us! Don't worry about Charlie. He's a sweetheart!" She reached to give Maya a hand as she climbed off the chair.

Afraid of dogs, she kept a leery eye on the pony-sized dog named Charlie. To her surprise, he must have sensed her fear and laid down at her feet. She bent a little at the waist. "Um... how do you do Charlie?"

Charlie nuzzled her feet a bit more. His weight was warm and reassuring. *Maybe dogs aren't so scary after all.*

"How are you doing?" Ms. Shirley took in, but didn't mention, Maya's red eyes and teary face.

"I'm good, Ms. Shirley. I need to get into my own space and start making plans. Do you still have a room for me?"

"Of course, sweetie. Right next to another long termer. Here you go, room twelve. Here are some complimentary eyedrops."

She smiled one last grateful smile at Ms. Shirley and braved a halting, friendly pat to Charlie, who nudged her hand gently while swishing his tail. "You are a good boy, aren't you, Charlie? You'll be gentle with me while we learn each other, right?"

Another nudge and little whine from the pup sealed the deal.

MAYA COMING to Rough Ridge was no random act. When she left Columbus, she recognized she had to go somewhere obscure. It would be easier to hide in a tiny town no one had ever heard of instead of hoping the anonymity of a big city would protect her.

When Maya's mother was younger, she took a tour of the country, often stopping in small out of the way places. Rough Ridge had been one of those places. Maya wished she had more information, like what room her mom stayed in all those years ago, but every time she asked her about her time in Rough Ridge or her sabbatical in general, her mother got sad. Eventually, Maya stopped asking. Her mom likely missed the freedom. Being a single mom wasn't easy.

"Mommy, here I am," she whispered. "I'm hoping I'll make wonderful memories here."

She opened her door, flicked on the light and scanned the small room. Quietly, she shut the door, placed her gun under the pillow and stopped to take in the space.

The scent of flowers wafted through the room, and it was clean. Those were the pluses. The minuses started with the decor that likely hadn't changed since her mom visited. Though, if she was trying to be positive, it was a plus. The building had good bones, and her best friend and sometime biz partner Shay would've knocked the decor out of the park.

It seemed like a million years ago they were tag-teaming on projects. Maya would design the building and Shay would dress them. Two Black women making their own rules in a field where there weren't many like them. She missed her Shay.

Maya checked the time on the East Coast, opened her laptop, launched her Tor browser, and pinged her girl's IM. She braced herself for Shay's attitude as she waited.

SUPER SHAY: "YOU BETTER HAVE A GOOD
EXCUSE FOR SLIDING INTO MY DMS AFTER RADIO
SILENCE FOR WEEKS."
MAYA: "I LOVE YOU TOO, GIRL."
SUPER SHAY: "MAYA, WHERE HAVE YOU BEEN?!
ARE YOU OKAY?"
MAYA: "YES."
SUPER SHAY: "WHERE ARE YOU?"
MAYA: "IT'S BETTER IF YOU DON'T KNOW."
SUPER SHAY: "OK, BUT YOU'RE OKAY?"
MAYA: "I AM. TELL ME WHAT OR WHO YOU'VE
BEEN UP TO SINCE I LEFT."
SUPER SHAY: "I MISS YOU TOO."
MAYA: . . ..
SUPER SHAY: "HE'S LOOKING FOR YOU."
MAYA: "I KNOW."
SUPER SHAY: "HE'S CRAZY ANGRY."
MAYA: "I KNOW."
SUPER SHAY: "DID HE HURT YOU?"
MAYA: ...
MAYA: "YEAH."
SUPER SHAY: "OH SWEETIE, I'M SO SORRY!"
MAYA: ...
SUPER SHAY: "ARE YOU PREGNANT?"
MAYA ...
SUPER SHAY: "MAYA?"
 MAYA: "YES."
SUPER SHAY: "OH HONEY ... WHAT CAN I DO?"
MAYA: "WHAT YOU'RE DOING RIGHT NOW. IS HE
BOTHERING YOU?"
SUPER SHAY: "NOTHING I CAN'T HANDLE. THERE
ARE PERKS TO BEING A PART OF THE FIRST
FAMILY."

Shay was a part of a bigger dynasty than Griffin's family — old money and high profile. Griffin was a monster, but he would never be stupid enough to mess with her.

MAYA: "I GOTTA GO, SHAY."
SUPER SHAY: "OK. BE CAREFUL BABE. LOVE YOU."

Maya disconnected the Tor browser, closed her computer, and for the second time that night, she cried.

MIKE

Mike paused at the sound of crying from the room next door. Alert, he waited to see if there was trouble. After a while, he heard the shower turn on, and the sobbing stop. Relaxing, Mike turned his mind to one of Rough Ridge Hotel's best features - the heated pool and hot tub. Even though it was spring, the air still had a bite to it and the warm water would get Mike's head straight and his thoughts off Maya.

He hoped.

It'd been a few days since she left the hospital and traveled straight to the Walters' home for recovery. Their last night together at the hospital was strange. She was contemplative, and it made him uneasy, but he respected her wishes and didn't push. He would have done anything she asked to be near her.

The last couple of days without her were a mixed bag. He wanted to see her, but the baggage he carried would only weigh her down. Their encounter at the store underlined that. He shook his head, trying to clear his thoughts, and headed to the pool.

Mike swam a few easy laps, enjoying the cool air kiss his skin as the heated water cascaded over it. He sensed her before he saw her, and the hairs on the back of his neck stood up. The water and the cold Colorado evening temperature climbed another ten degrees. Mike thought he'd convinced himself he didn't have time for distractions, but, as he swam near her, he had to admit Maya was one distraction he sorely wanted.[2]

She wore a long, thin, loose white cotton skirt with a matching bikini top. He watched as she slipped her legs further into the water. The outfit was demure and sexy, even if the reasons for it - her bruised body - were not. Shit, everything about Maya was complicated. Alarm bells were going off, but he couldn't take his eyes off her. She was fucking perfection.

She swished her long legs back and forth slowly in the water. When she would lift one out, the skirt clung to it like a second skin. He imagined her legs wrapping around him as he fitted to her. Then he took in the smooth dip of her waist and the shape of her fantastic breasts. He noticed the cold air doing the work on them he wished he could. She had an elegant neck with smooth skin complimented by high cheekbones, and a single, exquisite dimple. He lingered on her full lips and thick, dark lashes — the kind women spent hundreds of dollars to mimic. He finally was less of an asshole and focused on her eyes. They were wary.

He'd stared too long.

Her marvelous lips parted, her pink tongue darted out to moisten them, and he jerked slightly.

"Joe Friday, are you studying me for a lineup, or can I help you with something?"

There was a low hush to her voice that made him want to peel her out of those scraps of material, right there, in full view of Main Street.

"No, ma'am. Just wondering what you were doing out here on your own at night. It isn't safe."

"Oh, I don't know, a cop swimming in my new pool has got to be better than most security systems." She smiled.

Damn that dimple. He was fucked.

"You're staying here now?" he asked, finding himself somewhere between excitement and agitation.

"Yes, a girl can only depend on the kindness of strangers for so long," she quipped, her smile not reaching her eyes or even activating the dimple.

"You were making dinner a few hours ago."

"It was time," she said firmly.

"That's bullshit."

She blinked. Twice.

"Eliot Ness, are you calling me a liar?"

"I'm saying my bullshit detector is going off."

"Asshole."

"Is that your favorite word?"

Why was he teasing her?

"One of them." With an arched brow she continued, "I also like dipshit, dumb shit, and nosey fucker."

She was just damn delightful. Mike had never used that word to describe anything, but it fit her perfectly.

"You kiss your grandma with that mouth?"

"No."

He moved in to get a better view of her fantastic lips. Her breath quickened, and she bit her lip, which made him draw even closer. He stood between her legs, felt her shiver, and appreciated it wasn't from the cold.

"Would you kiss me with that mouth?"

He looked into her eyes and traced her bottom lip with his thumb, leaving glistening moisture behind. Those beautiful, brown orbs grew large with surprise, then narrowed at the challenge. She gently placed her hands on the sides of his face. They were cool and damp from the water, but his skin heated as she touched him.

Finally, she placed her mouth on his.

It was everything — good, sweet, and decadent, dirty, and carnal. What started off as playful and soft built quickly into a fevered, passionate embrace. He wrapped one arm around her waist and drew her into the water and into him.

Mike gripped her tighter and slid his other hand into that thick mass of coily curls like he longed to do since the first day he saw her. And Heaven help him, they were so much better than he imagined. *She* felt better than he imagined. Soft, warm, and damn it; she was electric. Her intense energy vibrated straight through him and on top of all that, she smelled like sugared vanilla.

He was screwed.

His tongue touched her lip, and he was even more screwed because her lips parted at his touch. He hungrily dove in. A deep, sweet sigh escaped her mouth and sent him over the edge.

Yep. Completely, totally, utterly screwed.

He slid his hands over her ass and lifted her. Using both hands to wrap those long legs around him, he pressed his hardness against her.

Trapped between him and the pool wall, Maya held on like she was drowning and squeezed him closer. She threaded her hands through his hair and began kissing along his jaw, leaving alternating hungry and feather-soft kisses.

The loud ring of his cell phone interrupted the magic and brought him back to reality. He'd crossed, no, obliterated the line, mauling her in public like a damn animal. *What the hell was wrong with him?* She'd obviously experienced intense shit before coming to town, and he was taking advantage of her. *Damn it!*

As he abruptly pulled away from Maya, he took in her half-closed eyes, swollen lips, and rapid breathing.

She was so damn beautiful, complicated, and mysterious. He needed to live a life that was open, clear cut and, honestly, he had nothing to offer her. He shouldn't be trusted with her or the promise she held.

Not trusting himself to say or do the right thing, he grabbed her with gentle, firm hands by the waist, lifted her, and softly deposited her on the edge of the pool. Next, he pulled his big body out of the pool in one smooth movement. Mike walked to the lounge chairs by the pool. He grabbed his phone and keys and hit the button as he walked to his room. As he pushed his door open, he heard a husky, irritated voice from the pool.

"What the hell was that?"

---

1. Refuse by Kevin Garret
2. Wicked Game by James Vincent

10

LOOKS LIKE WE'RE HAVING BREAKFAST TOGETHER

MAYA

Maya was stunned, pissed, and horny as hell.

She was also soaking wet in all the ways you can be and freezing in the chilly spring air. No way she was getting back into the pool after that shit, so after she grabbed her key, phone and the tatters of her dignity she marched back to her room.

She slammed the door closed and continued slamming things around until she decided she could be mad or horny, but not both. Digging through her bag, she praised the discount store gods for their bulk sale on batteries in Illinois.

Ten minutes later, Maya was in the throes of a second orgasm. She worked her toy, imagining Mike's hands and mouth all over her body. When the orgasm died out, she took a moment to catch her breath before getting in the shower. She was still pissed, but at least she could sleep.

MIKE

Mike listened to her moans through the paper-thin walls and jerked off to keep from knocking her door off the hinges and burying himself in her. Coming only helped a little, but at least it kept him from acting like an ass with Maya. Again.

MAYA

Maya spent the next week checking out the town, looking to find a new, more permanent place to live and trying to forget Officer A-hole. In between viewing condos and apartments, she also spent time at the library and county recorder.

She explored local real estate options for building the home she kept having dreams about and drafted several building plans. And by the end of the week, she settled on a condo where she could live until it was safe to build. She started the purchase process through her internationally registered LLC. Untraceable and established when she was sixteen, Maya was almost certain it was off the radar enough to keep the purchase from arousing interest.

The condo would suit her purposes until well after she gave birth - three bedrooms, an office, open floor plan, loft area, and wrap-around deck with a view of the Rockies. Most importantly, the master bedroom on the second floor held a safe room. She instructed the realtor to get information from the owner about where to purchase the nifty supplies they kept inside. Thinking about the peaceful view of the mountains, she hoped she would never have to use it. With weeks ahead until she closed on the condo, she put that negativity out of her mind and focused on not becoming strung out on a man she barely knew. A man that was heavy into playing games. He had arrested her, ruined her shirt, saved her life twice, bought her groceries, rejected her coldly, and kissed her as if his life depended on it, only to leave her hanging without so much as a backward glance.

No. Way too much drama.

She needed stability and to concentrate on getting things ready for her baby. Luckily for her, Mike appeared to be actively avoiding her as well.

Nighttime was the only time she couldn't avoid him. In the quiet of the night, her mind replayed all their interactions on a loop. The kiss.

How he smelled in the grocery store. The way he looked at her. The kiss. Those green eyes, staring intently. The quiet strength in his voice. The kiss. Every single night for a week, the hot and cold detective lived rent-free in her mind, and she couldn't get to sleep until she released the sexual tension built up inside her. It was getting ridiculous.

Maya was sitting in a booth at the Main Street Diner, (yes, the one diner on actual Main Street), with her back to the door, when Mike came in. She was in the middle of deciding between eggs and a peanut butter sandwich when she heard the change in conversation.

"I still can't believe they hired him. Like the town needs another Sheppard, especially on the force."

Some loudmouth had spouted their opinion on everything from the government to his neighbors, to the eggs since she arrived. It was seriously interfering with her thought process.

"Pipe down, Jessup," the butthead's dining companion replied. "He's one of the good ones, as straight as Cabot or Cap'n. Let the man eat in peace."

"Bull. All the Sheppards are bad, not a good one among the lot."

Maya hated bullies. HATED them. She'd spent a good part of her awkward youth being bullied left and right. And by awkward youth, she meant from age nine until her junior year in college. When you're a nerd, you're bullied, when you're a nerd too young for college who doesn't party and spends her time with her mom, you definitely catch static.

Sighing loudly, she recognized her mouth would get her in trouble again - this time before breakfast.

"Yeah, I'll tell ya, every one of 'em is on the take."

"Excuse me, sir? Yes, you, the one with the logorrhea."

"Loga-what?" the man he asked, confused, and miffed his rant got cut off.

"Diarrhea of the mouth," Maya snapped. "You've run down every person who has walked through that door this morning. Honestly. I've never seen a man gossip more than an old hen." The patrons around her laughed into their morning coffee. "Hey hon," she called to the waitress, "can you move my seat over to Detective Sheppard? All the hot air over here is a little too much first thing in the morning." She leaned over, looking the older gentleman directly in his eyes. "Or EVER."

The waitress could barely contain her smile. "Sure thing, honey."

Maya grabbed her tea and stood. Turning, she spotted Mike sitting at his table. She willed herself to keep walking toward those green eyes glaring at her over his cup of coffee. He wore a faded black t-shirt stretched tight over his chest, dark jeans, motorcycle boots, and his requisite badge. His thick hair was still drying from his shower and turning wild. The closer she got, the more irritated he looked. She realized she, not the gossiping men, irritated him.[1]

Well, he'll have to get over it. She'd made a public, dramatic play and aimed to follow it through. She slid into his booth and sat her mug of tea on the table gently. "Looks like we're having breakfast together," she said as cheerily as she could fake.

He didn't say a word. His jaw clenched.

"You should pretend to be happy to see me. I already made that big 'fellow citizen camaraderie' show."

He still didn't say a word.

"Or not. You can at least NOT act like I was the one who left you high and dry on the side of a pool. Or should I say, low and wet?"

"I don't need your pity," he growled as she lined her paper napkin on her lap. "Or your help. And you seem to handle any residual disappointment yourself ... nightly."

She jerked back in shock. The heat of embarrassment rose from her toes to the top of her head. Her scalp prickled with it.

She was caught vibrator handed.

God! How awkward is it he listened to me - wait ... He sat there listening to me ... sneaky bastard. I bet my case of batteries he rubbed a few out listening ... Damn. Now her nipples were straining against her thankfully padded bra.

She shifted slightly, clenching her thighs at the thought, pissed at herself for having it. Plus, there was the fact he was trying to make her look stupid. She swallowed the rest of her embarrassment and embraced the knowledge she turned him on.

"Good, because I'm not giving it - pity or help. I hate bullies - always have. And how often, how creatively, and how incredibly satisfying I handle ... tension"— she licked her lips slowly and dropped her voice low and husky — "is entirely my business alone." She licked her lips again as she watched him struggle with that information. Those green eyes laser-focused on her lips and when they dropped to her chest she heaved a small sigh. Satisfied she'd put him in his place, she smirked and turned her attention to the waitress who arrived to take both of their orders.

"I'll have scrambled eggs with cheese, applesauce, a peanut butter sandwich on wheat, no crusts with jelly on the side," Maya rattled off quickly.

"Ok, what about you, Detective?"

"Eggs over medium. Bacon."

"Ooh! Add a slice of bacon for mine as well."

"Sure sugar," she said, laughing. "That's a wild combo."

Mike sat staring holes through Maya as she ignored him. She played with her straw instead.

"Do you talk at breakfast, or do you simply scowl?" she asked the cutlery she was deeply engaged in arranging.

"Depends."

"On?" She fiddled with the sugar.

"On whether the person I'm with was in my bed the night before."

Her eyes raised to him in surprise.

"I thought that would do it."

"Do what."

"Get you to look at me again."

She sighed heavily. "Our little tête-à-têtes are... interesting I admit. And you have a certain je ne sais quoi. But the up, down, hot, cold drama thing is not for me. And I don't want to sit here while you use those magnificent eyes of yours to do a soul scan of me. Especially before breakfast. Now, we can eat like civilized people, or I can get my food to go and get out of your hair."

"Do you always say what's on your mind?"

"No. There are times I'm downright demure and retiring. You'll never see that, however."

His lip twitched.

She sat back and crossed her arms. "I'm an introvert no matter what people's initial impressions of me might be. I turn the personality on when I'm out, but then I need bubble time to recharge. I prefer quiet and solitude until I don't if that makes any sense. I have little patience for the bush beating. Things in my head move quickly, and if I must focus on massaging the message every day with everyone, it creates a log jam. Strategically, it's easier to say it. Often, it leaves my mouth before my brain has time to stop it anyway."

"Complicated answer." He sighed as he rolled his eyes. "An introvert? The first day you met me, you called me an asshole and told me to kiss your ass."

"That has nothing to do with being an introvert. You were being an asshole, and the only thing I wanted was for you to kiss my ass."

They were quiet again, as Maya busied herself by tracing patterns on the table with her fingernails. She licked her lips and sensed his eyes on her. His jaw clenched as he stared at her lips again. He looked hungry - and not for breakfast. He also looked like she made him angry, and she didn't understand why.

"Why are you here, Maya?"

"Here on Earth? In Rough Ridge? Relaxing here with you now, or what?"

"Cut the shit, Sunshine."

"You're stuck on being Officer Asshole, huh?" She glared at him in frustration, thinking about how much to say. She poked the bear a bit. "As far as being on the Earth, well, we all search for that singular purpose. I have mine and it's my business. No ulterior motives to being here in town or in this booth. I came to the town because I want and need peace. I came over here to sit with you because you come from a shit family. People paint you with a broad brush and it's a poop deal, so I said something. IF that offends your delicate alpha male sensibilities, well, my previous offer stands. You can kiss my ass."

This brought a slight, but devastatingly handsome grin to his face. Maya ignored it and the pleasure it gave her, choosing instead to focus on their arriving order.

MIKE

She was a nightmare. Her health had improved, and she radiated a glow that made it hard for him to take his eyes off her. He noticed she was at the diner before she made a scene and loved watching her walking toward him like she was wearing $1,000 designer heels instead of a pair of sneakers.

Everything about her said high class: she appeared to speak perfect French, she ate her food with a knife and fork like she was at high tea with the Queen, and she didn't appear to be overly concerned about getting a job in town. But her clothes, including her collection of t-shirts with smart assed sayings, and her mouth, said down to earth. He loved the way she parted her lips a little before she spoke. It distracted him, and then she would shock him by saying something crazy. She was used to being in charge, he could tell, but in charge of what?

She was a conflicted woman ... or a woman of contradictions. He hadn't figured out which one yet. Her smile didn't always reach her eyes and she had a way of saying everything while still keeping things close to the vest. Obviously, she had a fucked up past. All of it meant, "Danger Mike! Run the other direction!" But here he sat, like a jackass, watching her eat peanut butter and eggs with a knife and fork. She carefully cut her peanut butter sandwich and smeared jelly on top. Then she did the same with eggs and bacon and piled it all together for one gross bite.

"You're odd," she said when she finished chewing.

"I could say the same about you." He tucked into his own eggs.

"You can and should. I've been the resident weirdo all my life. I'm used to it." She smiled.

Another one that stayed south of her eyes. Fascinating.

"You move back to a town you obviously hate, to care for people who aren't sure they can trust you, even though you are obviously so connected to the purpose of your job you arrest lost visitors for apple juice."

Straight to the point. He didn't like the subject, but he liked how she said it. He liked her and he was still trying not to, so he switched tactics. Push her away before she got in ... any further. "I hated my father but love this town. My sister is dying of cervical cancer, and I don't give a fuck if they don't trust me. I got a job to do, which is to unfuck all the shit my father did."

She paused mid-smear, biting her lip and he watched the flash of brilliant white worry the soft skin of her bottom lip. It was sexy and sweet at the same time. *Fuck, more contradictions.*

"I'm sorry." Her eyes were wet.

He'd upset her. Good. Now she'd leave him alone and take all her sexy ass, sass, and the promise of a different life with her. He hated that it bothered him so much to see her upset, but this had to stop, so Mike fired another shot. "I said I didn't want your fucking pity, so mind your own damn business."

That stung her. She blinked twice, and he watched in surprise as her eyes lit on fire, the wet clearing as she leaned in.

"And I said I wasn't giving it. You mean, uncouth, neanderthal ingrate," she whispered viciously. "But you do have my empathy because I'm an actual human being and not some RoboCop who follows the rules without regard to others. You have my empathy because I watched my mother die from bone cancer for SEVEN YEARS. Watching someone you love being eaten alive from the inside is a pain few should ever have to endure. You also have my empathy because you seem bent on wasting your life paying a tab you didn't open."

His heart froze in his throat, and an overwhelming shame bloomed across his soul.

She sat back, shook her head, and crossed her arms as her foot bounced under the table in agitation. "You are gonna miss so much good life, shit ... for that ... I do... I do pity you."

She was shaking with rage as she quickly removed her napkin, crossed her knife and fork at the top of her plate like she was in a five-star Michelin restaurant instead of a diner in rural Colorado, and slid out of the booth. If she had slapped him, he wouldn't have been more stunned.

Fuck. Fuck. FUCK! Jesus, seven years? The hell it must have been for her and her family. He wanted to push her away, but damn, he didn't want to throw her own mother's death in her face. He felt lower than an ant's balls, and watched with remorse as she stepped to the counter to pay her bill, slapping down a twenty as she waited for service. She hadn't finished her breakfast.

MAYA

She was barely keeping it together. Screw beautiful eyes. Nothing excused his lack of basic human decency. His life was free and clear when others, like her, like the women in the shelters she stayed in after Griffin, had to leave everything and start over. He was throwing life away, sitting on crap he didn't even own. It wasn't noble; it was misguided and selfish. As she waited for the cashier to come back from topping off a customer's coffee, she felt him by her side.

His voice was low in her ear. "I can't let you do that."

His voice sent waves radiating through her, waves that concentrated at her heart, at the moist juncture between her thighs, and scrambled her mind. Luckily, being pissed won out.

"You are not in a position to 'let me' do a goddamn thing."

"You barely ate any of that weird shit you ordered," he said flatly.

"I lost my appetite." Which wasn't true, but the prospect of sitting with him one minute longer outranked her growling stomach.

He scrubbed his hand down his face, his shoulders rounding in weariness. "I'm sorry. Jesus... Maya, I... I didn't mean to be cruel. I'm... Let me pay for your breakfast at least."

He placed his hand over hers, sending chills up her spine and generating a searing heat where his hand touched. His hand was enormous, and it covered hers completely, which she liked. A lot. And it shocked the shit out of her when she whispered, "Okay."

His eyebrows shot up. "You're agreeing with me?"

She looked into those emerald eyes and heard her voice say, "Yes." Her heart beat with a new earnest rhythm. It was wonderful, exhilarating, and terrifying. She needed distance. Right now.

"Really." He sounded amused, shocked, and slightly suspicious.

"When you touch me, I can't say no," she whispered, shaking her head sadly.

Green eyes widened in surprise and flashed something else, but she didn't wait to interpret it as she snatched her hand out from under his. There he went, being warm again. Men manipulated. The back and forth, the not so innocent suggestions, the "their way or the highway," and soon you were at a loss as to what became of your life as you stared down the barrel of a gun.

She shook her head again as she backed away and then quickly strode out the door. She was halfway to the main drag of Rough Ridge before she registered where she was. Going back was not an option. She put more distance between them and dipped into the biker gear store.

MIKE

He lost sight of her.

Shit.

"When you touch me, I can't say no," her voice was in his head on repeat, and the expression in her eyes when she said it burned into his memory: honest wonder and fear.

He'd lost her in the time it took for him to pay for their breakfast and the breakfast of the man Maya told off.

"I am nothing like my father or the men before him," he told their stunned faces. "Call me if you need anything." The man was shocked but took his card.

Baby steps.

But those steps, steps he took every day since landing in Rough Ridge almost a year ago, gave Maya just enough time to slip away. He had to get to work, but he'd hear her voice in his head all day.

Dammit. Dammit. Dammit.

Mike didn't lie and he absolutely wouldn't lie to himself about this whole situation, not anymore. He was already gone for her, which was bad - for everyone - and now he had to undo all the bullshit he'd done. He growled to himself as he stalked to his Jeep and jumped in.

A FEW HOURS LATER...

"Come on man, you're new, but me and Stan had a friendly arrange-ment," the man said as he struggled in the big detective's grip. "I'd pay a fee or lend him a sweet piece and he'd let me carry on with my travels. I can cut the same deal... officer ... uh ... "

"Detective Sheppard," Mike bit out.

The man stopped trying to negotiate when he got a glimpse of the cop arresting him. Mike's face was taut and his eyes blazed.

"You must take after your mom," the slippery character mumbled.

"That's the smartest thing you've said all night, and you're still under arrest. Going down for a while, friend. Underaged girls, across state lines, and if you're as big of an idiot as I suspect, your hard drives in the back have the same girls, which will buy a bunch more time. Where are you headed? Who's taking delivery?"

"Man, I ain't saying shit. Call my lawyer," the pimp spat.

"Suit yourself, but I assume a large load like this won't go unnoticed. Whoever was taking delivery of the girls and the product won't be too happy with you, and that's likely to spread around your new residence. How'd you meet the girls? You work with a recruiter?"

"Go fuck yourself!"

Mike leaned in and murmured. "You realize Big Dirty is locked up right now, right? Big Dirty likes to play with his food before he eats it, and he hates traffickers ... "

The pimp's eyes narrowed with understanding. Big Dirty was renowned inside for his disdain for traffickers. He was creative and patient. This middle-manager-wanna-be-Don would have a hell of a time if they put him into gen pop.

"Good luck, buddy," Mike said, shaking his head as he pushed him into the back of the squad car, slamming the door and slapping the roof to let the officer know he was good to go.

Mike moved back to lean against his Jeep while he watched the rape counselor from the county hospital talk to the girls they found in the van. Paul came to him and clapped him on the shoulder.

"Good work man, two of those girls are only twelve years old."

Mike shook his head. "This guy was small-time, been doing it a while though." He met Paul's eyes. "My father knew about it."

"Jesus, Mike." Paul shook his head.

"How many women, kids are lost today because he looked the other way, or worse?" Mike asked, not expecting an answer.

"Mike, I know about dealin' with guilt. It'll eat you alive, man, and that's with guilt you bought. This is shit you're borrowing. You gotta find some peace."

Knowing where Paul was going, he shook his wild, dark head. "A good woman deserves a good man's name. My name ain't shit right now. Not in this town. How can I bring her into this?"

"If it's who I think it is, keep doin' what you're doin' and your name will be worthy. Hell, askin' me, it already is. It's the man attached to the name that matters." Paul gave a meaningful glance to his friend one last time, walked to his truck, and took off home.

Mike waited until he received the counselor's update, and the victims were safe on the police van headed for treatment at Rough Ridge County Hospital. The he hopped into his Jeep and headed back to the station where he figured his perp was singing like a bluebird.

---

1. Butterflies by Michael Jackson

II

TESTOSTERONE ALL UP

MAYA

Maya turned off the shower. Her "Purple Majesty" playlist was blaring from her mini speaker, and she was enjoying the funky Purple One. Groovin', she was going to town with the full 11-minute extended mix of Prince's Purple Medley as she applied a layer of concealer to the bruises on her legs [1]

They were almost gone. The pain was still there, in spots, but she hardly noticed it unless something hit her legs. She applied the setting agent and checked out her work. Today would be warm, and she was looking forward to shedding leggings and jeans for a little while.

She wrapped a soft t-shirt around her curls, before they dried and 'fro'd up, winding the long sleeves around her head and tucking the ends. Then she moisturized the rest of her body with shea and jojoba body butter, brushed her teeth, flossed, and belted out a few bars of "I Wanna Be Your Lover" while spraying on a bit of vanilla perfume she found at the outlet mall about forty-five minutes away from town. It wasn't her signature custom blend, but it would work until she found a different, untraceable source. As she flung open the bathroom door, the residual steam billowed out.

As soon as the door opened, she tensed. Wired, she knew someone was in her room.

Maya always took a shower with her gun because every self-respecting woman who watched TV understood the bad guys in the movies got you in your sleep, on your way to the car, and in the shower.

Tucking her towel extra tight around her, she slid her gun off the counter, eased off the safety, and took a deep breath.

She cautiously stepped out of the bathroom, gun raised, body tight, finger by the trigger, and pointed toward the door. Jake, Caine, and another big man stood casually in the middle of her room. The unknown man had a bald head, full red Viking beard, and hazel eyes. His face was too roughed out and hard to be considered beautiful but he was wearing an impeccably tailored three-piece suit and wire-rimmed glasses as if he was on his way to balance someone's books while simultaneously bench pressing a car. His sharp hazel eyes studied her with interest.

"You have got to be kidding me," she said, her voice hard, as she lowered her gun. "There are things called doors and you knock before you enter."

Stomping over to the bed, she slid her gun back underneath the pillow.

She moved to the drawer to grab her underwear, mumbling, glaring at them, and shaking her head the whole time, "It's a small town. Mayberry with bikers. One main street that is literally the Main Street. Where people say 'sass...'"

She put on her underwear under her towel.

"No one says everyone will be in your business, everyone will know the actual color underwear you're wearing, breaking and entering is normal and, oh yeah, most of the male population will be handsome, charismatic giants with no regard for personal space. THAT shit should be in the brochure," she finished in a huff.

The amount of maleness in her room and the weird vibe she got from Caine threatened to overwhelm her. This increased her nervous rambling. But like always, Maya powered through. She'd worked with men her entire career and you had to establish dominance in your space before they claimed it. Often, she accomplished this by acting as if she were unaffected by them. So, Maya continued her regular post-shower activities.

Taking her hair out of her t-shirt, she shook it out. Then, turning her back to her uninvited guests, she dropped her towel.

There was a simultaneous response from all three men: a sharp intake of breath, a chuckle, and an appreciative "Damn!"

If the situation wasn't so ridiculous and she wasn't terrified as to why they were there, she would have thought the whole thing was funny.

She slipped her white tank dress with shelf-bra on over her bare breasts as she kept mumbling. "Imma walk up in other people's homes, eat their food, and use up all the toilet paper..."

When she finished, she took a deep breath, grabbed the curly hair custard and, a wide-tooth comb off her bed, and finally, turned around to face them.

Caine - standing in the middle in a tight white t-shirt and jeans – had his head lowered, his big hand over his eyes, and his body strung tight. Jake, on his right, was biker cool with motorcycle boots, faded jeans, and tight, black, short sleeve t-shirt that revealed a large amount of ink decorating his forearms. His head was tipped in the air, staring at the ceiling with an amused smile on his handsome face. The third man, completely out of place in his suit, grinned right at her. The last two men's body language appeared casual yet their bodies were on alert, bookending Caine's coiled energy.

"Enjoy the show, gentlemen?" she asked, her voice low and steady while her eyes blazed and narrowed.

"Maya, what the fuck?" That was from Caine.

"No comment." That was from a smiling Jake.

"Hell yeah!" That was from the last man.

Maya rolled her eyes.

"Mace man, the fuck?" Caine bit out.

"What? She ain't *my* sister."

A strange thing to say, or more to the point, a strange way to say it. The name sounded familiar. Then a memory shifted into place. Sean "Mace" O'Connell was Caine's other best bud formerly of Vegas. Maya looked him over and decided the pictures she'd seen at the Walters' home didn't do him justice. He exuded charm, alpha maleness, and had great taste in clothes.

"Was that necessary?" Caine growled.

"Oh, I'm sorry. Did I make you *uncomfortable*? I'll try to be more gracious the next time three men I barely or don't know,"— she nodded to Mace — "break into my hotel room while I am in the shower."

Maya crossed her arms in front of her and continued, "Since you all are clearly not Santa, and this isn't Christmas"— she leaned in biting out each of her words — "what the fuck do you want?"

"Maya, darlin' we need to talk," Jake started with a grin.

"I'm not your 'darlin'', Matthews." She was not in the mood to share in the camaraderie they had before. Jake paused, then smiled again, looking at Caine.

"Sit." Caine barked.

"I am not a damn dog." She took another step toward him and, as she advanced, she realized she should be frightened. His face was scary with anger. And maybe she was a little scared, but this was too much drama for the first thing in the morning — and she told them.

"I'm sick of you mountain creeps trying to tell me what to do. I wanted a little fucking peace, and what do I find? I've been arrested, handcuffed to a bed — and not the good way — hospitalized TWICE, kissed, now a mid-morning break-in, investigated and..." Maya realized the reason behind the dramatic appearance of the men. "YOU. ASSHOLES! You've been digging on me!"

"Maya dar — " Jake stopped when Maya's blazing eyes cut toward him. "Maya, we can do this the hard way or the easy way."

Oh, damn, did she miscalculate who the good guys were again?

The only way out was past them or the bathroom window, but her gun was under her pillow. She retreated to the bed as the men watched her. She sat on the bed close to the pillow and, in what she hoped was a casual manner, slid her hand underneath it.

"If you're thinking about the gun under your pillow, I suggest you consider never using it," Jake said, his voice low in warning.

"That's gonna be automatic jail time," Mace chimed in.

"I have a permit. And no judge, even in this hick county, would begrudge me busting a cap into the three men who found their way into my room uninvited."

"Getting a permit under false ID is a crime, sweetheart," Jake said seriously.

She was strategically in a poor physical position and back in a situation where she had no control. She needed ... she needed to think clearly. The breeze through the window brought a hint of gunpowder—she thought. It was faint and her heart was in her throat. *I'm not crazy. He's not here. He's not here. Go for cute and charm them.* She climbed on a little stool by the bed.

"There. Eye to eye. Now we're in equitable positions."

Mace roared with laughter. "She *is* a goof."

Caine lost what little hold he had on his patience. He stormed to her and spat, "I asked you if you were trying to fuck with my family."

Maya had no idea what he was accusing her of, and taking in his outraged face, hers was a vision of confusion.

"What have I done?"

Hopping down, she walked a few steps away from Caine to peer at the other men in the room. "What did I do to any of you? You asked me who I was. I told you what you needed to know."

"Needed to know." Caine repeated, his deep voice dripping with sarcasm. "This chick is crazy, and she thinks I'm stupid." He waved his hand dismissively and glanced back at the men.

"Look asshole, I don't know what's got your testosterone all up," she said waving her arms, "but I assure you, I want nothing from you and would never hurt anyone."

"Maya Anderson didn't exist a few weeks ago. She first appeared in Vegas, where she bought a used Ford F-150 in cash, got her conceal carry license, and purchased a new gun. Your prints do not match the prints given for the license. Then this Maya Anderson drives straight to Rough Ridge, Colorado," Jake rattled off. "Because Maya's ID is nearly flawless, she must've had help."

Jake looked at Mace and continued, "There are only a few people with the chops to pull it off around there. Two never heard of you. One never gives up her girls."

Sarah.

"This 'Auntie' Sarah's got good reason to keep mum, because her specialty is hiding battered women and their children. Immunization records, birth certificates, the whole nine."

"Yeah, even leaning heavy, we got nowhere," Mace chimed in.

Thank God for Sarah.

"You put the women she protects in danger. If you found me, he will too." She leveled a scorching gaze at them. "The women I saw at Sarah's were frightened, but determined. Their children were scared," she said as her voice broke. "They were lonely and out of sorts. Sarah provides peace and hope when women can't turn to anyone else. When the system fails them and their families." She shook her head, her eyes watering. "And now because of me..."

"Who's looking for you?" Mace asked.

"It doesn't matter," she replied, her mind distracted by the thought of the women she may have inadvertently exposed.

"Why don't you tell us what's going on," Mace said, "because right now it isn't looking good for you."

Huh?

"The women and Sarah's operation will be fine," Jake said. "We don't leave a trace; we just want to know what you want from Caine."

Confused, Maya shook her head dismissively. "You obviously think I'm someone else, I — I want nothing from you," she said, looking at Caine directly.

Caine exploded.

"STOP FUCKING WITH ME, GIRL! You sleep with a loaded gun under your pillow, you've got 150 large in your nightstand and you suddenly appear in Vegas, then here. Who put you on me?!"

---

1. Thieves in the Temple (Remix) Prince | The Purple Medley by Prince can only be found online - YouTube specifically and for purchase through the Prince Estate.

12

Helluva Hustle

MAYA

Maya was, at first, breathless in the face of his anger. Then her anger matched his. In fact, it was bigger. Everything she held in, everything since the first time Griffin struck her, churned constantly inside her. And for the first time in weeks, she lifted the valve. The rage, the indignation, the horror, the embarrassment, the fear — everything. She gave Caine a taste of what lived inside her.

"What the fuck is the inside?!" she hollered as she stalked as close as she could get to him and still see his face without having to tip her head back too far back.

"I have lost EVERYTHING I worked my ass off for since I was a child! I walked away from my life and now I'm here." She threw out her arms, indicating the modest hotel room. "With a loaded gun under my pillow. With '150 large in my nightstand.' LIKE A FUCKING FUGITIVE! You don't know me, but this is NOT the life I planned. I had–I had plans, dreams. Now I have flashbacks. And nightmares. I sit carefully so I don't ache from my injuries, and you stand here accusing me of fucking with YOU, while you all broke in MY room pawing my panties and looking through my shit?!"

She shook and wheezed. Damn thin air, damn asthma, goddamn EVERYTHING.

Caine blinked, his face going soft as he reached out to her. "Where's your inhaler?"

"Fuck you," she bit out as she slammed her fists and forearms into his chest with all her might. "I don't need YOU, your help, your accusations..." her eyes filled with tears. Caine reared back.

Her body still shaking with anger, she walked around him to the dresser and snatched out her inhaler. Angrily, she turned her back to the men. Her physical weakness, what she'd revealed, embarrassed her. She shook her inhaler, carefully inhaling the medicine as she squeezed the canister. Holding her breath for thirty seconds, she slowly exhaled, repeated the maneuver, brushing irritating tears away the whole time.

As the men waited for her, the room's mood shifted from alert to concern, back to alert when her body went tight as she suddenly screamed "FUCK!" and threw her inhaler across the room. Her head fell back as she looked to the ceiling, her hands clenched at her sides. "You couldn't leave it alone." She sighed, her shoulders sagging in defeat. Lowering her head, she stared at the wall in front of her. "I could've been happy here. Free ... " she whispered.

She shook her head, walked to the bed, and pulled a small set of rolling luggage and a canvas book bag from underneath the bed. She tossed them on the bed before slowly sitting and moving her head from side to side, popping her neck. Maya took a deep breath, and crossed her legs with her back straight. An armor came over her as she radiated a calm command of herself and the room. Finally, she spoke in a deeper, quiet, measured voice.

"Matthews, tell me what you know, and I'll fill it in. When I am finished, you will stop digging for anything I don't give, and I will leave Rough Ridge by the end of the day. I also ask that no one, no matter how convincing they are, learns about anything I share, and please keep your families safe by not sharing with them either. That is imperative. The parties involved will not hesitate to take away everything you love to get to me." She then looked at Jake and waited.

He watched her thoughtfully. Finally, he spoke. "I had only the first name and your approximate age to go on. There are three Mayas in the U.S. that you could have been. Maya Pembleton is missing from her parent's farm in Maine. No registered identification is available. She's ghost."

"Poor girl, but that's not me."

"Maya Lawson – an addict from Vegas who used to be a part of a stick-up crew that ran with some dudes locked up with Caine."

"I assume this Maya has a rap sheet with physical ID and prints. None of which matches mine."

Jake nodded his head. "That left Maya Angel Walters."

She looked at the men with a raised eyebrow, eyes blazing.

"Maya Walters from Columbus, Ohio, who attended Ohio State."

"THE Ohio State University," she corrected.

Jake continued with a chuckle. "You graduated early with a degree in architecture after completing high school early. The same Maya Walters is listed as currently on sabbatical from M.A. Wall Designs."

"Google would have told you the same thing," she said with quiet accusation.

"Why do you have building plans of my house?" Caine growled.

Maya blinked and lost all demeanor again. "Oh, for shit's sake," she sighed. "You had me followed? Stalker ass muthafu–"

"Didn't need to. It's a small town."

"You people need hobbies."

She stood, crossed the room to the desk, and pulled a large metal tube off the desk. Pulling out three sets of plans, she rolled them out, paying attention to the order. "You already know I'm an architect."

"This is your house," she started. "It's beautiful, and it doesn't intrude too much into the surrounding landscape. It's also huge and energy inefficient. You're spending a fortune heating and cooling that sucker. And given how much laundry you all have and number of sex showers you and Tori take every week; you spend a ton on your water bill."

She flipped those plans over and revealed the second set. "This is why I have plans for your freakin' house," she said, pointing to the designs. "Are you going to come look or stand over there being an asshole?"

He still didn't move, but Jake and Mace did. "What am I looking at?" Jake asked.

"A solution that is ecologically friendly, saves sixty percent on heating and cooling over the first three years, and will eventually generate enough power to earn you back credits from the electric company."

She was back to speaking quiet, deep, and measured. She flipped open her laptop, typed in the password, and accessed a proposal. Scrolling to a particular section, she said, "There's enough snowfall in this area to fill an underground cistern that can cut the county water usage in the summer. You have enough land to do it and with creative landscaping you can make it blend into the background."

"That's sweet. How much would all of it cost?" Mace asked.

She pointed to a graphic on the laptop. "I have the initial investment numbers, which are substantial. BUT, if you phase in the changes over time - I have three options–that way you can spread out the financial responsibility while hitting your ROI in one to three years from each phase, depending." She scrolled to a new section in the proposal. "I also have the current and predictive green energy and improvement tax credits — if those dicks in Washington get their heads out of their asses and don't gut them. Fortunately, the Colorado legislature has comparable credits to take the bite out of your local property taxes, as the property will increase in value twelve percent more than it currently does per year."

"Twelve percent over?" Caine asked incredulously.

"If current trends hold," Maya confirmed. She had no idea when he'd walked over. She was so into presenting her ideas, it soothed her. "I've got 3D models as well." She located them, set the animation in motion, and stood back to watch Caine. He had the expression all her clients got the moment they saw the possibilities take shape. She aimed a slight smile at him, proud of her work.

"What about the third set of plans?" Caine asked quietly, gesturing to the desk.

"That's one of the dreams I keep having," Maya said as she moved to reveal the final set. "This is mine. LEED Gold Certification eligible. It would be platinum if I allowed public access to information on it. Low emission materials, small vertical footprint, geothermal heating, and cooling — the works. Yet, 100 percent a part of the land. Rustic on the outside with a concentrated focus and effort to blend in with the surrounding landscape." She opened the 3D model of her dream home, setting the animation going. "Inside is modern and comfortable with an open, nature focused design so you feel like you're outside with privacy. The entire home is self-sustaining, including waste. Human fecal matter isn't good for things like gardening, but there are companies, several within fifty miles of here, that use it for interesting things. It sounds weird hiring someone to haul away your poop, but true ecological impact goes beyond recycling. If I can build a minimal impact structure from the ground up, then why not? Design it better now."

"M.A. Wall Designs," Caine said.

"Yes." She looked at him again hesitantly.

"You've worked for them since the beginning," Jake said.

"You don't know as much as I thought."

"I know you are the work behind the 'Wall,' so to speak. Your partner gets the accolades and leaves you to make the speeches. It's a shit lot," Jake said.

"It is, but not for the reason you think." She stepped back from the men and went back to the bed and sat. "Since we're having a heart-to-heart," she took a breath, "I'm M.A. Wall." she said, throwing out jazz hands.

"Bullshit," Jake said.

"And the elusive white guy?" Mace asked.

"A struggling actor who looks the part and can deliver a helluva pitch. I do the work. He delivers the pitch, though much less now than in the beginning. I work the deal, create the designs, lead my team, attend the events and make speeches on behalf of the company."

"Why?!" Caine asked incredulously.

"The better question," she said, shifting to grab her spray bottle of leave-in conditioner, "is why no one wondered why his partner had all the answers to their questions and the "genius" didn't have any. If a white man was the figurehead, I got the business." She parted her long hair and spritzed her hair until it was damp. "A 25-year-old, black, female architect couldn't get a meeting even with stellar credentials, top internships, and design projects under her belt — and I have some pretty innovative ideas." She smoothed in styling cream and a light oil, then braided her hair into two long braids, making her appear much younger.

"A 25-year-old white man goes into the meeting. No one glanced at his credentials. They looked at the designs and the previous work. Period. Anderson is a friend from college, and I hired him to be my personal assistant because he needed a job flexible enough for acting gigs. One day, he walked into the conference room ahead of me to alert potential clients that I was running behind. He didn't know I was watching. I saw that when he introduced himself, they began speaking to him like he was the architect and when I entered the room, they asked me for coffee. I tried the same scenario again, but I sent my white female second assistant in. The next clients asked her to validate their parking. They asked me when the architect would arrive before dismissing me. I called Anderson in. They thanked him for having a meeting with them. I realized my company could die because I was the wrong gender and color or, at a minimum, those things might severely stunt its growth. I gave him a mild raise and a new title — "Dreamer."— We put his photo ahead of mine on the website and made sure he walked through the doors first."

The men were stunned.

"Helluva hustle," Caine said.

"Brave," Jake said.

"Bull." She shook her head in frustration. "A hustle doesn't begin to encapsulate the hoops I had to jump through, the mechanics of running a company and two identities ... It was and is two full-time jobs. And as far as brave ... I'm hiding in Colorado with giant mountain men who think I'm the Unabomber."

"No, we think you're my sister," Caine said bluntly.

Maya's head snapped back in surprise, then she smirked and rolled her eyes. "Hilarious." She continued smoothing her hair, wrapping a small, clear elastic around the end of each of the two braids.

"He's serious," Jake said, crossing his arms in front of him, watching Maya closely.

She noticed both him and Mace assumed subtle protective positions near Caine, which puzzled her.

"Whatever," she said dismissively. "I don't have any family. My mother, Elise, died when I was 21, as I'm sure you know," she looked at Jake and he nodded. "All her people are gone, and my father died before I was born."

"Are you sure?" Jake asked.

Sighing again, Maya closed her eyes and said, "He went to his death the next day." She said, using air quotes. "My mother said they had one magical weekend and then he died."

"We have the same last name," Caine said.

"It's a common last name. Why are you trying to make this a thing?" she asked, suddenly unsure and upset.

"You guys look alike," Mace said. "Especially around the eyes."

"Not all Black people look alike. You should know, Conor McGregor," she snapped.

"Why did you come here of all places, Maya?" Caine asked.

Maya shrugged. "Honestly? I was scared, running, trying to keep my trail erratic so he couldn't find me. My mom always kept framed postcards from her travels and had one of this hotel. I figured I'd check it out. No one would ever think to search for me here at a low-end hotel/motel in Colorado. It's nice, but I wouldn't keep a postcard for all those years... oh ... " A connection she never made crystallized in her mind. "No way. No fucking way," she muttered, shaking her head slowly.

"Your birth certificate says 'T. Walters.'" Caine said.

Maya wasn't listening. "She wouldn't talk about him," she said, mainly to herself. "She said she didn't know his family, and once she got sick, I didn't ask any more. I focused on keeping her happy and taking care of everything. I was her shield, holding everything back while she held cancer back... I always thought... I always thought I was alone after she left me." Her lip trembled. She looked at Caine working it through in her mind, "I guess it could be possible. I always assumed they met in Ohio... I'm sorry about your dad. Was it an affair? Am I the bastard child everyone worries is going to come to the reunion and cause a scene?" Shaking her head more, she looked at him again. "He was just a name on my birth certificate. Shit, not even a complete name ... God, I don't have a full name, but you would have known him, right? You were... nine? Oh... that sucks." Her eyes were large and sad, her hands worried the hem of her skirt.

"It was an affair," Caine said quietly, his face soft. "Our father's name is Thomas Walters, and he is still alive."[1]

Maya looked, really looked, into eyes suddenly so familiar for a long moment. She covered her mouth with her hand and breathed in deeply a couple of times, trying to keep herself in check. Suddenly, she rose and ran the length of the room crashing into Caine, wrapping her arms around his waist and holding on for dear life as she sobbed. He looked stunned for a moment, his large arms out akimbo, then he slowly wrapped them around her and held her close, placing his cheek on the top of her head. She cried harder.

"I always wanted a brother," she whispered, taking in big gulps of air.

He squeezed her again.

"Oh! Thank God I wasn't attracted to you," she yelped. Jake and Mace chuckled in the background.

"Same here."

She snorted. "I have nieces," she whispered.

"Yeah."

"My dad's alive."

"Yes."

"I have a — a family," she whispered so quietly you could barely hear it, but everyone in the room did and appreciated what it meant.

Caine squeezed her again so tight it hurt. The breath whooshed out of her body and she didn't mind one bit.

"Is it weird I don't want to let go? 'Cause I've got thirty years to make up."

"So do I," Caine rumbled, squeezing her again.

---

1. A Song for You by Donny Hathaway

13

BEARS. THEY'RE ASSES

MAYA

After Jake and Mace left to have a drink at the bar, Maya and Caine talked more about the circumstances surrounding their parents' relationships which was a tragic story. She was grateful that Caine suggested they walk over to join the fellas. She could've used a whiskey but settled for juice and Mace went out and got her a toasted deli sandwich, which she inhaled.

After a while, it was time for Caine and Mace to go. She needed to sit for a while and digest all the new info. As she walked with them to the car in front of her room, Caine took the time to circle back to what brought Maya to Rough Ridge.

"Maya, about the bruises--"

"I don't want to talk about it Caine, not even with you. Will you stop digging?"

"No."

"Caine—"

"You're my sister."

"Caine. My shit doesn't blow back on you, remember?"

"Why didn't you name him?" That question had bothered him since getting Jake's report.

"I did, Caine," she sighed.

Caine stopped and looked her in the eye. "There wasn't a report."

"That's because he didn't want there to be one." She stared back at him, her face hard, as she tried to drill into him what she was up against. "He gets what he wants, including making things and people disappear."

Anger radiated off him, but she pushed past that, understanding the gift of a family was also another devastating weapon Griffin could use. "Leave it be, big brother, or I'll have to go. I'll disappear before I allow anything to happen to you, Victoria, or the girls. And now you know I have the means to do so. Don't push this. Don't make me give up this blessing," she said, her voice cracking.

He grabbed her in a tight hug and surprised her by kissing her on the top of her head. She aimed a huge smile at him. "You never know what life has in store," she breathed, her eyes dancing.

"Hey lil' sis," Mace called. "You need anything, I put my number in your phone."

"How long were you all in my room?" Her face showed more than slight concern.

"Long enough to hear you can't sing for shit." He laughed. "And you have great taste in vibrators."

With an eye roll to her brother, she disappeared into her room.

THAT NIGHT MAYA WAS EXHAUSTED. She spent the rest of the day isolated by choice, too raw from the morning's visit. After ordering pizza and salad for delivery, she did yoga in her room, and put in a call to her security consultant for alternative bug out plans now that she had a family to watch over.

In case something happened, she ordered secure phones for her family. She also planned for safe house access for them, both in and out of state. Maya declined guards and video surveillance, mindful that while she wasn't hurting for money, she needed to be prudent. This could be a long-term endeavor and she may never return to her firm.

Griffin, his father, and even his grandfather were in excellent health and God still hadn't given any indication He'd do the pillar of salt thing anytime soon.

An added worry was that, in this small town, security would certainly cause talk. No matter how good the guys in Denver were, locals would sniff out people who didn't belong quicker than most people got their morning coffee.

No, I'll keep things as quiet as I can for as long as I can. She closed her Tor browser, slid her secure phone back into the hidden compartment in her purse and walked to the bathroom. She washed her face, pulled off her sweatpants and face dove into the bed.

"Quiet, Colorado mountain town. Yeah right."

I AM RUNNING through the woods. My breath tearing from my chest, the cold piercing my lungs, the wind and snow stinging my skin. My footing unsure, I pray I can stay upright. He's closing in, his breath on my neck, his growl in my ear. His claws break through my clothes, slashing, iron hot, through my skin and I am falling, falling through the dense night sky... before the weight of his body, his teeth are on me. Blood is pouring onto the snow as his teeth rip through me. A scream tears through my throat, raw and piercing, as I fight, fight even as the metallic aroma of my blood assaults my nose. Pounding, barking and teeth, screams, pounding and barking, someone yelling my name, barking and pounding...

The pounding continued as Maya woke, screaming, from her dream. It had been a little while since the last time she'd dreamed about the bear. The emotions of the day brought everything to the surface. The pounding disoriented her until she heard Detective Sheppard's voice yell, "Maya, I'm coming in!"

When it dawned on her the pounding was on her door, she stumbled out of bed and yelled toward it, "Wait! What? No! I'm coming."

She threw open the door. There stood Ms. Shirley in curlers, a ruffled pink housecoat, and fluffy blue slippers, patting an anxious Charlie on the head. Officer Asshole stood in nothing but his jeans, unbuttoned at the top. She took in his bare feet, moved up his thick, strong legs in well-worn jeans, lingered on the open top of his pants for a bit, then up to the happy little trail of dark hair that coursed down his stomach and disappeared into his zipper. The tour of awesomeness continued, as her eyes bumped along his abs, across his broad chest to his lickable neck and up the lines and planes of that stop-you-in-mid-stride face, only to land on brilliant green eyes that looked ... seriously pissed off.

Well, what else was new?

She realized she was standing in the door, facing Main Street, them - and Charlie - in her underwear and a tank top. Hopping behind the door, she tried to calm her breathing and shake the dream, and Mike, from her head. She studied Ms. Shirley as she asked what was wrong.

"We heard you screaming," she explained, her eyes full of worry. Charlie whined and moved forward a bit to nudge her hand.

"Oh gosh, I'm so sorry," she rubbed Charlie behind the ears, as she was suddenly more embarrassed about them hearing her have night-mares than she was about being in her underwear. "I had a bad dream - bears. They're asses. Right, Charlie?"

"You have 'em often?" Mike asked, still sounding pissed and her reaction was instant. Her head snapped back, and she launched into full attitude.

"Why? Is it a crime? Are you going to arrest me for a noise ordi-nance violation?"

His eyes blazed and the animosity coming off him built by the second. Green eyes locked on to brown ones and engaged in a heated stare down.

Ms. Shirley looked from Maya to Mike with a mixture of surprise, concern, and something else - maybe amusement. "If you're sure you're all right... I'll let you young people work this out for yourselves... Come, Charlie." After one last snuffle against Maya's tummy with his snout, Charlie followed Ms. Shirley toward the motel office.

"Sorry, Ms. Shirley," she called after the woman, never taking her eyes off his.

"What is your problem, Officer Asshole? First, you're banging on my door like a maniac and now you're staring at me like I was on the grassy knoll."

"You were screaming like a maniac was after you," he spat.

"Ok, so I'm awake now. Are we finished?" She started closing the door.

"Why did you open the door?" he rumbled quietly, still angry.

"What?"

"Why did you open the door? You just throw open your door when a man is banging on it? You didn't check your peephole. You didn't know who I was. You just threw it open in your damn pink panties."

"Fuchsia. And you were banging on it," she replied, looking at him like he'd lost his mind.

"Dammit Maya, it's not safe. Keep the door shut until you know who is on the other side."

She slammed the door in his face.

"IT'S SHUT NOW JACKASS!"

THE NEXT NIGHT...

Running through the woods, my breath explodes out of my chest as the bear crashes through the trees, closing in on me. His teeth scrape my skin and I scream ... Pounding and my screams ... pounding ... pounding...

Maya jumped three feet in the air in her bed, then fell out of it trying to get to the door. She yanked it open.

"I'm SORRY!" Her hair was wild with sleep and lack of care for the last two days. She blew out a puff of air to push some out of her face.

"Bear?"

"Yeah."

"When do you sleep, Sunshine?" he asked as he walked into her room uninvited. "And you did it again; opening the door in your damn yellow panties." His voice was hoarse with sleep and he was shirtless again.

Now I'm definitely not going to get any sleep.

"Sunshine."

"Hmmm?" She jumped at his voice, and hoped he didn't notice she was staring at his chest.

"Sleep. When? So I can time it out to where I can get some."

Her shoulders sank. "I'm sorry, I nap in the afternoons. I don't seem to have the dreams then. But that's when you're out getting the bad guys."

"Close the door, Sunshine."

"What?"

"Close the door. We're going to sleep." He sounded bone tired.[1]

This can't be happening.

"Listen, um, I'm sorry I keep waking you up I can—"

Mike stalked to the door, closed and locked it. He trudged back to Maya, scooped her up in his arms, and walked to the bed. She gasped, her eyes on his determined face.

"Hold on to my neck, Sunshine."

In a state of shock she did as he asked, and he took his hand from around her waist and reached into his pockets. He pulled out his keys, phone, and wallet, and deposited them on her nightstand. Putting his arm back around her back, he kneed up onto the bed, and laid her down facing the wall, sliding in behind her.

She got over her shock long enough to whisper, "I-I can't sleep this way."

"What?" he whispered back.

"I have to face the door so I can keep people from sneaking up on me." Her body was tense, and she hated how she trembled.

He stilled. Then he rolled over and faced the door. "Hold on to my back, Sunshine."

"What do you mean?"

"I'll watch the door and keep you safe. Seein' as you're a pain in the ass and like your control, you can hold on to my back and have my back. Together, we got this."

She hesitated, then rolled over, moved against his back, and slid an arm around his waist.

"Better?" he asked softly.

"Better."

He threw the covers over both of them and ordered her to relax.

When she didn't, he murmured, "Baby, you've got to sleep. You're safe with me."

He slid her hand from around his waist to underneath his arm and placed her hand on his heart. Soon its rhythm put her to sleep ... and kept the bears away.

Maya woke the next morning to the Colorado version of an alarm clock - loud, rude light pouring in from all sides. She realized Mike had left a note on the nightstand.

SUNSHINE –
OUT FOR A RUN. GO BACK TO SLEEP.
–M

She chuckled and tried, but it was too late. Wide awake and starving, she grabbed an apple, poured a glass of milk from the mini-fridge, and jumped into the shower. Deciding to twist her hair before she went for a run, she quickly dressed and got started on her hair. She collected the tools of the trade - a rattail comb, wide-tooth comb, clips, leave-in conditioner, and curling cream. Maya turned on her Love Groove playlist. Lauryn Hill sang about nothing mattering. [2]

Maya parted her hair into four sections, applied product, and began quickly parting and twisting smaller sections. It took her longer than usual because her hair was growing out — almost to her bra strap when curly and longer when straight — 'cause shrinkage was real. Working methodically, she cleared her mind of everything but the rhythm of her movements and the music. It was normal. Tactile. Comforting. A place of calm in a world where she couldn't seem to get her footing. She rounded the last section when Sade's *Sweetest Taboo* came on. She stopped briefly, laid back on her bed, and allowed the music to wash over her.

The jiggle of her door handle scared her shitless. She quickly rolled to her pillow, reached under it, and stood — her weapon ready for the second time that week — when the door opened. *"Wait until you see the whites of his eyes before you shoot sugar,"* Sarah's voice in her head said. She waited to see Griffin's dark eyes and instead peered into hyper-alert green ones.

"Maya, it's me," he whispered as he paused in the doorway.

"Okay."

"Put the gun down, Sunshine."

---

1. Lay Me Down (feat. John Legend) by Sam Smith
2. Nothing Else Matters by Lauryn Hill

14

DO YOU TRUST ME?

MAYA

"Right." She closed her eyes and exhaled slowly. Lowering the gun, she shook her head and engaged the safety. "Why do you have a key to my room?" She tried to distract herself from the jumpy, twitchy feelings she had. They continued to increase instead of going away with time.

"Because you're going to keep waking me up every night, and I'm going to bang on your door waking everyone else."

"Aaand Ms. Shirley gave you a key?"

"Of course. I'm an officer of the law. She's known me since I was born and I'm charming."

"Sounds like an abuse of power," Maya threw out, unthinking.

He stilled for a moment, and she realized her mistake.

"Oh! Shoot, I'm sorry. I didn't mean that like that. I meant about the charm," she stumbled. "You're charming and it makes women's knees weak. So ... they ... go ... along with..."[1]

"You think I'm charming?"

She chewed her bottom lip again, and his eyes zeroed in on them. "Yes."

Maya didn't think it was possible for a man that large to move that fast. One minute, she was reasonably able to exchange oxygen for carbon dioxide. The next minute, he was directly in front of her, his wide chest the only thing she saw, and her normal functions ceased. It wasn't an unpleasant view. Great actually, and it kept her from looking at his face. She focused on the weaved pattern of his deep green t-shirt right in front of her, counting the rows and columns and concentrating on not looking up.

"Sunshine."

"Hmmm?" *Don't look up. Sixteen by six stitches.*

"Maya."

"Yep?" *Don't look up. Seventeen by seven stitches.*

"Look at me darlin'," he coaxed.

She looked up, and his expression struck at the center of her soul. It was intense, questioning, and full of need.

"Do I make your knees weak?"

Her brain suffered from lack of oxygen, and it was her excuse for continuing the truth-telling road to disaster.

"Absolutely."

Sade sang in the background about how being with the one she loved made every day Christmas and every night like New Year's Eve.

She's got that shit right.

He placed a hand on either side of her face, tipping her chin further, and leaned in to kiss her. When their lips touched, a spark zinged like a pinball let loose, tagging back and forth between them. With the music in the background egging them on, Mike deepened the kiss. Gentle strokes at first, slow and languid, like he had all the time in the world. Maya leaned all her weight on him as, indeed, her knees got weak.

She molded her body to his, sliding her hands up his chest, exploring the hard muscles under the thin fabric of his shirt, around his neck, and finally into that thick, wild hair. A soft moan escaped her lips, and he responded with his own deep groan.

Maya could have kissed The Ohio State University 2014 National Championship Football Team right after they won and *still* not get remotely close to the way she felt now.

His kiss grew hungrier, deeper. Sliding a large hand down her back, he moved further south to her ass and grabbed hold of it. Tightly. He held on like it belonged to him and if he asked for it, he could've had it. Right. Now. Silver. Platter.

Instead, he let go with a sigh, ended their kiss, and stepped back.

Maya's eyes slowly opened as Mike looked at her hair.

"Your hair's drying and you're not finished."

"Come again?" How could he lay a kiss like that on a woman and then go back to regular conversation?

"Your twists ... they won't come out like you want them if your hair dries."

"Now I'm confused. You are a giant, wild, and yes, white, *man*. You lay this ambrosia, manna-from-Heaven-kiss on me, and then you spout Black hair care advice like you've been reading Essence Magazine. What dimension did I step into here?"

She looked past him and checked the room. "Yep, 1980s decor still intact and no wormhole to be seen."

He simply chuckled, and looked over at the bed. He gently pushed toward it. Pulling the clip from her hair, he ran his fingers through it. She suddenly remembered her hair. While she was having an Earth-moving, romantic kiss, she looked like she escaped a beauty salon to do it. *Ugh.*

She stiffened at his touch because this wouldn't be the first time someone treated the hair that grew out of her head as an oddity to explore. Yes, it could be romantic to run your fingers through a Black woman's hair during loving acts. It was something else entirely when it was "closed for maintenance," or if you were a stranger on the street.

His hands left her hair, and he sat on the flowered bedspread, his back to the cream walls, legs spread. He patted the space between his legs. "Sit down, Sunshine."

Instead, she scowled.

He laughed softly, reached one of his long arms out, and tugged her hand, pulling her into the bed. She reluctantly sat between his legs, back to him, and waited. When he lifted her comb and moved toward her hair, she ducked.

"Maya, do you trust me?"

"With a gun, yes. With my hair? Hell no."

He threw back his head and laughed full out. It was nice to hear and feel against her back. The deep belly rumble cocooned her as he wrapped his arms around her and kissed her neck.

"You don't trust me, Sunshine, but you will. Now scoot up a little."

"Do cops say scoot?" she asked as she followed his directions, preparing to have to redo her hair after he finished playing in it.

He parted her hair in sections, gently combing through her curls, starting at the bottom and working his way to her roots. He started twisting the strands together, slowly, and deliberately, until he was at the end. Finishing the twist, he swirled the end around his finger into a uniform curl.

She fingered the twist, examining it. It was perfect. Things weren't adding up. It freaked her out and turned her on a little. *A giant man with the body of a deity that can do your hair? What?!*

"How do you know how to do twists?!" she asked, turning and looking over her shoulder at him.

"Turn around babe," he said, grabbing the spray bottle and spritzing her hair a bit.

"But—"

"Turn around."

She turned around.

He kept sectioning, and his huge hands worked gently through her hair, twisting it carefully, and finishing with a curl at the ends. He worked with the same rhythm for each section, and the same quiet confidence that he always displayed. This went on for a while and while Maxwell crooned in the background about being ready "*Whenever, Wherever, Whatever,*" he spoke.[2]

"My father, grandfather, great grandfather ... all racists, all asses and generally wastes of human flesh, creating misery on Earth. They were junkyard dog mean. Said and did horrible things to people for decades." His voice was a bitter growl. "They tried to pass that shit on to me. Probably would have if not for my mom...

"She knew who my father was, knew what he came from, and loved him anyway. Even knew she was his second choice ... Optimistically, she thought she could love him hard enough, long enough to change him." He sighed. "Can't change a man if he doesn't want to..."

More sectioning and twisting and silence...

"Mom always said she didn't *see* color. Told me to judge people by what they did and how they treated others. After she died, I took my sister's advice and got shot of my father as soon as I graduated high school. I needed to get away from the shit he was doing, who he was. I traveled for a while, met people from all over the world, and finally settled in L.A. I joined the force and met Tina.

"One night over dinner, at the best restaurant I could afford — a little dive with cheap tequila, amazing guac, ribs, and Szechwan chicken — we were getting to know each other. I proudly told her I didn't see color. She patted my hand, smiled at me like I was a sweet boy, and told me that was the dumbest shit she'd ever heard." He laughed hard at the memory, dropping his head on her shoulder for a moment. Maya smiled, reached up, and stroked it absentmindedly. He moved to kiss her neck again and slowly got back to work.

"She explained that being a Black woman was a large part of who she was. That it was her culture, her history, and she was proud of it. She asked me if I would say the same to someone of a different religion or from a different country."

"'Would you ever say, 'I don't see Swedish?'" He said, imitating a woman's voice, and laughing even more. "She had a big ass point. Then she nailed me. She got serious for a moment and said, 'You have no right to dismiss parts of me that make me who I am to make yourself feel better or more comfortable.' She was right of course."

Maya nodded, taking it all in. "She sounds like an amazing woman."

"She was. My mom had the right heart. Tina showed me I still had a lot to learn, always will."

More silence passed between them as Dido's "Thank You" played in the background. He worked through her hair as she traced lazy patterns on the legs of his jeans.[3]

"She had a daughter, Abigail. A sweetheart through and through, but incredibly shy around me. She had almost as much hair as you and she was only five."

"Wow!"

Maya loved the smile in his voice.

"Yeah, and she was a terror when it was time to comb it."

"One day she asked me to do it instead of her mother ... I couldn't say no to that little face, so Tina walked me through the process and Abbie patiently sat still for *two* hours while I fumbled through it. She looked terrible,"—he chuckled — "but she loved it. Twirled like she was a fairy princess going to the ball ... That's how we bonded. I did her hair almost every day for three years. Mainly twists and ponytails. I can't get little braids..."

There was something in the silence. Something heavy. Maya almost didn't want to know, but she wanted him to understand he was as safe as he made her feel.

"You don't have to tell me."

"I don't keep secrets," he said, his voice gruff.

He continued on the last twist. She watched his fingers curl around the last strand. He brushed it off her shoulder with such tenderness. Wrapping his arms around her, he pulled her close to him. She relaxed her head against his chest and waited, her hands holding onto his arms around her chest. She felt his heart beating, yet he was so still.

"A drunk driver hit Tina and Abbie the same day they sentenced Caine to prison."

Her hands spasmed around his forearm as her breath caught in her throat.

"I was ... I was supposed to pick them up for Abbie's tap recital. She'd been click clacking around the apartment for weeks practicing. Running late and angry that Caine was going to prison, I told them I'd meet them there ... The driver ran the light and killed Tina instantly. Abigail ... she held on through surgery to relieve the swelling in her brain. They cut off most of her gorgeous hair, but it didn't matter because she was still so fuckin' beautiful. I remember checking her face for her mole. Praying they were wrong, and it was all a mistake. She had the cutest little mole right under her left eye ... " He squeezed Maya tightly, but the pain she felt was *for* him, not *from* him.

"She fought. Hard. But her little body ... she died the next morning. She was only eight years old. Eating cereal one morning, and the next morning gone. She never woke up and I never got to say goodbye. I should have been there."

Tears soaked Maya's face and his arms as they sat there quietly together for a while longer.

"Some lessons," he said as he kissed the top of her head, "you never forget."

Mike's phone rang. He slipped a hand into his pocket and swiped with his thumb. Still holding Maya with one arm, he cleared his throat and answered the phone. "Sheppard."

A pause.

"Yeah. That sounds like a load of bullshit, but I'm on my way." He tapped the screen with his thumb and kissed Maya's neck. "I've got to go, Sunshine," he whispered in her ear.

She scooted off the bed and turned to watch him get up. He used his thumbs to sweep her tears off her face and bent to kiss her. It was short and sweet.

"Thank you for giving me that," she said as she placed her hand over his heart. She closed her eyes, letting the rhythm wash over her. "And I am so sorry you lost Abbie and Tina." She swallowed to hold back more tears and clear the lump in her throat.

Mike kissed her again, and lifting his head slightly, he breathed against her lips, "I'd give you everything I have Maya. If you told me you wanted me. No games. No bullshit. You're the kind of woman a man would give his last breath. Didn't think I'd ever ... not again ... " He smiled sadly, kissed her nose, and grabbed his keys to go.

"Michael," she said to his back.

He turned and looked at her over his shoulder.

"It wasn't your fault, the accident," she swallowed as his eyes blazed. "Life sometimes ... it turns, and we can't control that."

He gave her a long look, then finally, he nodded. "Maybe someday I'll believe that." He turned and walked out the door.

Maya realized he left the key to her room on her nightstand. She wouldn't admit seeing it there bothered her. He was giving her the privacy and security she wanted, but she realized she felt more secure knowing he had a key. *Ugh ...*

Maya looked around the room at a loss for what to do with herself and all she was thinking. She could still get a run in and then go to the diner and regain every calorie she would shed during her run.

Yep. That's a good plan.

She laced her sneakers, grabbed her phone, earbuds, and keys, then headed out into the day.

MIKE

Mike didn't return until late in the evening and when he did, he saw Maya's light was out. He wanted nothing more than to open her door and slide into bed next to her. To sleep or otherwise, but he gave her the peace of mind he wouldn't use a key to get in. Her face when he came in earlier ... she was terrified. It was something he'd seen in the eyes of victims, far too often. Everything becomes a threat, everyone a person to fear. *Is she talking to anyone about what happened to her?* He decided he'd investigate that tomorrow. He had only focused on how excited he was to see her; it was stupid not to consider her reaction. He checked his watch; and realized it was close to the time Maya normally had her dreams. All was quiet. *Thank fuck she's resting.* After his shower, he crashed hard. All too soon after he drifted to sleep, he heard the now familiar cries of terror coming from her room.

Slicing through me like white hot iron claws ... I scream as his teeth tear... the pounding ... the tearing ... the pounding ... pounding ... pounding.

Maya tripped over her shoes this time, falling onto her hands and knees at the door.

"Freaking shit shoe bastards!" she yelped as she opened the door while still on her knees. "I'm up! The bear, go back to bed."

When she heard nothing, she sat back on her legs and took in Mike's surprised face. She waved him off. "Fell over my shoes. I'm fine, sorry. I'm going to stay up tonight and work on some things. Go back to sleep dear heart," she said sleepily and dazed.

"The fuck?!" he growled in anger.

Now she was awake. *Shit. Here we go again.*

He reached down and placed his hands under her arms, and he lifted her up so high her feet weren't touching the ground. And he acted as if it took no effort.

Wow. Hubba.

He glared up at her as she looked down at him in fascination.

"You're fuckin' killin' me babe you know that? You all right?"

"Yeah."

"Sure?"

"Yes!"

He lowered her to the ground and stalked into her room muttering. "Fuckin' killing me. Fuckin' killing, fuckin' me." Turning to her, he stared her down.

"It's the same damn thing, Sunshine. THREE fuckin' nights and you're still just opening doors. Now you're on your goddamn knees in your damn blue panties, not even LOOKING at who the fuck is at the door. You can't reach your gun on your goddamn knees in your little blue panties. THINK, for fuck's sake."

I guess tender time is over. She watched him stalk around her space angrily and uninvited, with growing agitation. And, as usual, his anger quickly triggered hers. Leaving the door open behind her, she threw up her hands in exasperation.

"God! What is your problem? I knew it was you and opened it!" She dropped her hands and settled them on her hips.

"You're not safe alone. Especially in those damn panties," he growled.

"Is it me opening the door, or my choice of sleeping attire that bothers you so much? Because for it to be so dangerous, the only one barging into my room at God knows what hour is *you*. Protecting and serving the hell out of me WHETHER I WANT IT OR NOT!"

"It's the panties."

Say what?

"It's all of it," he continued. "You being alone, you having those dreams, but right now it's the panties."

"Oh." She licked her lip, unsure what to say next. His body jerked.

"Don't do that," he growled.

"What?"

"Lick your lips. It's so damn sexy."

The dark heat of desire washed over Maya, radiating from her core. Her breath grew shallow. The rapid breath wafting over her lips made her moisten them again. Another growl escaped his throat that was as intimate as a touch. The damp heat in the underwear he was obsessed with grew. He crossed the room and next thing she recognized he'd pressed her against the side of the open door.

"You did it again," he said quietly, possessively dominating her space.

"Habit." She was all breathy. "I... maybe you should go, if it bothers you."

Girl! What are you saying?!

Her emotions were all over the place, but one thing she understood, to the very core of her soul, was she wanted to spend the rest of her nights with the man in front of her. No matter how many she had left, she wanted them to be with him.

They stood there. Close. Not an inch of space to spare. Each inhale brought them together, each exhale achingly split them apart. She was painfully aware of her heartbeat again as it pounded and rushed in her ears, reaching a deafening roar when he lightly rested his hand on her hip.[4]

"Do you want me to go?"

She didn't trust herself to answer. She closed her eyes letting his body heat waft over her, soaking him into her pores, taking him into her bloodstream, allowing him to course through her veins to where she would never be rid of him again. Not until her soul left her body.

"You drive me crazy," he said. "I'm a wreck watching you come and go. The way the sun hits your hair, the way you walk. Hearing you make yourself moan at night..." A breath escaped her throat. He slipped his second hand into her hair. "All I can think about is how good your lips taste. I tried to avoid you and this." His hands gripped her hair as he leaned into her, pressing his growing need against her body, and his mouth closed in on her lips.

"You can tell me to go. Tell me to go and I'll still watch over you. Protect you. Sit with you while you eat weird shit. But you have to tell me to go so I can stop the rest of this. I don't have the strength to ... not anymore."

A pause.

"I can't say it."

When you touch me, I can't say no.

They both remembered what she said in the diner. It was not only the truth, but a promise.

In an instant, his mouth was on hers, his right hand possessing her hair, while his left hand loosened its grip on her hip and pushed the door closed with a slam.

He curled his arm around her waist, crushing her to him. Their tongues hungrily explored, both were desperate to experience each other's touch, to fulfill the desire that had built to a fever.

Mike slid both hands from her waist to her hips and around to her ass. He claimed it as his with power, lifted her and she wrapped her legs around his waist. His tongue began tracing a trail down her throat and along the bit of her collarbone exposed by her tank top. Another moan escaped her lips, followed by a growl from deep in his throat.

Her body tensed and spasmed as he ripped the side of her panties away with one swift jerk. His mouth came to her ear. "I could feel your wetness on me the second I picked you up." With one hand he gripped one ass cheek and his other hand moved further, sliding a finger into her from behind.

"Michael," she gasped, her hands gripping his hair tighter as her hips moved against his hand. At the sound of his name on her lips he stilled, then slipped a second finger into her sweet, tight, wet space.

"Soaked for me," he growled. Backing up to the bed, he laid her on her back with him on top. He ripped her panties off the rest of the way as his mouth closed over hers, swallowing her cry of surprise.

Mike gripped her tank top, eager to see all of her, she lifted to help him take it off. He took his time moving his mouth down her chest, as his hands did most of the work. Kneading her breasts, his palm brushed her nipple in a circular motion, his rough, calloused hand provided electric friction to her rock-hard nipples. Maya spasmed and cried out as his mouth covered her erect, brown bud, sending her already primed body so close to the edge she could see forever. She grabbed his head, fingers entwined in his hair, arching her back, pressing into him.

"Don't stop, please don't stop," she whispered.

He suddenly paused, frozen, with a sheepish look on his face.

"I don't want to, Sunshine," he said haltingly, "but I'm going to have to..."

She turned to wood underneath him. "YOU HAVE GOT TO BE KIDDING ME!" She started squirming against Mike to get up, but he held her tight against him. "No. Let me go and get out," she fussed as he held her close.

"Maya listen, honey —"

"No. You're a, a — CLIT TEASE," she yelled.

He laughed a full throaty laugh that rumbled through her, including her soft, tight space that was still throbbing for him. THAT did *nothing* to put her in a better mood. He dropped his head onto her neck and kissed it, still laughing. His hair brushed her shoulders sending little waves of electricity everywhere it touched.

"I'm not a tease, I swear baby, listen," he whispered as she struggled. "I don't have protection."

"SO?! Your room is next door. Surely a man that looks like you has industrial size boxes of condoms. Or ... or ... there are stores open somewhere. Hell, this is a BIKER TOWN! Flag down a Billy Badass at the bar and bum one off him." She tensed against his laugh again, feeling herself get wet all over again. "Detective Sheppard, you need to get out and throw yourself in front of a bus."

"I'll leave, but first I'm going to make you come until you are so worn out you sleep without nightmares." His green eyes were dark with desire.

"Oh." She immediately relaxed and hated her body's response.

"Yeah... oh." His finger found the little hard nub that throbbed with need and as he circled it, electricity coursed through her. She tossed her head back as he worked her clit with his fingers and his mouth worked her breasts. It didn't take long for an orgasm to rip through her, making her cry out her release. Before she finished, he slipped two fingers inside her and slid his mouth over hers. "I figure it'll take three or four more to get you tuckered out plenty." His goateed mouth curved into a wicked smile.

"Three or four more and I may never wake up," she breathed.

"Let's find out."

"Okie dokie." She didn't die, but she damn sure slept through the night, and he was wrong. It only took two more to do the trick.

THE NEXT MORNING, she woke alone. She hadn't slept that well in weeks. It was a lovely Saturday morning, and the Colorado sunshine danced through her windows. She rolled over to smell Michael's scent on her pillow. She noticed a note on the nightstand.

> SUNSHINE —
> GOTTA RUN AN ERRAND, THEN GOING TO GET COFFEE, MUFFINS AND...
> DON'T GET DRESSED.
> -M

A thrill shivered through her, and Maya leaped out of the bed, scurrying to the bathroom. She took a quick shower, washed and moisturized her face, fluffed her hair, and decided fuzzy sexed-up hair would have to work for... well, sex. She would re-twist that shit later. As she brushed and flossed her teeth, she looked at herself in the mirror and her face fell.

"Maya Angel, what are you doing? He's gorgeous, does amazing things with his tongue and is sweet and as honest as they come. You're being hunted, pregnant with another man's baby and not even using your real name. This is going to end badly..."

She stood there considering her options, wondering how she could be straight forward with him and not get locked up.

"*Hey Mike, I'm on the run from a billionaire who promised to kill me. Wanna have sex? Or I have a limited time here on Earth, let's boink our way through it... Before you arrest me for false ID and whatever other associated crimes, let's use the handcuffs another way...*"

"Yeah... none of that works."

A knock at the door startled her. She threw a sleep shirt over herself and opened the door with every intention of ending the orgasm train. But a blur of hair hit her, hugging her tight.

"I have another sister!" Tori squealed.

"Oomph!" Maya said as two more people barreled through the door into her. Granted, they were much smaller, but they had a running start. "Whoa! Good morning y'all!" She laughed, miraculously keeping her balance, while thanking her stars Mike hadn't made it back. She made a mental note to tell him he was right about opening the door.

"Hey," Caine said, bringing up the rear with Baby Simone. "We're taking you to breakfast."

"I would have been here sooner, but Caine insisted we give you your space to adjust. You've adjusted enough."

"Ha! Okay, I'm going to breakfast," Maya said, throwing out jazz hands.

"Were those jazz hands?" Tori asked, her head cocking to one side.

Caine snorted. "What the hell are jazz hands?"

"A celebratory masterpiece of dance," Maya said, throwing her hands out, fingers splayed wide and shaking them briefly with a huge smile.

"Goofy," Caine mumbled.

---

1. Sweetest Taboo by Sade
2. Whenever, Wherever, Whatever by Maxwell
3. Thank You by Dido
4. Your Hands by Marsha Ambrosius

15

CUTENESS IS INSURMOUNTABLE

MAYA

MAYA WOKE when the SUV stopped and realized she slept the entire way back from the little breakfast spot about thirty minutes away. She looked over, and saw the girls and Tori were asleep.

"I'll walk you to the door," Caine said.

"The door is right there Caine, as much as it likes to pretend, it's not a hotel, it's a motel."

"I'll walk you."

Maya sighed, giving in when Caine opened her door. After one last check on her nieces, she slid out of the SUV. "Thanks for everything today."

"You gotta let us help."

"Caine—"

"Let me help. We've got resources, connections..."

"Not like him. And help with what? I'm not staying with you guys. I don't need money, and unless you want to go to childbirth classes in a couple of weeks, I'm golden."

He made a face at the idea of childbirth classes.

"See." She laughed. "It should be old hat by now, you're on number four!"

"If you want me to ... I will," he mumbled.

"You're an M&M. Hard on the outside and soft on the inside ... Thanks for the offer," she rushed on quickly, seeing him get grumpy about being compared to candy. "But I have a midwife and a doula. I will be fine. I love that you offered."

"Maya—"

"Caine. Stop. Don't ask, not anymore. If I do share, it will be in my own time, in my own way. Okay?"

His jaw clenched and unclenched.

"Please, Caine."

"Fine."

She hugged him tight and, noticing Victoria awake, she waved at her new sister and ducked into the room.

Maya snatched off her bra, tossed it onto the chair, yanked off her pants, and kicked them across the room. Another eventful day in a "quiet" mountain town.

"This place is a Shonda Rhimes dream," she muttered as she headed to the bathroom to wash her face.

She got halfway into the bathroom when she heard a knock at the door. She pulled her hair into a ponytail holder and grabbed her discarded pants to hold in front of her. Instead of throwing open the door, she stopped and looked through the peephole.

"I'M LOOKING THROUGH THE PEEPHOLE IDENTIFYING DETECTIVE SHEPPARD AS THE MAN OUTSIDE THE DOOR!" she yelled before opening the door.

Six feet six inches of mountain man grinned down at her.

"Good girl."

And praise kink activated.[1]

"I apologize and will never open the door without checking again. This morning I was attacked in my pajamas, thinking it was you. Instead, it was a high-heeled, pregnant assassin and her little minions whose weapon of choice is unsurmountable cuteness. And breakfast. They weaponized breakfast."

"Ah, the Walters family," he said, nodding. "Did you get my note?"

"Of course—"

"Yet you got dressed."

"Yes."

"And you left."

"Ye-ah, but in my defense, cuteness is insurmountable," she replied.

"Tell me about it," he grumbled, glancing at her, before walking in the door and kicking it shut with his foot. "I come bearing gifts."

"At least I know you're not a vampire."

"A vampire?"

"You always enter uninvited. That is against vampire lore."

Mike stopped and considered her for a moment. "What about the one guy that stalks the sad chick and turns into glitter shit in the sun?"

"I'm following the rules from the '80's classic 'Lost Boys' with the two Coreys, not that new wave bull, and I'm surprised you watched 'Twilight,'" she said as she laughed her ass off.

"Tina loved those movies." He grinned, kicked off his boots, and sat on her bed. Setting his gifts next to him, he looked at her expectantly.

"Make yourself at home," she mumbled, walking over to him. "If the gifts are coffee and condoms, I think it's too late for the first and too early for the second."

"Mmm... Is that why you left? Too early for condoms?"

"No, I told you, I was kidnapped by cuteness."

"Mmm ... hmm ... and I gave you a chance to have second thoughts. I won't make that mistake again. Why do you sleep with a .38 under your pillow?"

He nailed her with a look, and she couldn't turn away. The change in subject made her head spin. She recovered and shot back, "What's in the bag? It's too big for condoms."

"Is it?"

"Oh." The heat rose to her face as she remembered last night and the night at the pool. She considered it might not be big enough.

He watched her, a playful glint in his eyes. "I've got cookies. The best chocolate chip cookies in Rough Ridge." Then he took out a giant cookie and bit into it.

Maya's eyes lit up.

"But, until you're straight with me, Sunshine, you can't have any." His eyes gave her an unflinching glare.

Her face fell. "This whole town is nosey as hell," she grumbled.

"Small town manners, sweetheart." And he took another bite.

She considered him for a moment. "Same rules for you."

"A bite of cookie for info from me. And I'll give you,"—she walked over to the mini-fridge and opened it up — "two swigs of ice-cold milk straight outta the carton, the only way a real mountain man drinks it." She sat the carton down with a dramatic snap.

"Is that so..." he said with a slow chuckle. "You're on, but to be fair, I'm not hiding anything."

She walked over to the bed, slipped her hand under the pillow, grabbed her gun, and carefully checked it. As she put it in the night-stand drawer, he watched with his signature intensity. When she finished, she clicked off the light.

"Why—"

"The truth is easier said in the dark," she said. She crawled into bed next to him, crossed her legs underneath her and, without looking at him, she said, "Ask."

"Why the gun Maya?

"I'm a woman alone in Colorado."

"Bullshit Maya, now Imma eat your cookie."

"Which one?" She asked instinctively, before clamping her hands over her mouth. "I'm sorry that was—"

"Honest. Something you don't seem to shy away from in most cases."

A long pause.

"I keep it because I'm afraid."

"Of what?"

"Bears and wicked men."

"Yet you repeatedly open the door in your panties."

He has a point, though bears don't care about attire...

Instead of responding, she demanded a cookie. The first bite, she moaned in ecstasy, and Mike's body jerked. He roughed out, "Ask your question, Sunshine."

"Why do you call me Sunshine?"

"Because you brighten up a room. Your eyes sparkle, and when you smile everyone feels its warmth, even if it's not directed at them. And when you leave ... that warmth ... it's missed."

She sighed as she shifted a bit. "Wow ... I, uh, I thought it was because of the movie."

"What movie?"

"Harlem Nights... Never mind."

"Mmm, never saw it. Milk," he demanded.

She watched his profile in the shadows, taking in the raw masculine beauty in bed beside her.

"Is your gun legal?"

"It's registered to Maya Anderson, with corresponding concealed carry permit."

"That's a long way from a straight yes."

"That's my thorough answer."

"Dammit Maya," he said, snatching a pillow and jabbing it behind his back as he settled against the wall in frustration. "I'm a cop. Be straight with me."

"Does that tantrum usually work with bad guys?"

"You're a bad guy?"

She snorted. "Not by the farthest stretch of the imagination."

"What about us?" he asked, his voice low and rough.

Us? When did we become an us? Sure, I think about him all the time, and the multiple orgasms certainly indicate something's happening, but an us? With a cop?

She shook her head sadly. "We haven't known each other long enough to be an us."

Mike sighed, shifting a bit. "I've known you long enough to see you hurt, to see you sick and scared ... hear you cry out from fear at night. I've known you long enough to know your favorite color is white. You love tea, order weird shit for breakfast and you have a scary chocolate addiction ... I know that you have a kindness that's so fuckin' pure, people drop every wall they have and gravitate toward you despite the walls you keep up ... your music matches your moods, and it's as eclectic and nuanced as you are ... and I know right now you're building new reasons to keep me on the other side of that massive wall you compulsively add to..."

"I don't have a favorite color," she said lamely. "And, if we were an us, you would leave the law where you leave your boots–outside this bed. But I have no right to ask that of you."

They sat for a while.

"I come with baggage."

"Sunshine, my father the crooked cop ... the worst. He corrupted an entire police department... destroyed lives. His last act on Earth was to kidnap and torture a pregnant woman. He learned his charm from his father and so on. There is barely a person in this town who hasn't been blackmailed, assaulted, harassed, or worked over by someone with my last name. I let myself get distracted by Stan's shit, and I wasn't there to protect innocents."

"It's not your fault. You are a different man, a man with a good heart. And Tori doesn't hold it against you."

"She's uncomfortable."

"Probably because she turned your father into a shit stain on the sidewalk." She could tell he thought that tidbit over with a new perspective. "You are not your father." She placed her hand on his heart.

"There's a darkness in the men of my family," he warned.

"Here's what you don't see, Heart. That shit's not hereditary like eye color. It's learned. And someone taught you better. Nurtured you better. It's a freaking miracle, but here you are. Instead of carrying a chip on your shoulder like many would, you've opted to pick up the whole damn world. That's a burden too big for anyone."

They sat quietly for a while longer.

"You have a look too," he began cautiously. "Like you're on the run from the world."

She took a deep breath. "That's because I am. Well, not from the entire world, but a big part of mine."

She shifted to lay her head in his lap, facing away from him, and he stroked her hair, patiently waiting.

"He wasn't always a ... I could tell there was a dark side he never showed me. He was the first person I was close to after my mother died. I worked hard through high school and college. My sole focus was on graduating early so she could see me do it before cancer finally got her. From the time I was fourteen until I was twenty-one, my world was school–double loads, filling out scholarships–and taking care of mom–chemo sessions, doctor visits; and sometimes working part time ... a constant run against time. You can live a long time with bone cancer, but never long enough."

"I didn't date or go to prom or anything like that, so I was way behind in that department. He swooped in like a knight. Dazzling, rich, powerful, but none of that mattered. What mattered was he pretended to believe in me. *That* was what I needed."

She paused for a while.

"I made all kinds of concessions. They seemed small. He said he loved me, so I indulged him. Straight hair only–he loved my hair that way. All black clothing because he said it was chic and sexy. He did things like insisting on ordering for both of us in French at restaurants, even though his French was abysmal and mine was ... well, better. But it was a power struggle with him. We saw each other on his terms. No male friends, unless proven gay. Check in three times a day. Wait at his apartment until he got around to coming home. He said it was because he missed me. A compliment, then an order and an affectionate reward. He wore me down. Molded me. He was never violent or rough, it was coaxing and training... I convinced myself he was decisive."

"He was controlling," Mike bit out.

She nodded. "I know that now. One rule was absolutely no children. That was fine with me because at the time I had no intention of having kids. I wanted to expand my business to the West Coast. I'm afraid of dogs and allergic to cats. Shoot, I could barely keep a plant alive, and I had a housekeeper. Then ... I got an ear infection. Tired from battling with a client on a tough project, I got sick. I didn't know antibiotics decreased the effects of birth control. We didn't have sex regularly, and when we did, he was ... hit or miss. Now I know it was from too much 'E,' or he was too tired from screwing every chick on the East Coast ... Timing and fate are something else," she said.

"He demanded I get an abortion. I'd already considered it when I found out ... but his reaction woke me up to a lot of things. Chief among them was I really did want kids and not just someday..."

"What happened?" Mike asked, his voice tight, anger coming off him in waves.

"I defied him. No one defies him, and I found out why..."

"The bruises."

She nodded. "After he finally let me go—"

"Finally?"

She sighed again. "He held me in the wine cellar for three days while he beat/convinced me to agree. Or using his words– 'brought me to heel.' Like I was an animal." His hold on her tightened, his body coiled tight, but her memories tormented her. "I went into survival mode. And tried anything to get him to stop hurting me. I pretended to go along with it, got him to let me go... I walked in the front door of the doctor's office and out the back door, running to the police. They took my statement, took photos for the files. It was humiliating. Their questioning was less about his crime, and more about what I'd done to bring on the abuse. They asked if I liked it rough, reminded me he came from a prominent family, and then told me I could go to jail for lying. I was mortified, but not stupid. I may have been singularly focused for most of my life, but that doesn't mean I don't understand what it means to be a woman and, in this case, a Black woman dating a powerful white man in this world. The writing was on the wall. I stopped the interview, gathered my senses, and left the room. I walked out a wreck. Shaking, scared, and there he was, at the bottom of the steps. They had *called him*. I was in a ratty sweatshirt and jeans. He looked like a million bucks, with nothing to fear. He called to me, 'Darling, I'm going to kill you. No matter your reproductive circumstance.'"

"There were people all around. Lawyers, cops, no one said a thing, no one helped me. They knew who he was and didn't want any part of it. His father was with him, waiting in the car. He lowered his window from the backseat and, I kid you not, said 'Now is not the time, son.' Like it was a couple's spat at the country club." She cringed, her voice still portraying her disbelief at it all. "I'd never felt so low ... so utterly worthless in my entire life..."

She paused long enough to breathe through her rising anxiety. When she started speaking again, her voice shook.

"I caught a cab and waited outside until I could walk into my apartment building with other people. I ran to a friend's apartment instead of mine, aware his security team wouldn't burst in there. Instead, they waited and watched. By the time he and more reinforcements arrived, I'd already climbed out of the window onto the fire escape, and into another apartment below. They helped me get out of the service entrance with the maintenance crew. From there, I hit the public library, made a few hard-to-trace arrangements, and hit a couple of women's shelters. Eventually, I made my way here. I was lucky ... "

He jerked at her statement. "Lucky?"

"He underestimated me, and I have resources myself. I've been naïve, but not completely stupid."

He squeezed her hard.

"You left everything."

"On balance, I didn't have much, and what I did have wasn't worth my baby's life. It's my body and my choice, and I chose what I knew what was right for me..." She sighed. "You may have baggage, but yours is in the past. My baggage is still a threat, and another package is due to arrive in about six months. Too much baggage to be an us."

The hand that stroked her hair stopped. She braced herself for what he would say next. The acknowledgment it wouldn't happen for them. Her body prepared for the mental blow. Michael's hand slid over her still flat belly and held it protectively.

"That's not baggage. That's a blessing," he whispered.

Sudden sobs rocked her body at his words.

"Sunshine," he quietly soothed as he slid her fully onto his lap and kissed her forehead, and tucked it under his chin, "the load you carry is too much to wrestle with alone, baby."

"And you carry three plus generations of steamer trunks. You don't need mine," she said, muffled into his chest.

"I've got big shoulders."

"I've noticed." She looked at him and he kissed her gently. Maya didn't know what came over her. It was wrong. She should have told him right then the rest of it— who she was, who was after her, be upfront about everything— but she ran with what she wanted right then. Wrapped in his compassion and care for her she wanted to stay in that moment. To remain there, together in the dark, making it last for as long as she could.[2]

So, for once in her life, Maya let go and let herself *enjoy*. It was stupid, selfish, and if she'd been able to see the future, she would have done the right thing. The smart thing. Instead, she deepened the kiss, darting her tongue over his lips. He grabbed her tight, receiving her invitation and greedily took from her mouth all he could. Deep and rough, he expertly communicated his own need and Maya had every intention of filling it. Repeatedly.

She broke from him and began trailing kisses along his jaw, stopping to nibble his earlobe. She pulled at his t-shirt, jerking it impatiently over his head, and attacked his neck, moaning at the taste of him.

He growled at her touch and repositioning them he lay on top of her. His hands were inside of her shirt exploring, and when his hand palmed her breast, he brought his mouth over her nipple while she arched her back eagerly. He took that opportunity to slide her top off. Raising up on his knees, he looked at her.

"Gorgeous." He gently traced his fingertips along her body, gliding them along her collarbone, over her chest, along her rib cage, across her stomach... lingering along the edge of her underwear, then jumping to the sensitive skin on the inside of her wrists. Slowly, torturously, he lightly stroked her arms. Everywhere he touched left a trail of fire. Maya never felt more cherished and more turned on in her whole life.

"Michael..." she moaned, pleading.

"I want to memorize every inch of you," he rumbled, his eyes hungry and intense.

She was writhing. "It's like I'm on fire," she breathed.

His face changed. In an instant his mouth was on hers, his hands slipping down her waist, across her stomach, and jerking clear the thin lace of her underwear. Another pair destroyed. And she didn't give the first flying flip. She would order panties by bulk if he got off ripping them off her. She'd have Amazon ship that shit on a weekly basis. Anything. Anything if she could keep having this— having him.

His hand slid through the delicate, slick folds of her sex. He circled around her clit slowly until Maya was coming apart with need. Then he grazed across her sensitive bud and Maya exploded. Intense waves of warmth and light washed over her, rocking her body with its intensity. She cried out his name, raw and hoarse in her throat.

He gave a deep, sexy chuckle. "That's what I like…"

He slid slowly down her body and dipped his head to feed as the residual waves of her orgasm continued to torture her. The next wave built quickly as Mike shifted Maya's legs over his shoulders. He reached under and cupped her ass, giving him better access to her sweet wetness.

His hair tickled the sensitive skin of her inner thighs, while his powerful hands gripped and kneaded her ass, still careful of her injuries. He teased, nipped, sucked and lapped at every inch of her. It was almost unbearable.

Almost.

She was so close, and she looked down at him. When their eyes met, he grinned mischievously and slipped his tongue *in* her, using his hand to lightly tap a sexual rhythm on her clit.

That was it!

Her second orgasm came harder and lasted longer than the first. She was certain she'd break in his arms, disintegrating into shuddering shards of orgasmic dust. Vaguely aware she held his hair and head in a vice-like grip, she dug the heels of her feet into his shoulders and arched to meet his mouth, offering even more of herself as a loud, deep wail flew from the pit of her stomach.

Her body shook all over as he kissed her legs and shifted them off his shoulders. He quickly unzipped his jeans, shoving them and his underwear off in one swoop. Maya moved from panting from the orgasm to panting for something else. All that something else. And amen, there was a lot there. He snagged a condom from his wallet and tore it open with his mouth. She rose and took it from him. Sliding close, she wrapped her hand around as much of him as she could and stroked him.

"Let me do that for you."

She dropped her eyes and slowly, teasingly, stroked him with her hands until a deep, aching moan rose through him. Her mouth watered at the sound, and she quickly maneuvered herself to all fours, arching her ass in the air as she lowered her mouth so she could wrap her tongue around the tip of his dick. Swirling her tongue around the head of his shaft a few times, she loved how he tried to anticipate her movement. His body was tense, his ab muscles bunching tight. She lifted her gaze to him and almost shivered. His eyes were almost black with desire.

She kept her eyes on him as she clasped him firmly in her hand and took him as far as she could into her mouth in one swoop. His strangled groan turned her on more, so she moaned around him, allowing the vibrations to flow freely from her throat around his shaft. She used her tongue to massage the sensitive underside of his dick as he grasped the sides of her face.

"Ah ... fuck ... shit... babe."

She half expected him to take over the rhythm and begin thrusting into her mouth, but he let her control how she pleasured him. That alone earned him her best effort. She smiled with her eyes and bobbed, taking him in and out earnestly, using her hand to stroke the parts of him that wouldn't fit into her mouth. She tried Shay's trick: relaxing her jaw, she exhaled and took him even deeper until he reached the back of her throat, then she swallowed.

"Fuuuck ... "

She hallowed out her cheeks and increased the suction, adding a twist to both her hand and her mouth as she sucked him in and out.

"Touch yourself," he demanded.

Using the hand that massaged his balls, she reached between her legs, where she was dripping. She moaned as she massaged her clit and the more she massaged, the harder she sucked, the more Mike swore until finally he swelled in her mouth.

"Babe, God, you gotta stop now I can't hold—"

She kept working his shaft and herself until she starting coming. Her whimpers drove him over the edge, and he fisted his hands in her hair as he released into her mouth with a shout. And she took all of him. The saltiness coated her tongue and ran down her throat. She swallowed again. The movement over the tip of his shaft at the back of her throat sent another deep moan and shudder through his body. She took one last long suck, releasing him gently.

Rising to her knees, she kissed his chest and ran her hands over his abs and ass. Maya delighted in the heat of him. She nibbled at his neck when something hard poked her in the stomach. Surprised, she pulled back, breaking his hold on her, and looked down.

"Already?" she asked, laughing.

"Have you seen you?"

Practically giddy, Maya slid the condom on him.

She met his eyes and, holding them, she sat back, tossed her hair over her shoulder, and spread her legs.

His eyes dropped from hers, down her body, to her glistening sex.

"Prettiest pussy I've ever seen."

"Take it."

His eyes flew back to hers.

Eyebrow raised, mouth slightly parted, Maya felt powerfully feminine. She'd had a couple of lovers, none of them that great. But she'd never been shy about sex, always taught that a body was nothing to be ashamed of or embarrassed over. Still, something in her remained reserved until she met the man kneeling before her, his eyes full of adoration and desire.

Mike gave her another slow, sexy smile. Slowly covering her body with his, he cupped her face, keeping his weight on his forearm, his heavy thick member hot and pressing at her opening.

---

1. Leave the Door Open by Bruno Mars, Anderson .Paak, Silk Sonic
2. Lose Control by Ledisi

16

HIS TENDER CARE

MAYA

HE GRABBED her thigh and lifted it to position her when she gave a surprised squeak of pain and grimaced.

Mike froze. "Maya?"

"It's fine, baby. Keep going, please." She closed her eyes and braced.

"Maya, look at me."

Her eyes flew open in irritation. Light brown hit green.

"Maya—"

"Dammit Michael, if you stop this again..."

He squeezed her thigh in the same place. She jerked despite herself.

"Fuck no, you're hurt." He sat back, looked down at her, his face soft.

"Son of a..." she muttered to the ceiling. "I. Am. Fine."

"What else hurts, Maya?"

"What?"

"What else?" he demanded quietly.

She sat up quickly, growling as she pulled her knees to her chest. "Drying up like the Sahara here."

He wasn't amused.

"Maya. You've been through a lot. I don't want to take advantage of you or worsen any ... injuries. I need to know so I can take care of you."

She got what he was trying to say. "He didn't rape me," she whispered. "Some of my injuries may never heal completely, but that one isn't a concern. I *want* to *be* with you. Well, not now of course."

He gave her a long stare. "This is a safe space, Sunshine." His hands gestured between the two of them. "I am going to make sure you're good, even if it's uncomfortable or a mood killer. Always."

"Now..." he whispered, placing a soft hand on her knee, "what hurts? Show me."

She released a heavy sigh. "Not until you put on pants. No way I'm looking at all of that right now." She waved her hand up and down his body.

Smirking, he reached down, grabbed his black boxer briefs and slid them on. He walked into the bathroom and after a while the toilet flushed and Mike washed his hands. He strolled back in and turned on the small desk lamp. Shifting to her dresser, he opened the top drawer, then the second drawer, looking through her underwear.

"That's unnecessary, Heart. Don't need it. You've seen everything already."

"No way I'm looking at all of that, Sunshine."

"Touché." She yawned deep.

He roughly dug through the drawer. "Don't you have any granny drawers?"

Maya lit up and snorted with laughter. "Granny drawers? I'm no granny! And 'drawers?!'" She cackled more.

"What about that time of the month pants?"

His suggestion edged on desperation. It was hilarious.

A handsome, big, ol' mountain man, a cop, in his underwear, looking for lady 'drawers.'

She shook with laughter. "I'm pregnant and left with the clothes on my back. No need to have any."

"Fuck Maya, where are your ugly underwear? All this shit is sexy."

"I've got boy shorts in there."

He pulled out cotton boy shorts, held them up, and grimaced.

"These are the kind where the ass cheeks fall out. Fuckin' sexy shits." He growled, crumpled them into a ball and threw them back in the drawer.

Maya laughed so hard her stomach hurt. "I'm gonna pee!" she hooted, hopped off the bed and stumbled, naked, to the bathroom.

MIKE

A few minutes later, she came out, walked past him standing in the same spot, and went to the bottom drawer. She handed him a package of maternity underwear. The full brief kind.

"There. That's the ugliest I have. Grey and huge. I don't think they'll fit now though."

"Put these fuckers on. NOW."

She sat on the side of the bed still cracking up. Her naked body alight with amusement, breasts gently jiggling, the throaty husk of her laughter turned him on even more. He groaned in frustration and adjusted himself, which did not help. Instead, she laughed harder. He grew harder, and tears rolled down her face. She snorted and fell over onto her side, giggling like a maniac. It was an emotional release after the tough conversations and intense physical tension. But he was determined.

She looked up at the sound of the package ripping and saw him advancing on her with a giant pair of "drawers."

"On."

"You want them on, Caveman, you do it." Her eyes glittered as she taunted him.

"Pain in my ass," he mumbled as he positioned her like she was a toddler and slid the underwear up. He looked at his work. It looked like she wore bits of saggy elephant skin.

"Better. Those are fucking terrible."

She shook with giggles as he slowly and full of regret, slid a tank over her breasts.

Dropping beside her, he looked into her eyes, then stroked her face and hair, waiting for her to calm down into quiet chuckles.[1]

"Sunshine... serious about this babe. I'm gonna go slow. You tell me what hurts and how it hurts, yeah?"

Maya's gentle giggles died, leaving her looking incredibly vulnerable. She closed her eyes briefly, and when she opened them, he saw a brick in her wall fall as she nodded a silent yes.

He spent the next dark hours of the evening carefully, tenderly mapping her injuries in his mind. He listened with all his senses to her responses from the gentle prodding of his fingers. And he kissed every hurt encountered. He couldn't put into words why he needed to nurture ... to minister to her in this way. A small part of him hoped to heal her little by little with his touch and care. A lot of her healing would come from within, but his heart filled in a way he couldn't have imagined when she told him his quiet, thoughtful gesture started her on her journey.

For Mike, a journey started as well. Each injury discovered was a dagger through his heart, tearing at the control he kept over his emotions. Every time he touched a gentle lip to her tender, wounded skin, he made a silent promise to inflict infinite pain on the man who caused it. Each confirmation of the monster's brutality added dry kindling to the pit of his soul until an ember of the dark Sheppard flame blazed to life.

---

1. Red Dust by James Vincent McMorrow

17

GIVE ME PEACE

MAYA

Maya stood in Dr. Flemmings' third-floor office at Rough Ridge County Hospital, staring at the woman's credentials like the map to the lost gold of El Dorado hid in them.

Flemings' office was cozy, not clinical. A granny squared Afghan decorated the proverbial shrink couch on one side of the room. Throw pillows and an area rug in a colorful Native American pattern softened the gray commercial-grade carpet underneath. The room, painted a soft butter yellow, boasted billowy cream curtains and personal touches of decorative pottery and fresh flowers. It made Maya think of "living room" not "shrink-one-floor-beneath-where-they-put-the-long-term-psychiatric-residents."

Clever.

"Maya, what happened this week?" Dr. Flemmings asked, again, after she went silent.

"What didn't happen is a better question, Dr. Flemmings," Maya responded, voice calm. "I'm either falling apart or getting it back together again. I don't know … you're the expert. Several times over." She nodded toward the plaques on the wall.

Maya moved on from the mounted frames of diplomas, awards, and accolades and peered through the good doc's bookshelves. *A mixture of professional and classic literature - interesting.* She slipped out *"I Know Why the Caged Bird Sings"* and started thumbing through the pages.

"My mother's favorite book. Her favorite author," she mumbled. "I'm named after her," Maya told the doc with a quick glance. "Maya Angelou walked on water to my mother. She would say 'Mother Angelou captured what it meant to be living as human…'"

She snapped the book shut and finally sat across from Dr. Flemmings in the "conversation area" of the office. Two large, broken-in, club-style chairs faced each other, with low slung tables on each side. The patient's side held a clear acrylic carafe of water with a matching cup, cloth napkins, and a clear acrylic tin of cookies.

"Saturday night I spent the evening having each of my injuries - largely unseen - being kissed so softly," Maya whispered. "He was patience and strength personified. It scares the shit out of me. Nothing about Michael and our relationship makes sense. I'm supposed to be low profile, but here, I *feel* different. I should be wary of all men … None of this makes sense."

She absentmindedly pulled a pack of M&M's and a bag of celery and carrot sticks out of her purse and munched, deep in thought.

Mike and Maya had been apart for almost a week. She wished they had *that* night as the last memory of each other, but Biscuit got in the way. The Biscuit Incident, her inability to sleep, the constant fear and anger under the surface, and the strange attachment she'd already developed with Mike and the town of Rough Ridge meant she reached the point where she couldn't ignore her mental health any longer.

"Monday afternoon, all hell broke loose. Tuesday morning, I called you and submitted to this intense thing you call 'progress.' Tuesday afternoon we talked until I was hoarse. Later I took your advice, tried to make myself feel safe sharing. I went boxing with my brother, later to the gun range by myself. And I couldn't do it."

"You couldn't do what Maya?"

"Fight back." Her eyes filled with shame. "I couldn't pull the trigger at the range. I learned right then it didn't matter if I had a gun. When the time came, I would never use it. He would win." She rushed on, full of anguish. "Everyone says, 'Imagine I'm him.' I do ... and ... and ... all I do is freeze. I couldn't hit Caine at the gym. I couldn't hit anyone. When he took me to that cellar? I never fought back!"

She shook her head angrily, pissed at herself. "I begged. Pleaded. Rationalized. Appealed to his humanity, his vanity ... I prayed, and I cried, but I never fucking *fought*."

"And how does that make you feel?" Dr. Flemmings' voice grew soft, as the older woman looked at Maya with intense kindness.

"Weak and stupid ... Vulnerable ... That Gr ... he was right."

"Maya, you understand what happened to you is not your fault. None of it. How you reacted is how you reacted. You survived, and your survival is what's important."

Maya nodded her head. "I understand that intellectually, but I like control. I solve problems and this..."

"Is not a problem that has a logical solution," Dr. Flemmings said, nodding. "You come across those often in life unless you close yourself off."

A little light bulb illuminated in Maya's head. Dr. Flemmings switched topics.

"Why won't you reveal who he is to the people in your life?"

"No," Maya said, her voice hard. "No one gets involved in that. They are already making moves, putting themselves in danger, moves I'm going to put a stop to— soon."

"Maya—" Dr. Flemmings leaned in, her face calm, her eyes telling a different story.

"No doc, that isn't a mental health issue."

Dr. Flemmings adjusted in her seat, made a note on her little pad, and studied Maya.

"What happened Wednesday and yesterday?"

Maya's smile was partly wicked and partly triumphant. "I woke the fuck up and started fighting back."

Dr. Flemmings blinked.

THURSDAY | THREE DAYS AFTER THE BISCUIT INCIDENT | JAKE'S GUN SUPPLY & RANGE, TEN MILES OUTSIDE OF ROUGH RIDGE, COLORADO...

"Ok cupcake, are you gonna bitch about this like yesterday, or are you going to do it?" Laila asked Maya.

Rough Ridge officer Laila outside of uniform was no less polished than when she was on duty. She wore a pristine tank top and jeans. Her dewy olive-toned skin was without makeup, except for a bit of gloss, which Maya guessed was Vaseline. Maya expected her nails to be shorter, but they were long, elegant, buffed to a shine. If she didn't exude extreme bad-assery, she could be a fresh-faced skincare model joyfully tossing water on her enviable skin.

Tall, Laila moved with a calculated feline grace. She was self-assured and dangerous. What Maya liked about Laila most, however, was how her face changed when she smiled. Even the bat shit crazy-pants glee she got out of incidents of violence transformed her into something extra beautiful. It was a glimpse into what was under the Kevlar vest and watchful gaze. Her eyes never left Maya as, in rapid practiced movements, she loaded bullets into gun clips and sat the clips down in neat, ordered lines on the long table.

"No bitchin' Laila. Let's get it going," Maya replied. She pulled her hair into a ponytail and reached for a pair of shooting goggles from the table.[1]

Laila looked the woman over for a few seconds. "Hmmm... Dark leggings and tee. Nice stance. Legs apart, feet firm. You're not making yourself smaller. Definite progress. You're getting there sooner than I expected, but the faster the better. You were on the road to cracking up and taking folks with you." She paused, assessing her again. "Mmm ... You're getting off on this now, aren't you?"

"I'm getting off on feeling less like Bambi waiting for the hunter."

Laila laughed a bit while smoothing her tight, impossibly neat bun. Without warning, she grabbed Maya by the throat. Maya, caught by surprise, inhaled sharply and tried to jerk away. Laila squeezed and barked out, "FIGHT!"

Maya struggled a second more. "FIGHT DAMMIT." Laila squeezed more. Maya paused a half second, forcefully blew out air while dropping her chin and pushing her body into Laila's hand. At the same time, she reached and pulled Laila's thumb away from her throat with both her hands as she drove her body toward the woman. When she was close to Laila, she quickly delivered an elbow strike.

"STOP HOLDING BACK MAYA."

"Laila, you're not wearing any gear," Maya noted. She was breathing hard already.

"Stop being a punk and hit me. Follow through. You need to experience skin on bone. If that bastard Biscuit, Pop Tarts, or anyone else comes after you, they won't be wearing gear either."

"That's crazy," Maya huffed. "I can't hit you full on. What if I hurt you?"

"Unlike you, I'm not a princess in a tower waiting for someone to rescue me. I can handle it."

Maya got ticked. Quick.

"What is that supposed to mean? I handle my shit. I'm here, aren't I?"

"Monday, five men came to your rescue. Five. And you stood there shaking and apologizing and throwing tears."

"What the fuck was I supposed to do? Yell 'I got yo' ass!' and kick the man in his balls?"

"You didn't *have* to say *anything*. Control your emotions and you could have defused, deflected, or defended even after you did what you did," Laila said, looking Maya in the eyes. "You're a mess of conflicting emotions. In battle, you need to be clear. Rage will power you through, but it'll cause you to do things you regret. Fear will heighten your senses, but if you're not careful, it can also make you freeze in your tracks ... like you did just now."

"I recovered."

"Yeah, so what? Want a cookie?"

"Actually..."

"Sheesh, you *are* pregnant." Laila rolled her eyes as she walked past Maya. She then suddenly reversed and grabbed Maya with a bent arm across her throat and jerking Maya tight to her body. Maya instinctively dropped her butt low and turned her throat toward Laila's elbow, breaking the hold and allowing her a bit of air. She hit Laila with a low elbow strike to the ribs. HARD.

"Shit," Laila wheezed as she quoted a movie. "Ooh yeah, sucka, that's what I'm talkin' about."

"Finally, someone on this dang mountain who has seen *Harlem Nights* besides me and Caine," Maya yelped. "By the way, I've been watching the defense videos you sent me Tuesday."

Maya reached over to the table, grabbed a bottle of water, and took a deep drink. She offered it with a shake. "Squeeze bottle, no backwash."

Laila waved her off. "I think you may have bruised my ribs. Good job princess." Laila breathed hard, adjusting her side. "Next time follow through. You are not hitting me; you're hitting *through* me. AGAIN."

For three hours, Maya and Laila worked through strikes and escapes. Maya was in no position to initiate an attack. She needed to get the basics down before her pregnancy brought a shift in her balance. Repetition, muscle memory, and getting quickly over surprise were what Laila focused on. At the end of the session, she stopped and met Maya's eyes. "What's your job?" she barked.

"Run," Maya said, panting hard, her hands on her knees.

Sweat ran down her face and dripped onto the dusty ground. Yes, the ground. This was not self-defense at the local YMCA with mats and safe words. It was something else entirely, and Maya liked it. All her terrifying experiences occurred in regular clothes, in the ordinary, real big world.

"If not run then?"

"Incapacitate." Maya stood watching Laila prowl back and forth.

"HOW?"

"Completely." Maya looked away from Laila's eyes down to her sneakers. They looked out of character for the hard ass Maya has gotten to appreciate over the last couple of days. Hot pink with neon orange piping.

Super cute.

"You don't sound convinced."

Laila jerked Maya by her navy *"MYODB is a vibe, mood, lifestyle and combat style."* t-shirt and stood nose to nose with her. "Will the man who did this to you hesitate to kill you?"

Maya swallowed and shook her head no, eyes wide.

"Princess, you need to speak," she barked. "Is he going to hesitate one fucking moment?"

"No," Maya whispered.

"Will. He. *Hesitate*. To hurt *anyone* you love?"

"NO."

Laila jerked her tighter. "And this is when I get to watch the internal fight play out in your eyes. Fear, anger, the thousands of thoughts regular people have when faced with their mortality. And yeah, I'm pushing it. You were a mess two days ago. Boo hoo. I'm no white knight, but I believe in giving women a chance to save their own asses. Will you? I'm taller than you, stronger than you. Even in those ridiculous wedge sneakers, which are the most indecisive footwear invented. I intimidate you. And what are you going to do about it? Nothing. What about him? If you can't get away. If you *can't* bring him to his knees. If you know in your heart of hearts you're going to die. What the FUCK are you going to do, princess?" Laila's voice dropped to a deadly whisper.

Maya's mind was completely blank. She couldn't move, she couldn't do anything but listen and feel. Scared and angry. Confused and frozen. She stared into the dark brown eyes of the crazy woman in front of her. There was something cold there. Dark. They reminded her of Griffin. No, scratch that. Griffin's eyes had a void, a blankness to them that was inhuman. Her mind perfectly recalled exactly how his eyes looked when he held the gun to her head and, just like that, she was right back at that moment. In the wine cellar. His custom cologne clogging her nose. The inky midnight hue of his shirt, the metallic glint from the light reflecting off his watch. His breath on her face like Laila's was now. Then— something settled on her spirit... a knowing.

He would have killed me. He would have killed me then, and he will kill me when he finds me.

It wasn't an if, but a when. She didn't understand *how* she knew, but she knew it like she knew her own name. *What will I do? What will I do when he finds me, finds my baby or Caine, Tori... the girls? What can I do?*

The answer came in a moment of true clarity. It caused her eyes to clear, her breathing to still, and her body to relax. She focused back on the dark eyes in front of her and stated with absolute certainty, "Take that fucker with me."

For a moment, Laila's eyes widened in shock, then narrowed in delight as she grinned big. She let Maya go and backed away to the table, chuckling. "Ice cold, baby. THAT earned you a cookie, but first hit these shots. Let's see if yesterday was a fluke."

"That's what you said yesterday," Maya replied quietly, distracted by the idea she was preparing to take another person's life. "You keep putting them in front of me and I keep putting bullets in paper heads. No fluke. Just another weird ass stupid human trick."

"A useful one, unlike people who can hula hoop or turn their eyelids inside out. Plus, today, I've added a couple of elements. Blood packs! Every money shot you hit, you'll get splatter."

"And the point?" Maya joined Laila at the table, pulling her own .38 out.

"Putting bullets in humans is not like on TV ... It's messy, it smells, the sounds are unimaginable from when the bullet hits the body to when the body drops, and you need to understand that."

Maya was clearly disgusted and disturbed by Laila's grin.

"You're likely going to deal with multiple targets, babe. If you need to take down multiple perps to take care of you and yours, you DON'T want to freak out after the first one because it's the first time you've heard and smelled it—well, the chemical equivalent. Even I'm not crazy enough to keep stacks of blood on hand."

Maya twisted her lips with a look that said she thought Laila was definitely crazy enough to keep blood packs on hand for such an occasion.

Laila rolled her eyes and moved over to the control panel. She placed her hand over the button to start the targets moving.

"First round is all stationary. Pop your cherry easy. Second round is when things get interesting. Remember, there is nothing behind or beside you. Shoot only within the range lines. I don't want to end up in the ER because you got spooked. Call it when you're ready, princess."

Maya checked her gun, positioning her next clip close. She took her stance, rolled her shoulders, popped her neck, and yelled "Ready!"

"Such a drama queen. Keep it ice cold," Laila said as she pushed the button.

---

35 MINS LATER...

"Not bad," Laila called as she sauntered to Maya. "How do you feel?"

Maya turned to Laila, took one look at her and vomited all over Laila's shoes.

"So ... no cookie." Laila's head tipped to the side, face calm, like Maya's reaction was perfectly normal.

Maya puked again.

WEDNESDAY BEFORE DAWN | TWO DAYS AFTER THE BISCUIT INCIDENT

So ... twenty minutes to there ... a half hour to there ... that's cutting it close.

She checked the map again and looked at her watch. She wished the two weeks she spent in Girl Scouts taught her something about finding her way in the woods. Not their fault, honestly. Right now, she was relying on slapdash info from the internet. She checked her watch quickly and set off, moving through the darkness until she found her spot.

Gorgeous house...

She paused, waiting until the alarm vibrated. She waited as he took off on a jog, then sprinted toward her target.

Forty-five minutes later...

Maya clutched the stitch in her side. She ran most days, and was slowly getting used to the thinner air, but hiking the side of a mountain in the early morning darkness was something entirely different. She used her inhaler, and peeled off her all-black top, while she waited and watched from just behind the tree line. Same as before ... She waited until they were distracted. The male headed to the shower, and the woman smiled, tossed her long, red hair, and joined him. Maya waited a few more minutes, then took off.

Thirty plus minutes later, Maya looked at the house built into the side of the mountain and shook her head.

Freakin' cat!

She checked the area and took off, sneezing down the mountain. *Damn cat allergy.*

As she arrived at the motel, she saw Detective Paul Cabot parked in her space. The morning sun reflected off both his mirrored glasses and thick, blond hair. His mouth set in a grim line. Anxiety clawed at her throat as she whipped her truck into the space next to his.

Her first words were, "Is Michael okay?"

"Sure kid, but he might be a little pissed to know you've been out since before dawn. Where ya been, Maya?"

An obstinate gleam flared in her eyes as she crossed her arms and leaned against her truck, mirroring Paul's posture.

"Is there a problem Detective Cabot? Surely, you don't keep tabs on all your citizens like this."

"The problem is my boy Mike asked me to keep an eye on you while he's gone, and the first day I do, you're gone at a time when there's nothing open in Rough Ridge or anywhere else that's close. I'll ask again, where were you?"

"I've been taking care of myself a long time Detective, I don't need you, Michael or anyone else chasing behind me."

Paul considered her for a moment.

"He cares about you," he said. "Enough to where he's finally considered having a future instead of making up for the past."

Well, I was not expecting that.

"I wasn't with another man, if that's what you're thinking."

He snorted. "That's obvious. But I think you were likely doing somethin' stupid that'll put you in danger."

She didn't know how she should take that "obvious" comment. She popped her neck.

"And he'd be better off not adding me to that future."

"Maya—"

"Understand this. I was making myself safer, not less. Now, if you'll excuse me."

He tipped his chin, and she pushed off the truck. Hitting the locks, she left her bag inside. She'd come back and get it after he'd gone.

When she got to the door, she noticed him watching her, so she asked.

"Why did you say it was obvious?"

He watched her with his head slightly cocked, then he gave her a half grin and shook his head. Wordlessly, he got into his truck, started it, and drove off.

WEDNESDAY NIGHT JAKE'S GUN SUPPLY AND RANGE...

Jake stood in the office door at the gun range. His sharp eyes glanced through the targets Laila handed him like a proud momma duck. Frowning a moment, he looked over at Laila and gave a bemused look. "Ninety percent kill shots?"

"Yesterday she couldn't even fire it," Laila said. "Scared shitless. Now she's getting pretty frosty."

"One day?" he asked again, looking beyond Laila through the window to the woman standing outside, eating what looked like a pecan roll and an apple, her second since Laila came in.

"She can calculate that stuff," Laila said, shrugging. "Made it a math problem for her and, like a teacher's pet, she ate it up. She's got a crazy IQ and is like a freaking pitbull if you give her a problem to solve. Plus, she's lonely, horny, and doesn't have shit else to do right now."

He took in Laila's excitement and leveled an eye on her carefully. "You're not teaching her to defend, you're teaching her to kill," he said flatly.

"I'm teaching her to stay alive. It's not my business, but this isn't your regular deadbeat, abusive boyfriend. He's got bank and boys."

"She tell you that?"

"I looked into it."

The man watched Laila closely. "She wouldn't be a distraction, would she?"

"Fuck no."

"Don't get me wrong, you need a distraction, a life, Laila. There are these people called 'friends' and you see them when you're not working."

"NOT now, Jake."

Jake had seen a lot, done a lot, and some of it he didn't want to remember. And he recognized the two women in his presence right now were the biggest bouts of trouble the town had seen in a while. Pretty, skilled, and completely fucked in the head. "Next thing you know, you two will be wearing little black dresses and drinking cosmos," he called as a parting shot.

"Not in this century." Laila tossed over her shoulder as she walked through the door of the range and threw it open. Maya propped herself on the table and ate Brussels sprouts from a disposable plastic container.

"Hey cupcake, ever tried getting out of a chokehold before?"

TUESDAY MORNING | THE DAY AFTER THE BISCUIT INCIDENT ...

Maya sat on the edge of the bed, looking out the floor-to-ceiling windows in Caine and Victoria's guest bedroom as the Colorado sun bathed her in light. She checked her phone, saw the three messages from Mike she avoided listening to, and dialed his number.

"Babe. Seriously? Are you fucking shitting me right now? I was this close to rollin' up to the Walters, and that's not something I want to do. That shit goes down and I don't hear from you for hours? I gotta tell you, babe. I am. NOT. Real happy right now."

Maya slowly closed her eyes as she listened. Not happy was an understatement.

"Heart, I was tired and needed space." She started tracing a pattern on the pale lavender bedspread with her fingers.

Mike breathed deeply through his nose. "Space."

"Yesterday was ... intense." Maya hoped that would explain the whole needing space thing.

"Maya, you need to see someone. Professionally."

"I noticed," she sighed, her voice strained. "I made an appointment before I called you. Emergency appointment at noon."

"That's good, Sunshine, but understand we need to talk about this. We do this? We do us? Then *I* protect you. Period. Unless I am in a position where I can't be there right away. You come to ME. Not Caine or anyone else."

"Wait. What?" She did not like his tone or what he was saying. *Who did he think he was?*

"I get that you've got friends, and the men that had your back are the men I'd pick to have it. But you're not layin' with them every night. You're with me, then you're with ME. I get you haven't had a man like me before. But bottom line, how it went down yesterday and you being reticent to call until close to fourteen fucking hours later is NOT how that shit goes."

Maya didn't reply. She was stuck on the force and tone, and Michael using the word 'reticent,' and the message itself, and the uber alpha caveman shit she was hearing. A small voice in her head piped up, *"I guess he told you."*

Why was her inner monologue petty?

She wasn't sure she liked this possessive club and drag vibe she felt coming off him. *Club and drag to bed? Yes. This? Meh.*

Mike took in her silence and continued his mini rant.

"Now it's bad fuckin' timing, but I gotta go out of town for a few days." He sighed again.

"And I can't get in touch as often as I'd like. But what I do know is when I call you—answer. If you can't answer, you get back to me quick and not fourteen fucking hours later."

"I've already had a man keeping tabs on me. I'm not interested in going back."

"Fuck, Maya," he ground out. "You're pulling that? I'm nothing like that piece of shit and you know it. Don't make this a brick in your wall."

He took an audible deep breath and exhaled, his voice going quiet again. "I'm giving this to you quick and to the point, and I realize I'm not being gentle, but I just spent the last fourteen hours worried out of my fucking mind. I'm tired, and I'm standing in the airport instead of wrapped in you. I'm not trying to keep tabs on you, Maya. What I am asking you is to give me peace of mind. Give me the peace of mind of knowing you're okay, and that the baby is okay."

She closed her eyes again and smiled as warmth spread through her.

"Ok, Heart."

"Ok?"

"Ok."

"No smart-ass comments, pop culture references, or shit?"

"No, I appreciate you need that and I understand. You going all alpha male on me is freaky, but I understand."

"There it is," he muttered.

She ignored him and asked after his sister.

"No, my sister is the same. I've got to head to L.A. and help a friend on a case."

"Sounds important. How does your boss feel about it?"

"They're paying me to come out, and I go there wearing a Rough Ridge badge to help the big boys in L.A. It proves he was right, and he likes that." Mike sounded like he wore a smile.

"Right about what?"

"Hiring me. It wasn't an easy sell, bringing me on the force, and there was push back. Since then, folks have been waiting to rub his nose in it."

"Heart..."

"It's all good, Sunshine. This trip will help me spearhead a pilot program here in Rough Ridge. Meeting's is in a few months before the town council."

"When will you be back?"

"Not sure, hopefully by Friday, but when I do, we're going out."

"Out?" She stopped tracing patterns on the bed.

"Yeah, out. Out of that damn motel room, out."

"I, uh, okay." Something slightly disturbed her, and she couldn't put a finger on it.

DING

Maya looked down at her secure phone and saw a text message.

M. SECOND HIT ON YOUR NAME IN TWO DAYS.
FEDERAL ACCESS. NOT G.L. LIKELY SOMEONE
YOU KNOW. CHECK YOUR PEOPLE.

"Shit. I gotta go, Heart. I've got something I've got to take care of before I go out for the day. Be safe, love you bye."

MIKE

Mike looked at his phone with irritation. *"Be safe, love you bye."* Did she mean that? What was going on that she had to get off the phone so fast? He looked at the plane sitting on the tarmac, the sounds of new arrivals and final calls going on around him. He chomped on the toothpick in his mouth, hearing it snap. If he left now, he could be back in Rough Ridge in an hour and catch a plane out of Denver later this evening. He paused, one hand on his hip, the other gripped tight around his neck.

She is fucking killing me ...

He pulled his phone out of his pocket and called Paul's number.

"Cabot."

"Hey Paul, I'm heading out in a few. Do me a solid and look after Maya for me while I'm gone?

"Sure brother, anything up?"

"Not sure... My gut's picking up some shit I can't put a finger on."

"Got it. I'm on it."

"Thanks."

"Anytime man, do us proud with those pretty boys in L.A."

---

1. Hard by Rihanna

18
NO!

MAYA

Maya and Mike had an intense Saturday. Instead of the sexual intimacy her body craved, his tender care left a mark on her soul she wasn't sure her heart could handle.

After her mother's diagnosis, people, friends, and colleagues of her mother fell by the wayside. A long cancer battle and impending death are uncomfortable for people and, unfortunately for Maya, she was seen as a capable adult when she was fourteen. The adults that should have stepped up slunk into the background with hollow platitudes of "call if you need anything" while simultaneously high fiving her for being so mature and on the mark. Honestly, what choice did she have?

After YEARS of being her own fortress, of keeping every relationship superficial, the idea of someone looking out for *her*, caring about *her*, being ... tender with her, was almost too good to be true. Yet she'd found that here, with the family she'd met so far, and in Heart.

Sunday, they spent all day together. They were both worn out from the emotional roller coaster of Saturday and slept 'til mid-morning. Then they played a quiet game of Scrabble that was way more challenging than Maya expected. She loved that about him. They'd ordered food in and simply held each other, talked, napped, and talked some more. They learned each other's favorite books and why they loved them. Maya read to Mike from a book of poetry she thought he'd love. It was bliss.

THE BISCUIT INCIDENT

Monday looked to be a normal day.

A normal day in a small Colorado town, Maya thought as she got out of the shower. The nerves she suffered with for days hadn't settled, but she was determined to put them on the back burner. She wrapped a towel around herself, finished her morning routine, and began digging for something to wear.

Her cell phone rang. *"Blake calling"* She swiped the screen and hit speaker.

"Hey Blake!"

"Hey baby girl," his voice drawled.

That was nice. Terms of endearment seemed to be big around town and Maya felt accepted when the "darlin's" and "baby girls" flowed freely. She smiled as she thought of the friendships she'd made in her short time there, and that smile was in her voice when she spoke to Blake.

"Got that second part you asked for. Bring that heap of yours in and I can put it on today."

"I'll take care of it."

"Maya, that was cute before. No way you are pulling that shit again at the shop."

"Right," she said sarcastically. "See you in twenty."

She slid on her jeans when her phone dinged again. Seeing which phone it was, she froze. She pulled her cream tank all the way down and walked cautiously to the phone like it would bite her. There hadn't been an update in a while other than *'all clear.'* She lifted her secure phone and read:

BD: INQUIRIES ABOUT YOU HAVE INCREASED. GL
HAS INVESTIGATED EAST COAST
ESTABLISHMENTS. STILL IN THE DARK IN RE:
YOUR LOCATION. SOMEONE ELSE IS LOOKING
INTO YOU AT COLUMBUS POLICE DEPARTMENT.
HACKED ACCESS OUTSIDE OF THE NETWORK.
CURRENTLY, CPD IS UNAWARE OF BREACH.
ACCESS TO SEVERAL OTHER FILES IN THE SAME
BREACH SHOWS ASSAULTS WITH IDENTICAL MO
AS YOURS. YOURS IS STILL CLASSIFIED AS JANE
DOE AND BURIED. ADVISE.

M: I MAY KNOW WHO IT IS. SEND ME A COPY OF
MY FILE TO PROVIDED EMAIL ADDRESS. GIVE ME
UNTIL THE END OF THE WEEK TO FIND OUT.

BD: COPY.

Maya sighed, zipped the phone back into the hidden compartment in her purse, and chewed her bottom lip for a moment. She had a good idea who was behind the hack and why, but she couldn't believe they were being so damn annoying. She finished getting dressed, quickly logged into her computer, checked the shipping on her package, and signed out. They were costing her a small fortune with their antics. Her jumpiness grew as if she'd drank a giant cup of coffee. Closing her eyes, she breathed deep as she steadied herself, threw on gloss and mascara, grabbed her keys, and headed out the door.

A quick shot down the street put her in the shop's forecourt. She killed the engine, which stopped Jay Z from having "99 *Problems*." Hopping down, she called to Doc who waved from the office. She swallowed her issues as usual and put on a cheerful face.

"Hey Maya honey," Doc called. "Blake says you're fixin' to install on your own."

She looked at Doc, took in his serious face, crossed arms, and warm brown eyes and told him the truth.

"I need to do it, Doc. I need to do something with my hands to take my mind off some things. You get me, right?"

He studied her for a second. "All right then, pull into the third bay and help yourself."

"Doc!" Blake exclaimed, making his way over to them, frustrated.

"The gal said she can do it, let her do it. Get her some coveralls Blake."

Blake stared at his father, looked at Maya, and exhaled. His face full of resigned annoyance, he stalked over to his office.

"At least bring the truck in the garage for fuck's sake." He looked back at his father and Maya. "Flash a dimple, and the man loses his damn mind."

In a few minutes, Maya appeared, clad in huge blue coveralls. She suspected Blake selected the biggest ones to make her look ridiculous. Doc, Blake, and the boys at the shop snickered as she rolled the sleeves, wrapped a hair tie around each, and tucked the legs into her socks '80s style.

Maya blocked out Blake's grumbles and spent the next several hours going over the truck, changing the oil, replacing belts, checking and replacing seals, etc. She lost herself in the work, the smells, and the sounds.

Her elderly neighbor Sir Ernest Q. Jones - his real name - taught her everything about cars. From the time she was seven until she was sixteen, he'd patiently answered every question, listened to every story, and taught her about the church of getting your hands dirty.

"Maya child, every ponder you've got to ponder can be worked out right here," he would say, patting whatever broke down heap was leaking oil in his driveway. "And at the end of the day, when you've got grease caked so thick you can't tell your hand from a carburetor, you might have figured it out."

She asked him once if he always figured it out in a day. "Nope, been working on the same problem for thirty years child, ain't figured it out yet, but when I do, the good Lord will give me something else to think about."

He'd never told her what it was he was working out. When he died a little after his eightieth birthday, she wondered if he'd finally figured it out and, with no more ponders to ponder, the Lord called him home. When she'd done everything down to replacing the wiper fluid, her stomach signaled it was time to go. She hadn't solved much of anything, but maybe tomorrow. She looked longingly at the engine one of the guys was rebuilding.

"Don't even think about it," Blake grumped as he walked past.

Welp that answers that.

As she was finishing up, a Harley pulled into the forecourt. She reached into the cab of her truck and pulled out a bag of M&M's as a peace offering to Blake. Walking out to the forecourt, she tossed back some water.

"I don't fucking believe it," a large biker spat out, looking at Maya with contempt.

She stopped short, confused. She'd never seen the man before in her life and she would've remembered that scruffy blond beard, bald head, and big physique that said he fed on a steady diet of junk and beer. He looked closer to delivering a baby than she was.

She continued to beeline to Blake, the biker's gaze blazing through her.

"You let pussy in your garage?"

Pussy?

Maya looked around, still slightly confused, more uneasy, and shifting closer to angry. Blake's body tightened next to her. Not wanting the drama, she placed her hand on his arm, dragging his attention from the biker to her right away.

"I'm finished. Thanks, I—"

"What kind of shop lets pussy in the garage?" the man continued on loudly.

"When your name's up on that sign? Then you can question me." Blake pointed to the large "C.J.B. Harley Inc." sign in Old West font looming large over the parking lot.

"The old man know you got pussy in the garage?" Harley man asked, jerking his head toward the office.

Maya had enough. Jangled nerves and the quest for consecutive normal days thwarted, she took the challenge not meant for her.

"Asshole. Stop calling me that." She placed her hands on her hips, feet wide apart, her gaze furious.

The man leaned in, narrowed his eyes, and proclaimed, "Pussy don't touch *my* bike." He jerked his thumb toward himself.

"The way you look, I'm not surprised," Maya shot back.

Blake and a couple of the fellas chuckled.

"What you say bitch?" he asked as he stalked toward her.

Blake stepped in front of her. "Biscuit, cool down. Now.

"You takin' up for that bitch?" Biscuit's head jerked in surprise. "I've been coming here for fifteen years!"

"Yeah, and you've been a pain my ass for all of 'em," Doc said, stepping out of the office.

Maya remembered herself and decided to stop partaking in or creating any more drama, especially with a pot-bellied biker named Biscuit.

What kind of biker name is that? Biscuit? Might as well call himself Pancakes or Apple Strudel. She stood behind Blake and slipped out of the coveralls.

Stepping out from behind him, she offered Blake the coveralls and the candy. "That's for the trouble." She nodded to the treat.

Blake looked down and cocked a half-smile. "No problem, baby girl."

"All I'm sayin'," Biscuit said, pushing his luck, "is no bitch is touchin' my bike. Even one with tits like that." Leering at her chest, he grinned.

Rage Maya tried to keep buried bubbled to the surface a bit.

"No bitch?" she exclaimed. "How does that explain your bitchass Biscuit?" She flicked her hand, indicating him. "Your doughy ass is the *only* bitch I see, and yeah, your tits are fantastic." She cupped her hands out in front of her like she was cradling breasts.

The men roared with laughter. Biscuit took in the defiant woman in front of him, looked at the men laughing, and popped, lunging at Maya. Blake deftly tugged her back behind him, using his finger hooked in her belt loop, and getting this close to the biker's face, his voice deadly.

"You sure you want to make that move?" Blake growled, sounding more beast than man. There was an arctic blast in his voice that clearly communicated his words were a promise, not a threat.

Eye-to-eye with Blake was not where most men wanted to be, so Biscuit smartly retreated, passed a face-saving glare through the people standing outside, and stalked to his bike. Hopping on, he brought the custom Harley Road King to life with a roar. He cast a tight turn around the forecourt and sped away.

"Hey darlin' you good?" Blake asked as he touched her arm. She jerked it away instinctively, still staring at the space the rude biker had vacated.

Maya was tight. Her teeth clenched, hands balled at her sides, a headache formed like a band wrapping around her skull, and she was still freaking hungry.

"Maya."

She blinked at him and took in his concerned face.

"Are you good, baby girl?" His warm brown eyes searched hers, a deep frown creasing his brow.

She took a deep breath and nodded, more out of politeness than anything. "He pissed me off."

White teeth rimmed with an overlong salt and pepper beard grinned at her. "I think the feeling was mutual."

She sighed, looking guilty. "I'm sorry I cost you business." She looked over at Doc.

"He'll cool off and come back," Doc said as he walked away.

"But he'll still be mad," Blake warned.

"Why?!"

"'Cause I was thinking of hiring you. Part-time of course."

"Really?" Maya was shocked and pleased.

"You do good work. You'd have to get certified to be full time here. How are you at school work?"

Maya snorted with laughter. "I do all right. Can I think about it?" A job meant money coming in, but it also meant paperwork and going into a system somewhere. She'd have to plan that carefully.

"Sure darlin'."

Maya nodded to him and moved back to her truck. She backed out as Caine came in for the afternoon shift. He tipped two fingers. She waved, and ducked her unsmiling face, blasting Amy Winehouse's "You Know I'm No Good," as she peeled out.

Blake waited for Caine to unfold himself from the 'Stang before he started talking.

"I can see why y'all like her. That girl is salty and sweet. Smart too. She ran Biscuit down," Blake told Caine, chuckling. "Had the whole place laughin'."

Caine watched his sister as she drove away. "How did he take it?"

"Not well, you know how he is. He'll be all right though." Blake looked closely at Caine. "What's up brother?"

"Somethin' I gotta tell you, Blake," he said, looking at his friend and business partner.

A FEW MINUTES LATER...

Maya purchased a big salad to go from the diner and drove over to Jake's. She reached across the passenger seat, popped open the glove compartment, and took out two slightly warm, meaning awesome, packets of M&M's. As she grabbed an empty plastic food storage container, she swore as she noticed a wrench sat on the passenger seat. She slid the wrench into her back pocket to remind herself to drop it back off, and walked into Jake's.

Maya threw a wave and gave a "Hey everybody," as she slid onto a barstool next to Regina. Jake came from around back with a keg on his shoulder, moving the heavy item like it weighed no more than a case of beer. Once again, she marveled at how freakishly handsome he was, like seriously hot. Her teenage dream standing right in front of her.

He was in a tight black tee, one arm rolled, revealing an intricate black tattoo. The man was, what, in his mid to late forties and put many a twenty-year-old to shame. He looked like at any moment he could be on the field with a pro team. His linebacker body was still good and firm, with tight abs and thick muscular thighs. His six-foot-four-inch frame meant his beautiful face always stood shoulders above everyone else. Hazel eyes sparkled and his meticulously trimmed full beard emphasized his square jawline. *Boy, married or not, you were required by ovary oath to admire this man at least once or twice ... or three times.*

He grinned at Maya. She grinned back a little too hard.

"What do you want, baby girl?"

Sigh.

"I've got a huge craving for peanuts and pork rinds and I'd also like something to drink with no caffeine to go with my salad." She plopped her grub on the bar along with the M&M's and plastic ware.

"Seriously?" Leslie asked, coming over from bussing a table. "That salad looks like a sandwich without bread."

"Oh yeah, isn't it awesome?" She unwrapped her salad and dug in.

Jake tossed her a small blue bag of bar nuts and pork rinds and laughed as she licked her lips and poured both packages into the plastic ware. She added the soft M&M's, closed the green top, and shook it. Now Regina and Leslie were watching her in amusement. Snatching the lid off, she dug in, getting all three ingredients in a bunch and popping them into her mouth.

"Mmmm. Heaven. Try it," she said, passing the mixture down to Regina and going back to her salad-wich. "Gotta get some of everything in one bite," she informed them.

Regina popped the mix in her mouth and chewed. "Damn, this *is* good."

Leslie and Jake tried a bit.

"Girlie, that sounds like a pregnancy craving," Regina said.

Maya choked on her food.

Regina whacked her on the back while Leslie jumped to get her water. Jake leaned in, and, after she swallowed painfully and got her bearings, quietly asked, "You all right?"

Maya nodded, then mouthed an embarrassed "Yeah." Leslie reached out and gave her a squeeze. Maya figured Jake would share her situation with his wife and gave her a squeeze back. Jake walked back to the backroom of the bar for something, and Maya nursed her food more carefully.

"Why do you have a wrench in your pocket?" Regina asked with her gap-toothed smile. She was either curious or checking out Maya's ass—which one was debatable when it came to Regina.

"Oh, I forgot to leave it at Blake's. I was there this afternoon," she said, reaching back and dropping the heavy tool onto the battered wooden bar carefully.

"You fix Harleys?" Regina asked, her eyes wide.

"No, I tinker around on cars. My neighbor taught me when I was a kid." Maya sipped the juice Jake brought her. "I'd love to learn about bikes."

"Not sure too many men will let you fix their bike," Regina said into her beer.

"Yeah, I figured that out today," she mumbled to no one, shaking her head.

Maya absentmindedly, nervously, flipped the wrench over and over on the bar. Her salad sat half-eaten as she chewed on the straw from her drink. Leslie looked at the door.

"Hey Biscuit, what's got your shit stirred?"

Oh damn.

As heavy footsteps approached, Maya tried disappearing by concentrating hard and staying still. It didn't work.

"This bitch." Spoken from right behind her.

Oh damn. Damn.

"Now Biscuit," Regina said, sliding closer, but miraculously keeping her ass on her stool.

"You need that sweet ass taught a lesson. I bet you like it rough, too." Biscuit grabbed Maya's shoulder and spun her around roughly on the stool.

Before she could think, her body reacted.

Maya was not coping. For weeks, her brain and body tried to heal. For weeks she tamped back the emotions, released them only under duress, then quickly buried them again.

The dreams, the talks with Heart, finding out about her family, learning a new place and people. Covering her tracks ...

It was all too much.

Her brain and body stayed primed for a fight these last weeks. She thought she was making progress, but mentally she was at her end.

And. She. Snapped.

She snapped in a way she never imagined. Tears, shaking, crying ... that she could understand. But this? This was different.

Biscuit saw a soft target. What he did not count on was stepping on a landmine covered in curly hair and soft, feminine curves.[1]

I bet you like it rough too...

Maya was back in the precinct in Columbus.

I bet you like it rough too...

They were taking photos of her injuries and smirking.

I bet you like it rough too...

They were leering at her.

I bet you like it rough too...

Maya didn't remember grabbing the wrench as he yanked her

around. But vaguely in the back of her mind, she heard a woman scream, *"No."*

Maya also didn't remember bringing the heavy wrench across Biscuit's face and neck area with all the strength she had in her.

It felt like she was watching a Hi-Def movie.

Biscuit flailed back in surprise. She watched, outside herself, as a woman on a stool launched herself in an attack, bringing the wrench down again and again. Hard metal met soft flesh again and again.

A woman in distress screamed, "NO!" over and over and over ... Then Maya was in the air. A powerful pair of gentle, iron-solid arms wrapped around her, pulling her back. Slowly. Gently.

"Careful Logan, she's pregnant." Jake's voice registered in her periphery.

Leslie's face swam in front of hers. Eye to eye asking her something, but what she asked for made little sense.

"Maya honey, it's okay. It's all right sweetie." Leslie spoke in a soothing, calm voice. "Maya, can I have this? Can I have it now?"

Maya looked down to where Leslie was gripping her hand firmly, but gently. Everyone was being really gentle. Why?

Maya suddenly recognized the heavy wrench held so tightly her hand was throbbing, the metal biting into her skin painfully. She looked from her hand to Jake, who pulled a bleeding, worse for wear Biscuit off the floor, and reality washed over her. Her mouth dropped open as she immediately opened her hand. The wrench clattered to the wooden floor.

"Oh my God," she whispered.

"Deep breaths, Maya," Leslie cooed. "Deep breaths."

Jake looked behind her to Logan. "Office. Now."

Logan lifted Maya gently and walked with her to the office in the back of the bar, with Leslie following close behind.

"Did she knead Biscuit with a wrench?!" Mac guffawed. "And don't tell me Logan's back. Jesus it's Monday!"

"Call Caine," Jake said.

"Caine?!" Mac started. Jake nailed him with a look and Mac waved him away as he lifted the phone, punching in Caine's cell.

CAINE

Caine swiped at the screen. "Yeah."

"Caine, it's Mac. You need to come down to the bar quick. Maya just freaked out and tanned Biscuit's hide with a wrench."

Caine's head snapped up and met Blake's eyes. "It's Maya."

Both men took off toward Caine's car.

Mike was coming down the street when Caine and Blake blew past in Caine's black Mustang and flew into the parking lot of Jake's. Mike knew Jake liked to handle his own trouble, but every so often it spilled out of the bar into the community, and with Caine and Blake on the move, it didn't look like it would spread but explode. Hitting a U-turn, he sped down the street and into the lot. The men were already inside the bar as Mike hopped out of the Jeep.

When Caine and Blake arrived, Jake was gripping a severely disgruntled Biscuit, who sported several angry-looking welts and one big bloody cut by the neck of his shirt. Caine and Jake locked eyes and Jake tossed a nod toward the back. "Office."

"Crazy bitch," Biscuit grumbled.

Caine stopped and got nose to nose with Biscuit.

"Biscuit you can't lie low, can you?" Regina muttered. "I'm glad my young and dumb days are behind me."

"Caine, come with me please," Leslie called softly from behind the bar.

Caine, his jaw flexing, stared at Biscuit until Biscuit dropped his eyes. Turning on his heel, Caine stalked to the back, followed by Blake, who gave Biscuit his own hard look.

"You're done. Find a new shop for your shit."

Caine, following Leslie, made his way to the back office but as she went in, he stopped at the door frame. He hardly recognized her.

"Maya—" Caine called from the door.

"Is he okay?" she asked quietly.

"Maya—"

"Is. He. Okay?" she uttered, her body so tight it could snap in half.

Caine and Blake walked further into the little office as her hand continued tracing erratic patterns on the old couch, shaking like she was being hit with a steady electric current.

"Biscuit is built like a brick and as dumb as one," Blake offered. "He'll be fine."

She was dumbstruck. "I can't believe I did that. I was outside my body watching it happen. What does that mean?" She didn't look at anyone in the room, instead focusing on the walls in front of her.

"It means you've had a traumatic experience and Biscuit triggered a reaction with his ham handling of you," Leslie said. She walked closer and squatted low next to Maya. "Honey, have you talked to someone professionally? Heck, anyone about what happened to you?"

"Only Heart," she whispered, her mind a thousand miles away.

Caine and Blake looked at each other reacting to the name they didn't recognize.

"Honey," Leslie continued, "you should, so you can get past it."

Maya looked at Leslie, her eyes large, face anguished, voice hollow. "How do you get past being beaten and locked in a basement for three days? How?"

Blake sank onto Jake's desk in front of her. "My God."

---

1. Crawling by Linkin Park

19
THIS IS A COURTESY

MIKE

Mike's captain called him right as he hit the steps of Jake's, so it took him a few minutes to get into the bar, but when he walked in, he clocked a variety of strange activities. Ahead of him and to the right was Laila, obviously on her day off, sitting in a relaxed position that belied the high alert expression in her eyes as she kept watch on everything. Everyone else's eyes were on the men to his immediate right.

Turning slightly, he took in Jake and Biscuit. The latter was sporting an interesting collection of marks, including a decent-sized cut across his cheek, jaw, and neck. He was holding his shoulder close to his body. Mike noticed Mac didn't have his blade out, so that was something. Mac could fillet a man and julienne a tomato with what he carried. It was why Jake hired him and why no one messed with Mac or his construction foreman husband.

"'Sup Jake?" Mike asked casually.

"Nothin' Mike, want a beer?"

"No thanks ... Looks like somethin' here though," Mike pressed.

"You know I like to tend to my own yard," Jake said with a slight grin.

"And we don't mind it, 'cept when the trash blows into your neighbor's backyard," Mike replied, eyeing Biscuit.

"Nothin' blowin', right Biscuit?" Jake shook the man by the back of his jacket collar.

Biscuit spat on the floor. "Right," he grunted.

Mike eyed the men when movement in his peripheral brought his attention to Maya, Caine, Blake, and Leslie appearing from the back office. Caine and Blake moved with purpose, and Maya shook like a leaf as Leslie talked quietly to her.

Maya looked up and her eyes got wide when they locked on Mike's. The look on her face shot through his gut like a bullet. "Am I under arrest?"

"Under arrest? Why—"

"I'm so sorry," Maya said in a panicked voice, looking over at Biscuit. Mike's eyes sliced to Biscuit in understanding and heat rushed from his neck up.

He caught Jake looking from him to Maya with interest.

"Accidents happen, right Biscuit?" Jake said, shaking the man again.

"Accident," Mike ground out.

"Yeah," Regina offered. "Biscuit here slipped on Maya's wrench and landed on his face. Repeatedly."

The bar tittered.

As Caine led Maya past Mike and out of the bar, Blake covered her from behind. She looked like she'd seen a ghost. Mike cut his eyes to Laila and saw her give a slight, almost imperceptible head shake. And he knew he should let it be. For now. He turned and gave one last hard glance at Biscuit, then rushed out to check on Maya.

"Maya, wait."

"The fuck man," Caine growled.

"It was an accident, Sheppard," Blake said.

He ignored them and walked to Maya, getting close to her and tucking a cloud curl behind her ear. He rubbed her jaw with the back of his knuckles and looked her in her eyes.

"Sunshine, baby, are you all right? Did he hurt you?"

He watched her eyes slide to the side, disconnecting from him. His gut twisted painfully.

"No, I want to go home." Her voice was barely a whisper.

Caine and Blake looked over Maya's head at each other.

"I've got her," Caine grunted, yanking open the 'Stang's passenger door, sending a clear statement.

Blake looked at Sheppard. "You good?"

"No."

"You gonna make trouble for her?" Blake asked. "Listen, your heart is in the right place, fight-your-daddy's-demons-by-the-book-cop-shit, I get it. But Maya doesn't need that right now."

This sonofabitch.

"Her home? Is my bed." Mike locked eyes with Blake before slicing them to Caine. "I'm taking her home."

"Oh," Blake replied, blinking in surprise and throwing his hands up. "Yeah, oh."

"You gonna be home all night like she needs?" Caine asked.

Mike didn't like Caine's tone or his insinuation, and he also didn't like the attachment he seemed to have to Maya. Mike didn't get a chance to answer because his phone rang.

"Fuck..." Yanking the phone out of his pocket and swiping it, he barked, "Sheppard!" His jaw got tight. "Yeah. No, I understand. Yeah, in ten."

"Like I said. I got her."

The muscles stood out in Mike's neck as he bit down on the toothpick in his mouth and kept eyes with Caine. *Ten, nine, eight...*

"Heart."

All three men's eyes collectively moved back to her. She looked so small. Diminished. It rubbed him raw to see her like that.

"I'll go home with Caine. Go put on your cape and save the day. I'll call later."

Mike closed his eyes, slowly marshaling every instinct at that moment so as not to put her through any further trauma. He got hold of it, but barely. When he felt he could speak, he opened his eyes, took his hands, placed one on each side of her face, and pressed his forehead to hers.

"Okay, Sunshine. I'll call you when I'm through. You go straight to the Walters and stay there, yeah?"

"Yes."

He kissed her softly on the nose and the forehead and guided her gently into Caine's car. Once she was in, he stood and Caine closed the door. The men stood facing each other, assessing. Laila walked up and glanced at Caine before sighing and shaking her head.

"Mike, can I holler at you a sec?"

Mike allowed himself to be pulled away as Caine gave a head nod to Blake, jumped in his car and took off.

As Laila explained what happened, he watched Blake walk the few short blocks back to the shop slower than his usual long-legged stride, his hands shoved into his pockets.

IT WAS after midnight when the big man dragged himself home. He parked his bike in the shed and rounded the house over patchy, dead grass. He clomped past the overgrown rose bushes that someone who once gave a shit planted. As he took the wooden steps to the porch, they groaned under his weight and from neglect. His was the worst house on the street, and clearly, he didn't give a fuck. It simply existed like he did until someone put both out of their misery.

His gait showed that his head and shoulder were killing him. The small bag he carried marked a trip to the drugstore.

Mike waited for him in the shadows on the porch.[1]

When Biscuit hit the front door, a light flared from Mike's match as he lit his cigarette. It briefly illuminated his wild, dark features. Biscuit, a man not smart enough to fear much, looked uneasy as he glimpsed the man's green eyes and what was no longer hidden in them.

"You lost a woman to a madman a while back," Mike started, his voice low and seemingly patient, "so this is a courtesy. That kind of thing can tear a man apart, make 'im mean. Take away rational thought ... but if I hear of you touching another woman in a way that could be *loosely* interpreted as aggressive, you stop livin' free for a long time."

"You're knockin' yourself out tryin' to prove you're a saint. You ain't gonna fuck wit that," Biscuit said bitterly.

"The law is the law. You've got history and the way you've been bitin' at every man, woman, and beast since she passed ... It's well document-ed." Mike waited a moment before continuing in a quiet, iced-over voice, all mock casualness gone. "You know better than anyone the lengths a man will go to for his woman. Make her feel safe ... so I trust you get me."

Mike waited, allowing Biscuit to consider and take stock of him while he took a second drag off his cigarette.

"I get you."

"You will not breathe her air. She comes in the bar, you leave. She walks down the street; you find someplace better to be. She even thinks of your existence again; I'll be back. And you're either not breathin' free or ... "

Biscuit watched again as Mike took another long drag off his cigarette. He savored the sweet familiarity of it. Flicking the almost whole cigarette into the grass off Biscuit's porch, he exhaled slowly, the smoke curling around his long hair and framing his face in the shadows.

"Been years since my last cigarette," he said, almost as an aside, as he popped a toothpick into his mouth and pulled himself to his full height. His shadow grew more menacing in the darkness.

"Gotta be careful fuckin' with shit that'll end your life."

Mike chuckled, as he suddenly loomed close. He held Biscuit's eyes for a moment and watched them grow wide in alarm. Satisfied the biker understood him, he casually strode off the porch, into the darkness of the unlit sidewalk and into the street of the ramshackle neighborhood.

Climbing on his own bike, Mike watched as Biscuit waited, straining his ears to hear him driving away, but he gave him nothing. It wasn't until Biscuit was in the house, sitting at his kitchen table, staring at what Mike guessed was a photo of his late wife that he finally gave him the gift of his Harley roaring to life. He aimed the headlight from his bike directly at Biscuit's living room window. After a long, satisfying moment, during which Biscuit jumped up and snatched the faded curtains closed, Mike drove his Harley away, roaring into the night.

MIKE SAT in Maya's room. She hadn't answered her phone all night. He was on a 9:30 a.m. flight to L.A. and he didn't have his woman tucked into him. Standing, he grabbed his bag. Her comb felt smooth and cold under his fingers as he adjusted it on her desk. Next, he moved her running shoes out of the middle of the floor so she wouldn't trip. The cool air of the refrigerator hit his face as he made sure she had plenty of milk and apples. He did everything but be with the woman he needed as much as air.

Loneliness settled in on Mike as he took one last glance around the room. He didn't like this shit one bit. When he got back, he would have his girl, and he would never let her go.

---

1. Desperado by Rihanna

20
PEACHY KEEN

MIKE

Mike stood in line at the front of the sweeping, modern hotel, waiting his turn to check out. Its glass and chrome decor with pops of color was quintessential L.A. - ultra-cool, modern, and perfect to the point of impersonal. After spending the week in his former city, he didn't miss it as much as he thought he would. He knew the difference in his life was Maya. Wherever she was, that was where Mike belonged, and he was eager to get back to her.

His eyes restlessly swept the room and identified the source of his wait. Two new trainees manned the desk. He took in the impatient, rushed glances of the folks in line and realized his little Colorado mountain town beat the big city in several areas.

The case was more intense than Mike bargained for, so they didn't connect as often as he wanted. Still, Maya kept her promise. She sent him quick texts, answered when he called and as the week wore on, sounded more grounded. He hated leaving her in the aftermath of the "Biscuit Incident." The tight feeling in his chest came back with a vengeance every time he thought about it. Shaking it off, Mike pulled out his phone and tapped her picture on his home screen. She answered on the second ring.

"Heart." Her voice was husky with sleep.

"Mornin', Sunshine." Mike stared at his boots as he waited for his turn in the queue. "You just wakin' up?"

"I've been working late," she said with a yawn.

"You're trying to keep the dreams away." He tried to keep the worry out of his voice. He looked at the line as it moved ever so slowly, half-heartedly listening to the grumbles and wondering why he didn't do e-checkout.

"Well, yes, plus I had things I needed to get on top of. I'll finish soon."

"I'm checkin' out right now darlin' and when I get there, I'm taking you to have some fun."

"Fun. Commissioner Gordon, you know how to have fun?" As she teased him, she sounded a bit more awake.

He grinned back down at his boots. "I think your pussy knows the answer to that, Sunshine."

"Oh my."

Mike chuckled, working the toothpick in his mouth. She was cute in the morning and when he caught her off guard. He realized it didn't happen too often. Some men liked easy-going and quiet. Mike wasn't one of them.

His mind on Maya, he almost missed Detective Martinez coming in the sleek double glass doors of the hotel lobby.

"Should get in from Denver around six. Pick you up at your room at seven, wear something pretty."

"Heart, listen ... we should talk about..."

"Mike. You almost done?" Martinez asked, looking antsy.

Mike heard Maya's hesitation but saw the grimace on Martinez's face and chomped down on his toothpick for an altogether different reason.

"Damn. Darlin' I gotta go. Call you when I'm close, yeah?" He didn't wait for her response as he clicked off.

"You don't look like you're coming to take me to the airport with warm hugs." Mike leveled a gaze at his friend.

"The witness recanted," Detective Martinez said without preamble, running his hand roughly through his short brown hair in frustration. "Suddenly her mother's got enough money in her account to cover her bills for a little while."

Mike sucked in a deep breath through his nose. "She was edgy. Fuck. You got a trace on it?"

"No. We've got a cash deposit, no hit on ID from the video. First National Bank, in and out."

"I've got a plane to catch at one. Let's go." Mike growled in frustration as he strode to the front of the line, apologizing to the folks that were ahead of him. Flashing his badge, he said quietly, "I need to get this taken care of right away."

The trainee smiled brightly and tossed her reddish hair with a wink. When she was done, she smiled even bigger, and her lips parted as she scanned him from top to bottom. In another life, Mike would have considered the unspoken offer. Now, he made tracks to catch his Sun.

FRIDAY 5:45 P.M.

MAYA

Maya looked amazing. Better than amazing. She opted to skip out on her scheduled session with Laila, citing the need for a break from blood packets, to which Laila called her a 'cupcake.' She kept her daily session with her therapist, emotionally purging for the day. After, she took off to the mall with Victoria and Leslie where she spent way too much money.

Today's warning from Dr. Flemmings weighed on her, but Maya figured she'd have a fun night out with her male *friend*, take part in an adult, open chat about the dynamics of their relationship with her mountain man hottie *friend*, scratch the sexual itch with strict parameters in place, and all would be fine. Ok, she didn't believe that, but she hoped by the end of the day she'd convince herself.

And so, she bought three dresses instead of one. And four pairs of shoes, and a set of new bras. Pregnancy made her boobs spill over the tops of her old ones and she had a bit of a pooch now, but Victoria - a fashion school dropout – picked the 'fits. Two dresses masked her little baby's appearance and one celebrated it with enough give for several wears. Not that she'd have many places to wear a white, four-hundred-dollar Prada dress in Rough Ridge, but what the hell.

By the end of the shopping spree, Maya successfully convinced herself that she, in her super awesome dress, could convince Mike to keep things casual. What guy wouldn't want to have friendship and casual sex with a woman in this dress?

She took in her reflection in the mirror. Shimmer body butter gave her skin a glowy, dewy appearance which complemented her figure-hugging, muted gold jersey dress with ruching at the waist that camo'd her bump. A demure boat neck sheath with cap sleeves, the bottom of the dress hit above her knee. It was a simple dress until you caught the back. There wasn't one. Not until you reached about a half-inch above the crack of her ass.

It was so freaking gorgeous she couldn't stand it! She pulled her curls to one side, so they cascaded over her shoulder, added borrowed diamond hoops from Victoria and a deep smokey, golden eye. The gold sandals she wore had a thin little strap across her foot and around her ankle and made her legs look fantastic. Maya turned and looked out the vast windows in Victoria's guest room and felt calmer than she'd felt in weeks. She shifted a small bundle into her regular bag, took a deep breath and stepped out into Victoria's living room, where the girls were waiting.[1]

"Girl! That dress is dangerous," Victoria yelped.

"Ten bucks they don't make it out of her room," Leslie giggled.

"NO WAY," Maya said. "All of this prep work, shellacking, priming, primping, and taping? This," she said, gesturing to herself from top to toe, "is going *out* for fun. Likely overdressed for said fun, but fun anyway. This is going to be the last time I look like this for months, so yeah ... " she added, rolling her eyes hard.

The women laughed loud at Maya's expression.

"I wish you could take the 'Stang instead. It would go perfect with that dress. But Caine's off with the fellas at Jake's."

"Only Victoria could recommend a car to accessorize an outfit," Leslie said, shaking her head.

A shadow passed over Maya's face and disappeared as quickly as it came.

"Maya, are you all right?"

"Oh yeah super, peachy keen even, I gotta go though, I've got stuff to drop off," she said in a rush.

"Take my car," Victoria offered, "so you're not climbing up and down of your truck in that dress."

"No thanks. I've got stuff in my truck to drop off and don't want to move it from one to the other. It's ok." She moved quickly, kissing them both on the cheeks, gathering her clutch (also new), keys, and hoofin' it toward the door. "Thanks for today girls, it's been a blast!"

MAYA CHECKED THE TIME. It was almost six. She had time to get there, have gnashing of teeth, possibly get arrested and get back down the mountain to fun with Heart. If they didn't have her arrested. She didn't know all the players in this, but she needed to make her case before they blew everything to hell. After snapping on her seatbelt and backing out of the drive, she slid her headphones in and called Heart.

"Hey Sunshine."

His smooth voice washed over her, sending tingles from her head to her toes.

"Hey yourself," she said, smiling. "I think I may be on time, gotta make a quick stop."

There was a long pause.

Oh no.

"Sunshine..." his voice was hesitant.

"You can't make it," she said quietly, disappointment sinking into her bones. She looked in the rearview mirror and, seeing no cars behind her, she sat for a bit at the intersection.

"The case hit a snag with a witness. It took longer to get them back on board and I missed my flight. I just got out of the room with the D.A. I'll still be there tonight, but it will be late, around eleven."

"I understand, maybe something tomorrow," she said in what she hoped was a perky voice that sounded fake, even to her.

"Sunshine ... Don't bullshit me, honey. I know you're disappointed. I am too."

"They needed you," she said firmly. "It's ok. We'll have fun soon." Her eyes stared a hole through the hem of her dress.

BEEP!

Maya glanced in the rearview mirror again.

"Heart, I'm driving, I've gotta go. Text me when you get in, okay?"

"Ok darlin'. Are you sure you're okay?"

HONK! BEEP!

"I gotta go Heart, see you soon." She clicked off, resisted the urge to give the people behind her the finger, and tossed her phone on the seat next to her. It bounced off the seat and hit the floor. *Yep, brilliant decision to get the damn case.*

Hitting the gas on the truck, Maya pulled off and tried to convince herself that casual meant if it happens cool, if not, that's cool too. She desperately tried to ignore the stitch in her chest and the lump in her throat. Instead, she focused on her next stop - a problem she could fuckin' solve. She had to.

---

1. Golden by Jill Scott

21

STAY WITH ME A LITTLE LONGER

FRIDAY 6:15 P.M.

CAINE

He arrived at Jake's a little early. Climbing the steps to the house built into the side of the mountain, he rounded the wraparound deck to find Jake sitting in an Adirondack chair, beer in hand, feet on the rail, taking in the heavily wooded view.

"Hey brother," Jake said.

"Hey," the big man greeted back, his eyes on the view, body tense.

Jake studied his friend. "You're worried."

"She makes him seem like he's the bogeyman," Caine said, his voice heavy.

"She—," Jake started.

"She's sure she's going to die."

"Caine, man—"

"She asked me to be the guardian." The taste of the words was bitter in his mouth. "She begged me to take her baby if something happened to her. Said she had money set aside and that her baby wouldn't be a bother ... "

"Jesus man." Jake shook his head slowly. "I hate to say it, but she's got good reason to worry." He stood and clasped his friend on the shoulder as Paul, Mace, and Blake climbed the steps. Jake gave a chin up in greeting and gestured they should go inside. Walking to the large glass patio door, he slid it open carefully to keep his large, fluffy, snow-white cat Jake Jr. in as the men followed him.

They filed into Jake's house, each accepting a beer from the fridge and sitting at Jake's giant, dark wood dining table. Jake's wife Leslie and their son Colt were out with friends, ensuring the men had plenty of time to go over what he'd found.

"Are we waiting on anyone else?" Paul asked expectantly.

"Nope," Caine said.

"Her and Mike are tight man," Paul warned.

"If she wanted him to know, she'd tell him," Caine said, his face set hard.

"She doesn't want *anyone* to know," Jake reminded his friend.

Caine crossed his arms and glared stonily at the men before him.

"If we kept something like this about Victoria from you—" Paul interjected.

"No," came a growl of warning.

Paul threw up his hands in frustration and the other men looked at each other and shook their heads.

"This ain't gonna end good," Blake muttered, taking a long pull from his beer.

Caine ignored him and looked to Jake, jaw clenched, showing the conversation was over and he wanted the details of the investigation. Jake waited for a beat and looked at Caine with a big grin.[1]

"Your sister is brilliant. There is a reason I initially hit a brick wall. Griffin Levy, heir to the Xenia Lux Corp fortune, assaulted Maya." The atmosphere in the room went alert.

Jake dropped the photo of a tall, dark-haired, dark eyed handsome man in his thirties alongside his father, well-known business magnet Marion Levy on the table. He also threw out a printout that included the logos of over a dozen world recognized clothing and real estate brands the company owned.

"To most of the world, the son is an All-American eligible bachelor in his early thirties. Three-hundred-dollar haircuts, custom suits, athletic build created by weekly celebrity personal training sessions and a short stint as a rower before he got caught rigging regattas in college."

"The family is worth close to ten billion dollars, is the richest in Ohio and a couple of other states," Mace bit out. "His team keeps him untouchable, and the family name is on practically every building in the city. Nothing he does makes the press or the precinct, at least nothing that sticks. But things are pointing to him being a complete nutbag underneath that All-American smile. He's the kid who gets caught kicking puppies and in his defense his parents spend a million bucks convincing the world it doesn't need puppies."

"That smile hides something the Levy family tried to love, buy, and rationalize out of him since he was a kid. Apparently, his father tells anyone who will listen that Griffin needs maturity and a 'good woman, not a waitress, personal assistant, or bottle girl with stars and dollar signs in her eyes.'"

Jake threw two sets of photos on the table. Each young woman pictured had severe bruising and bite marks over the lower half of their bodies.

"Autopsy photos," Paul said roughly, gesturing to the metal table the women were on.

"The police ruled them suicides," Jake said, pointing to a blonde woman around twenty. "Took pills. And this one," he went on, indicating a brunette around thirty, "hung herself. At least that's what it looks like."

The mood in the room went from electric to heavy, thunderous anger with each man thinking the same thing. Maya experienced the same abuse the dead women suffered. The tension and anger in the room were suffocating.

"Maya's injuries ... they match these?" Blake asked Caine quietly, face set in barely controlled anger.

Caine was wooden. His heart in his throat made it hard to breathe, but it also kept back the bile that threatened to roll up. He stared at the women until his vision blurred. That could have been his sister. His baby sister could have been laying on that cold, hard steel. Dead before he'd ever known her. His daughters would have never known her. Caine's rage coursed through his body and as he pressed his fists into the table, it vibrated with the repressed energy he was containing in his arms. After several moments, he tore his gaze away from the photos. Instead, he concentrated on a bare spot on the table. Eventually he nodded to Jake with an angry jerk.

"Poor girl," Paul muttered, his voice thick.

Blake, with his focus solely on his friend, asked Mace without looking at him, "What else?"

"She is brilliant for a variety of reasons, the first being she got away. She didn't get tagged by a tail and she kept her assets and money exchanges hidden. Then she secured a new ID and has continued to run her business completely under the radar. The clients think she's taking a break, and no one can trace her internet activity back to her."

Mace dropped stacks of papers detailing assets, holdings, and other various items on Maya. "She uses a Tor browser to cloak her internet activity and taught women at the last shelter she was at how to use it." Seeing the men's confused faces, he elaborated. "The Tor network uses volunteer servers and computers to bounce a person's internet activity from their IP address to addresses around the world. It's usually used by political dissidents, black market sites, and the like, but average citizens use it as well - usually for porn or drug buys."

Jake dropped photos of Maya from her high school and college graduations. Her braces and shorter curly hair in her high school photos hinted at a budding beauty, perhaps behind the other girls her age, and then morphed to a beautiful, confident woman in her college photos. Two things were consistent between the two photos - her dimple and bright, determined eyes.

Jake pulled out more paperwork - transcripts, letters of recommendation, etc. that marked the passage of time and accomplishments in Maya's life.

"Beyond that, Maya graduated from high school in two years and college with her undergrad and graduate degree in architecture from OSU in half the time it takes mortals. She speaks at least three languages and started that firm, getting it running after she spent two years interning at top firms in France, China, and New York."

Jake looked as proud as if she was his sister. He laid out the last big stack of what looked like court papers. "She also successfully argued for emancipation from her mother."

"Why? She loved her mom," Caine asked roughly, shaking his head, still reeling.

Mace's smile was sad. "By declaring herself an adult she'd have power of attorney over her mother's affairs, able to make medical and financial decisions for both of them. The girl lost her childhood the moment they diagnosed her mother. Instead of giggling at sleepovers, she was taking double course loads for college credit, sorting the dozens of medications her mother was on, and working part time on and off. I talked to an acquaintance from high school. She was coming out of her shell, made the cheerleading squad her freshman year, and before the first game, her mother received her diagnosis. Maya quit the team and went into adult mode. Two years later, she made it official. By making it legal, she was providing a level of safety for the two of them if her mother passed away before Maya reached eighteen."

Caine sat back in his seat at Jake's table. The weight of all he learned pressed on him, bowing the big man's shoulders. The fuller picture of Maya's life 'til this point, what his sister endured and the daily strength she showed, humbled him.

"Caine, I need you to stay with me a little longer," Jake whispered. He watched Caine's head jerk once in agreement, his eyes focused on the floor. "The report you said she filed. It's been buried or never entered. If it is there, I can get to it, but they may be watching access, which means tipping off whoever is helping him. Digging more could make him jumpy and increase the incentive to find her."

The men watched the muscles in Caine's shoulders and neck bulge and tighten.

"He's got resources, opportunity but,"—Mace sighed, — "he also has a new girl. It may be enough to distract him from Maya. How long that'll last for both women ... "

"This guy has Teflon coating covered in slime, so nothing sticks. Drugs, rape, assault, you name it, all under the rug. Victims retract, witnesses suddenly can't remember or take long luxury vacations, evidence is lost, or damaged, and local media won't report it. He does his dirt almost exclusively in the area where the family influence is the strongest, though there have been incidents overseas. But he's lazy. Most of his shit is opportunistic and impulsive. Bottle girls, stylists, waitresses. Maya's firm designed a building the grandfather wanted to be built as a shelter for battered women, which is how she got on his radar, completely against type in the sense that she was his equal, his better."

"Sick bastards," Paul spat out, his eyes still on the photos of the dead girls. "They know he's a predator and they cover for him and then make a play for public goodwill."

"His parents are damage control, but word is the grandfather sees him for what he is and has been pushing for the parents' to do something for years. There have been rumblings about the sick fuck's activities for a long time, but no one's doing anything about it. The parents have cut him off a few times. The grandfather, who built the company, revoked his trust after the fourth drug incident. Now he exists on a generous allowance and covered living expenses. He's got standard protection for a family like his, except his personal bodyguard is a goon, not with the security firm. He's also an asshole."

Mace slapped down a photo of a beefy man with cold grey eyes, pale, pockmarked skin, bald head, and thick neck.

"Foster Hitchens. Dishonorable discharge from the Army for beating a man to death who accused Hitchens of assaulting his wife. You name it, he's done it. Enforcer for loan sharks, B&E, runnin' women ... he hooked up with Levy after being his dealer for ecstasy and coke. It's a match made in sick fuck heaven."

The men absorbed the information in silence, with an eye to Caine, while thinking about the young woman they'd gotten to know over the last couple of weeks.

"Now what?" Blake angrily broke the silence. "'Cause I know what the fuck I want to do."

"We wait for him to make a mistake or dig deeper and force his hand," Jake said.

"Does she know about the other women, Caine?" Paul asked.

He shook his head no, still not looking up.

"She needs to know," Jake said.

Raising his head slowly, Caine spoke in a voice both rough and full of anguish, "She is afraid all the time, she's angry ... you saw what she did to Biscuit. She's getting help now, but it's only been a few days. No way she can handle this."

"Speaking of which, she wants to make peace with him," Blake volunteered. The men's heads snapped to Blake's quick. "She texted asking for his information. She wants to apologize."

"Biscuit doesn't make-up," Jake said.

"I tried to tell her, but she seems set," Blake said, taking a long pull on his beer. "I wouldn't tell her shit, but she's smart as hell. It won't take long before she has it."

"Fuck that. I'll talk to her," Caine barked, his frustration growing while his hands balled into fists. "Let's wait to tell her about the other women, monitor him Mace, tell me the cost and I got it. Until we have something for her to be worried about, I want her healing, buying baby shit, and playing with her nieces, not chasing down bikers and looking at dead bodies." He slammed his fist down on the table suddenly.

"The least she needs to do is get out of the Rough Ridge Hotel to someplace more secure," Jake said. "She can come here."

Caine shook his head more and took a drink. "She won't. She won't stay with Victoria and me either. She's stubborn as fuck."

The men looked at each other with small grins, knowing that was a trait her brother shared. "Wonder where she got it from?" Jake asked pointedly.

"There are those condos on Hillside. A few have safe rooms," Paul said.

"Those cost a whack. She won't take my money and she's got about one hundred large on her and that's gotta last," Caine muttered.

"Oh yeah," Mace said, a smile slowly growing across his face. "She's loaded. A couple mil at least personally, the company is worth much more and privately held. You sure you don't want me to send her my bill?"

MAYA PULLED UP THE DRIVE, took in the number of cars, and narrowed her eyes. The anger that still coursed through her veins bubbled to the surface again. It wasn't a blinding rage like her outburst with Biscuit, but she also didn't expect miracles with a week of counseling. She took in the house built on the side of the mountain with its lights ablaze and for the second time; she was there uninvited. At least she drove this time versus parking a mile away and hiking it through the woods. She gathered herself, snatched her giant bag with what she needed in it, and carefully hopped out of the truck because if she fucked up her shoes, there would be hell to pay.

JAKE LOOKED over his shoulder suddenly, his eyes narrowed. He moved to the door as the men took guarded positions, watchful as Mace gathered their findings. Jake looked from the deck through to the room, his face blank as he waited for the unannounced visitor to ascend the steps to the deck. When the men saw who it was, they froze for a moment while Blake muttered a barely audible, "Oh fuck."

Mace slid the file off the table, never taking his eyes off Maya as she sashayed through Jake's house, giving them a small finger wave.

"Maya, you look..." Blake started.

"Like liquid sex," Jake finished, following behind Maya.

"Hey man, damn." Caine ground out.

"She does," Jake shrugged. He tipped his bottle to her in a manly kudos. "You do."

"You can thank Leslie and Tori for that," she said with a small smile. She took a small, slow runway model three-quarter turn and there was an inhale of breath when she showed the exposed back of her dress. "I'm going out tonight."

"Alone?" Caine said, looking unhappy.

"I'm going out tonight," Maya said, ignoring Caine's question, "and I need the 'Stang."

"Why?" he asked in surprise.

"Because hopping down out of my truck in these heels doesn't work and climbing up in this dress isn't great either."

She dropped the keys to her truck in front of him and turned her palm over. "Victoria's idea. She said it would look hot with my dress." Maya grinned full out.

Caine sighed, reached into his pocket, and dropped the keys in her hand.

"Thanks dear," she said and walked toward the door. "Oh, I forgot one other thing," she said softly, snapping her fingers. She turned, walked back to the table, looking in her giant bag that didn't match her outfit. She took out several pieces of paper and unfolded them and turning them face down on the table, she began smoothing out the wrinkles carefully. Then she set a thick file next to them. The file was nearly identical to Mace's. She twisted her neck from left to right and Mace noticed her hands were shaking. Watching the men, she took in the bemused looks on their faces, the beleaguered expression on her brother's, and the watchful look on Mace's.

---

1. 1 Heathens by Twenty One Pilots

22

YOU FORCED MY HAND

MAYA

"Nice file you have on me, Mr. Mason Robert McCutchins of 1237 Golden Hook Grove. Comprehensive if not complete," she said, her voice low and controlled. Flipping over the papers, she started spreading them out on the table. Caine sat back as if they were snakes, turning his head away. In fact, all the men looked away. Mace looked down briefly, grimaced, then looked back to Maya.

"CPD doesn't realize the breach yet," she said, leveling Mace with a steely stare. "I'm still alive, so they buried me another way. As if I need another alias ... Look gentlemen." She gestured to the photos spread across the table.

"You're so fired up to be involved. Look closely."

Maya held one of the photo printouts. It was of her own battered legs and thighs.

"This is the picture they took when they asked if I liked it rough."

She flung it to the table, frisbee style. Another photo showed her spread legs, only clad in panties, a small ruler held against bite mark injuries on her inner thigh to show scale.

"Bonus - you get to keep on your underwear if you weren't raped, but you still have to spread 'em. Did I mention there were no female officers available for my 'low level' case?" She tossed the photo aside.

"Here it is, boys, the full report of Jane *Fucking* Doe." She turned to Caine, who wouldn't make eye contact with her. "I asked you to stop. I got word about pings on the case and of others with the same M.O. One good thing - I never learned their names, now I can be specific when I pray for their families. Thank you, Mr. McCutchins."

"Mace."

"I'm sorry?" she said in her professional voice.

"You've obviously been in my home. Those who have, call me Mace," he ground out. His gaze on Maya was scorching. She guessed it was a stare that made many grown men rethink the trajectory of their lives. Maya didn't blink.

"Don't worry, I didn't read anything else," indicating his work files. "I don't sleep well as is. I don't need anything extra."

"You don't?" Jake asked distractedly.

"Not since all this," she said, sweeping her hand toward her police report. "Whatever he's paying you, I'll double it if you stop." Maya said, abruptly turning to Mace and losing a bit of her armor.

"It's not about the money—" Mace started.

"Ok, fuck it then," she cut him off. "Here's the deal boys,"—her eyes blazed, body strung tight — "this shit stops tonight or I need you all to draw straws on who gets to put a fucking bullet in my head now. Spare me the trouble of wondering when the hell he's going to show because you're all excited to throw on capes and white hats."

She abruptly flew back to her purse and started tossing things - files from Jake's home office and pieces of Leslie's jewelry, Tori's jewelry from Caine's safe, a SD card marked McCutchins files - into a pile on top of her own police report.

The room was electric with a lot of angry men. It was suffocating, pressing in as each man realized what Maya had done.

"Jesus Maya," Paul started, seeing the situation deteriorating and putting on a gentle voice. "Darlin' this—"

"Paul, if I learned you were in on this bullshit, I would've made a point to drop by and visit your family as well."

"Now listen—" Paul started again, his voice taking on an edge.

"NO! YOU LISTEN! LISTEN TO ME!" She hit herself hard in the chest. Paul blinked, and his head snapped back. Caine's eyes finally moved to his sister. "You're all pissed as hell right now. You feel violated. I've been in YOUR private space uninvited. I crossed boundaries that are unacceptable. Does it matter if I say I did it because I care about you? Because I want to keep you safe?

"Maya," Jake growled. Maya looked Jake directly in the eye.

"I am NOT afraid of you." Her eyes swept the room. "Of *any* of you." She whipped her head around to the men on her left, nailing each one in the eyes.

"Blake, would you beat me, a few weeks pregnant, with a repeated and dedicated focus to the same spots for three days? Just as the throbbing ebbs, you come at it again and again." Blake's scowl drained away as Maya revealed details of her torture.

"Paul, would you get off on firing your gun so close to my head I can feel the heat of it? Smell my own singed hair? In the morning you'd have your gourmet coffee and your gun, afternoons likely a protein smoothie - because you've gotta keep that six pack - and your gun. And in the evening, a nice cocktail in an heirloom glass in your left hand and a bespoke Wilson handgun in your right. Is that how you'd teach me a lesson?

"Anyone wanna break a two-thousand-dollar bottle of Château Le Pin over my back when I scream a little too loudly? And then you know, you're all buds, maybe you'll get together and rip off my clothes," she said, tugging on her dress, "and discuss among yourselves what you want to do to me when I 'take care of it.' It being the baby you. *Slam.* Helped. *Slam.* Create! *Slam.*"

The slamming of her balled fist on the heavy wood table punctuated her last words. She prowled around the room as she spoke. "Of course not. You're good men. The best. Be angry at me if you must, but I needed to prove two points - what you are doing, the man you are going after won't hesitate to do that to your families, *your wives,* if he feels threatened. And if I recognized you're digging, he'll notice you're digging, and there are billions of reasons and ways to stop you."

When she made her way back to the head of the table, her voice was low and quiet. "You men, as wonderful as you are, are violating me all over again."

She swallowed hard. Her were eyes wet and her body vibrated hard to keep them from overflowing. She took in their stricken faces, closed her eyes, and continued.

"I haven't been to Blake's house for dinner yet, but he already knows what the battered inside of my thighs look like. I haven't sat at a fishing hole with Jake, but he knows the intimate details of what happened to me. And I can only assume their wives know, too. You took the choice of when and with whom to share my trauma away from me." She stared into eyes identical to hers and continued, "I brought the report, but you forced my hand."

Caine looked like he'd been slapped and it stung. Maya closed her eyes a second time, swallowed past the growing lump threatening to choke her. "You wanted to save me before you really knew me," she said, nodding, her voice hushed. "That's a beautiful thing." She walked to her brother and took his face in her hands, kissing him softly on the head and staring into his eyes. "But I'm *no one's* victim," her voice turning hard. "And my shit doesn't blowback on any of you, your families, or *this town.*

She snatched her oversized bag, now mostly empty of its contents, and Caine's keys. With anger still coursing through her, she moved swiftly into the open kitchen off the dining room, fussing the entire way.

"This shit has got to stop. You want to help me? Help me put together baby furniture. Help me move into my condo when it closes, make me laugh, bring me food, and trust me to identify when it's time to call in reinforcements..."

She walked over to a big chocolate cake sitting on the butcher block island and the men watched as she hacked a big ass piece.

"Pains in my asses ... every one of you..." She snatched open drawer after drawer until she found a fork. "Costing me a lot of money ... Got me running around like a freaking Navy Seal at Zero Dark Thirty to prove a damn point because apparently having a dick means ignoring simple commands like 'Don't investigate' and 'Mind your business'..."

She snatched open more drawers until she found a large freezer bag with a Ziploc closure and returned to the cake slice, dropping it into the bag along with the fork, still muttering loudly to the men and to herself.

"I'm hungry, horny, and this is likely the last time I'll be this hot in at least a year because in a few weeks I won't be able to see my fucking feet..."

She looked at the men sitting there watching her in shock at seeing this side of her. The men, their collective hotness and the variety of yummy flavors available, pissed her off more, and she declared loudly, "I'm surrounded by the fucking dream team of mountain men," she said, gesturing wildly with her cake-in-a-bag-clad hand, "and none of you can help me out with any of this."

She stalked gracefully out to the door and stopped. Without looking back, she asked, "Please, stop digging. What I do will be my call, my time. Don't take that away from me."

Maya strode out the door, down the stairs, and out into the night.

Caine was out of his seat and down the stairs before she got to the car. It dawned on her that the thin air must make the men move faster than someone of their sizes should. She sighed as she sensed him behind her.

"I'm not sorry," she said to the night.

"I'm not either," he said, his voice gruff. "I'm not sorry for wanting to protect you."

He reached out and placed a hand on her shoulder. "I *am* sorry for not realizing how it would make you suffer. I only want to keep you safe. You're my sister Maya. I want you out from under this. Even if you weren't blood, I'd want to help. All you've been through ... you deserve your time to breathe free, baby girl."

She sighed, turned, and dropped her head to his chest. "I'm not sorry I broke into your testosterone meeting and cat burgled, but I am sorry you all had to be confronted with this shit."

Caine gave her a squeeze, "You didn't do this, HE did ... They already thought you were a badass, to go through what you worked through and to be who you are, but now they think you're a badass, crazy chick."

"And that's a good thing?"

He chuckled a little, "Yeah sis, it is."

"Mmm..."

"Let me help."

After a full minute of silence, she spoke. "Only if Mace lets me pay him. It's a monitor-only operation and I'm kept in the loop completely. I have a security team monitoring aspects of this. Mace coordinates with them."

Caine clenched her tightly, growling out, "Fine."

"And no one tells Michael."

"Fine with me," he said too quickly.

"He's a good man, Caine," she whispered.

"Too much baggage."

"No more than mine. I want to tell him myself. Things are ... weird right now."

"It shouldn't be. He's either with you or not. Period."

"I haven't been open, Caine," she said, stepping out of his hug. "Have I made this easy on you?"

He didn't reply.

"That's what I thought."

He grumbled something under his breath, rubbed his hands up and down her arms absentmindedly, then looked back down at her.

"Go, get food. Bring my car by the house tomorrow."

She smiled at him, waved with the cake in a baggie hand, and slid into the muscle car. She started it and grinned at him as it purred beneath her. Fiddling with her phone, he watched her scroll through her playlist, connecting it to the car stereo. Rolling down the windows, she turned the volume way up.[1]

CAINE

Caine chuckled as the hard-hitting strains of Rihanna "*Bitch Better Have My Money*" boomed through the quiet area as she peeled off backward down the driveway and into the night.

"Drives like a maniac," he mumbled. He relayed her requests as he drained his now piss warm beer. He looked at the men who'd been by his side through thick and thin. "Still want to help her?"

"Help her? I want to hire her," Mace said.

"And buy her a steak," Paul said.

"And get her laid," Jake said, grinning at the table.

"Did she really put cake in a bag?" was all Blake asked.

---

1. Bitch Better Have My Money by Rihanna

23
OBELISKS

MAYA

Maya arrived at the second place, outside of Denver, where she could have a bit of fun - the Friday night scene at Jake's bar. Now she wasn't just a little overdressed, but HUGELY overdressed for a local bar where the men wear nothing more than jeans and leather motorcycle jackets, and for women, clothing was optional. With a deep breath she opened the door.[1]

The bar was completely packed, a live band rocked out to Aerosmith, and a few people were dancing. Most eyes shifted to her when she walked through the door. She barely fought the intense urge to back out and disappear into a black hole. Mac picked the perfect time to whistle loud and long - right as the band finished their song, guaranteeing everyone else's eyes snapped from Mac to her.

Well Shit.

Heat flushed to her face.

"Come on, golden goddess," Mac yelled again from behind the bar. "I got your mix."

Maya locked eyes with good old Regina sitting in her usual spot. Other regulars lined along the bar, and she relaxed a bit. She walked carefully through the crowd of locals and bikers and sat on the stool next to her. Mac, brown eyes sparkling, provided her with water and a bowl of the peanut, M&M, and pork rind mix. Maya smiled gratefully. She was still hungry even after she stopped to eat dinner at the diner. Pregnancy was ridiculous.

"Where are you headed to or coming from looking like a sexy Cinderella without a ball?" Mac asked casually, as he filled drink orders and monitored the people around them.

"I had a date, but he had to work."

"And no sense in letting a good outfit go to waste, right?"

"Pretty much," Maya mumbled.

"Mike know you out on the town looking like you do?" Regina asked.

"What makes you think Michael has anything to do with what I wear or who I go out with? Last time I checked, I was a grown woman," Maya said evenly with a smile.

"What Regina is trying to say is with great ass comes great responsibility," Mac said with a laugh. "This ain't the big city. You're surrounded by bikers and, girlie, you're lit up like Christmas. Tonight could get hairy if you don't watch it."

"I'm good Mac," she said, meeting eyes with the man who was clearly skeptical. "I've met demons and not much outside of them scare me anymore."

Mac paused, took her in, and nodded slowly, eyes concerned.

Maya turned to Regina. "What's that dance they're doing?

"Come on, I'll show you," she said, pulling her hand as she slid off the stool.

Maya produced fervent, silent prayers: *Dear Lord, Regina actually moved. Dear Lord, don't let her die on the dance floor.*

After briefly worrying her bottom lip, Maya shrugged, saying, "Don't let me trip and embarrass myself."

"No chance, girlie."

"I got your purse, honey," Mac called.

Maya glanced over her shoulder to see him stow her gold clutch behind the bar.

Regina shocked the shit out of Maya as she walked her through the steps a couple of times, and before she realized it, Regina was twirling with Maya around the floor, with the energy of a woman half her age.

Maya's laughter came as easy as the steps under Regina's tutelage. After a few songs, the band slowed it down, the two of them left the dance floor, and Regina resumed her permanent perch on her stool. When Maya got back, she realized Mac had sent someone to the store to get her baked chicken with steamed veggies. He laid her clutch beside the to-go box.

"Gotta keep baby fed," he whispered loudly over the music.

Maya smiled softly and blew him a kiss.

"Oh! Do you want cake?" Maya asked a confused Regina as she dug in her purse and produced the baggie with cake and a fork. "Leslie made it."

"Why is it in your purse?" Mac asked.

She shrugged with a sheepish grin. "I was hungry."

Regina and Mac roared with laughter. They were still chuckling when Leslie came in and took Mac's place behind the bar while he hit the tables. Maya snacked on her food until another regular asked her to dance. Half the night Maya was out of her seat dancing, having a good time as regulars and not-so-regulars took turns cutting up the floor with her. Even Logan, the lead singer of the band, got in on it and danced a couple of songs while the drummer took over vocals.

"I didn't get a chance to say thank you for the other day," Maya said as Logan took her hand into his large, callused one.

Logan shrugged his big shoulders and put her through a series of turns. "You did what most folks in this town have wanted to do for a while. Biscuit ain't been right a long time. His grace period has passed."

Maya blinked a second at his speaking voice. It was the required mountain man deep, but with a slight Australian-like accent. She realized she hadn't heard him speak much.

He was almost the same size as Mike, as tall and nearly as wide. He worked out regularly, given the size of his arms, but he didn't appear to be a meathead. His jet-black hair was pulled back in an elastic showing off his appealing hazel eyes, and his slightly bigger eye teeth gave him a wolfish appearance when he smiled. He wore a vintage Aerosmith t-shirt, a small charm on a braided leather cord necklace, broken in black jeans, and motorcycle boots. Honestly, he looked like he'd stopped in for a beer and decided to sing. He was relaxed and chill. A little too chill about Maya's encounter.

"Don't say that. There's no excuse for my behavior," she admonished.

"All I care about is that *you're* okay. I haven't seen rage like that in a while."

She looked at him and cast her mind around for something else to say.

"You know, you look a lot like the Rock with hair," she blurted out.

He considered her before giving her a turnout. "I've heard worse. We're both Samoan, my mother is, so there's that. And don't think I missed you changing the subject."

Maya laughed and shrugged herself. "Your accent?"

"You notice it? Most people don't. I went to school in New Zealand, spent the summers in the States a few years, other years the arrangement flipped. When I was in the States, I spent time here with my grandparents and with my mum in Hawaii. Now ... it's safe to say you find me attractive. How about a meal after I finish my set?"

"You're flirting with me."

"No, I'm tryin' to get in your pants" — he glanced down at her attire — "correction - dress," he said as he gave her a wolfish grin.

Good Lord. When it rains, it pours. Where is Shay when I need her? She'd be able to handle all of the raining dicks.

"I—" she started as she tripped over her words and her feet.

Logan steadied her with a brawny hand and a laugh. "I had to try. In case that cop hadn't made a move."

"How do—"

"Anyone here the other day could tell he wasn't responding to a regular bar squabble, he was a man ready to rip another man apart for touching his woman. Even if she can handle herself."

"Oh, you're teasing," she said, sounding relieved. She threw her hands up in the air in the groove.

"No. I'm not. If I had a shot, I'd have you out of that dress as quickly as possible."

Maya glanced at him, expecting a smile, and saw he was dead serious.

"Wow," Maya said. "And I thought I didn't have a filter."

"Life's too short for bullshit."

"Yes, but you're like one step from slappin' your dick on the counter." She laughed, barely keeping in a snort.

"Well, that would be rude."

Maya actually snorted, stopping mid-dance, cracking up. "Not to mention unsanitary!"

Logan's bark of laughter rang out.

"A definite health code violation," he said between breaths.

"Not the nuts I ordered," she hooted loudly, unable to hold it in.

"Footlong for table five?" Logan guffawed.

"Are y'all making dick jokes?" Mac asked while on his way past with a tray of drinks and nachos.

"Absolutely." Logan chuckled deeply.

"Because we are now sixth graders." Maya giggled, holding her side.

"Dick is serious business," Mac said, his eyes full of mirth.

"Of course," Logan said. "Like Big Ben."

"The Washington Monument," Maya chimed in.

"Obelisks," Logan said, his face serious but his eyes laughing.

"Ah yes, The Black Obelisk of Shalmaneser III is, of course, a historically big Black dick." Maya spoke like a professor in class, quickly switching her tone and inflection to a clipped, affected diction.

For all a half-second, the three of them kept a straight face. Then they were roaring with laughter.

"I've got to go to the restroom." Maya laughed as she stepped away, hiccuping and giggling.

WHEN SHE FINISHED in the restroom, she began making her way back to her seat. Logan joined the band again, and Mac was on the other side of the room. The dense crowd made it take longer to make her way back to her seat next to Regina. Midway, a guy she'd seen a couple of times around town stopped her.

"Dance with me, sweetheart."

Maya hesitated for a second when he added, "Come on, give an old man a thrill."

She relented, though she was ready to go home. As they moved through the dance, it called for switching partners and coming back. When they switched, she found herself with a guy she didn't recognize.

MIKE

Mike found out about Maya dressed in gold as soon as he hit town. Outside the convenience store, he ran into Paul, who was on a late-night diaper run. Paul clocked her having dinner at the diner and heading over to Jake's. It struck Mike as funny and kind of cool that Maya made it a night without him instead of waiting for him to come home. It was funny until he took in her outfit in the middle of the dance floor of a dusty biker bar.

As he stood in the doorway, the music registered. So did the crowd, but the only thing he cared about was her. Gold shimmery material slid against her skin as her body moved in time with the beat. The exposed area of her back was a beacon as she moved around the floor, her arms outstretched, graceful, with a small smile on her lips ... She was pure beauty.

It was a punch to his gut that radiated down to his groin and back to his heart as he realized that dress was for him, and he'd almost missed it. Her eyes glowed, their color more prominent against her smokey makeup. Her skin glistened, and every time she smiled, it was with sumptuous, glossed lips. And it was all for him.

Mike also recognized he didn't like her smile, lips, and glow in the arms of another man dancing her around the floor. And he really didn't like how the dude's hand dipped lower and lower every time he spun her out and brought her back. He saw Maya's friendly distance and that asshole's eyes on her tits. When he leaned in, Maya leaned back to avoid him. Mike's body automatically moved in their direction.

"Oh shit," Mac muttered when Mike moved past him quickly with a focused purpose. He looked to Maya, who gracefully, but purposefully, danced further away from an increasingly handsy dance partner.

Mike moved through the packed house like he was made from water - fluid and powerful. His hand reached out for the biker's wrist as his hand moved to Maya's ass.

---

1. Crazy Aerosmith

24

WHAT ARE YOU ASKING ME

MAYA

Maya dipped outside of her "dance partner's" reach while grabbing his arm first and applying painful downward pressure to a sensitive point on his wrist.

"No, no." Maya scolded gently. Laila's words were in her head. *Diffuse. Deflect. Defend.*

The man grunted and jerked his hand away roughly.

Maya jumped a little when she realized Mike was right next to her and their eyes caught. Stepping further back from Mr. Handsy, she said brightly, "Oh Mike, you're here!"

She turned back toward the handsy man and tried to keep things light. "I've been saving Mike a dance, and he's here to collect — you understand, of course."

"You've been a dick tease all night," the biker spat. "He can wait until I'm through."

"The lady asked nicely," Mike said calmly.

"Fuck you."

"Aw hell," Maya muttered, stepping even further back as she saw where this was going. On TV, the girl always gets cold cocked trying to step in between battling men. Maya had no intention of catching a wayward punch. She was entirely too cute tonight for that shit.

As Maya wisely stepped back, the dickhead further proved his stupidity as he attempted to grab her arm to stop her from going. He didn't make it an inch before Mike quickly and easily deflected the big dummy's hand away and moved him back two feet on his knees with his face on a table with zero effort.

"I think I just had a mini-orgasm," Maya muttered low to herself.

"Me too, honey," a chick in a skin-tight miniskirt and tank leaned in and whispered conspiratorially.

"Me three, babe," Mac quipped, walking past with another tray, confident everything was under control.

Mike's face never changed from that quiet control he exuded regularly. Tonight, he was dressed in head-to-toe black. Tight tee, jeans, and motorcycle boots. Yum.

"Like I said, dance over," Mike said, letting the man up.

Mr. Handsy stood, eyes narrowed, and assessed Mike like a challenge.

"He's a cop, genius," Jake said, coming up behind the man, clapping him on the shoulder. Caine flanked Jake. "That's his girl's ass you tried to grab. Walk away."

Finally, the biker backed down and slunk away, making his way toward the door.

Maya caught Logan's eyes and mouthed the word "slow." He nodded, cued the band, and the first guitar twangs and keyboard twinkles of Norah Jones' "Those Sweet Words" began as she turned to Mike. Stepping close to him, she placed her hand over his heart.[1]

"Hey handsome, how about a dance?"

At her words, Mike stopped watching the biker and looked down at her. She gave him a big smile with full dimple. Something passed over his face she couldn't read, so she joked, "You can lead."

"That's a given, Sunshine." His voice was gruff as he wrapped an arm around her waist and pulled her close, his large hand spread across the small of her back, making her feel delicate, possessed, covered.

It was a good feeling. A superb feeling.

He took her hand at his heart in his own and kept it close to his chest. He began moving her around the floor slowly. Maya was falling so hard for him, it stopped her breath. She forced herself to exhale slowly as the heat from his hand scorched her, branding her as his.

When she tipped her head back, she saw the expression in his eyes. It was the same one she'd seen Caine give Victoria, Jake give Leslie. His face was soft, like the man delighted in her.

Forget falling. She was already there, airborne. Wind rushing into her face, the sky wide open. She'd flung herself off the cliff, and of course, she feared the bloody, catastrophic brokenness that would surely follow. But right there, in his arms, his emerald eyes focused solely on her, time stopped. It was only Maya, Michael, and the music.

The second song began.

"You dance well, detective," Maya said, sounding impressed.

"You ain't seen nothin' yet, Sunshine." His voice was rough like gravel as he whipped her out into a turn and snapped her back to him, bringing her in close. He laughed at her, eyes wide in surprise, and getting dark when she licked her lips.

"Oh my," she whispered.

He grinned and dipped his face to hers, never breaking time with the music, and kissed her gently on the lips. He barely raised his head before he took her through another set of turns that included moving her behind his back, out and whipped back, her curls dancing on the wind he created with her body. Mac whooped loudly from the bar, but all Maya heard was Mike's low, heated growl. "Beautiful."

The couple moved together, in sync, fast and slow, the rest of the night until the last call. They smiled at each other, laughed close, danced closer. They shared long looks and stolen glances.

Maya feared everyone could see how far gone she was. News travels fast in small towns. She recognized she should have been more concerned, more private, but at that moment, she couldn't find it in her soul to give one care. When she took her eyes off Mike for a few moments, she noticed Caine watching them closely, appearing uneasy. He held up her keys and placed them on the bar, getting his own from Mac. After draining his water, he gave a chin-up to Jake, and took off.

MIKE

Maya talked to the band while Mike ran to get her purse and whatever she told them must have been hilarious. They were in stitches. Leslie reached behind the bar and pulled out Maya's purse, setting it in front of him. Then she pulled out a half-eaten to go box of baked chicken with veg from the cooler and a freezer baggie with a mostly eaten slice of chocolate cake.

Mike tipped his head slightly, grinned, then looked over at Maya who was still talking. She met his eyes and called, "Don't forget my cake!"

He grinned full out and waved the baggie in response.

God, she is adorable.

She smiled and turned back to the band. Mike looked back at Leslie and noticed her watching him.

"She comes with both, you know."

"Both what?"

"Light and dark. Like you do, hell, all of us." Leslie nodded. "She's burying whatever hers is and you're scared to death of yours, determined to good deed it out."

Mike's face lost its humor as Leslie said her piece. She took that in, and to her credit, kept going.

"You've been given a gift, the two of you." Her eyes narrowed, and she crossed her arms. "Don't blow it."

She fixed him with a glare then yelled over to Maya, "Hey Goddess, get your ass in gear unless you're sweepin' and pickin' up empties tonight."

"That's my cue fellas - you were righteous tonight!"

Maya hustled to Mike, who met her halfway across the floor and held his arm out to guide her through the door.

"Bye!" she called as she sailed through the door into the warm Colorado night.

"Let me take you back, I'll bring your truck 'round tomorrow darlin'," he said in her ear as the whisper-light brush of his fingertips across the lowest part of her back caused her to shiver. She looked up at him through her lashes and gave him a wordless nod, biting her lip.

There was heat and intensity behind her eyes. He took a moment to brush his knuckles across her cheek, then leaned in to brush his nose across hers, slightly touching her lips. When he raised up, he saw her eyes slowly blink open like she was waking from a dream and he got hard as a rock. Forcing himself to focus on getting her home safely and not throwing her in the back of his Jeep and taking her right then, he lifted her and placed her inside.

A small rush of air escaped her lips as he did, and he clenched his teeth at the sound. Shit, everything she did turned him on. Five blocks. Five blocks to her room. He had to focus. He walked around the hood of the car to the driver's side, chanting five blocks in his head over and over. His eyes never left the woman shimmering under the bright lights of the bar's parking lot in the front seat of *his* Jeep.

"Fuck. Five blocks," he said, jumping into the truck.

"Hmm?" Her eyes searched his face, curious and aroused.

"Five blocks 'til I can get you out of that dress." Mike peeled out of the parking lot.

Maya sucked in a breath, then chuckled in mock shock. "Detective Sheppard, you're setting a terrible example for the good people of Rough Ridge. Mind the speed limit." She slid her hand across his thigh and his foot hit the gas. Her laugh rang through the night as he covered the five blocks in record time, sliding expertly into the space in front of her door.

He jumped out of the Jeep, strode to her side, lifted her out, and slid her along his body slowly until her feet hit the ground softly. Her breath hitched, and she released a slow moan as he greedily took her mouth. Another of her moans slid down his throat and he matched it with a deep, gravelly groan of his own.

She tasted sweet - like chocolate, mint, and Maya. Deepening the kiss he pressed her to him reveling in the sensation of her hands exploring his back. After a while, he broke the kiss long enough to slam the Jeep door closed, grab her hand and drag her quickly the few feet to her door. Mike slipped the keys out of her hand and opened the door, stepping back to allow her to step through.

Maya inhaled sharply. "What the?" she whispered.

She stopped in the door, her eyes roaming over the sight before her. Mike pressed against her back. He looked down and to the side to see her expression. It looked like the late-night picnic was a success. Spread out before them was takeout from the Mexican restaurant the next town over, candles, sparkling cider, and a bowl of M&M's. He wrapped an arm around her middle and softly nudged Maya further into the room so he could close the door behind them.

"Heart, I..." she whispered softly.

She turned and looked at him, and his heart stopped. Her eyes were sparkling, her face soft. She looked so happy and genuinely surprised. In an instant, he became addicted to making her happy.

"This is beyond sweet," she said, her voice hoarse. Maya swallowed hard. "How did you do all of this?"

"Ms. Shirley came in, lit the candles, and reheated the food when I called."

"Heart, we have got to stop waking that woman up!" She laughed softly.

"She didn't mind at all. She was the one who suggested I call. I take it you like surprises." He smiled at her, dipping his head low to capture her lips with his.

"I don't think I've had any in a long time, not good ones like this." She answered honestly, her mind suddenly deep in thought.

He took her beautiful face in his hands, swept his fingertips along her cheek, and said, "This makes me sound like an ass, Sunshine, but I like that I'm the one who's gonna give that to you."

She smiled hesitantly and, suddenly shy, she dropped her eyes. She wasn't used to being spoiled; made a priority, he could tell. Mike captured her chin with his hand and tipped it up to him. Her eyes followed.

"Hungry?"

"I hate to say yes, but yes. I'm hungry all the time now."

"Let's get my girl some food." Mike grinned, dropped Maya's purse in the chair near the door and her leftover cake into the trash. He tagged her mini speaker and synched his phone to it. Anthony Hamilton's "*The Point of It All*" filled the room.[2]

He led her to the food laid out on the floor and helped her down to the blanket. He held in a groan when she gracefully sank to her knees and then to one hip, her gold-heeled feet curled behind her.

She reached and pulled him down next to her and when he placed his outstretched legs on either side of her, his front to her side, she snuggled into him close. "This is beautiful."

"You're beautiful," he countered. He bent down and kissed her shoulder gently. "Now, my plan was three cheese jalapeno dip with tortillas, a foot massage, and then I'll fill you in another way."

"Oh, wow. That's ... well ... " She shivered again slightly and tried to control herself.

"That's me taking care of you in every way I can," he said as he nuzzled her ear. "I've missed seeing your face for a week. When I left here, things weren't good. Now I gotta atone for lost time and you gotta let me."

He reached down, grabbed a tortilla chip, scooped up some dip, and held it out for Maya to bite. She hesitated for a moment, then he saw another brick fall when she leaned in and took a bite, closed her eyes, and moaned in delight.

His fingers bit into her hips in response, and her eyes flew open as she smiled.

She reached down and gathered a chip and fed it to him as he watched her eyes get heated again, watching his mouth. He loved that she got turned on by being with him. The feeding game passed back and forth for a while until Maya was panting slightly and fully in his lap. He was hard as a rock pressed against her hip and licking the remnants of spicy cheese off her lips.

Maya shifted, changing into a straddling position as Mike slipped one hand around her neck and his other hand around her lower hip, cupping her behind. Mike moved his hand from Maya's ass and slid it slowly from her thigh to her knee, rounding her knee and down her leg to her ankle, taking in the smooth length of her until he reached her golden strappy sandals.

"I love these shoes," he growled against her mouth, "we'll keep these on for a while."

"Anything you want, Heart," she whispered back.

Mike's body stilled for a moment.

"Anything?" he asked in that quiet voice of his searching her face.

She blinked slowly, her breathing quickening. She focused on his face. Her eyes cleared, and she whispered, "What are you asking me Heart?"

"You said 'anything,' are you ready to give me everything? All of you?"

He watched her face, waiting for another brick to fall, praying another brick would fall when her eyes shuttered. A gate came crashing down, and she locked herself away from him. *FUCK!*

He dropped his forehead to hers and forced out a deep sigh as the pain in the side of his chest grew.

"Sunshine."

That one word said everything. There was a pain in it and a plea.

"I don't know what you want from me," she said, which both recognized was a lie, "but I know what I need from you."

She raised to her knees, and she pressed tight against him, moving her mouth over top of his. He hesitated at first, but as her tongue prodded his mouth gently, he broke. A loud groan came from deep within him and he quickly flipped her onto her back, pressing his heavy weight between her legs. She moaned softly as he roughly kissed and sucked her neck, leaving a mark that would last for days. Mike was swinging himself out there. He should get a handle on her mindset before they finally fucking went where they both needed to go, but the smell of her, the feel of her - dammit, her. Just her.

She planted her heel and rolled him, climbed on top and licked his corded neck from the base of his collarbone to his jaw, nipping at the skin at his goatee while ripping his shirt out of his jeans and pushing it until he took over to take it off. She laid flat on his chest, kissing him deep, wet, and long, appearing to lose herself in the smell and taste of him.

He yanked her dress up and paused when he encountered the smallest pair of underwear he'd ever had the joy of encountering. Sitting up, he slid her off and turned her around. She was on her knees; he was behind her and he took both hands to the dress, sliding it off her hips and over her head. Mike sat back on his haunches and took in the sight of her from behind with that teeny, tiny G-string almost the exact color of her skin and lost it. His finger glided slowly from the back of the G-string to the front, and into the front of her soft curling hair and into her.

Her head dropped back, landing on his shoulder, her face in his neck. "Heart," she whispered.

"Gorgeous, buy more of these, a lot more," he growled before he slipped his finger out, turned his hand, gripped the delicate lace, and tore them away.

Her body jerked, and she moaned, pressing her ass into his hardness.

"Let me get you in the bed, baby."

"Heart—"

"I'm not taking you for the first time on the floor of a motel, sweetheart," he explained.

He quickly lifted her off her knees to her feet while still on his knees and she gave a small cry of surprise at the movement.

"I love when you do stuff like that. It's like you bench press logs or something."

He chuckled as he stood and took her in his arms again, backing her gently back to the bed. Mike's phone began vibrating across Maya's small dresser, interrupting the music.[3]

"I hear nothing," Maya said.

"Fuck!"

"Exactly. That's what is happening." She said stubbornly as she angrily yanked at his belt.

"Babe."

"Dude."

He squeezed her hard, took a deep breath inhaling her scent, and reached out his arm, tagging his phone.

"Not a good time, man."

"Mike, we've got another van, headed to Denver, coming through here in thirty," Paul said.

"That solid?" Maya turned to wood against him.

Dammit.

"Brick. One girl from the other bust kept her ears open, looking for a way out. Sat on the info until they'd be close, so you'd handle it. She called in and got Laila's desk."

Mike sighed, looking up as Maya stepped away, and began slipping on a cute little nightgown.

"Fuck. There in ten, man."

He jabbed his finger at the screen.

Maya started pulling her hair into a sloppy bun. "You're hard and it's after 4 a.m., doesn't that count for something?" she said, arms crossed.

"Yeah, blue balls," Mike sighed as he snagged his shirt from the floor.

"Three detectives on the town's tiny force. Why are they always dragging you out of bed?"

"I'm single, no family. This is a case that is my specialty *and* connected to a previous case," Mike said as he slipped on his boots. "I asked to be put on call first, didn't have anything keeping me in bed."

"You do now," she mumbled. He met her eyes and waited. She looked away.

"I'll make you coffee, go get your travel mug and I'll fill it up."

Mike kissed her softly and sighed. "Be back in a minute."

He sensed her watching him walk out of the door, then he heard movements that sounded like she was getting started on making coffee in the little electric kettle.

---

1. Those Sweet Words by Norah Jones
2. The Point of It All by Anthony Hamilton
3. Scandalous by Prince

25

IT MEANS YOU'RE MINE

MAYA

Within minutes Mike was back, badge around his neck, holster armed, face frustrated, and travel mug in hand.

"I'm coming back to finish this," he said, his eyes on her, clearly indicating what he meant.

"I will remind you I've been up all day and most of the night. I am also pregnant and sleep with a loaded .38. You wake me before noon and I'm gonna pump you full of lead, as they say."

He chuckled. "Outside of corny movies, no one says that."

"Really?" She smiled at him and filled his mug. He wrapped his arms around her from behind as she worked, his chin on her shoulder. It hinted at another level of intimacy. Things were shifting with them. She noticed it, liked it, and struggled against it. She screwed the cap of the mug on tight and turned to him, looking into those emerald eyes, and saw he felt the same, without the struggle. His face was soft and settled.

SHIT.

"Don't run."

"Go," she said gently. "Thank you for a beautiful night."

He paused and met her eyes. He searched her hard, but she knew he still didn't see what he needed to see, and she wasn't trying to be coy.

There was so much more at stake. Her heart, if she needed to run again ... Putting Mike in danger ...

"Tonight. Be ready for The Treehouse at seven."

And with that, he turned and walked to the door.

"What's The Treehouse?"

"Seven, Maya. Lock up behind me."

"Be careful."

He nodded, smiled at her, and walked out.

She walked to the door, locked it, and continued to the bathroom to wash her face, snatching up another torn-for-nothing pair of underwear and dropping them in the trash along the way.

"Is there a such a thing as blue ovaries?" she muttered.

SHE WOKE AROUND NOON, starving, with Dr. Flemmings' warning playing over and over in her head, *"Romantic relationships that start under times of stress rarely last."*

Shit. She was right. You read about it all the time. People falling in love with first responders during a disaster or crisis only for things to fizzle out when the excitement and emotion of the incident wore off.

Her Saturday was full. A hair appointment, a desperate search for food, and learning whatever crazy shit Laila wanted her to learn.

Plus, she still needed to convince herself that she was doing the smart, rational thing as far as Mike was concerned. After all, Dr. Flemmings was correct about other aspects of her therapy. She felt better, less angry, and on edge. She could apply the same rational principles to this aspect of her life.

In the blazing Colorado summer sunshine, she could see and think clearly. There was no romantic music and dancing, dressy clothes or Dear Lord, emerald green eyes and soft, rolling thunder voice to change her mind or muddle her thoughts. Today, Maya Anderson was back on track. And for the next hour, she was clear on the idea that The Treehouse was likely a barbecue joint, that a friends with benefits arrangement was possible, and that she could still live a life of quiet anonymity in a tiny mountain town in Colorado.

SATURDAY, 3:45 P.M.

"Sorry love, The Treehouse is high class, pricey, and a serious date," Tammy, hairstylist to the town and wife of Detective Paul Cabot, said. Tammy was a former model turned hairstylist who came to Rough Ridge for a quiet vacation, took one glance at Paul's blue eyes and fell hard.

Now they had an adorable, blue-eyed, giant baby boy that sat on Maya's lap, drooling down her shirt as he tried gumming her chin, necklace, and anything else he could get his hands on. Tammy was giving Maya a deep, penetrating head massage while letting the conditioner work in her hair. She came in for a wash and trim. Mac saw her arrive and tagged along. Tori chatted as she got her nails done.

"I'm not looking for a relationship. At all. I can't," Maya said to everyone and no one.

"Sweetheart, you showed up at that bar looking like golden sex," Mac said, "danced the night away with him, giving him all the eyes, hair, legs—"

"Ass and tits," Tammy cut in.

"And you think he's not gonna want to take it up a notch?" Mac finished, eyes wide.

Maya closed her eyes against the thudding of her heart, trying to block out the night before.

"I don't see what the problem is. He's hot, you're hot..." Tammy kept going.

"He needs a biker chick or sweet mountain flower, not..." Maya left the rest unfinished.

"Not what? What do you think you are?" Mac asked, his voice softer — well, soft as it got for Mac.

"I've always known who I was, what I was doing, and where I was going. Now everything is up in the air. Wherever I'm going, it makes little sense to drag someone else around in the dark with me. He doesn't need awkward Midwest girl or non-cooking roaming chick, or whatever ..."

"What about beautiful, worthy woman?" Tori cut in.

Maya sucked in her lips against the words of her sister-in-law, willing herself to not get emotional.

"I'm canceling," Maya said firmly.

"What?!"

That was Tammy.

"Aw hell."

That was Mac.

"Maya—" Victoria tried to cut in.

"No. I need to stop this before it starts. It isn't fair to him." She pulled her phone out and punched in her text with one hand as she rubbed her other hand along the fussy baby's back.

"Let me see that," Tammy said, snatching the phone away from her and reading the text out loud as her eyes widened in horror.

> "Hey, thanks for the invite tonight. I don't think dinner is a good idea."

"Honey, that is awful," Tammy said, handing the phone back to her, picking up her baby, and settling him in the playpen near the front of the salon.

After a few minutes, it alerted Maya and the rest of the salon to Mike's return message.

"Shit," Maya whispered.

Tammy leaned over her shoulder and again provided an oral transcript.

> "Where are you?"

"I'll ignore it. Wait a while until I can talk."

"I wouldn't do that." Mac warned. "He knows where you live."

"And the town's like eight New York blocks long," Tori chimed in.

"Right," Maya said.

She thought for a moment and then typed something that was friendly and polite. *Send.*

"Last night was super fun. I appreciate your friendship."

Now reading her own text out loud, she felt the eyes of horrified women throughout the whole salon.

"Oh God, that was worse," Tammy said as she shook her dark, glossy head and gave Maya a look of deep disappointment, like she selected a bad dye job or something. She began to blow dry Maya's mass of curls straight.

"I have never heard you utter the phrase 'super fun.'" Tori said. "No actual human has ever said that in actual conversation. Ever."

Ting!

"The fuck? Where are you?" Maya read out loud.

"Does Rough Ridge have a witness protection program?" Mac asked.

"Doesn't matter, he *is* the police," Tammy giggled.

Maya sat there, trying to figure out her head. She sat quietly through the rest of the blowout and as Tammy trimmed her ends.

"Maya, are you okay?" Tori said after a while, sticking her legs straight out so she could see her pedicure past her baby belly.

"It's all good," Maya said quietly. "We'll talk later, and I'll explain."

"Explain what?" a smooth, deep voice behind her asked.

Maya looked at Tammy's eyes in the mirror. Tammy gave her an 'I told you so' eyebrow and turned Maya's chair around to face the voice.

Judas.

Maya cleared her throat. "Hello, Detective Sheppard."

"Detective Sheppard," the wild man repeated.

He looked so out of place in that top to bottom, pink-polka dotted oasis of female beauty it wasn't even funny. His face blazed and his voice had a definite edge.

Maya stood and straightened her shoulders. "Perhaps we should talk outside."

He put his hand on the back of his neck, the other on his hip, and took in a deep breath. Maya didn't think that was a good sign.

"Looks like you've explained plenty to your crew here, so clue me in Maya."

His manliness was overwhelming, especially in the middle of the salon. He looked good and smelled good.[1]

Seriously, how many tight shirts did he own?

"I—I understand what you're trying to do, but it's unnecessary. We don't have to date; we should keep it casual."

"Casual."

The room tensed as Mike's mood darkened considerably. She sucked in a breath and powered through.

"Relationships started under duress rarely work out, Dr. Flemmings said. Until things die down until I figure out ... well ... everything ... I thought we might try out the whole ... friends with benefits thing people do. Maybe it's more like a Fortune 500 benefits package," she rambled, "but you know ... friends."

And for some insane reason, Maya Angel Walters, CEO of M.A. Wall Designs, Phi Beta Kappa, Mensa member, punctuated her remark with ... jazz hands.

"Oh My God. Jazz hands?" Tammy stage whispered.

"Jesus be a fence," Mac muttered.

Mike took two long steps to Maya and grabbed her outstretched hand, yanking her to him, wrapping an arm around her waist, and lightly sliding his other hand up her back to the base of her neck. He got close to her face and spoke in a husky voice tinged with exasperation, "Do you dance with your friends like you danced with me last night?"

"I haven't had a lot of dancing friends so I—"

He squeezed her a little tighter to him, interrupting her.

"No," she breathed out.

"Ever had any friends hold you like I do at night?" he asked, tracing a finger lightly down the side of her face and along her jaw.

"That would be the benefits part," she whispered, sliding her hand up his chest, distracted.

"Any *friend* make you feel on fire the way I do?" he growled low, pressing her even closer.

"C-Suite, golden parachute type benefits," she said as her breathing shallowed.

"Nothin' about us is casual, Sunshine, and you know it. Got a lot of friends, none I want on the back of my bike."

The salon gasped. Mike and Maya ignored them; or the noise didn't register.

"You know what that means?" he asked her.

"I need leather and a helmet? I'm not sure, I don't speak biker."

He chuckled low. "It means you're mine"—he kissed her softly — "and I'm yours." He kissed her gently again. "Tonight. Seven o'clock. No helmet."

"That doesn't sound safe."

She could feel her eyes sting, threatening to spill over. Didn't he understand how awful this would hurt in the end? Her heart thudded in her chest.

Mike tagged her hand and placed it over his heart. Her eyes closed on their own briefly, opening again when he spoke.

"I trust you with mine. You trust me with yours, everything else we go for the ride. Starting at seven."

He bent and kissed her once more on the lips, then stepped back. He looked over.

"Sorry to interrupt Tammy. Mac. Tori." He nodded, giving her a small grin.

Mike then nodded to the room at large. "Ladies." And strode out.

When the door closed, a collective sigh and shudder traveled through the salon. Maya was still standing in the same spot with her hand pressed to her lips. He made it seem so simple ...

"Somebody take her pulse," Tammy called, laughing. "I think she's flatlined!"

------

1. I Belong to You by Lenny Kravitz

26

EVERYTHING YOU ARE

MAYA

At 6:50 p.m., Maya was in the middle of a freak out. At 6:55 p.m., she took a puff of inhaler and at 6:59 p.m.; she crammed M&M's in her mouth, trying not to get them on her white dress. Then, she spit them out and swished water around her mouth to make sure she didn't have candy in her teeth. At 7 p.m. on the nose, there was a knock at the door. She weighed her options, including pretending she moved to Argentina. At 7 p.m. and eleven seconds, Maya took a deep breath, said a quick prayer, and opened the door.

Maya had a visceral reaction to Mike standing in the doorway. *Is it possible to look at a man and get pregnant? ... Again?*

He wore a crisp, white button-down shirt open at the collar, dark rinse jeans, and a navy blazer. The white shirt popped against his tanned skin — and the wild man had been tamed. His goatee, neatly trimmed, and long, wayward hair pulled off his shoulders with an elastic made one hell of an impression.

Maya always thought the whole "Man Bun" thing was contrived. Few pulled it off without looking like pretentious Instagram pretty boys, but Mike should give a class. The style made his square jaw more pronounced and his eyes more striking. He was simply raw man magnificence.

"My God, you're beautiful," she said.

Mike blinked, his face registering shock and then a tenderness she'd never seen before. He grabbed her by her waist and brought her close to him. Sliding his hands up her sides, glancing over her breasts, and ending by cupping her face, he said in his quiet voice, "You're proof."

"Of what?"

"That God exists."

It was Maya's turn to be shocked. She lost purchase on her feet, leaning all the way into him. She pulled his mouth to hers and they lost themselves in each other. After what seemed like a lifetime, he groaned and finally pulled away.

"You keep kissing me like that we won't make it to dinner," he teased.

"You keep kissing me like that and I won't care."

He smiled big and chuckled, but stepped back. "Let's go, Sunshine."

"Wait, so am I wearing this or that?" she asked, pointing to the bed.

He took in her white, form-fitting dress with a thin, deep v in the front displaying a tantalizing glimpse of her well-rounded cleavage. The dress had long billowing bell sleeves, and the skirt hit right at her knee, highlighting her shapely silhouette.

Her hair, blown straight, hung long and swept to the side, covering one of his love bites on her neck. She wore dramatic smokey makeup, simple earrings at her ears, and a wide, polished silver cuff at her wrist.

"There's an alternative to this?"

"Well, yeah. You said back of your bike, so I didn't know if that started right now with a bike or..."

Mike threw back his head and roared with laughter. She grinned and wanted to laugh too but preferred watching him. His green eyes danced as he looked over to the bed at the alternative outfit. His eyes roamed over skinny, black leather pants that laced from the ankle to the waist for her growing belly. She ordered them on a whim while she hid in the store after the diner fight with Mike. She also ordered black, thick heeled motorcycle boots and a scrap of black suede with a sunburst embossed onto it. Darts in the front formed under the bust, and laces that crisscrossed the back, held it together. It was a top, in the sense it covered the necessities, but it was far and away different from what Maya normally wore. It was biker chick cool.

"Damn." Deep in thought, he looked from her to the bed and back again. He rubbed his goateed chin and said, "I'll make love to you in that dress tonight and when we wake up, I'll take you on a ride so you can wear that"—he pointed to the leather outfit — "then I'll fuck you in the top and boots. Yeah … that'll work. Let's go eat." He nodded his head and clapped his hands together like he'd solved world hunger while Maya struggled to keep her panties dry.

"I—uh—shoes," she said as her mind whirled at his announcement/solution. She sank into the chair by the door and bent to pick up her white peep-toe booties with a spiked silver heel when Mike took the shoe from her hand and, after kissing each foot, he slipped each shoe on. She was jelly-kneed before, and now she'd lost all the bones in her spine.

She rose with as much grace as she could muster, with jelly knees and a spine of goo, and took one last glimpse in the mirror. Normally, she'd stare at her belly and smile, but her face fell as she met Mike's eyes in the mirror. "I'm starting to show."

"A little. It's cute, and you look amazing Sunshine."

"People will think it's yours."

Understanding crossed over his face. "I don't have a problem with that."

"If this doesn't work out—"

"Maya," he said, coming close to her back, his eyes never leaving hers in the mirror, "I don't know what's in the future, but darlin' I'm here and I'm not going anywhere. When I said you're mine, I meant it and that includes…" He paused as he pressed a gentle, but firm hand over her little rounded belly, " … everything you are and all you bring, including that beautiful baby girl you're carrying."

Her eyes closed, and she sucked in a breath, trying to steady herself. She finally spoke out loud one of the million things she feared.

"Is this about Tina and Abbie?" He tightened around her. "I don't want to be a substitute," she said in a rush. Her eyes were still closed as she readied herself to receive his response.

"Maya, look at me."

Her eyes opened slowly and focused on him.

"There isn't anything you can't ask, nothing from me to fear. I don't lie and I don't keep secrets. I must keep discretion in my work, but my life, to you, is open."

She turned and looked him in his eyes.

"I'm afraid of this. Of so much ... "[1]

"I know, honey." He ran his hands through her hair, watching it fall around his hand and arm. He looked back at her and said quietly, "I loved Tina and Abbie with everything I had. When I lost them, I squandered years looking for something, anything, to fill the hole. Women, work, adrenaline, anything ... The only thing that helped was time."

He took her face in his hands and brought his face to hers, whispering against her lips. "I wanted you the moment I looked in your truck window. The first time you called me an asshole, I knew you were for me. When you flipped me the bird, I wanted to give you babies. And I knew I wanted to cherish you for the rest of my life when you looked into my eyes and tried to get my head out of my ass outside the grocery store. This is fast, babe, and I know it's not like anything either of us has been through before. But for me, Maya baby, it's you. This is right for us, and I'm done bullshittin.' I'm not playing it cool or anything else people do to waste time so they can feel like they checked a box on a relationship scorecard. You gotta know, Sunshine, you could never be anyone's substitute. You're it for me."

Maya sucked in a breath and clutched his hands at her face.

"Can we start with dinner before we get to forever?"

Mike kissed her and chuckled. "We can but heads up— forever started the moment I saw you."

---

1. The Only One for Me by Bryan McKnight

27
A HEIFER

MAYA

"Sunshine, wait!"

It was too late. She leaped out of the Jeep in awe, taking care not to trip in her heels. It didn't dawn on her to wait for Mike to open her door. She scrambled to the front of a large wood and glass structure designed to appear like it grew naturally out of the forest floor, then kissed by architect fairies.

The Treehouse was *literally* a treehouse made of wood with floor-to-ceiling glass windows and a partial glass roof. The two-story structure — built high between eight huge, closely grouped trees — extended on stilts into the side of the mountain.

"Oh, I should have brought my sneakers," Maya cried as she took off underneath the structure, with Mike moving quickly to keep pace with her.

She observed the fairy light-lined, wood-planked path that weaved through the forest and back to the restaurant, and ran her hands over the support beams, making mental notes the whole time. Then she bent at the knee to study the railing of one of the two staircases that wound in a circular fashion up the side of the building. A clever combination of iron, wood, and repurposed branches gave the illusion the branches grew together to form the rail. It was beautiful and solid.

Maya paused when they reached the landing of the outdoor dining area, smiling at the retractable leafy canopy awning before continuing to the main floor of the restaurant.

The crisp white linens, fresh mountain flower arrangements, and sparkling glasses popped against the natural wood finish of the structure and its furniture. Maya especially liked the green napkins. They looked like leaves that had floated down to the tables just in time for dinner.

As they walked through the entrance, Maya loved the sense of comfort and hushed intimacy. The restaurant balanced between a "one with nature vibe" and understated glamour.

Mike seemed content to watch Maya as her eyes moved over the building from ceiling to floor, taking in the large trees growing through the center of the two-story building. She was delighted when he asked the hostess for brochures that shared more information about the creation of the famed almost local restaurant. She grinned big and slid them into her clutch, drawing herself closer to Mike and slipping her hand into his.

This would have been a good time to at least start with "I'm an architect." But she chickened out when she noticed Tank Ass Snyder at the restaurant.

She'd lost the blue velour sweats of the grocery store and instead, opted for a skin-tight black velvet dress for the evening. Her fresh and severely dyed blonde hair curled in tight ringlets that reminded Maya of an old movie about a former child star who wouldn't let go of her babyhood fashion of ringlets and painted doll face, even though in her elderly years it took on a gouache, menacing appearance. Her eyes widened when she saw Mike and narrowed when she saw Maya.

"Oh dear," Maya started speaking low. "She rubs up against you again I get to kick her in the kneecaps."

"That's assault, baby."

"Of you or her?" Maya shot back, her voice full of humor.

Mike's body shook with repressed laughter as they followed behind the hostess to their booth. Maya had experienced her choice of fine dining and an array of interesting, dazzling, and infamous business dinner partners, but none of them, not even Griffin, when their relationship was new, made her feel the way she felt with Mike. She'd never looked forward to and feared an evening as much as this on.[1]

After they placed their drink orders, Mike took Maya's hand, looked her deep in the eyes, and said, "You sing like a sick cat."

Maya's eyes grew wide with shock and then she quirked her brow. "You have never heard me sing!"

"Sweetheart, every morning, you fire up your phone and get to wailing. Every evening when you drive up to your room, the windows are down and you're howling. Blake said it was more like a wet cat. I'll take his word for it."

Maya nearly doubled over in laughter. "It's true. I can't carry a tune in a bucket," she said with a shrug. "But you have to sing along to good music. It's the law of the universe. I try not to disturb anyone—too much."

"Something the great Maya Anderson can't do," he said as he sat back with a slow, sexy grin. "It's a miracle. Beautiful, you can dance your ass off, fix cars, and make me smile. Regina said you make a mean bar mix. With all of that, it's nice to know you're human."

"Oh, I'm extra human, if that's possible. Seems like I spent a large part of my life out of sync with everyone else. I'm socially awkward. I say things I shouldn't say all the time and I don't cook well, which people seem to think means I should turn in my woman card."

"With you taking care of your mom, I thought you'd cook more."

She played with his fingers in hers. "No time. We ate restaurant food, healthy stuff, mostly vegan for my mom. I had a deal to tutor the owner's kids in exchange for meals for years. It made things easier. I make two things well - baked beans and potato salad - and my lasagna is ok. Do you cook?"

"I—"

"Maya!"

Maya looked up to see Mace, and who she figured was his wife, Shannon, making their way toward them.

Oh shit.

Maya masked her anxiety by greeting the couple. Shannon looked gorgeous in a little black dress with her dirty blonde hair swept in a low bun and Mace ever dapper in dark slacks, button down and leather jacket. And were those? Yep, suspenders.

"Good to see you, gorgeous," Mace said softly in her ear before looking over at Mike with a friendly smile and cautious brown eyes.

Maya introduced the couple to Mike, and Mike gave a small, but easy smile as he greeted them.

Shannon sat across from Mike and Maya and gestured for Mace to do the same.

Mace sighed, dropped his body in a seat, and shrugged apologetically. "She has no boundaries."

"I simply want to chat up Miss Maya and her male friend here and get to know them a bit," she said, cheerfully dismissive to her husband. "I've been back home settling my family's estate, so I've missed out on almost everything happening here." Turning to Mike, she smiled and tilted her head a bit. "You know you should think about changing your name. There was a horrific man that lived in Rough Ridge a while ago—"

"Yeah, I know. Imagine being his kid," Mike interrupted with a small, self-deprecating smile.

Mace dropped his head back to stare at the ceiling. "Shoot me now, love."

Shannon flushed red as a tomato. "Oh, damnable hell. I—"

"Don't worry about it." Mike waved it off. "I'm used to it."

"No, that was an appallingly rude thing to say," Shannon said, reaching out to place her hand on his. "I deeply, deeply apologize."

Mike turned his hand to squeeze hers and responded sincerely, "Darlin', it's okay. The truth is the truth, but thank you. Don't give it another thought. How about a glass of wine?"

Mike signaled their server and ordered two selections from the wine list. The conversation turned lighter after, with Mike turning on the charm to make sure Shannon felt at ease.

While things were going well, Maya excused herself to visit the ladies' room.

As she returned, her ears peaked as a sweet, teasing, and lustful voice carried above the din of conversation.

"Mike Sheppard, as I live and breathe, I never thought we would see you back this way," the voice said.

Maya observed the woman attached to the voice - tall, thin, with long, gleaming chestnut hair, wearing an impeccably tailored dress. Her face was interesting, with wide-set eyes and a full, pouty mouth Maya suspected she wasn't born with. She looked like she'd stepped off the runway straight into the restaurant.

Suddenly, Maya was self-conscious. She wished she could pass it off on pregnancy hormones, but Michael was an incredibly handsome man. Women were always doing a double-take when they saw him, and she was on track to be whale-like sooner than later.

Old feelings came to the surface. She was back to being the youngest, most awkward kid in the class all over again, with poofy hair, a flat chest, and a brain so big that even the smart kids didn't want to hang with her. She upped the ante with a mom dying of cancer, which was a social calendar killer if ever there was one.

As she got closer, Michael caught her eyes, and in them, she saw desire and pride. She had his full attention. She gave him a small smile, shy about being the source of his intense focus. Inside, she was doing a goofy dance in celebration. As she walked, she stole a glance at one of the floor-to-ceiling windows and the woman looking back at her was pretty fucking fantastic.

That's right, I am Maya Freakin Walk- uh- Anderson.

Her smile broadened, and she brightened as she walked the rest of the way to the table. Mike stood and reached out a hand to her.

Sigh. I could walk to him forever.

"Sarah Beth, I'd like you to meet my Maya," Mike said in that quiet, smooth voice of his.

HIS Maya. Sigh of a thousand sighs.

Mike placed his hand casually on Maya's hip as she reached out her hand to Sarah Beth for a handshake.

"Hello Sarah Beth, I'm Maya."

Sarah Beth swept her from top to toe slowly and clearly was not pleased.

"Charmed," she uttered with a simpering smile that was as fake as her lips, still never taking Maya's hand.

Maya dropped her hand and looked over at Shannon and Mace. Shannon's eyes were wide, then she rolled them so hard Maya worried about them falling out of her head. It made her grin, and she aimed that grin back at Sarah Beth, who apparently inherited her mother's sensibilities.

"Sarah Beth, that's a beautiful dress and you look amazing in it," Maya said, still making a decent effort.

"Vera Wang. I modeled for her in Paris."

She *was* a model. Of course.

"And yours is cute as well," she continued. "Is that Prada? Last season I suppose."

This bitch.

Mike's hand clenched at her hip. Maya could tell he was not pleased. Sarah Beth either missed or ignored the shift in his mood.

Maya, relaxing more, threw out a dismissive hand. "I never pay attention to that sort of thing. When it's made for you, it's timeless." She leaned into Sarah Beth conspiratorially and added, "Plus, when you have a man that looks at you the way Michael looks at me in this dress, you'd be a fool not to wear it. Right, baby?" she asked as she tipped her head back and to the side to look at him.

Mike looked down at Maya and his own body relaxed as he tried to hold in laughter. He bent down and kissed her. "Right, babe," he said against her lips.

"Of course, I've always admired plus-size women who have learned to embrace their 'curves.' You carry off the pooch well."

"Bi–" Shannon started before Mace covered her mouth as she geared up.

Maya wasn't exactly plus-sized, but the fact this chick acted like it was an insult to be plus, thick, curvy, fat or whatever pissed Maya and Shannon both off, and Shannon wouldn't stand for it. Before Shannon could jump in, Maya simply smiled wide.

"Thank you so much. I worried about wearing this dress because I'm showing, but not enough for it to be an obvious baby bump. Lucky for me, Michael can't get enough of me. You know what they say, 'once you go Black...'"

Mace turned red with laughter; Shannon raised her wine glass in agreement while Mike slid his hand protectively across Maya's stomach. She threaded her fingers through his as he bent to chuckle into her neck from behind.

"It was great to meet you, Susan."

"Sarah."

"Right," Maya said, smiling as she slid into the booth.

Mike slid in beside Maya as Sarah formulated her parting shot.

"Bon coupoeil à cette Mike," she said in an affected French accent as she waved.

"I'm sorry?" Maya asked, her face icy. Shannon joined her in, staring.

Sarah Beth repeated the phrase slowly, like Maya was a child. Her eyes catty with a hint of a smirk playing on her lips, she lied to Maya's face.

"It means 'be happy.'"

"No. It does not," Maya countered and in perfect French replied, "Bon coupoeil à cette, means 'good luck with that.' Soyez heureux means 'be happy.' You truly must be careful with the translation and indeed pronunciation, otherwise the French will think you are a bubble-headed, American twat." She shrugged as if they were girl-friends.

"If you are truly happy for him, Sandra, you might say 'Il n'y a qu' un bonheur dans la vie, c'est d'aimer et d'être aimé,' which means 'There is only one happiness in life: to love and be loved.' Or even simply, 'Félicitations à vous,' which means congratulations. 'Bon coupoeil à cette' could be interpreted to mean you are less than thrilled with his relationship with me, which, I know, you would never be that rude and make yourself look like a—"

"A heifer,'" Shannon cut in.

"Right." Maya confirmed, "'A heifer.' Great to meet you again. Sheila."

"Sarah."

"Right."

Sarah turned and runway stomped away, which in a real-life setting, was odd as hell. Shannon laughed hard. Mace shook his head, grinning, and Mike threw his arm around Maya and pulled her to him. He touched his forehead to hers and asked in his low voice, "Are you okay?"

"Yeah."

"Sunshine."

"Ok, it was like a quick trip through the bad parts of high school and college again, but I'll survive."

"Survive?" Mace rasped. "You roasted the woman. Where did you learn to speak French?"

"In France, I was there on an internship," Maya said quietly. Mace took in her change in demeanor and glanced briefly at Mike.

"Aretu vas bien?" Shannon asked, like she was sharing a joke.

"Bien entendu," Maya replied with a strained smile.

"Mace honey, sitting across from these sexy people it feels like a tequila and reverse cowgirl night," Shannon declared loudly. "Order shots." She winked at Maya.

Maya relaxed, realizing even though Mace likely hadn't told his wife everything, she saw a fellow woman in need and distracted the table from her. She settled into observing their interaction, avoiding eye contact with Mike.

The rest of dinner continued without incident, with delicious food, great conversation, and laughs. Mike won over a cautious Mace and Shannon. In turn, they learned a lot about Mace and Shannon's courtship. It started with a testy road rage incident followed by high stakes drama in which Shannon saved Mace's company from corporate sabotage and Mace rescued Shannon from being lost in the woods during a storm. Their relationship moved quickly and before anyone noticed, they were married with a baby on the way.

Maya saw a pattern among these mountain dudes - grumpily meet a woman, claim her, and waste no time getting her onboard and in bed.

Hmmm...

She also reflected on the wisdom of Shannon's words as she sat next to Mike in the Jeep on the way home. *"Sometimes you're so worried about it making sense, you miss that it's right."*

Mike held Maya's hand as he drove and yes, it felt so right, but clearly, none of it made any sense. Rational Maya turned it all over in her head - so fast, so intense. Maya was a realist. Life was lines and curves. Perfection took time, patience, and research. Relationships took the same, especially after the colossal disaster that was her last one. Maya planned life and worked according to the plan.

But you're not on a plan or schedule now, are you? Her petty inner monologue reminded her. *And you're living more than you have in a long time...*

"How long did you study in France?" Mike asked, sending Maya's thoughts to the wind.

"A year." She hoped she sounded relaxed. *Tell him.*

"And you learned French so well in that short amount of time?"

"I took a bit in college in anticipation," she replied, tighter.

My name is Maya Walters. My brother is Caine Walters, the one your dad framed for murder ... Shit. Nope. Don't say that.

"Still, you have a gift for languages."

"Mmm ... Something like that."

MIKE

Talking to Maya about her life outside of Rough Ridge was like interviewing a freaked-out witness. It killed him that he needed to tiptoe around her life like this, but he recognized going slow was important to gain her trust. Once he had it, he would make sure the man who hurt her paid for it.

He promised himself he wouldn't touch the file his contacts had gathered on Maya until she let him in, but it was hard. Every day he passed it on his desk. If he moved on the information, she would see it as a violation of her privacy. A violation of her right to reveal her life to him. But he wasn't stupid enough not to have the information on hand in case something went wrong.

A beat ...

"What were your favorite places and things to do while you were there?" he asked, moving her to a safer conversation. She relaxed and became more animated as she described all the people she'd met, the funny little quirks of her neighbors, and the hidden gems she'd discovered.

She sounded wistful when she talked about exploring the French countryside.

"It's everything people describe and more." She sighed.

"You miss it."

"I do. I didn't realize how much until now. You should go on the off-season or anytime. It's beautiful no matter what. Off season, it's quiet. Everyone's friendly and once they get to know you, they fall in love with you forever."

"I think that happened because you're you, Sunshine," Mike responded with a low chuckle.

"I went to school for architecture."

His hand in hers flinched slightly, and the whole car held its breath. Metal, and human alike.

---

1. Boo'd Up by Ella Mai

28

THE WORST HOTEL EVER

MAYA

Maya studied his profile, completely taken by his warm heart. How was it possible to seem so connected to someone so quickly? She looked at his rough hand in hers as best as she could see in the dark car, making out silvery lines of healed cuts across his knuckles. Gosh, she even liked his knuckles. The half-circle scoop of his cuticles, the rounded curve of his nail. She pulled his hand to her mouth almost unconsciously and kissed it. Softly, as soft as his hand was rough.

His eyes were on her. When he turned back toward the road, she spoke.

"Yep, I went to school for architecture." *Baby steps, breathe.*

Mike cleared his throat. "Your love of buildings ... "

"Since I was a little kid. I love math and art ... it's what I did. That's why I was in France."

"Amazing opportunity for you."

She was grateful he wasn't pressing, letting her go at her pace. *God, he was wonderful.*

"I still have friends there, though I haven't seen them in years."

"You ever go back?"

"For work," she said tightly. "Never enough time to visit, though."

"You worked a lot before moving here. What did you do to relax?"

"Work was relaxing. Well, mostly, but when I wasn't working, I read about people doing it better and thought about how I could be a better architect and business owner. I worked out, had a non-work-related dinner occasionally, but I'm most comfortable at home ... Damn, that sounds boring."

"Not boring Maya, focused."

"To the point of boring." She snorted. "I'm from Ohio. My town has tons of things going on all the time. I missed a lot of it being so focused."

"Ohio - the heart of it all." Mike muttered a tourism slogan for the state. "And that explains the Buckeye obsession."

"I bleed Scarlet and Gray. 'O-H-I-O!'" she bellowed, doing the hand gestures known around the world.

"You're so damn adorable."

Mike's phone vibrated across the dash and Maya reached out, swiped across the screen and held it to Mike's ear, whispering, "At least I have clothes on right now."

Mike grinned when he answered, "Sheppard."

His smile froze, then died, and he took his hand off her thigh and pressed it to the phone. Her delicious meal started roiling in her belly.

"How long?" he bit out.

She sat up straighter, checking to see how close they were to Rough Ridge, as the restaurant was an hour away from town. They were about ten minutes out.

"There in an hour," he clipped and tossed the phone onto the dash.

She waited for him to speak. The mood in the Jeep continued to darken, and he struggled with control, the muscle in his jaw jumping.

"My sister..."

Maya's throat got a familiar lump, and she swallowed, trying to push past it.

"Is she..."

"Not much time left."

"Heart, I'm so sorry. How long will it take us to get there?"

He glanced at her briefly then turned back to the road.

"I'm taking you home."

Maya was confused.

"But ... "

"Your mom died of cancer; you've done this hospice shit. I'm not putting you through that again."

"Heart honey, this isn't something you do alone."

"No."

The finality in his tone meant there was no further discussion. She didn't like it, but she didn't argue. She took his warm, rough hand in hers and held it tight until they arrived outside the motel.

Mike pulled up to Maya's room door and lifted her out like he always did. He placed her gently on her feet next to him, took her keys and, still holding her hand, opened the door to her room. After hitting the lights, he scanned the room. He walked in, stopped to move her sneakers out of the way, then walked through the room to the bathroom. Satisfied the space was secure, he came back to her, taking her face in his hands.

"My beautiful Ohio girl who studied architecture," he whispered.

His eyes swept her face. He leaned in and kissed her nose, then her lips softly. "My talented, French speaking girl, thank you for tonight," he whispered against her lips, kissing her again.

She placed her hand on his heart. "Please, let me come with you."

"Baby, I'm protecting you. You don't know what effect going will have on you and you've been through enough." He took a hand off her face and placed it on her belly. "Both of you have. Stay here. I'll call you. I promise."

He kissed her again and walked out the door. He stood on the other side until she locked the door's top lock, then he moved to his own room. She was still standing in the same spot when the Jeep engine started about five minutes later.

Maya remained there another minute as she allowed her brain to go back several years.

The scent of her mother's room at the hospice care facility came back to her—lavender and antiseptic. She remembered the beeping of machines, the hiss wheeze of the oxygen and footfalls of busy hospice staff outside the door. Her mother, frail and fading, appeared like a mirage in front of her. The overwhelming loneliness hit her again — a weighted blanket drawing her shoulders down, bowing her back. Maya gritted her teeth as she remembered how she wished for someone outside the nursing staff and the occasional friend to be there. How she wished for family.

As the memories, tough, but dulled with time, flashed through her mind, one theme stood out: she'd endured her mother's death - alone. The preparations - alone. The funeral - alone. The return to their home - alone. Sorting through her mother's things - alone. Utterly. Painfully. Alone. People were there of course, but there weren't many deep connections. She oversaw it all, and it was the hardest job she'd ever done.

Maya dropped into the chair beside her door with a heavy shudder and snatched off her two-hundred-dollar shoes like they were flip-flops. She dug into her clutch, looking for her phone, and called Tori. Then she called Jake.

It took two seconds for Maya to toss her four-hundred-dollar dress on the floor, and six minutes to throw on a bra, tee, and jeans; stuff a couple of changes of clothes and her prenatal vitamins into her big bag; swipe makeup wipes across her eyes and face; grab a significant amount of cash from her stash and slip on her running shoes. She was on the phone with Ms. Shirley, giving her a heads up as she swung out of the parking lot. As she hit the town limits, she requested Siri to get her directions to Denver because there was no way she would let Michael endure the hell that was to come alone.

THE DRIVE to Denver was a blur. His hands were sore from gripping the steering wheel. During the drive, his mind tumbled with memories from his childhood. He and Rose playing explorers, spending hours in the forest looking for treasure. Rose pointing out edible plants as they tried to lose themselves outside to avoid going home. Rose singing to him. Her giving him all her meager savings from her dead-end job so he could go to school. He blinked up at the hospice care facility and choked back the emotion threatening to freeze him to his seat. Willing himself to move, Mike stepped out into the night.

HE WALKED into the room bracing, he thought, for whatever he would find.

He still wasn't ready.[1]

His big sister lay in the bed, machines all around her. She looked small, frail, and so pale she was translucent. Only a few wispy strands of her thick, beautiful, dark brown hair around her hairline remained. She had no eyebrows or lashes, but for the first time in weeks, her eyes were open and remarkably clear. Beautiful green eyes twinkled when she noticed him.

"Mikey," she said, her voice hoarse and weak.

"Rosey-Cakes."

He gave her a grin he didn't own, walked over to her, and sat on her bed, placing one hand on the outside of her legs. They were mere bones under the blankets.

"How's my beautiful big sister?"

"Great Mikey, except I'm dyin', darlin'." She pulled a half smile. "Figures. I get clear up here," she used her eyes to indicate her brain, "and it's at the end of everything."

When Mike dropped his eyes, she moved her hand to cover his. It was cooler than he expected.

"I heard them talkin', but I figured it out a while back," she smiled. "So many code blues in this joint, it was either a place you come to die or the worst hotel ever."

Mike laughed out loud at her joke, even though it hurt. It HURT. For so long, his sister wasn't herself. Now her mind reconnected for what would likely be only hours.

MAYA

Mike's laughter led her to the room number Jake gave her. She rocked back on her heels a moment, then smiled to herself, glad he'd found something to laugh about. Her plan was to wait for him outside of the room. To listen for when he let out what she thought of as 'The Sigh.'

The Sigh happened when activity stopped for a moment and you looked around, spent. The Sigh sometimes came before a panic about what was to come. Other times it came after a scare, or in the middle of the night when sleep was elusive. It was always there. She heard it in the rooms she walked past tonight, just like she'd heard eight years ago. It was the outward exhalation of inner agony.

As she stood outside the door waiting to get a nurse's attention, she heard what must have been Rose's voice.

"Mikey?"

"Yeah Rosey-Cakes?"

"I want Momma's rosary. You know, the one with the beads that smell like roses? She always said the Pope blessed it."

"Ok Rosey, I'll get it," Mike replied, his voice rough and thick.

"Thanks Mikey," Rose said weakly as she yawned.

Mike called in the nurse to ask if there was time. It would be at least a two hour round trip and Maya sensed they were getting close before the nurse confirmed her suspicions to Mike. Her heart broke when he thanked the nurse, his voice wrought with emotion.

Maya turned on her heel and took off toward the lobby. She thought about it for about point three seconds before she hit his name. He answered on the second ring.

"Mace? It's Maya, I need a big favor of the not legal variety, but it's for a good reason and then I need you to tell the cops after you do it - well, Paul."

"This should be good," Mace sighed into the phone.

MAYA

Maya paced back and forth in front of the Sunrise Hospice Care building, waiting for a local officer to deliver the rosary. Maya explained the situation to Mace, knowing that not having a key to the Sheppard home wouldn't pose a problem. He located the rosary and Paul arranged for a uniformed officer to take it, lights flashing, to a waiting highway patrol officer who relayed it to a waiting Denver officer. The officer called a few moments ago to say he was close.

The whole transaction took maybe forty-five minutes, with Mace and Paul getting out of their beds and leaving their families to help. While she waited outside, Maya used her phone to order them all enormous bouquets of roses and large bottles of premium hooch. Now she waited on an Officer Joshua S. Greatt - his real name.

Mike still didn't realize she was there, and the nursing staff kept her extreme delivery efforts quiet. It was on the fourth or fifth pass in front of the building that she saw the flashing lights. It surprised her to see an unmarked SUV with lights on the dash. A tall, handsome Latino man folded himself out of the SUV with eyes on her. He was wearing a black button-down, black blazer, black jeans and leather Converse. He might have been a year or two older than her.

"Are you Maya?"

Maya ran to him in relief, threw her arms around his waist, and hugged tight. There was lots of muscle and resistance before she came to her senses and backed off the poor man.

"Officer Greatt I hope? Otherwise, this is embarrassing."

"Detective Greatt, though not for long," he replied.

She took in his dark eyes, chiseled jaw and close-cropped black hair and asked the obvious.

"Leaving for a modeling gig?"

"Becoming a firefighter," he said, his mouth drawing into a lazy half grin. Freakin' Colorado.

Maya's eyes moved to his hands, where he was withdrawing a small velvet bag from his front shirt pocket. Her eyes welled up.

"Thank you," she whispered. And to her surprise, he handed her a real-life handkerchief as the tears spilled over.

"I'm sorry. I should get back in there," Maya mumbled in between sniffs.

"I'll walk with you," he said, and steered her with a sure, steady hand back through the doors. Maya had been in and out so often in the last hour the front desk automatically buzzed her in.

When she arrived at Rose Marie's door, she stopped again. She trembled as her own memories came back, and she became worried about Michael's reaction to her being there. Detective Greatt placed a firm hand on her shoulder.

Maya focused on his patient, dark eyes as he leaned down.

"Take a breath."

Doing as she was told, she used that moment to fortify herself as she eased the door open with a light tap of her fingernails.

"I have your mother's rosary," Maya said softly as Mike's head whipped around to her, his eyes unreadable. She swallowed hard and forced herself to move her eyes off him to his sister, who was awake.

"You look like an angel," Rose Marie said to Maya with a smile. The bright hallway light shined around Maya, who was dressed in a white tee and jeans. "Though don't reckon God makes angels with bodies like that."

Maya's eyes grew wide at the unknowing mention of her middle name, and she pressed her hand to her mouth, trying to stop the laugh from the mischievous expression on Mike's sister's face. Her body shaking, she couldn't stop a snort from escaping.

"A woman with a sense of humor," Rose Marie hoarsely forced out. "You should ask her out, Mikey."

"Already did, Rosey darlin'," he said with a smile and a small shake of his head.

"Smart cookie."

Maya crossed the room to Mike and pressed the small pouch into his hand.

"I'll be right outside if you need me."

"Mikey, can you pray the rosary with me?"

"I don't ... I don't remember how," Mike replied softly, his voice cracking.

"Oooh Mikey, Momma would tan your hide," she replied, her weak laugher followed by quick, shallow breaths.

"Angel?" she called softly, stopping Maya's retreat. "You think you could find someone who knows how to do this?"

Maya looked from Mike to Rose Marie, whose hand clutched the pouch tight. Maya nodded as she moved further into the room.

"Ten years of Catholic school. I could do an entire mass if I needed to."

Rose Marie offered another weak smile as Maya walked to the other side of the bed opposite Mike. He moved to grab her a chair, but Maya shook her head no, slid a chair quietly to the bed on her own and sat down. She nodded toward the bed.

"You're allowed to climb in with her. It helps if you turn on your side. More room."

Mike looked at her for a long moment. Careful of the monitors and tubing attached to Rose Marie, he slid onto the bed and gently tucked her to him.

"I used to hold you like this when you had bad dreams or when daddy was in a fit, remember?"

"I remember Rosey-Cakes," he replied, stroking her arm softly.

Maya slid open the small, wine-colored velvet pouch embroidered with the seal of the Pope in gold thread. She unfurled the rosary and carefully straightened it out. She placed part of it in Rose Marie's open hand and held it partially in her own. The scent of roses filled her nose as Maya made the sign of the cross and prayed. Rose Marie settled in and closed her eyes.

MIKE

For close to two hours Maya prayed with and for his sister - a woman she'd never met before today - with all the love and compassion she could give. During that time, Mike realized Maya made several calls, including to Jake and Blake. When both men walked in, Rose Marie's eyes opened briefly, and she gave the barest hint of a smile.

"Hey."

"Hey, darlin'," Blake whispered.

She smiled again, closed her eyes, and when she squeezed Maya's hand, Maya continued praying. The men settled in quietly, standing sentry over the soul preparing to leave the world.

After a while, a nurse came in as Rose Marie's breathing became more labored, rattling in her chest. The nurse ran through her routine checks and Maya waited to make eye contact with her.

It would be soon.

The nurse placed her hand softly on Mike's shoulder and stepped away. When the priest arrived, Maya ended the Hail Mary prayer she was on and closed Rose Marie's hand around the rosary, placing it on her chest. A chest that was rising and falling with breaths that grew more shallow with each pass.

She moved out of the way as the priest began offering words of comfort, support and prayer for everlasting life. As the priest ended his prayer, Mike began whispering sweet memories against his sister's ear. His beautiful, broken champion. She was the first one to tell him to get the hell out of Rough Ridge and never look back.

"You were my first love, Rosey-Cakes. No one was smarter or more beautiful. It was you and Momma, remember? I told you I was gonna marry you both, and we'd live in a tree house. You asked me where you would put all your shoes..."

Inhale ... exhale.

"When it got bad, you'd sing Ave Maria and I would concentrate on your voice and not the yelling ... "

Inhale ...... exhale.

"You gave me peace, Rosey-Cakes."

Inhale. .... exhale.

"Say hi to Momma darlin'."

Inhale. .... exhale.

Maya moved to silence the heart monitor. She watched as the seconds between the blips on the screen stretched until the long single line signaled his beautiful sister was gone.

The hospice staff entered and confirmed through quiet whispers his fragile sister was free.

He put a soft, reverent kiss on her temple, closed his eyes and prayed. "Our Father, who art in heaven ... "

---

1. 1. Cancer by Twenty One Pilots

29

SOMEONE WALKING OVER YOUR GRAVE

MAYA

Maya looked down at her phone and clocked the time - it was going on one in the afternoon. She'd been awake for well over 24 hours. She yawned and looked around the hotel room. At first, she thought Tori had gone a little overboard with the reservation, especially for two people who lived in motel rooms. The two-room suite was gorgeous with a sleek modern living room area - smoke gray couches, bamboo and glass accents, and beautiful, black and white photography of the mountains.

Those same beautiful mountains greeted her courtesy of the floor-to-ceiling windows along two of the walls. A huge California King bed boasted thick Egyptian cotton sheets and large plush pillows over the top of an exquisite slate gray duvet. It was an oasis, and the more she thought about it, the more she realized Victoria had the right idea. A quiet, beautiful place to retreat, reflect and prepare.

She looked over her to-do list, scratched out on hotel stationery, and reflected on the morning. When Rose Marie slipped from this life, it left Mike with the business side of death. He completed much of the preparation when he first arrived back in Colorado, so there were only little details left, such as when the body would arrive in Rough Ridge, what day to hold the service (Wednesday), and whether the family would use a limo - that was a big fat no. Turned out Rose was a Harley babe and Mike would ride his to the service in her honor.

Still, those little details, and the surrounding discussion, took a lot out of Mike. Maya helped where it made sense, which was why she sat in front of her laptop, shopping for burial attire for Rose. The funeral home never communicated to Mike that clothes for her burial were necessary. Once Maya emailed her selections for Rose Marie and something dark for herself to the personal shopper at the mall, she checked off the second to last item on her list.

Her phone vibrated in her hand. Well, vibrated again. It had been going off all day. Maya coordinated everything via text with her friends back in Rough Ridge. Mike finally agreed to rest for a few hours, and she didn't want him disturbed. Especially not for calls about flowers and potato salad.

MACE: ROOF LEAK AT THE SHEPPARD HOME. NOT BAD YET, BUT SHIT MIGHT GET MESSED UP.

MAYA: DARN IT. OK. I'LL RESEARCH MOVERS, CLEANERS.

MACE: SECURITY COMPANY FOR PAPERWORK, ETC.

MAYA: GOOD CALL GENIUS (LOL)

MACE: POT. KETTLE.

MAYA: TOUCHÉ ...

MAYA: THNX FOR YOUR HELP. IT MADE A DIFFERENCE TO HER; SHE HAD PEACE.

MACE: NO THANKS NEEDED. THE WIFE LOST HER SHIT OVER THE FLOWERS. AND BOOZE. THX

Maya added another note to her list, then took a deep breath and tried to keep the nausea away. She thought she had missed morning sickness. At first she was only nauseous when she busted blood packets with bullets, which was more of an eww-factor than growing a baby. But now the baby was kicking things up a notch.

She closed her eyes, rubbed her little belly, and suddenly her eyes flew open. Alert, Maya looked around the room, and seeing the curtains closed, she understood she wasn't being watched. Still, she couldn't shake the eerie vibe. Her mom would always say it was 'someone walking over your grave.' She rose, checked the door, made sure the curtains in all the rooms were closed tight, and headed to the shower, careful not to wake Heart.

THE YOUNG WOMAN blinked open her eyes and smiled. She took in the lush linens and the heavy arm draped over her waist and remembered last night like it was a fantasy. But it wasn't - here she was in the arms of one of the most eligible bachelors in the city, no state, no world (!) the morning after he had swept her off her feet, wined, and dined her.[1]

"Good morning, my beautiful angel," the voice of a god said in her ear.

Callista couldn't believe it. Griffin Levy had stopped her on the way to work and asked her out. Right there in the middle of High Street in front of the posh restaurant where she worked and now, she was in his bed - a first for her - and he was looking at her like she descended from heaven.

Callista pulled her hair in anguish at the memories. "Stupid Callista. Stupid, stupid, stupid."

She rocked as she tried to blot out the memories of her happiness from a few weeks ago. She didn't know much time had passed since she had last been let out because there wasn't any natural light in the basement. Callista half-walked, half-crawled around the room again. Dusty bottles of incredibly expensive wine, her piss bucket - outside the locked posh bathroom - and the stairs that led to the double-locked door. The same as yesterday and the same as the day before that and the day before that, or maybe the weeks before ... *Dear God, how long have I been down here?!*

Tears leaked down her cheeks as she heard them. The footsteps meant he would be beside her soon.

The first lock turned. And her stomach heaved.

The second lock turned, and her body trembled violently.

"Angel, I'm home," Griffin called. "Good god babe, it smells atrocious down here," he muttered. "Hitchens, arrange a bath for Angel and a stylist. The whole nine. We are going out tonight, baby."

Callista kept her eyes on the floor, her arms wrapped around her knees, desperately trying not to scream. He didn't like that. He didn't like when she screamed, and it hurt so much when she did things he didn't like.

"Angel love, look at me," Griffin called.

She looked up from the shiny, butter-soft leather shoes, slowly up the sleek custom-made slacks, past the belt that likely cost more than her entire wardrobe, to the crisp, custom-made, French-cuffed shirt to the face of the man that was a man in name only.

"Where are your contacts, Angel? Your eyes are a beautiful, intense amber brown. I like them that way."

Her eyes were not light brown, they were almost black, Angel's were light brown, and Callista now hated this Angel woman.

"They hurt," she whispered.

He considered her for a moment. "Indeed Angel, let's take care of that," he smiled indulgently, "and I won't consider it misbehaving ... this time."

Thank God.

"We have much to celebrate!" he said, clapping his hands. "My mother is dead and though there were complications, I now understand what I must do to claim what's mine and you're a part of that, darling. It must be exciting for you."

She stared at him blankly. A new sick game.

God help me, she prayed silently as she walked up the stairs to the splendor of the thirty-million-dollar mansion she'd been kept captive in since that very first morning.

GRIFFIN

Griffin watched the woman in front of him. She wasn't *his* Angel, but she'd do. She was lucky to have him. From waitress to the mother of an heir, *this* Angel was much more pliable. It wasn't lost on him that as soon as he let his pregnant muse slip through his fingers; he needed her. It was an unforeseen complication, but he was Griffin Levy. He could create another Maya like other people changed underwear. Everything and everyone had a price.

Maya... he had come so close to training her. This *new* Maya broke too easily, but she'd serve his purpose. He smiled, watching her ass as she moved up the stairs, shoulders bowed, head low.

Hitchens appeared at the top of the stairs, waiting to escort her to the bathroom.

"Everything is ready for her. The viewing is still on, and no news on the other Angel."

CALLISTA

Callista tripped.

She got away. They must be looking for her. What happens to me if they find her?

Griffin took Callista's jaw in his hand at the top of the stairs. He hit her with his megawatt smile, nuzzled her neck, and licked her ear. "Now, do you like Prada?"

Callista lowered her eyes and forced her head to nod.

"Be prepared to be spoiled," he said as he slid his hand down her exposed thigh and squeezed where he'd left his mark. She flinched but didn't cry out. He ran his hand up her thigh and grabbed her roughly. Callista gave a small cry against the pain.

"I am the best you've ever had, aren't I?"

Callista bit back tears and nodded.

He stroked her hair. "Yes, prepare to be spoiled."

---

1. Creep Acoustic Cover by Sean Mikes

30
IT HAS NO LIMITS

MAYA

Jake calling...

Maya swiped her ringing phone as she sat on the floor near the toilet. "Yeah?"

"You sound like shit."

"Morning sickness."

"You need help with anything?"

"Nope, unless you can solve a plague on the pregnant female kind. Then you can cut me in on the profits." She chuckled wearily.

"You need rest."

"On my list, friend. What can I do you for?"

"Your senator friend called trying to get in touch with you, and I didn't know if I should pass on your number."

Maya sighed and thought for a while. "I'll call him from my secure line. Sorry about that, Jake. Should have figured he'd call back."

Jake was silent for a moment as Maya counted the white flecks among the beige of the marble flooring. "You handled that well today, Maya. It wasn't easy."

"No, it wasn't, but rage helps."

"I'm not just talking about that bitch of a doc. I mean, the way you took care of Mike. Stood strong for Rose Marie. You did good, kid," he said softly. "You need to tell him everything, Maya. Don't hesitate."

"He's dealing with a lot now, but as soon as we get past the funeral, when I know he's okay, I'll tell him."

"He won't be okay for a while, Maya. The longer you wait..."

"I know... I've got it Jake. Thanks."

Jake sighed, and she imagined he was shaking that magnificent head of his. "Call your friend, then get some rest darlin'."

"Will do. Promise." And then Jake was gone. Maya promised herself she would sit through the call and then haul her ass to the shower and bed.

"ETHAN."

"Maya."

Senator Ethan Blackwell was a good businessman, attentive husband, and hands-on dad who befriended a young girl and her mother while his own mother was also going through cancer treatments in Ohio. His mother survived, Maya's didn't.

They had an easy friendship and one of Maya's first design projects was his wife Vivian's vision for their remote home in the Virginia hills that Vivian described as the Apocalypse Glamping Chic.

It was a crazy idea Maya had pulled off with Shay's help. The home was gorgeous and completely off the grid. The perfect vacation home. During the process, Maya made Ethan a sustainable design believer, and he took his climate change-focused platform to the U.S. Senate. His business dealings kept his wife in designer duds, his conscience kept his ass in office, and Maya loved him to life. He was one of the few conservative senators who crossed the aisle on climate change and renewable energy. They disagreed on a lot of other things politically, but they had a bond outside of politics.

"You were right, management of that hospice has a nasty habit of putting bed turnover higher than care. Fifty-three complaints over the last two years for that facility, several against that doctor specifically.

"Not sure still if it's only that site, but..." he paused. "Heard you elegantly tore the doctor a new one."

"Can that sort of thing be done with elegance?" Maya replied. "She had it coming with her 'You need to wrap it up here.'"

She heard Ethan suck in a breath.

"Yeah, that happened."

"Damn, Maya."

Damn was right. About five hours ago Maya lost her shit, as the fellas say.

FIVE HOURS EARLIER...

Mike hadn't said goodbye to his sister, but ten minutes before the attending doctor popped her head in and saw he was still there - they all were. Maya thought it was strange but said nothing. When the doctor came back five minutes later, the frustration was evident on her face.

"You need to wrap it up here," she said to no one in particular. Maya went from sad to flaming hot in about half a second and her response was immediate.

"Get. Out," Maya said, her eyes blazing. As she watched the doctor flounce out, she stood and motioned Jake and Blake to the door. Mike had moved to a chair next to Rose's bed. His eyes hadn't moved from his sister's body. She placed her hand on his shoulder and as she walked away, he clutched her hand, so tight it hurt.

"Come back to me," he spoke with a hoarse urgency that warmed Maya, pressed painfully on her chest, and made her even more pissed at the doctor.

When she arrived in the hallway, the men's dangerous energy met her. Jake and Blake stood near the nurse's station and watched Maya move her head from side to side, lightly cracking her neck.

"This is gonna get interesting," Blake muttered.

"How dare you?" Maya spoke, low and harsh.

Most people expected Maya to yell, but she had long ago learned, when she wanted to get her point across, to speak barely above room level. Her low, clear voice made you lean in and the authority she radiated demanded your attention.

The doctor turned around from the nurse's station, startled.

"You need to wrap it up here?!" Maya repeated, her body strung tight with controlled rage. "How dare you speak to a grieving family like that? Where is your oath of compassion? Of service?"

The nurse's station that normally buzzed with activity stilled. Doctors, nurses, staff, patients, and visitors simply stopped moving, all completely focused on the drama unfolding in front of them.

"My-my shift..." the doctor started.

"What?" Maya asked as she drew herself to her full height and placed her hands on her hips, legs braced apart. She leaned in ever so slightly. It wasn't a threat, but she made her point. "What about your shift? Was it ending? Full? Busy? Is there a single viable excuse you can provide that justifies speaking to someone as you spoke to us in that room? You are not only an appalling representative of your field, your apparent lack of character and compassion casts a pallor over this entire establishment, making me wonder not only about the level of ante-care given here, but about premortem care as well."

The doctor tried to speak, to which Maya immediately raised her hand to stop her. "I'm through with you," Maya said dismissively. Turning to Jake, she asked to borrow his phone.

She had a rapt audience as she dialed. The nurses were both impressed and amused; it would appear the good doc was not well-liked.

In full view of the entire staff, Maya proceeded to have a phone conversation that made Jake and Blake realize how different executive Maya was from hanging out at the bar eating candy Maya.

"It's me," she started authoritatively into the phone. "I hate to drag you out of your bed on a Sunday, but I have a situation that cannot wait. Find me the parent company of Sunrise Hospice Care in Denver. I need their board of directors. I also need stats on their holdings and profits. Last year will be fine and whether that is a decline, rise, or stagnant. Also, while you're looking, who authorized the purchase of thirty super soakers and a crate of bubble mix?"

Listening...

"Sabbatical does not mean I'm not paying attention."

Listening...

"Sounds wonderful. The kids will love it. Make sure they are aware it was a donation, do not accept payment for it. Were there enough for staff, and by staff I mean did you get me one? I want the biggest. Don't let him have it. He has a penis complex."

The doctor narrowed her eyes at Maya. Maya smiled at her and said, "Advocare owns them? Who do we know?" Listening closely, Maya smiled wider. "Connect me. And Selene? You're brilliant as usual. Miss you."

Listening ...

"Vivian honey, this is Maya. How's Mika?"

Listening ...

"She's at that age. Be happy it was pot. How did the counters hold up?"

Maya smiled at the person's response. "Being able to withstand joint burns and bong water isn't in the brochure, but sounds like it should be. Listen, honey, where is that husband of yours? I apologize for it being criminally early, but I need to bend his ear."

Listening ...

"Senator, how are you, sir?"

Listening ...

"Not so well, Ethan. A good friend lost his sister to cancer today." Maya sighed. She nodded her head, and her voice was thick with emotion. "I'm at Sunrise Hospice in Denver, and I'm disturbed. Sunrise Hospice is a part of the Advocare Network and you're on the board, aren't you?"

Listening.

"Ethan, as a friend and with you running for re-election, I wanted to give you a heads up before I filed a formal complaint and the media got involved."

The doctor paled, the nurses snickered behind her, and Blake cleared his throat.

"It's not a good story the way they are going to frame it - a hospice facility pushing grieving families out of the rooms so they can flip the beds quicker. The media are all over this kind of 'big medicine vs the little guy' scenario. You saw what happened to Pharma Bro."

Listening ...

"It *is* a shit way to hit their profit margins," she said, parroting the Senator's response. The swear word sounded funny coming from Maya's quiet, professional voice. The perfect diction on the word 'shit' sent one nurse over the edge and there was a loud snort from the station.

"Advocare turned three hundred million in profit last year, and I'm concerned that is part of the motivating factor for doctors to pose as airline stewardess for the dead and grieving."

Listening ...

"I couldn't tell you if it's systemic"—she turned slightly to observe the nurses' station better — "but the doctor's behavior would be unusually bold for a well-functioning facility. She saw one nurse in the back nodding fervently when she said "systemic." *Fuck.* She wanted to believe their experience was a messed-up anomaly.

"I have to say, the nurses,"—the room froze—"are fantastic. They remind me of our gang back home..."

Listening ...

Maya smiled a sad smile and spoke, her voice thick again, "Yeah, I remember. 'Angels of the Underworld.' It was corny then, and it still kinda is. It works on a t-shirt though." She saw the nurses share a sad smile.

Listening ...

"Thanks Ethan. I appreciate you looking into it for me." *Pause.* "Right. Hug the girls for me, especially the weedhead. Goodbye."

She tapped the button on the screen and skewered the doctor with a heated gaze.

"When you took your oath, you understood it has no limits, no dollar amounts, no bias. If you are unable or unwilling to display the basic level of respect and compassion the average citizenry expects of its healers, then you need to get the hell out of the business."

She leaned in close.

"Pray God has mercy on you. Pray you don't experience a doctor with your bedside manner in *your* time of need."

Maya turned and walked back to Rose's room, followed by Jake and Blake. Stopping outside the door, she hugged and thanked them for coming. Blake offered to drive her truck back to Rough Ridge, and after talking quietly for a few moments, she excused herself to get back to Mike. As she opened the door "Doctor, Director McGhee is on line one, says it's urgent" flitted across her ears. The words gave her little satisfaction as she thought of the countless families rushed through their grief.

PRESENT TIME...

"I would have paid to see you take that doctor down," Ethan said. "I'll replay in my mind the takedown you did of the specialists who messed up Elise's medications. But I'll make your chest bigger and take off the braces with M&M bits stuck in them."

Maya covered her mouth and laughed quietly into the phone until she snorted.

"There she is. There's that kid that would peek out from behind the sixteen-year-old elderly woman I met at the hospital," Ethan said, his voice smiling. "Are you doing okay? I know it brought up a lot of memories."

"I can deal. I'm just worried about my friend."

"Lucky friend ... Are you going to bring him out to meet us?"

"Why, so pot-smoking Mika can get him hooked on the wacky weed?" Maya cackled.

Ethan sighed loudly. "Fourteen. She's fourteen! I went ballistic. Vivian was so laid back about it I wondered if she'd smoked some too."

Maya giggled softly into the phone.

"Mom misses you Maya. When is this bullshit sabbatical going to end?"

"I don't know Ethan," she whispered.

"I know it's not my place—"

"I'm fine Ethan, I just need time."

Pause.

"Independent Maya." He sighed. "Ok. I'll back off, but I'm here - Vivian and I both. I even know where you can get weed if you need it."

"Thanks Ethan, I've gotta go get in the shower," she said with a tired chuckle.

"Don't fall asleep in there. You sound dead on your feet," he warned.

"Thanks for everything, including making me laugh. I'll talk to you soon," she whispered. "Bye."

Maya tried to force herself up. An achy tiredness seeped into her bones, down to the marrow. After a pep talk, she finally hauled herself up, washed her face, brushed her teeth, tried not to gag, and yanked off her clothes. She took two seconds to put her phone on *Do Not Disturb* mode and fell into the bed on the far side, so she didn't disturb Mike. As she drifted off, the bed moved and a pair of powerful arms wrapped around her, hauling her against a big, warm body. They both sighed, and it was lights out.

MONDAY MORNING...

SHANNON: THEY CAN LEAVE IT ALL?

MAYA: YEP, EXCEPT THE PHOTOS AND THE BED. THAT'S CREEPY. I'M GOING TO ORDER ONE ONLINE AND HAVE IT SENT THERE. MIKE SHOULD HAVE SOMETHING COMFORTABLE AFTER THE FUNERAL.

SHANNON: OK, I'LL COURIER OVER THE DOCS AND THEN YOU'LL BE A HOMEOWNER. I'LL INCLUDE THE ADDENDUM DOCS IF MIKE IS ON BOARD.

MAYA: YIPPEE. THIS WAS A WEIRD TRANSACTION. SHANNON: DIVORCE IS LIKE THAT. THEY GAVE UP AND SPLIT THE PROCEEDS INSTEAD OF FIGHTING.

SHANNON: ARE YOU TAKING IT EASY?

MAYA: MOSTLY. THUMBS ARE GETTING TIRED THOUGH LOL

SHANNON: GET SOME REST. TOMORROW IS GOING TO BE LONG. I'LL GIVE YOU THE KEYS AT THE FUNERAL.

MAYA: K, THX SHANNON

SHANNON: NP

Maya closed on a condo quicker than expected because of the

owners' divorce. Now she needed to order crap for it and have the movers install it... in 48 hours.

Geez, this would cost a mint. But she'd have a home again. With rooms. Yay. She glanced at the time when the shower started. If today was like yesterday, it would be a day of quiet and rest. She and Heart had room service and slept most of the day before. She had him approve the funeral program, and the rest she took care of. Funerals were like planning a grim-ass picnic. With a Catholic priest. There was a joke or a horror movie in that thought somewhere, but she couldn't find it because she was exhausted and looking at beds. Bad combo.

She picked the same one she had back in Ohio, but in a California King and called it a day. Then she texted Caine and asked him to pack her stuff. She didn't want poor Ms. Shirley finding her cash stash or her gun and thinking less of her. She'd ask too many questions that Maya couldn't answer without saying she was a drug dealer or telling the truth.

Life was complicated. Small town life was a clusterfuck.

Maya clicked over to Amazon and ordered towels, bedding, dishes, and a shit load of designer, finely made panties in three styles - thong, boy cut, and low-rise Brazilian - ten pairs in each color, in two sizes. Mike was quiet and exhausted since Rose died, but sometimes men needed to "screw through their emotions." Or at least that was what Victoria texted her that morning. Crazy text to receive, but there you go. She was prepared for panty ripping for the next couple of months, whenever it happened.

Maya shopped online for at least forty-five minutes when she realized the shower had never turned off. She quickly checked out - having to text Shannon to get the address to her new home (crazy). Next, she called room service and rushed to the bathroom. She saw him through the glass door. His beautiful body wet and slick and his long, dark hair hung limp around his face as the water beat on his neck and back. He was unparalleled, the most beautiful man she had ever seen in her life, and at that moment, he was also the most broken.[1]

His hands pressed against the wall underneath the shower nozzle, head bowed, almost like he didn't have the strength to move. The water had to be freezing by now.

Maya slipped off her clothes down to her underwear, opened the shower door and braced for ice-cold water. Instead, it was still warm, and Maya made a mental note to give a positive Yelp review. She grabbed one of the little bars of hotel soap, a washcloth, and gently washed Mike's back. She cleansed him all over with care and love. Stopping briefly to kiss his lips, she carefully washed his beautiful, ravaged face with a fresh washcloth. Then she washed his hair, doing her best on someone so tall. Maya took special care to massage his scalp deeply as she applied conditioner. She wasn't sure if alpha mountain men used conditioner, but she was winging it.

One might have found it odd he didn't move the whole time she bathed him. But she understood because she'd been there - holding life together through a sliver of sheer will. He responded silently when she asked him to close his eyes while she rinsed his hair. Other than that, his eyes never left her face.

"You'll get through this," she whispered to him, her eyes locked on his. "It's going to be hard, but you are not alone. You will get through this. And you will make your sister and your mom so proud. You already have."

Mike closed his eyes, nodded, and sighed. It was long, hard, and it sounded like it hurt, but he relaxed a little. He would, eventually, be okay.

---

1. Unsteady by X Ambassadors

31

ASTEROIDS, LOCUSTS OR WILDFIRES

MIKE

They laid Rose Marie to rest on Wednesday. The days before and after were a jumbled blur. The things Mike remembered were like snapshots, but the one thing he didn't miss: every step he took, Maya was there. He was dumbfounded by the funeral director's request for clothing for his sister. Maya simply asked after Rose's favorite color and took care of it.

He buried Rose in a beautiful yellow dress with a matching head-scarf. There were five huge sprays of yellow roses, beside the two he had already purchased. Two of them were from Maya, one each from Jake and Blake's family, and one from the Walters family - an enormous shock that Mike still hadn't processed.

Maya was the reason half the town came out for the service despite his family's reputation. She managed the food after the service along-side Tori, Leslie, Mac, and Tammy - Paul's wife. Maya rescued him several times from conversations he couldn't focus on. She spread the word about him riding his bike in Rosey's honor and everyone who had one rode theirs as well.

He hadn't noticed at first, but when they drove back from Denver the day of the funeral, she wore elegant navy, slim-cut slacks, a loose silk navy blouse, and boots. When they arrived at the motel, he went to change, and she walked down to see Ms. Shirley. Finally, it was time for him to meet the officials at the church. It was then he realized why she was wearing boots and slacks. Maya walked out with Ms. Shirley, slipped her purse into his saddlebag, put on her sunglasses, and quietly waited by his bike. She truly never left his side. Hyperaware of her pregnancy at that moment, he asked her if she was sure.

"It's safe for me because I'm comfortable with it," she said quietly, "but if you don't think you can roll this behemoth safely enough for me, then you shouldn't be on it today either."

Mike rode the few miles through town and back with the utmost care. The trail of bikes rolling at 10 mph from the church to the cemetery was long, loud, and Rosey would have loved it.

Honestly, he spent most of the day in a state of shock — from both the reality of Rosey being gone and the outpouring of support. One of the biggest shocks of the day came when the soloist began singing 'Ave Maria' during Mass. The voice that sang his sister and mother's favorite song was so achingly beautiful and clear that it physically hurt to listen. The voice reached in and grabbed your soul. Daring a glance at the soloist, it floored him to see it was Officer Laila.

Dressed in a white choir robe, her dark brown hair loose around her shoulders and her hands clasped prayerfully in front of her, she looked like the Angel of Mercy instead of a Soldier of Fortune he'd taken her for. Maya gripped his hand and shared the same shocked look, though he seemed to get over it faster. Maya looked torn between crying, laughing, or fleeing, and he thought she whispered something about cupcakes and princesses.

He shook his head at the snatches of memories assaulting him. Presently, he sat on the edge of the bed in a fully furnished condo Maya forgot to tell him she bought. He moved to the deck off the master bedroom and stared at the mountains. It was a beautiful space, and had to cost a lot of cake. Was her long money legal? Should he review her file now? His mind went back to this past week...He had just buried the last member of his family. His Rosey. And it gutted him. If Maya hadn't been there ... He shook his head, realizing she had done all this herself at twenty-one years old. A baby. She was a good, compassionate woman, and his heart told him she'd never risk exposing him to something that would destroy him or his career. Mike ignored the concern gnawing at his gut and decided to wait it out. She'd trust him. He had to be patient.

He walked back into the house to look for her and found her passed out on the couch, mouth hanging open with her hand curled around her small baby bump.

There was a bottle of water, crackers, and a big stack of notecards on the coffee table in front of her. Reaching down, he read through them. His heart caught when he realized she was writing out thank-you notes to those who attended the services, sent food or flowers. There were more than a hundred cards already finished. Some she signed "Mike," some "Sincerely, Michael Sheppard" and a few were "Hugs, Mike and Maya."

Mike and Maya.

Mike knelt next to the woman his sister called an angel and kissed her gently on the forehead. "I love you," he whispered against her warm skin.

He moved and kissed the small swell of her belly. "I love you too, little one ... can't wait to meet you." Then Mike lifted his woman and put her to bed.

MAYA

Maya's eyes opened, and she looked at the clock. It was after midnight and she felt Mike's body heat next to her, his arms wrapped around her, his face in her hair. Boy, she loved this, and she could stay this way forever, but she was hungry and had to pee. She tried to slide out of Mike's arms when he gripped her tight.

"Where you goin'?" His voice was jagged with sleep.

Oh yum.

"Gotta potty," she replied. He chuckled, kissed her neck, and let her go. She later wandered from the bathroom to the kitchen and started rooting around in the fridge. Nabbing cold Chinese, granola, milk, and an apple; she hopped up on the dark granite countertop. Maya had a mouth full of noodles when she heard him chuckle. She froze and looked guilty with chopsticks poised to shove more in her mouth.

"Hungry?" he rumbled, a small, sexy grin playing around his mouth.

"Starved. Was I too loud?"

"No, I missed you."

She smiled and put the noodles down as he walked over to her, his black boxer briefs hanging low on his hips and all his marvelous chest and abs on display. He had a nice smattering of happy trail hair coursing down his abs to that yummy patch at the base of his manhood. Now Maya was hungry for something else.

"Don't stop on account of me, darlin'," he said in his low, quiet voice that never failed to give her a tingle.

Is this the screw his feelings out portion of the grieving process? Maya was slightly ashamed to be hopeful about it. Slightly.

Mike grabbed the takeout box of noodles, picked around, and fed Maya a few bites slowly.

"More?"

She bit her lip and shook her head. He smiled slowly and moved away, looking through drawers.

"I forgot to buy silverware," Maya croaked, then cleared her throat. "There's plasticware in the other drawer."

Mike shrugged. "I wanted to cut your apple for you."

Instead, he bit into it and then offered the apple at the bite mark, holding it close to her mouth. She wrapped her hands around his and took a bite. It was his turn to bite his lip.

Mike stepped closer between her legs, pulling her to the edge of the counter and nuzzled her neck. After inhaling her for a long moment, he pulled back and placed a hand on either side of her thighs. He looked over her face, his own expression going soft. Gently, he leaned in and kissed her nose.

"I love you."

Maya choked on the last bits of her apple. Her heart slammed into her ribcage, then dropped to her feet. She was elated and grateful and terrified ... she felt so damn much she couldn't even think how to unstick the apple.

Mike stepped back in alarm and yanked her arms up in the air over her head to help her stop choking. When she had got her breathing under control, she felt sheepish. "Sorry about that."

He leaned into her again, his face set in what was supposed to be admonishment, but his half smile made him look anything but serious. "I love you, so don't choke to death."

"Right. That would be unfortunate," she whispered.

"You took care of me," he said, his lips close to her ear before he was back to nuzzling her neck. "Took care of my sister, showed her more kindness than she's had in a long time. All week, every step I made. Every time I needed someone, hell, before I knew I needed anyone, you were there. All because ... "

He paused, shaking his head and dropping his eyes. He wanted to hear it and she wanted to say what her heart knew weeks ago and say it for real, not by accident hopping off the phone.

"Because I love you."

His head snapped up, and his green eyes pierced hers. She reached out to hold a hand against his cheek. Dropping his forehead to hers, he roughed out, "Sunshine." He was tense, his body agitated.

"I do. I love you," Maya said, nodding her head and moving her hand down over his heart, her fingers electrified by his taut, soft skin over hard muscle, and the rhythmic thump that gave her so much hope and comfort. "I wish I didn't. It would be easier if I didn't. But I love you, so much it makes it hard to breathe."

"Damn, it's good to hear you say that, baby," he growled as his arms gathered her up and held her so close.

"I can't believe you're mine," Mike said as he traced his fingertips lightly up the outsides of her thighs and dropped his head, shaking it once more. "You sure as hell can do better, Sunshine, but any other man sure as hell won't be right."

Mike removed her hand from his heart, turned her palm up, and kissed it, moving up to the sensitive area on the inside of her wrist where he licked lightly. He kissed further up her arm, stopping to suck the sensitive, neglected skin on the inside of her elbow, trailing kisses, nips and sucks until he reached her shoulder, where he pulled the strap of her camisole down.

"All mine," he growled again.

Maya giggled softly. "Are you going to drag me by my hair back to the bedroom?"

"No..." He pressed himself close, his erection against her core. She instinctively wrapped her legs around him and he lifted her off the counter as she let out a small yelp of surprise. "But I am gonna pull your hair if you like it."

"Oh," she breathed.

"And tie you up if you wanna try it."

"Ok." Her brain got foggy and breath shallow as her vivid imagination took off.

"I want to test how flexible you are."

"Quite. I made the cheer squad."

"You don't say?"

It was his turn to sound surprised.

"Gonna have me swinging from the chandeliers, huh?" she joked, her voice husky with desire.

"I like swings."

"I'll never see the playground the same," she mused.

"Not those kind."

Maya's eyes went wide as she thought about the sex swings she had seen in a catalog once. She swallowed hard, making a mental note to go back online and shop more.

"We're going to do everything we can think of, but not tonight," he said, laying her across the bed. "Tonight I want to make love to you, finally,"—he slid his hands up her waist and slipped off her camisole — "slow and steady." He removed her ponytail holder and fluffed her curls. "All fuckin' night."

"Wait!"

He stopped, confused.

"What about work - any cases, pimps, trap queens or murderers waiting for you?"

"Off duty 'til Monday, Sunshine."

"What about illness? Are you feeling ok? Everything working as it should?"

He glanced down at his marvelous erection. "Everything's workin' fine, darlin'."

"Shh..."

"Babe—"

"I'm listening for asteroids or locusts or wildfires or whatever the interruption is going to be ... "

"Beautiful, tonight—all night—it's only me and you," he said with a lazy grin, his voice deep and rough.

"Whoo hoo!" Maya yelped, throwing her hands over her head in victory. She kept herself from doing jazz hands, but barely.

Mike froze, then roared with laughter, falling on the bed next to her, covering her with his body, careful to keep his weight off her bump. "God, I love you." He chuckled as his hand slid between her breasts, down her stomach, to the lilac lace panties. His fingers stroked along the edge of the lace, and he tugged a little, then stopped.

"You won't have any underwear left if I keep at 'em," he said, playing with the lace a little.

"You see that dresser over there?" Maya said, lifting an elegant finger to indicate a long, contemporary, eight-drawer dresser with a dark finish. "The first three drawers are stuffed full of panties. Every color you can think of and in the styles, you seem partial to..."

Mike's hands gripped the lilac lace almost on instinct as he stared at her.

"I guess I'm saying have at—"

She didn't get to finish the sentence before he jerked. She gasped, and lilac flew on lace wings across the room.[1]

Mike kissed Maya hard and sweet as their tongues played and coaxed. His mouth swept down her throat to the hollow at her collarbone while his hands slid slowly over her body, leaving burning heat tattooed on her skin wherever he touched.

She was writhing with fevered need by the time he dipped his head and drew one of her nipples into his mouth and sucked deep. A vibrating moan escaped her lips and her hands clasped around his head as she arched to him. The tickle of his goatee on her breasts felt delicious as every nerve in her body seemed alive, and exposed. The feel of his body on and against hers. The weight of him, the hard to her soft... She was alive in a way there was no coming back from.

Maya felt drugged. High on Mike—everything about him gave her a buzz. The feel of him, the sounds he made when she touched him, the smell of him, the taste of his skin. He acted like he could stay between her legs all night, her reaction fueling him. Her hands gripped his hair, her thighs slid and moved around him frantically with need. Her leg over his shoulder, pressing into his back with her heel as he slid his fingers inside, angled up to engage that sensitive bundle of nerves within her while his mouth concentrated on her pleasure bud.

He was like a man possessed, determined to drink her dry until she burst from her release. He teased and rewarded her until she fell over the edge. Then he began building her for the next orgasm before she had finished with the first. The second orgasm took her by surprise and as she quivered and clenched around him, he slowly made his way back to her flushed lips.

She tasted herself on him. *Damn, just when she thought she couldn't get any more turned on, he found a way.* Greedily, she arched to him as he positioned himself at her opening. She needed him inside her. Needed to join with him. She ached and only he could soothe it.

Heavy, thick, hooded muscle pressed gently at her opening. As she looked into his eyes, she saw both his love and restraint. His neck muscles grew tight as he paused.

Afraid of their track record for getting close without sealing the deal, she whispered, "Come home, Heart," and slid her hand between them down to her sex. Maya positioned her hand so her fingers splayed open. "I want to feel when you enter me."

That simple movement tore the last of his restraint and he surged into her with a powerful roll of his hips. As he entered, the intense pleasure-pain from the stretch to accommodate him overwhelmed her. A small gasp escaped her lips.

"Are you okay?" Mike was straining, beads of sweat forming along his shoulders from the efforts to still himself.

She smiled. "Oh yeah."

"I'm big honey, any time it's too much, let me know," he grunted. He slipped his fingers to her breast and began teasing her nipple, gently rolling as he placed slow kisses and sucks along her neck. Her body relaxed to accommodate him. His teasing manipulation smoothed any discomfort.

Maya tipped her hips, causing him to slide in further, and he groaned, dipping his head to her throat. She clenched and released her inner walls rhythmically and whispered, "Please ... make me yours."

A growl released from deep within him as he moved with lovely, slow, deliciously long, amazingly deep strokes within her.

"Mmmm, fuck yes," she moaned as her hips worked in concert with his movements. She slid her hand down his back to hold on tight to his ass and she wrapped her leg around his waist. He filled her, so sweetly touched her and so powerfully claimed her. His eyes, made dark with desire, connected with hers before he dipped to take her mouth, kissing her deep as he drove harder. She held on for the ride, desperate to get more of him. He slid his arms underneath her and the next thing she knew, she was up in the air as he sat back on his haunches. Her legs straddled his thick, muscled thighs as he kept them connected, never breaking the rhythm.

Oh. My. Damn.

They were chest to chest, their breaths mingling, arms wrapped tightly. Her arms around his shoulders, her hands in his hair. He kept one hand in her hair, the other arm wrapped around her at her hips, driving her down as he thrust up.

Slow.

Deep.

Smooth.

Powerful.

Beautiful.

She complimented his thrusts by tightening herself around him. Each time she did, he audibly inhaled or groaned deep which only made her more desperate for him.

"Fuck Maya, baby, what you do to me?" he said against her lips.

If she could speak beyond the gibberish in her mind, she would have asked him the same thing. His powerful muscles moving all around her, in her. As she gripped tighter, desperate to touch him everywhere, he increased his pace, thrust deeper, pulled her down harder, and her cries grew louder.

Over, and over, and over again, until her body had to release. It was pressure, a horizon that she climbed toward, afraid she would fall apart when she reached it. He angled friction against her clit while his dick stretched her pussy, repeatedly stroking that special spot. They called it a G spot, but at that moment it felt like he had control of the whole damn alphabet and a couple of Greek letters as well.

Then she came.

Hard.

Her back arched as she clung to him, her hair flying out behind her, everything stringing tight. Mike slid his teeth and tongue across her chest as he stroked faster, his own release on the horizon. He dropped them both back down, and she wrapped her leg around his waist as he took her there another unbelievable time.

"Michael, oh Heart I'm—"

"Come for me, beautiful," he growled low.

And she did, bringing him with her over the edge, with her into bliss - his body tensed as goosebumps erupted across his flushed chest, his muscles bulged, a deep, rough groan released powerfully as he pulsed inside her. And she milked every drop from him.

Maya was a being of light, shattered, scattered and reformed. There was a deep whooshing in her ears, a kink in her toes, and a raw, gritty texture to her throat. Her skin tingled all over as he glided slowly in and out. She softly stroked his back, staring into his eyes.

"I love you," she breathed.

Grabbing her hand from his face, he placed it against his heart, "Always, Sunshine." He let his forehead rest against hers for long moments, waiting for both their heart rates to return to normal.

"Let me clean you up, baby," he said after a while and kissed her nose. He turned her palm up, kissed it, and pushed off the bed.

She enjoyed watching him walk away. That glorious, amazing body on display. She decided then and there she would get a roll of quarters and practice bouncing them off his ass. First, she'd try it with M&Ms. *Am I a freak for wanting to bounce and eat M&Ms off his ass? Yes. Yes, I am.*

She also enjoyed the view coming back because of the sated,

peaceful look in his eyes and the casual, relaxed power with which he moved. In one smooth motion, he slid into bed and between her legs. Gently pushing her legs open further, he cleansed her, taking great care with her delicate, swollen treasure.

"Tender?" he asked, his face gentle as he looked into her brown eyes, her hair spread wide across the pillows. He looked at her like she was his fantasy.

"Maybe I will be tomorrow. I've never had ... well, size-wise ... endowed or skilled." She hid her face behind one hand sheepishly.

"Now she gets shy ... we forgot condoms," he said, his voice taking on a serious and cautious tone.

She thought back with relief as each test had come back negative since she became pregnant. Griffin was as paranoid as she believed. He didn't trust anyone but her, to not get pregnant to trap him and secure a piece of his family's money. She looked at Mike questioning.

"Celibate for over a year darlin' and yearly, force-required check-ups," he said as he quirked a brow her way.

"All good here, and I can't get double pregnant."

The question hung in the air.

"I liked it," she drawled. "Feeling all of you."

He kissed her inner thigh, and she quivered. "You're okay with us raw? I sure as hell don't want to go back, not when I've had you like this." He nuzzled the neat, curling hair at the meeting of her thighs. She let out a soft moan.

"This is sexual coercion," she complained.

"This is merely a discussion. Coercion would feel more like this ... "

And he showed her. With his amazing mouth. Before she could come down from her orgasm, he was inside of her again, claiming her as his own. He was rougher, intensely possessive of all of her. Holding her arms above her head in one of his large hands, he used the other to explore her body. It wasn't gentle; it didn't hurt; it was wow.

He had made love to her, worshipped her with his tongue, and now he was plain ol' fucking her—well.

It was the best night of her life. And after they climaxed together, Maya was so satisfied, so relaxed and so exhausted she would have agreed to be a rodeo clown if he asked.

"Do you agree ungloved is best from here on out?" he asked as he gently cleansed her again.

"Raw and free. Woot," Maya murmured, giving a weak thumbs up and lopsided grin with dimple.

MIKE

Mike chuckled softly, kissing her gently at her core, then on her softly rounded belly, between her breasts, at her collarbone, behind her ear, and finally her forehead. He heard her gently snore, and bit back a laugh as he looked down at her, already in a deep sleep. He tossed the wet wash rag in the bathroom's direction and reached down to pull the covers over the both of them. As Mike gathered Maya in his arms, he tucked her tight to him, her back to his front so he could slide his hand over her belly and bury his face in her hair.

Mike didn't pray often. The first time in many years was at Rose Marie's bedside as her soul left this Earth. Tonight, with his woman in his arms, hearing her gentle snoring, his hand around the place growing a special new life, he felt compelled to pray for the second time. This time it was simply to say:

"Thank you."

---

1. Hrs and Hrs by Muni Long

32

GRIIIIIITS

MAYA

Maya woke with a fresh new perspective on life and a song on her heart. Sliding gently out of the bed and Mike's arms, she strolled butt ass naked to the kitchen. She turned on Jill Scott's "*Whatever*," grooved quietly to Jill singing about a monumental night of passion and grinned to herself as she really understood what "Jilly from Philly" was talking about. Mike pulled some tricks out of his sleeve last night. [1]

And God, she was so content she could purr. In fact, she was certain she purred at one point and now she wanted to cook for the man. "*Is it the Way*" came on as Maya giggled and sang out "griiiiiits," as she stirred hers. She checked the bacon, poured OJ, and warmed the last chocolate croissant she had. *Damn, I'm really in love with this man to give him my last croissant...*

Unfortunately, as the eggs touched the pan, the smell struck her completely wrong, and she took off running to the bathroom. Morning sickness was a constant companion now. She sank to the cold floor, waiting for the waves of nausea to pass, when Mike appeared, already dressed, leaning against the doorway.

"What can I do?" Mike asked as he walked in, wet a washcloth, and crouched low beside her, pressing the cool cloth to her head.

"That feels good," she muttered. "I made you break–nope can't say it, but it's in the kitchen." She covered her mouth and closed her eyes, breathing deeply through her nose. After a few minutes, she was okay enough to stand and motioned to Mike that she was getting up. He carefully helped her up and lifted her onto the counter next to the sink. He nonchalantly grabbed her toothbrush and dabbed toothpaste on it. With a small smile on his face, he handed her a small cup of water to rinse and watched as she brushed.

This was yet another level. She was ass naked on the sink, vulnerable with sickness, and he was taking care of her. Watching her brush her teeth. They were comfortable together in this moment, no pretense or worry — just them. When she finished brushing, she rinsed again, and he patted her mouth with a towel.

"I take it you're not hungry." His smile widened as she shook her head, rolling her lips tight inside her mouth.

"You need ginger."

"How do you know that?"

"That '*What to Expect When You're Expecting*' book," he said, tapping her nose. "I picked it up at the airport in L.A. I also got the book on the Bradley Method and another one by a midwife, Ina something."

Maya blinked at him. Twice. Mike stepped in between her legs, pressing in, and Maya's eyes dropped half-mast.

"You know that's sexy, right?" she purred, leaning into him while drawing him closer. "You reading those books, on your own for me ... A lot of men would show up at the hospital, yell 'Push!' and happily receive their pats on the back."

"I'm not a lot of men."

"Damn right. You're amazing." She kissed him long and soft. "That doesn't come around too often."

"Sore?" he asked against her lips as he patted her pussy.

"A little," she croaked. "Whisker burn too." She grinned, rubbing her raw cheek. "Worth it."

His hands tightened on her hips as she ran her fingers along his jaw, touching her forehead to his. A low growl escaped his throat. He stepped back, reached in the shower, and turned on all the showerheads. The almost 360-degree spray of water kicked to life, and Maya watched as he stripped off his clothes, slowly, in front of her.

Greedily, she gawked, relishing everything about him, including that quiet power he radiated. She could see why he was such a good leader, why men followed him. And he gentled that power for her.

"You love me," she said breathlessly as reality hit.

"Sunshine."

"You love me and my baby," she said, looking at him, her eyes shining with unshed tears. He reached down, taking her face in his hands, his emerald eyes alive and smiling.

"To my bones darlin'."

He lifted her off the counter and, taking her hand, he led her to the shower to show her how deep his love was. Then he showed her again on the bedroom floor and once more in the kitchen after he reheated his food - minus the eggs - and fed her plain toast and weak tea. Then he tucked her back into bed and left for groceries.

"He loves me a lot," Maya said out loud, yawning with a giggle. She patted her still damp hair that had reverted to a fro and tried to get up the energy to at least put on her bonnet. Fingers paused deep within her curls, she drifted off to sleep. She slept right through the sound of her phone ringing several times.

MIKE

Mike didn't recognize the number, but picked it up as he looked through his cart, mentally checking off items for dinner, some staples, and a variety of ginger items for Maya.

"Sheppard."

"Good afternoon, Michael, this is Ms. Kate," a woman's voice rang over the line. "I wanted to let you know we are almost finished at the house, but there were a couple of things we wanted to bring to your attention."

"The house?" Mike asked.

"We tried to call your wife several times, but she isn't answering," the woman named Kate replied.

"She's napping," Mike said distractedly, not even pausing as someone referred to Maya as his wife.

"Ah, la bambina," the woman said knowingly. "Would you have time to go through the home with me today?"

"Ms. Kate, I'm not following," Mike said, as he stared unseeing at the aisle of food before him. His neck got tightened as he realized what home she was talking about. But Maya wouldn't have ... he made a third silent prayer that she didn't do what his gut was telling him she had done.

"Your parents' home at 32 Mountain View Lane," the woman replied, sounding slightly puzzled.

Mike almost threw the phone. Seeing red, he left his cart and stalked through the aisles out of the store. The patrons cleared a wide path for the man whose eyes blazed and looked like he would break anyone in his way.

"Be there in ten," he spat.

Mike ended the call, jumped in his Jeep, and peeled out of the parking lot, headed to the one place he never wanted to return.

MAYA

Shaken out of sleep, Maya yawned and answered her phone.

"Mmm-hello?"

"Ms. Anderson?"

"Mmm hmm?"

"This is Bishop from Security Solutions. I'm at the Sheppard residence and we have a situation. Detective Sheppard was not aware we are working on this project."

"I know. I hadn't had time to update him. What's the problem? Do you need clearance for something? I can get him on the phone."

"Ma'am, he's already here," Bishop said, followed by a lengthy pause.

"Okay ... " Maya was still knocking the cobwebs out of her head from their energetic night and morning and not following the conversation well. She looked over at the clock and distractedly realized she only had an hour and a half before she needed to meet Laila at the warehouse before heading to her doctor's appointment. Touching her hair, she realized she had a partially wet, flat afro from shower sex. She needed at least thirty minutes to get it fluffed out properly.

"Detective Sheppard is here, was not aware we'd be here," he repeated, "and is less than pleased with finding us here."

"Wait? What? Ok, I'll call him and explain. Sorry about that, Bishop."

"I think you should come up here."

"Oh, no Bishop, it's fine. I'll talk to him. Hold on, I'm going to the other line."

Maya punched in a few buttons on her phone, putting Bishop on hold and calling Mike's cell. He answered on the first ring.

"What?" he barked into the phone so loudly Maya had to pull her ear away.

"Heart, honey, what's the matter? I'm sorry I didn't get a chance to tell you about the folks finishing this week. I didn't mean for them to take you by surprise—"

"Are you shittin' me Maya?" he interrupted.

"Why–"

"I don't want to talk about this shit. Don't come here, just get them out of here. Now."

Maya stopped, looked at the phone, and took a deep breath, "Heart, I'm coming up. Hold tight, honey, and we'll talk about what's happening."

"I said I don't want to talk about. This. Shit."

His voice had gone quiet and cold, and tears stung in the back of her eyes. She didn't understand what was wrong, but it wouldn't get fixed over the phone.

"I'll be there in twenty," was all she got out before she hit the display to reconnect to Bishop.

"I'm twenty minutes out, Bishop," she mumbled as she blinked back tears.

"Better make it fifteen darlin'."

Shit.

Maya took a quick washcloth to her top and tail and threw on the first things she found in her hyper-organized closet. She snatched on white, super soft sweatpants that hung low on her hips and a white gauzy hooded sweatshirt with a white cami on underneath. She sprayed a good amount of leave in conditioner in her hair and wrapped a silk scarf around as a headband. Fluffing her 'fro with one hand, she grabbed sneakers in her other hand, snatched her purse, and literally ran out the door barefoot. Quickly slapping a shoe on her driving foot, she took off, making it to the home in 12 minutes - thankful she hadn't gotten caught by one of Mike's colleagues along the way.

She had never heard him that angry before, not even when she answered the door in her panties on her knees or when he made that grumpy call before he took off for Los Angeles. Something was ... off.

Maya threw open the truck door and tossed her sneaker on the ground. Hopped down on one leg out of the truck, she jammed her left foot into the waiting shoe. She rushed to Bishop who was leaning against his big black SUV while his crew waited, looking casually badass and eyeing her with interest. The cleaning crew Maya hired stood around in groups, looking uncomfortable.

"What happened?" she asked Bishop in a hushed tone.

"Your man came up a while ago, took one look at the activity, lost his shit briefly, listened long enough for us to explain, then he ordered everyone out and has been standing in the same spot ever since."

Maya took in what Bishop said, bit her bottom lip, and then seemed to decide. She tossed her purse and phone back into the open window of her truck, ignoring the plunk of the phone bouncing off something - again - and took off toward the open door.

"Ms. Anderson?" Bishop called.

She stopped on the threshold and looked at him.

"I hear something I don't like; we're comin' in there and we won't be polite," he promised.

Maya took in his badass form - tight black tee, cargo pants, boots - and the similar attire of his crew. She allowed herself a moment to study his unusual gray-blue eyes. They were dead serious. And while she gave him a small smile and a smaller nod, Mike would never hit her. She should have reminded herself there are other ways to inflict pain.

---

1. Whatever and Is it the Way: Jill Scott

33
CLUE IN

MAYA
MAYA

"Heart," she called as she walked in the door, looking over the home that was in various stages of packing and cleaning.

"You don't listen."

She froze. To her left, she saw Mike in a formal dining room with his eyes on neat rows of tablecloths and other linen mementos including baby blankets, each with a note detailing who had created the item, which relative had used it, and the year in swirly, lovely penmanship. On the floor were boxes of books organized by subject in alphabetical order. The crews she hired were efficient and methodical. Sorting, organizing, and cleaning the Sheppard home in record time.

"Heart, love, I can see this was a shock and I should have told you it was happening, but I didn't want you to worry with everything happening with Rose. I thought I'd help get things organized, so when you were ready to go through them, it would be easier. The roof had sprung a leak. Mace mentioned it after he got the rosary. I didn't want your family's treasures to be damaged…"

She trailed off when he turned slightly and nailed her with a cold, hard stare. He looked like he was physically restraining himself. Maya quickly flipped through the likely causes of his fury in her mind. She arrived at one of two possibilities. She spoke again, albeit much more carefully. "When I say treasures, I don't mean I'm trying to carve up your family's estate for sale or anything. I mean pretty things like those linens that someone, I'm guessing your mom, carefully stored and kept a record of."

She took a couple of quiet steps in and pointed to the table. "Ms. Karen said some of these are over 100 years old and that's why they have them wrapped that way. The cedar chest they were in got wet, but they stayed dry thank goodn…"

She stopped again because Mike had quietly shifted and moved in front of her, so close that when he inhaled, he almost touched her with his chest.

"Did I ask you to do this?" He clipped.

"No, but I—"

"A few minutes ago, didn't I tell you not to come here?" he barked louder.

"Yes, but you were upset and I—"

"I, I, I, I - fuck Maya, do you know any other pronouns?" he spat out, his hand waving dismissively at her.

Maya reared back like he had slapped her.

"You. Do not come to this place and do shit without my permission. You. Don't bring your ass here when I clearly told you to stay the fuck away."

Each "you" growled out so roughly it sounded like glass and flames were flying out of his mouth. Each "you" hit Maya with the force of that glass and flames, and it was *painful*.

Still, she took a bracing breath, swallowed, and said in what she hoped was a rational voice, "Sorry for overstepping." She sounded awkward, but didn't want to repeat the offending pronoun.

"That's a massive fucking understatement," he growled as he turned and stalked to the table with the linens. "You don't get to decide when I deal with this IF I deal with this."

"You're right, I'm sorry, Heart."

Mike stared at one tablecloth closely and asked in a still, angry voice, "Where is everything else?"

"Most of the items are in a storage facility. They compiled, scanned and placed all the documents on a hard drive in a safe in the same facility, with a digital backup with one of the security company's vendors. The things the cleaners and security team deemed top priority or of sentimental value are in the small bedroom at our condo, except for what is still here. They are moving room by room." She watched his muscles bunch at her reply.

"Our?"

Shit. Everything I say is pissing him off more!

Dropping the "I," she explained further. "Figured since we were back, and the condo closed, we'd move out of the motel."

"Clue in Maya - I'm no one's kept man. You don't buy a million-dollar condo and decide to keep *me* in it. And yeah, I know the table-cloths are antique. I watched my mother clean her blood out of this one after he smacked her around at the dinner table. She paid no attention to herself. She wanted to keep that piece of shit tablecloth clean. And you think I want that in my face every day?"

His voice was so quiet she could barely hear him and so rough it sounded like it hurt to produce a sound.

Maya's heart was bleeding, gushing at his expression. "Honey ... I didn't know. I'm so sorry. After Rose Marie wanted the rosary—"

"Don't throw that shit in my face to justify this," he bit out, still looking unseeing at the array of linens.

Maya's mind was moving a million miles a second. She understood he was upset, but this was much, much more. Panicked, she had to get him to understand, but she didn't understand what was happening. He was closing down, slipping away. She took a step toward him and placed her hand on his heart. He jerked back, and it was like a physical blow. In response, she quickly withdrew, wrapping her arms around herself at her middle.[1]

"Don't. You don't belong here."

That was all he said.

Maya gulped in big breaths silently and tried one last time to get through to him. "Heart. Where are you right now? Talk to me please..."

Silence.

"Your mother loved you. She saved these things for you and your sister. There's nothing of him in these. Let me help—"

"I AM NOT ONE OF YOUR FUCKING PROBLEMS TO SOLVE!" he roared as he lifted the heavy mahogany dining room table and tossed it - along with all the carefully cared for linens - against the wall. Turning to Maya, he never took a step, but continued to bellow, "YOU GONNA RENT A BITCH TO HOLD ON TO MY BALLS NEXT, MAYA? You don't fucking OWN ME!

Maya was stunned. She couldn't feel her heartbeat, but she assumed it was still pumping. She couldn't feel her feet, but somewhere she recognized she was backing away. She couldn't feel her mouth, but she heard herself whisper, "You're mine, and I'm yours." The table flying, his yelling didn't register, only his words. And fuck did they hurt.

She saw him freeze, but her mouth, her freaking ever moving Maya mouth, kept going. "Your pain is mine, Heart. Any home of mine is yours ... " She touched her hand to her belly, swallowed, and swiped away tears.

Maya continued to retreat until she made it to the front door. After bumping into Bishop - who had, true to his word, moved in - she seemed to come to herself. Mike took a step toward her, his face going from dazed to soft like he was coming out of something, but she threw her hand in front of herself to stop him.

"Whatever this is," she said, waving her hands around the home, "it's fucking your head up and you want to take it out on my ass. This is not simply about this house or the condo. Not three hours ago you *loved me*, fucking my brains out across *several* rooms of the condo I'm supposedly keeping you in, and *now* I can't even touch you?"

He took a step toward her again.

"Stay away. God, I'm sorry, Sheppard, but you stay the fuck away from me," Maya said, her voice trembling, but getting stronger. "I overstepped, and I apologized, repeatedly, but so you know — I had paperwork drawn up so you could buy into ownership of *OUR* home if you wanted because I knew that shit would be important to you. A home I began acquisition of BEFORE we were together, so don't throw that kept man shit in my face."

She shook her massive 'fro. "Packing up the dead *hurts*. Packing them up alone is an unimaginable pain, and for that reason I wanted to be there beside you whenever you did it. BURN IT ALL FOR FUCK I

CARE." She pointed to him in an angry jab. "And you're right. I don't fucking belong here."

She pressed her other hand to her chest absentmindedly, turned, and walked through the door.

On the front porch, she paused for a second, nauseous and retching a bit. When she glanced over her shoulder, she noticed Bishop stood there looking irritated. She glanced around at the workers and, embarrassingly, realized they'd pretty much heard everything. Maya sucked in a couple breaths and, holding her head high, she walked down the steps as Bishop followed her.

"Do you need a ride home?" he asked as she reached the bottom.

"No thank you, I'm fine. Plus, I have an appointment at the gun range."

His eyes widened in surprise.

"I'm learning to clear a building today," she said as an explanation that made his eyebrows shoot to his forehead.

"Why?"

"Why not?" Maya replied distractedly, as she moved to her truck. Grabbing her keys, she took the house key set off and handed it to the tall security expert. She noticed his curiosity had increased exponentially, but she did not give a flying fuck. "Could you have all the items at our, er, my, eh... the condo returned here? Please add it to the bill. I left so fast I didn't turn on the alarm."

Bishop nodded and tossed the keys to one man in his crew. Maya then walked over to the cleaner's crew. "I must go, but Ms. Kate, thank you for your time. We're going to end the work now. Obviously, I will pay the full contract through the end of the day."

The older woman tried to argue, but Maya, worn out, worried, sad, and holding her emotions together with a rapidly fraying thread, did what she always did - focused on problems she could solve. She reminded Kate that business was business and pulling in her entire crew on this project meant she wasn't collecting billable hours with other clients. Giving Kate and Bishop a small nod, she hopped in the truck and backed down the drive until she could turn around, then peeled quickly out of sight.

1. Fool of Me by Michelle Ndegeocello

34
CALL A MEDIC

MIKE

The gravel churned as she drove away. He stared at the spot where Maya last stood. The same spot where his mother stood the last time his father hit her. His mother's eyes were so swollen she couldn't see. He could hear the screams, see the blood pool on the floor and the splatters on the wall. He could still see his mother and he could now see Maya press her hand to her chest like she was trying to stop a deep pain.

He was so fucking stupid. Warring with himself, he was still angry she had interfered, but he was the one who first said the words "You're mine and I'm yours," and then kicked her ass because she believed in them as she should have.

God, her face.

Mike shook his head and looked around his childhood home. He looked down at his mother's handwriting and the pain and shame of his childhood and what he'd done to Maya flooded over him. He didn't want Maya or the baby anywhere near this godforsaken place. Instead of saying that, he had exploded. *What the fuck is wrong with me?*

"Mothers, they keep things, envisioning a time when they are long gone, and those things serve as reminders of the love they had for their family."

Mike looked over his shoulder at Ms. Kate, the woman who had become intimately acquainted with the items of a place he spent sixteen years wishing he could leave. Ms. Kate was another town staple, having built her small cleaning business one house at a time until she branched out into commercial cleaning and multiple locations. After putting her entire family through college with her business, she sent herself when she was fifty. She wore her midnight hair tied neatly at her nape. She still had a kind face, though she looked disappointed with him right now. He took in her rose-colored blouse, slacks, and pumps. It wasn't lost on Mike that she was helping to see to this account personally.

"Your wife is a mother now and is thinking as a mother thinks," Kate said, looking at him with a critical eye. "She only saw the good."

"There's no good here."

"Then it is you who is not 'getting it,'" Kate said. "Your father was a complete waste of skin, but your mother, she loved you. She raised her babies in a home with constant danger, anger, and sadness, yet took the time to care for the things that make a house a home in hopes you'd carry them with you. If you don't understand that, then you are allowing him to steal one of the little pieces of hope she held on to."

Jesus. Mike bent in a low squat to the floor and fingered the pink baby blanket now tossed haphazardly to the floor, tracing his mother's handwriting on the small linen card pinned to it: "*Rose Marie.*"

"I knew your mother for years. Knew things were bad here, though not how bad, not 'til the end. Your mother disappeared from town after she married him, taking that beautiful smile of hers with her," the woman said, staring out the window, lost in her own thoughts. "She became a shell of herself, but we saw glimpses of the old Mary ... when she was with her children. Did you tell her, your Maya, how bad things were?"

He said nothing.

Kate turned to Mike and hit him with a piercing gaze. "The whole town's talking about what a good man Mary's son has become, his stellar reputation in Los Angeles. How he has won the heart of our beautiful new neighbor, but today? Your mother would be so disappointed. It is okay to get angry. Men, women, we speak different languages ... we yell, fight and throw things, but you always fight fair, and today, Michael Andrew Sheppard, you fought dirty and crushed that girl. Now, what are you going to do about it?"

"YOU SHOULDN'T BE HERE," Laila said, her eyes not moving off the screen.

Mike, Laila, and, oddly, Bishop from the security company stood inside the control center of the warehouse rigged for practice. There were a half dozen monitors showing the various rooms of the warehouse from a multitude of angles, a control panel that determined the timing for the targets, the angles on the cameras, lighting, and overall sound system. The room set at a high angle in the warehouse with a large, bulletproof glass front. Darkened glass kept the participants in the warehouse from seeing those inside the control room.

"Laila," Mike whispered. "I gotta see my girl."

"And who is this mountain?" Laila said, looking briefly at Bishop, who leaned his tall, built, bald self against the wall. He crossed his obsidian arms in a relaxed way, his odd blue-grey eyes alert.

"I came to watch her kick his ass," Bishop said, flashing a small grin at Laila.

BUZZ!

Laila moved to hit the button on the speaker as she looked at Mike and held a finger to her lips.

"One hundred percent on the kill shots, cupcake," Laila called through the microphone.

Maya spoke clearly into the mic rigged to her. "I know." Her breath was coming fast and heavy.

Laila looked over at the monitor that controlled the targets and shook her head.

"Any reason you put a bullet in the brain of every male target in this warehouse, except the kid with the teddy bear, regardless of their threat?"

"They are all a threat," Maya said.

"And the women you didn't shoot even if they were holding a weapon."

"They likely had a good reason, like some asshole man."

Laila took her finger off the speaker button and looked pointedly at Mike. "You should go."

"I'm not going anywhere," Mike said, crossing his arms.

Laila shrugged. "Your choice. She might use live ammo..." She put her finger back on the speaker button.

"You know that means you technically failed, right?"

"Yep, but I feel much fucking better." She ejected her clip with practiced ease, a grim expression on her face.

Bishop's small smile passed into a full-on grin at that announcement. Laila rolled her eyes and asked, "You gonna do it right or you gonna keep wasting time and bullets?"

"Kiss my ass, Laila."

Laila took her finger off the button again.

"Last warning, Sheppard."

Mike didn't say a word. He focused on Maya's image on the monitor.

"She's pissed, pregnant, and has a gun." Bishop laughed. "You bought every inch of this man, but you should listen to the pretty lady."

Laila's eyes narrowed at Bishop with such fierceness he threw up his hands in defense.

Maya's voice came over the speaker in the control room. It was clear she was losing her patience. "Run it again," she barked. "And put on my music."

"With music you can't hear the targets, you'll have to rely on sight only," Laila warned.

"Don't care."

"Cupcake—"

"GOD! I'm hemorrhaging here, Laila! HE CUT ME. De-ep." Her breath caught on the word. "I was stupid 'Take Charge Maya,' messed up, and he sliced. Me. Open."

Maya snatched off her protective glasses and blinked rapidly, her hands resting on her hips.

"I can still feel his skin on mine," she touched her lips absentmindedly, "and he wouldn't let me touch him. I didn't know ... I didn't know it was that bad for him. And *I* was scared and hurt, and I yelled at *him* before I left. I don't know if I can fix it. This hurts so much. And his pain ... It was like he was in hell. And I forced him there ... " she said, almost to herself.

"Maya—" Laila started, her voice softening a bit.

"Please," she whispered, sniffing sadly. "I need another focus. Go back to being a cold-hearted bitch with blood packets and let me shoot pretend bad guys."

Laila watched him as Maya spoke. He had a gaping wound, too. Maya didn't realize it, but she had delivered a direct hit. Bishop focused on his boots, had lost his grin. Mike didn't know where to look. It was all kinda hazy. The prickling in the back of his eyes might have had something to do with it.

Laila, never taking her eyes off Mike, reached over and hit the speaker button again. "You got it, Maya. Listen for the buzz."

Mike turned his gaze from the floor back to Maya and he watched her wipe away at her eyes and slam her glasses back on her face. He had a deep burn in the middle of his chest that had grown as Maya spoke. He couldn't breathe. It hurt so bad.

Laila dug into Maya's purse, grabbed her phone, and connected it to the warehouse speakers. Mike realized Laila and Maya had grown close because, without asking, Laila moved through Maya's music and selected a playlist. "*Sucker for Pain*" blared out with hard-hitting beats.[1]

He watched as Maya took a deep breath and began bobbing her head in time with the music as she got into a zone.

"You're an asshole," Laila said harshly, never looking away from the monitor.

"I know."

Over the next half hour as Tupac, Metallica, DMX, and Twenty One Pilots blasted through the speakers, Maya cleared the warehouse twice, getting one hundred percent each time. The program randomized targets so Maya couldn't anticipate. She was thorough, alert, and in Laila's words - "ice cold."

"That's the sexiest shit I've ever seen," Bishop muttered.

"I know, right?" Laila said. "Forget a push-up bra and pumps."

Bishop snorted. "How long has she been training?" he asked Laila.

"I think she's had ten sessions now," she said, shrugging. "Her third session on the range she was at sixty percent. From then on, she has pretty much nailed them ever since."

"Bullshit," Mike said.

"Before she came to me, she would pull her gun, but not shoot it. She was terrified," Laila said, her eyes hard on Mike. "She told me she hadn't shot it since she bought it and then it was only twice. We talked about the science behind it, made the range a mathematical problem, and she went in. You, of all people, should know not to underestimate her."

Mike, watching her on the monitor, swallowed. His corded throat struggled with the action. "I'm going down there."

"Call a medic," Bishop mused from the background.

Laila pressed the speaker button. "Hold on, Cupcake, human coming down."

Mike walked across the cold room and snatched open the door that led to the warehouse. He approached Maya from behind, checking to see her hands were empty. Her music was still pumping through the speaker. Anthrax's "Bring the Noise" was on, and Maya paced back and forth. As he reached out to touch her shoulder, Maya suddenly turned, swinging his arm off her and striking him in the chest. She quickly delivered a devastating punch to the jaw before taking off to a defensive position on the other side of a table.

The warehouse exploded with laughter as Laila and Bishop's voices boomed over the loudspeakers and Anthrax cut off.

"Oops Maya, I forgot to tell you the training was over," Laila giggled. Yes giggled. A deep voice chuckled over the speakers from further away.

Maya's eyes landed on him as he mumbled, "Yeah fucking right, she forgot."

"SHIT!" Maya ran around the table to where Mike stood, rubbing his jaw. "I thought you were a trainer."

"Your trainers come in without protection?" he asked, amused and looking at her, impressed.

"Yes. Laila said I needed to feel skin on bone. You didn't defend yourself; I should have known."

He shrugged, dropped his hand, and green eyes met brown. "Maya, baby... I'm so sorry."

He watched as a tear escaped her eye. *Fuck*. He fucked this up. He took a step toward her, and she stepped back.

Shit.

"I flew off the handle. You didn't deserve that. I–I was completely out of line."

"I get being upset, but you were on another level. I've never seen you like that. I was an ass sending them there. I should have listened to you, respected your boundaries instead of coming up. But your reaction ... It wasn't you. Or was it?" She took a step back. "We only have known each other a little while. Where were you?" she asked, pointing to her head.

"I haven't been back to that house since I left at sixteen."

Maya's eyes widened.

"Sixteen years I lived in a special hell with my mother and sister. Stan was as big of an asshole to us as he was to this town. Bigger maybe. That place is my nightmare, and not only did I not want to be there, but I have never wanted anything from it, and I especially never wanted you to bring all your goodness into that place." He sighed, frustrated, running his hands over his face. "It sounds crazy, but it all came back. The fear, the hatred, the oppressive control. It was like a... cloud of dark memories when I walked through that front door. You were trying to help, but all I could see was his control. Hear his voice.... her screams. See her blood."

He swallowed hard. "Seeing you in there it scared me. That his stink would touch you like it touches everything else in this town. I was angry. I wanted to warn you away, protect you. Instead ... I'M the one that hurt you."

He walked to her, and she didn't move. Taking her hand and placing it on his heart, he watched as she inhaled sharply and closed her eyes.

"I've got a lot of shame and anger burning inside me from that place, but that doesn't compare to the shame I feel right now for what I said to you, how I treated you," he said his voice low and tight. "I wish you had asked me first, and I need you to listen to me. I gotta know that I can trust you, Maya. I'm working hard as hell to earn yours. I gotta know that I can give you mine. None of that excuses my behavior, taking all that out on you, reacting like I did. I ... Please, Sunshine, please forgive me."

The time from when he asked for her forgiveness and when she nodded was like 10 years. But eventually, she did nod, and he could feel his heartbeat again.

Mike blew out the breath he'd been holding and pulled his woman into his arms, her exquisite softness against him. "My Maya," he breathed against her hair, his voice full of relief. "God, I'm so, so sorry."

"I'm sorry too, I didn't think, and I should have been more sensitive," Maya said into his chest. "You need to talk to someone. This can't fester. Believe me, I know."

She tipped her head back to peer at him, and he leaned in to kiss her. Hard. It stole both of their breath, and soon they pressed into and ground on each other against the wall, Maya's legs wrapped around his waist before either of them realized where they were. That is, until the loudspeaker clicked on.

"You fuck in my warehouse. I shoot you both."

Maya and Mike's laughter filled the air.

---

1. Sucker for Pain by Twenty One Pilots
   Holler if Ya Hear Me by Tupac
   Purple Lamborghini by Skrillex & Rick Ross

35

MAKE THAT TWO

MAYA

"You ready to see and hear your baby?" Lilith Moon asked Mike as she squirted clear gel on Maya's belly. Maya wanted to laugh at his turn-around. The man was now damn near giddy. Before, when he was first introduced to Lilith, he was very skeptical.

Lilith was a third-generation midwife, nurse-midwife, and apparently was used to skeptical fathers. She looked too young and free to be delivering babies, but after she explained her expertise, her background - including teaching midwifery to more than 500 students to date - he relaxed.

If Lilith was surprised to see Mike at the appointment, she didn't show it. She was as she always was - calm, efficient, and welcoming.

She positioned the handheld device on Maya's stomach, and the whoosh whoosh whoosh of a new life filled the room. It was Maya's third time hearing it, but it still took her breath away.[1]

Mike looked mesmerized. He squeezed Maya's hand tight, his green eyes were wide and sparkling. "That's her?" he asked, closing his eyes and listening close. "Isn't her heartbeat a little fast? Sounds like she's running."

"Nope, they all sound that way. Her rate is perfectly fine, but if you want to make sure she's not running, look."

Lilith turned the monitor toward them, and Maya sucked in a breath softly.

"She's so different from the first time."

Mike leaned in close to the monitor over the top of Maya. "Holy fuck. She's gorgeous."

Maya cracked up laughing. "You don't know she's a girl and how can you tell she's gorgeous? This isn't one of those 3D sonograms!"

"She is the most gorgeous little baby I have ever seen in my entire life."

"Heart." Maya bit her bottom lip and smiled.

"Do you want to know the gender for relative certainty?"

Mike looked at Maya and shrugged. "It's up to you, babe. I already know it's a girl."

Maya snorted. "I want to be surprised. Wait ... I think. I don't know. Um ... "

"Why don't I put it in an envelope, and you can decide whether to open it?" Lilith grinned at them.

"Perfect," they said together.

MIKE

The Colorado late afternoon summer sun blazed. It was especially warm in the long hospital parking lot where the Women's Clinic attached to the main Rough Ridge County Hospital. Maya had declined to wait at the front door for Mike to bring the car around, preferring to take the walk across the expansive lot for exercise. They held hands as they strolled to his Jeep. Maya looked ahead to where the main road leading out of Rough Ridge shimmered from the heat.

"Do you think you can resist looking?" he asked.

Maya looked at him, smiled slightly, and nodded. She had gone quiet at the end of the appointment until now.

"Sunshine, what's the matter?"

"A lot of difficulties today. I'm just tired."

Shame and sadness hit him again. "Baby."

She waved him off. "It's okay. Couples fight, right? I need sleep, that's all. It feels like I have had so little in months. I'll be fine once I get home and get a normal week under my belt. Can you take me around to the warehouse? I need to get my truck. That way, you don't have to drop me off before you go home."

Mike had a splitting pain in his chest. They were going to separate places. He had made clear his concerns about the condo, and his place in it, with little tact. She listened and took it to heart, but it felt wrong. She was tired and stressed and he had added to it, keeping her up, adding to the emotional weight she was under. Fuck, maybe he wasn't good enough for her, for the baby. Seeing that precious little girl on the monitor changed him. He pushed down those feelings.

"Let's pick up your truck, then we'll go back and talk," he said, studying her.

She simply nodded and climbed into the passenger seat of the Jeep.

MAYA

That was when the air around them electrified and exploded. Mike shoved Maya to the floor of the Jeep and covered her body with his while reaching for his gun in between the seats.

The sound was deafening. It was nothing like the gun range - controlled, hollow, and in one direction. This was shots all around them, the pinging of bullets against metal, the pffft sound bullets made hitting the upholstery, the crash of glass shattering and tinkling as it rained down on them. She realized the sounds made when bullets hit flesh were absent.

After a brief pause in the shooting, Mike barked out, "Stay down!" And he took off.

"Oh my God!"

No sooner had that left her mouth the shooting began again, but it was further away slightly and sounded like it was from a single gun. *Mike's gun!* Boots hit the ground in a run and car tires squealed. *He drew the fire away from her.*

Maya looked around, hoping Mike kept a spare gun in the car, but found nothing between his seats. Blindly, she opened the glove compartment and searched, slapping and sliding her hand around. Nothing.

"Fuck!" Maya whispered, of all times not to have her own gun with her. Of course, a drive by hadn't been on the day's itinerary. Now, Mike was out there alone and cop or not, he needed help. She found her purse and dug in, scrambling to get to her phone while she raised her head quickly once, then a second time after seeing it was clear. And that's when she saw him.

She had always figured Mike for a badass. Giant man, that quiet, powerful energy, a cop ... but nothing prepared her for the view from the blasted-out driver side window.

He was crouched behind a car as two men from another car got out and were closing in. Both were a little on the taller side, they both were in all black, but one was a dirty blond and the other had dark, shaggy hair and beard.

She wanted to shout a warning to him, but her voice caught in her throat as she watched Mike spring up and—in a maneuver she could only describe as action movie superhero stuff—disarm and incapacitate the first one while using the man as a shield and a weapon against the second man.

Mike's movements were so swift Maya's brain had to slow it down and replay it for it to make sense. Each hit he landed looked painful for the bad guys and any counterattacks they made glanced off Mike. It was like the other men stood still. In seconds, they were limp on the ground, their weapons in Mike's control. She watched him scan the area and turn back toward the Jeep. When their eyes met her heart jumped into her throat. She had fucked up.

Shit. Classic mistake. She took her mind off her surroundings and focused too much on the action. She turned and stared up at a big reddish-blond man with a big black gun. Heavily muscled, with shitty-looking homemade tats all over his arms and neck, he outweighed Maya by a lot and none of her practiced stuff would work from this angle. He flicked the barrel of his gun.

"Out."

Dammit.

Maya slid awkwardly out, careful to make a big show of putting her hand on her belly to show she was pregnant. She pushed out her belly more. The man's dark blue eyes dropped to her belly, then back to her eyes again. His eyes told her everything. He was a stone-cold killer and her being pregnant meant nothing to him. Maya absentmindedly wondered why they all had that same cold, dead stare. How many times had this man or Griffin killed before they earned that stare?

Forcing herself to focus and try to stop shaking with fear, she looked around him at the security guard creeping near, Taser drawn, looking all of nineteen years old. She looked away and swept her eyes to the other side, where there was only a little room to get by him, and she doubted she could move fast enough. She brought her eyes back to the man. He bared his teeth.

"Nowhere to run, sweetheart. You and me are going to go for a ride."

Watching him, she quickly calculated distance and velocity as he clamped a meaty hand around her wrist. Clearing the Jeep, she struggled against him.

"Let her go."

Mike's icy voice sent shivers down her spine.

"You cost me a lot of money, Sheppard," he said. "But this fine piece of ass should work off some of the loss. I'll try it out myself first, though."

Maya saw the muscles in the large man's arm bunch, and knew she had seconds. As soon as he tried yanking her to him, she clamped onto his wrist with her other hand, dropped her butt down, and lifted her feet, swinging herself using his arm and momentum to become a pendulum. Her sudden movement took him off balance and he lurched to the side as her ass and the rest of her skidded along the side of, then past him, and out of his grasp.

That was all the distraction Mike needed. As swiftly as he had disarmed the others, it was no harder with this guy. Maya saw the bad guy's gun skid under the Jeep, and she looked to see Mike land three swift, bone-crunching, precision blows. The man dropped, his head hitting the concrete with a sickening thud.

"Cuff 'im, call it in," Mike growled to the guard who was looking at Mike like he had just walked on water, which Maya understood because she was looking at him the same way.[2]

Mike stepped over the perp, not glancing back or breaking his stride until he was next to Maya. He only paused to lift her carefully and place her on the hood of someone's car. He looked her in the eye and said fiercely, "Baby. Breathe."

Maya blinked and slowly realized the burning in her lungs from not breathing and exhaled. It came out rough. The same with the first intake of air and a bit of a wheeze. While she focused on the simple exchange of oxygen and carbon dioxide and used her inhaler, Mike checked her over thoroughly, checking for broken bones and other injuries.

Maya hissed sharply when he touched the side of her hip where she slid. Mike ripped her white sweatpants the rest of the way to see her injuries.

"Fuck. Road rash," he said, pissed off as he bent over to check it out. "We need to get that cleaned and bandaged." He straightened and looked at her hard. "You're all right."

"Are you asking me or telling me?"

"I'm telling you. You're all right. It wasn't your ex; they were after me. You're relatively uninjured and made a smart move back there." He closed in on her, taking her face in his hands. "You're all right. No panic attacks, no bad dreams, no loss in the progress you've made. Got it?"

Ah. She got it. Though she was pretty sure that wasn't how it worked, maybe her psyche responded well to badass alpha psychology because she did seem all right. Jittery, but overall ok, so she shrugged and nodded.

"I'm all right."

He gave her a small smile, kissed her nose, and demanded, "Stay here."

By now the parking lot was crawling with cops, medics, and looky loos. Mike stood talking with a grim-faced Paul as the shooters were being loaded into separate squad cars. Officers were rolling out crime scene tape and little yellow plastic tents with numbers on them. Further up the parking lot, the same was happening around the car that the shooters drove.

Maya watched the security guard give his statement and held back laughter as he described Mike. "Then that guy came through like

MegaCop and took the guy down in three hits! He didn't even watch his body drop; he breezed past him to get the girl. It was like a fucking movie!"

Paul chuckled, and Maya turned to see him and Mike approaching.

"Looks like you got a fan," Paul grinned, his blue eyes mischievous.

"Fuck," Mike muttered under his breath. "Shut up man."

Maya grinned at them both. "Make that two MegaCop."

"All this and she busts my balls," Mike mused as he leaned down and kissed her neck.

"I need to get your statement Maya," Paul said.

"Get it inside. She's got an injury," Mike said tightly.

Paul leaned over and looked at her thigh, his face clouding over.

"It's not that bad," Maya assured him.

She saw a news van arrive and turned her body away. "A scrape. But no statements."

"You've had enough injuries to last a lifetime," Paul said hard. "This shit will not touch you again. I'll see you inside after I finish here," he said, giving her knee a quick squeeze and walking away.

"You want to wait for a wheelchair?" Mike asked.

"Oh gosh no, I can walk. I don't need—"

She lost her sentence as Mike swooped her into his arms and carried her across the parking lot to the hospital entrance.

"You know this picking me up all the time is—"

"See! Fucking MegaCop," the security guard shouted excitedly.

"Fuck me, they're gonna kill me at the station," Mike muttered, which made Maya laugh so hard she forgot to be annoyed. She was ordering that on a custom t-shirt tonight.

---

1. Lady by Brett Young
2. Who Shot Ya by Notorious B.I.G.

36
RELIEF

MAYA

There's this thing called normalcy. Call it boring, call it routine. Maya had a craving for it — stronger than her constant craving for chocolate.

The week had been so awesomely normal. Blissfully normal. She was tempted to buy khakis for Heart and a twin set for herself - without the sense of fashion irony of pairing it with spikes, but with real pearls. Then she realized what now counted as normal for her still didn't go with pearls, and Heart in a pair of khakis might be the breaking of one seal of the apocalypse.

She didn't move on the uniform of suburbia, but she moved forward with ordering a drafting table for her office and some other kick-ass accessories to make her home more ... homey. She also investigated automotive certification at the local community college as a backup.

Plans.

Normal.

She had lunch with her sister-in-law twice. Lunch with Heart twice, and breakfast with her brother and father once.

Okay. That wasn't normal. It was normal for other people in the world, but for Maya's now crazy life, lunch with her previously unknown father and brother was not normal ... but it was nice. She'd met her dad because of her negligence.

After the drive-by, Maya should have checked in with those who would worry about her — like her family. Instead, it never occurred to her they would find out about bullets flying through Heart's Jeep, because why? She was from Columbus where these things made the news, but often dropped in the bin of "city life." Color her surprised when she got a series of frantic texts first thing in the morning.

TORI: CAINE HEARD YOU WERE IN THE DRIVE-BY YESTERDAY. YOU SHOULD HAVE CALLED HIM.

MAYA: I DIDN'T THINK OF IT. I WAS EXHAUSTED.

TORI: HE'S ON HIS WAY WITH THOMAS.

MAYA: WHAT?!

TORI: YOU'VE GOT ABOUT TWENTY MINS BEFORE THEY GET THERE.

MAYA: SUPER.

TORI: IS MIKE THERE?

MAYA: NO, HE WENT INTO WORK EARLY TO WORK THE CASE, OR GET IN THE WAY AND TAKE OVER FOR WHOMEVER IS WORKING IT.

TORI: GOOD, 'CAUSE CAINE'S PISSED. YOU NEED TO TELL MIKE EVERYTHING SOON, HONEY.

MAYA: I WANT ONE WEEK OF NORMAL.

TORI: NEW SUBJECT: YOU GUYS COMIN' TO THE PARTY? CAINE'S PULLING OUT THE BEAST.

MAYA: IDK, MIKE IS WEIRD AROUND YOU GUYS.

TORI: WHICH IS WHY YOU SHOULD TELL HIM.

MAYA: IN MY OWN TIME VICTORIA.

TORI: B.S. AND YOU KNOW IT, BUT GET READY FOR THE GUYS. TTYL

Maya put her phone down but had to grab it again when another flurry came in.

JAKE: IS THERE ANY REASON I SHOULDN'T BE AT THE STATION RIGHT NOW?

MAYA: BECAUSE YOU'RE NOT A POLICE OFFICER? I DON'T KNOW HOW TO PLAY THIS GAME.

JAKE: DRIVE-BY.

MAYA: I THOUGHT YOU DIDN'T TEXT.

The OSU fight song ringtone sounded on her phone. Shit.

"Jake, I don't have time to go over this, Caine is enroute with my father whom I've never met and I'm still in bed smelling like I've been fucking all night," Maya said in a rush as she hopped out of bed and ran to the bathroom with morning sickness.

She rinsed her mouth and pressed the phone to her ear. "Still there?"

"Unfortunately. That was gross."

"You call first thing in the morning. That's the risk you take," she said, putting the phone on speaker as she turned on the shower. "I can't hear you over the shower, so I'm going to shout it out and you can then tin-can this to the rest of the town."

Maya ran over the details of the drive-by in the second-fastest shower she had ever taken and was finished by the time she hopped out.

"Now I'm going to brush my teeth and try not to vomit, and you can say your peace," she said as she rushed through her morning routine on serious waves of queasy.[1]

"You sure this isn't him?"

"No, they seem certain it's related to Heart's case."

"I'll check it out."

"You and everybody else," she said, but it sounded more like "goo an ebodee elsh" with a mouth full of toothpaste.

"You tell Mike yet?"

"Gotta go."

"Darlin' ... "

"Bye!"

Beep.

The twenty minutes before she met her father was a lifetime. After Maya showered, she fussed with her hair and gave up. Then she tore through outfits until she settled on white slacks and a soft white tee with a screen print of the Eiffel Tower on it - a mix of casual and dress to show the importance of the occasion and to put her father at ease. She put a white ribbon in her hair. Then she reminded herself she wasn't six and snatched it out. She ran back to her room, shoved everything into the closet, and took the time to breathe in a few deep breaths and swipe on gloss. Before she realized it, Caine walked in the door, disarmed and re-armed the alarm, and tossed his keys down on the kitchen counter.

"Maya?" he rumbled loudly from her kitchen.

She took one more glimpse at herself and kicked off her shoes. They were too formal.

"Coming!" she called as she tried not to pee herself walking down the hallway. The fridge opened and closed and a low, deep rumblings of male voices met her ears. *My dad has a deep voice!*

She ambled down the steps and rounded the corner. There he was, with eyes like hers. He was a mahogany version of Caine; older, of course, but very handsome and tall. He gave her a gentle smile.

"Wow. You look just like Elise," he breathed. "Except your eyes. You have my eyes."

Maya smiled shyly and stuck out her hand. "Hi Mr. Walters, I'm Maya Angel. Wait! That sounds too formal. I'm Maya, your daughter. Shit, you already know that! Fuck, I swore in front of my father!"

Maya threw her hands in front of her face while Caine laughed. Thomas' deep chuckle made her glance up with a bigger, but shy, smile.

"You've got her dimple too ... absolutely beautiful." His voice was gruff. He took in a deep breath, and said, "I know you didn't want to see me; I don't blame you. I just wanted to see for myself that you were okay after yesterday."

He looked uncomfortable, jumpy even, and Maya rushed to put him at ease. "I wanted to see you. I was ... scared. In case you were disappointed or mad that you didn't know about me or embarrassed or..." She shrugged. "It's a lot to take in ... bastard child of an affair and all that."

"No, it's not, and you're not anything but the daughter of two people who cared a great deal for each other," he said, his voice deep and firm. "Never say that again."

Maya worried the hem of her blouse for a moment, then crossed the distance between them quickly, throwing her arms around Thomas. "It's really nice to meet you," she breathed. He promptly wrapped his arms around her and hugged her tightly.

He was warm and smelled nice and Maya was glad she forgot the mascara when he said into her hair, "I'm sorry I wasn't there for you."

"You didn't know."

"I'm still sorry."

"So am I."

They held each other a while longer and then slowly let go. Maya motioned for him to sit at the kitchen island, while Caine thoughtfully poured Maya a glass of milk and grabbed juice for himself and Thomas.

Maya looked over at Caine across from her, then to Thomas sitting at her side. "How much do you know about me?"

"Everything Caine knows."

She nodded. Sipping her milk, she traced a pattern on the counter with her other hand.

"What we want to know now is why were you in a drive-by shooting last night?"

Maya shrugged. "Wrong place and wrong time. Heart—Michael— and I were coming out of my appointment. Wait, you know—" She paused, gesturing to her belly.

"That I have another grandbaby on the way, yes," Thomas rumbled and nodded encouragingly for Maya to keep going.

"Right," she said as she grinned slightly and rubbed a protective hand over her bump. "We were there, and we were getting into the car when wham, everything went crazy!"

She told them everything, from Heart drawing the fire away from her to the takedowns to her minor injury.

"And Caine says you're ... involved with Sheppard."

"Heart and I are—we love each other, yes." She nodded slowly. "I know his family and ours have a fuc, erm, messed up history. But he's nothing like his father. He spent more time away from him than with him and he treats me like a treasure. He looks at me ... like ... Caine looks at Victoria. I wasn't looking for it. Neither of us was. He doesn't know who I am, but it happened."

She breathed out roughly and took a long drink of milk.

"I know better than to judge a man by his father," Thomas said, looking at Caine long. "When he first arrived back here, he sought me out. Caine too. Apologized for what his father had done. Took responsibility for what he considered his family's shame. That took an honorable man to do that. He has my respect. That said, being the wife of a cop isn't a simple life," he said, looking at her gently. "Especially when they are targeted. It also won't be easy in this town attached to a Sheppard."

"Caine told you everything about me?"

Thomas nodded.

"Then you know I have a knack for not doing things easy."

"Much like your mother," Thomas said, his eyes never leaving hers. He reached out a gigantic hand, covering hers and gripping it. "I'm glad."

"They shot at you Maya. Because of him, people shot at you at a hospital," Caine bit out, unable to hold it in anymore. "You need someone who doesn't add to your problems."

"And what's going on with me could easily get him killed," she said, nailing him with a stare. "Besides, when I do tell him, no guarantees you'll have to worry about our relationship. I don't know what he's going to say. I want one week of normal before it could all go away."

"Nothing normal about having to hide who you are, your family. If he loves you like you says he does, he wants all of you," Caine said.

When she said nothing for a long moment, Thomas suggested they go out to lunch. Instead, Maya wanted to cook for them. She felt like a little kid wanting to impress her father. She held back another round of sickness while she made BLTs for them and cut fruit for herself. Then she excused herself to go heave for a while. When she got back, they spent more time talking.

The conversation wasn't always easy, especially when Maya told Thomas more about her mother's illness, but it was nice. Thomas was funny if not cautiously open with her. He seemed self-conscious, and Maya caught him several times staring at her when he thought she didn't notice, his expression soft and sometimes sad.

Thomas and Caine stayed with Maya for about four hours, shooting the breeze and getting to know each other. When it was time for them to go, Caine leaned in and kissed his sister on the top of her head.

"Are you coming to the party?"

Maya paused, looking uncomfortable.

"Tori wants Mike to come."

She looked into his eyes. "What about you?"

Caine shrugged as he jiggled his keys restlessly. "My beef with him is you being safe and happy. If he can do that, I guess I don't have a problem. He fucks up, I'm gutting' him balls to throat. Simple."

"That was both distinctly vague and violently specific," Maya said, her eyes wide in both horror and amusement.

"You're not the only smart one," he said with a deep chuckle.

Maya walked to the island and dug in her purse. She produced a secure phone and handed it to Thomas, explaining its uses.

"I know it's all James Bond-ish. I want everyone to be safe," she said with a shrug.

"It's this bad," Thomas said, his voice on edge, his warm brown eyes turning hard for the first time Maya had ever seen.

"I don't do easy," Maya said, trying to make the moment lighter. Her attempt at a joke fell flat. "I don't want it to be, but I won't have my family hurt."

Thomas held her again, tighter, this time, so tight she almost couldn't breathe.

"I am in no position to tell you anything about your life and how you live it. I don't have the right. But this isn't normal, sweetheart. Living a lie will tear you apart."

"HAVE you ever considered what you believe to be normal is simply another way to control things around you?" Dr. Flemmings asked.

Maya was back in the saddle, or on the couch, again. It'd been more than a week of phone sessions as Maya helped with Rose Marie's funeral and everything that followed. She hadn't had time to come in and then she was a little afraid after the drive-by.

"Did you know my mother, grandmother, and her mother all died before they were forty-five? Cancer, heart attack, farm accident?" Maya asked suddenly.

"No, I didn't know that Maya," Dr. Flemmings replied, looking like she was not liking where Maya was going.

"I wonder..."

"You're attempting to control things, Maya, now your time of death."

"I don't want to die young!" Maya barked. "But you have to see there's a pattern here and with Griffin after me. I just..."

"Perhaps you don't, but you are trying to fit your abuse into a framework that makes sense, while taking away the uncertainty of one of the most uncontrollable aspects of life," Dr. Flemmings countered. "Nothing about what happened to you makes sense... other than abuse is all too common, no matter your education or care in picking a partner. Nothing about the men coming after your boyfriend makes sense. Your mother dying so young — it's out of order of how things should be. Life doesn't make sense, Maya. Not all the time. All you can control is how you respond. And how you respond is what defines you and frames your reality."

Maya sat there, not speaking. She stared unblinking at the bookcase.

Dr. Flemmings watched her for a moment.

"Maya, have you ever grieved your mother's death?"

"Of course. I wore black, cried, ate a gallon of ice cream..."

"How long?"

"I thought there was no timeline on grief?" Maya said, getting irritated.

Dr. Flemmings sat patiently, irritating Maya more.

"I gave it the weekend. I had an internship starting a week from when I buried her and I needed to focus."

"And after the internship?"

"I had another one."

"And then?"

"I started the firm."

"And then?"

"I worked my ass off for years, then I got my ass kicked, then I ran, and now I'm in this place. I spent seven years grieving her before she died. I think that's enough."

Dr. Flemmings said nothing.

"You're judging me."

"No Maya, of course I'm not."

"Yes, you are. You're better at hiding it. And why not? I'm judging me!" Her hand wildly traced a pattern on the chair. "What kind of daughter doesn't grieve her mother? What kind of daughter would rather be on the cheerleading squad or going to prom than be with her mother waiting, watching her die?" she ranted, her voice getting louder and louder.

"And the one time I took my eyes off the ball," she said, shaking her head. "The one night I had YEARS worth of stupid, irresponsible, crammed-into-one-night-fun, she goes and dies, and I almost didn't get a chance to say goodbye. I've always been responsible. Always good. And ALWAYS on watch. Every morning, taking a deep breath before you open the bedroom door, hoping she didn't die overnight. Managing nurses, medications. What was there to grieve? Especially when you're so fucking glad it's over!"

Maya gasped and covered her mouth.

"I can't believe I said that ... I gotta go." She jumped up.

"Maya, we still have time—"

"No. This is ridiculous. I don't know who I am anymore. I'm all over the place. Pretending shit ... I almost bought a fucking twinset. With pearls!"

"Maybe you're discovering who you are beyond who you have allowed yourself to be."

"Everybody wants to be Yoda." Maya snatched her purse and stalked out.

MIKE

Dr. Flemmings got down out of her SUV and looked around.

"It's a beautiful piece of land," she said, slipping her sunglasses off and taking in the tall trees and babbling brook nearby.

"There's a lake up the path aways and I own everything from there to there." He showed a vast expanse of land on the mountain. "The land isn't the problem, Doc. It's the house. I have a woman I want to make my wife, and I can't bring her home."

Mike looked at Dr. Flemmings. "I need to fix that."

MIKE

That morning, Mike woke at dawn, kissed Maya goodbye, and took off for the station. Maya understood he needed to be there to make sure what happened at the hospital didn't happen again. He explained to her why the drive-by happened - he had interrupted several crimes in progress, and that the men who shot at them directly benefited from the revenue of said crimes. What he didn't discuss, even after she asked about it, was why the man would go through such pains to personally take him out.

Sharp as a tack, she remarked it seemed like a huge risk, but he changed the subject by kissing her and, well, she stopped talking except to scream out his name and say things like, "Harder," "Yes," and "I'm coming." Sure, it was a limited number of words, but given his relief that Maya and the baby were okay, he had made it his personal mission to make sure she said them often through the night.

Now he was standing in the middle of his childhood home for the second time in recent days, trying to remember anything positive from his childhood.

"All I want to do is burn the whole thing to the ground," he said after a few moments.

"What's stopping you?" Dr. Flemmings asked.

"What? I thought you'd say something like, 'it won't take away from the feelings I get when I'm here.' Or 'that's covering the problem,'" Mike replied with a slight grin.

"You can work through those feelings without living in the building where you can still see your mother's bloodstains," Dr. Flemmings said seriously, gesturing to an old, darkened stain on the wood floor. "What do you feel when you come up the drive?"

"It's a mix. I love the land, spent tons of time out there exploring, getting away from here," he said, looking around.

"It's the structure that bothers you the most?"

"That, some things in it..."

"And the thought of it being gone?"

"Relief."

"Then it sounds pretty simple to me, Michael."

"Do people actually pay you for this?" he said, chuckling.

"People pay me to listen. Most of the time, they already know what they need to do, and those that don't often only need to be pointed in the right direction."

"Like Maya."

"Michael Andrew Sheppard, it's been a while since you were a patient, but when you came to me at fourteen years old, what was the first thing you asked me?" Dr. Flemmings asked, crossing her arms and looking at him sternly.

"Could a police officer find out what I talked about?" Mike replied gruffly, as he remembered his fourteen-year-old self sitting in Flemmings' office, scared, eye swollen from a fight at school - his tenth that year. He worried his father would find out he was coming to see her and would know he had confided about his mother's abuse.

If it hadn't been for Dr. Flemmings, he would have never created the plan to graduate early. It was also Dr. Flemmings that kept him out of jail the night he laid Stan out with a baseball bat when he was fifteen. It was the last time Stan put a hand on his mother, too.

"The answer hasn't changed," she replied unsmilingly. "You'd do well to remember that young man."

"I'll try," Mike said, heading for the door, itching to get out of the home.

"Do it or don't kid, forget this trying business," she said, walking through the door he held open.

"Yes, Master Yoda," Mike said with a deep chuckle.

"Great minds."

"What?"

"Nothing," Dr. Flemmings mumbled, with a slight smile, as she climbed into her SUV.

---

1. Under Pressure by Queen & David Bowie

37

DENIAL IS INTOXICATING

IN COLUMBUS, OHIO...

CALLISTA

Griffin stood in the middle of the exquisite private room, his back to the scene taking place behind him. The lush interior reflected the type of clientele that visited. Ruby red, buttery leather seating, artistic yet unobtrusive mood lighting, sensual and tasteful art adorning the walls, low-lying contemporary designed tables. Everything was chic, expensive, and completely innocuous to the eyes of outsiders.[1]

The private rooms of the exclusive Club Columbus were places where power brokers with particular tastes, both local and visiting, unwound. Ninety-Nine percent of the people in the large, buzzing, Midwest city didn't know the club existed. The multi-million-dollar club fees, exclusive invite-only admittance, and deep background checks for all members made sure of that. The tastes of members varied, and Griffin made sure every desire, no matter the depravity, was indulged for the right fee. Some members were mild; they enjoyed a private sex show. Others came to take part in sexual trysts of various configurations and kinks. Still, others took part in the secret, high stakes world of buying and selling human bodies. All had exclusive access to the finest sexual offerings on the east coast because of the machinations of the Xenia Lux Corp heir.

While there were backroom whispers that there was a new mega rich player in the high-end flesh market, there was so much smoke and so many mirrors, no one knew who it was. No one except the people currently in the room.

"Well, that's quite a specific request on behalf of both my mother and father," Griffin said thoughtfully. He looked over to Hitchens, his bodyguard. "That changes things a bit." Griffin sighed. "This is beyond the pale for them, truly. My bastard child is to inherit *my* fortune. And you're sure that it must be my child with Maya Walters?"

Callista watched the man to whom Griffin was speaking. It was understandable why he was slow to reply. Tears streamed down his face as he sat on the chair in front of a live sex show. His eyes were lowered, but the sounds were unmistakable.

Griffin looked from the lawyer to the show, almost as an afterthought. "Ah yes, your daughter. You must admit she is talented. That level of flexibility is highly desirable."

The sound the father made as he reacted to Griffin's comment and, seeing his daughter "perform" forced Callista to close her eyes and remind herself to breathe. If she showed any emotion, she'd earn his wrath, and now that she wasn't needed as a breeding cow, she didn't know what would happen.

"Mr. Johnson. Your attention, please," Griffin warned.

The older gentleman looked at Griffin as he repeated his question. He appeared to gather his feelings. "There is nothing that can be done. The terms are ironclad."

"You have another daughter, correct, Mr. Johnson? One a little less exuberant than your oldest child. If you remember, this daughter,"— Griffin gestured toward the one-way mirror— "has been on this path a while. It's fortunate I was able to find her a safe home here with us instead of the other clubs that are a bit more ... public. And we also make sure she safely uses. Meth is such an epidemic these days. Even good families are affected."

Hitchens snorted and Callista burned in response, working harder to control herself.

"If by fortunate you mean taking advantage of a vulnerable girl, drugging her and keeping her here while I violate the law and every one of my morals to disclose the confidential terms of your parents' wills and trusts. You may think yourself a gentleman, Griffin, or clever. You're simply psychotic. You always have been."

Mr. Johnson stood and Callista watched, amazed, at the backbone of the older man. She would have cheered if she wasn't terrified.

"Don't play games with me, you bastard. Say what you want. I can't change the wills. Your father has not been located, but we have no reason to believe he's dead. Whatever you have done is sloppy, as usual. Your mother may not have survived the car accident, but that doesn't change the terms of her identical will."

Griffin considered him for a moment.

"Of course. This must be distressing. The evidence of your failure as a father 'deep throating' like a champ right in front of you."

Griffin paused and smiled warmly. "All that I want is what is due to me. I am a Levy. The money, company, and legacy belong to me. Now, I want you to get creative in getting it for me." He turned and motioned to Hitchens, who walked out for a moment.

Griffin waited in silence as the show ended and the lights dimmed on the little private show's stage. When Hitchens returned, Callista's heart stopped. A young girl of around fourteen walked in with Hitchens at her side.

"Amanda." Johnson's voice broke.

"Daddy?" the young girl whispered as she ran toward the man before Hitchens snatched her back.

"She's unspoiled, blond, and sweet. Our clientele will pay a premium for merchandise of this exquisite quality," Griffin said. "Her debut video, however, has significantly higher residual revenue opportunity. And your son is twelve, I believe? I have clientele that would love a bit of bareback with a tight little soccer player."

Johnson dropped his head. After what seemed like an eternity, he spoke in a hollowed, defeated voice.

"Your only solution is guardianship of the minor child. A trustee and a guardian controls the trust."

"And I take it you know who the trustee is?" Griffin grinned.

Johnson looked at his daughter with tears in his eyes.

"Me."

Callista lowered her eyes to the floor, and for the first time in weeks, she allowed herself one tear.

FOURTH OF JULY WEEKEND 10:15 P.M.

MAYA

Denial is intoxicating. The ability to create your own reality in the face of hard truth is an overwhelmingly comforting concept. Once you've had that first self-medicating hit, it's a tough habit to kick. Maya had been an addict these last couple of months. She realized that now. Her life in Rough Ridge was a coward's life. An escape within an escape.

She stood in the middle of Caine and Tori's living room, her heart and brain concussed. A dozen emotional time bombs had detonated. One painful hit after the other. As the emotional debris floated around, her mind traveled back to the night of the drive-by a week ago.

THE NIGHT OF THE DRIVE-BY, after they had finally arrived home, she loaded the Tor browser and checked her messages. There were the usual from clients that could wait until morning, a few funny memes from Shay, and a message from Anderson. Clicking on it, Maya smiled right away.

> M. I wouldn't have said anything in case it fell
> through, but I got a call back for a big. No. BIG.
> Role today. We are talking movies - and likely a
> sequel. There are going to be a thousand callbacks
> before they cast it, but I've gotten this far. Let's
> talk soon about Plan B.
> -Anderson

Plan B. Maya's plan to come clean to the architecture community about who runs her company. It wasn't complicated, executing a specific narrative - the truth - rolled out with careful timing. She thought a moment about what it would mean for it to happen now and became more weary.

She also told herself not to worry, because Anderson's last big role with a sequel was a man who contracted crabs in the first film and herpes in the second. Anderson was a brilliant actor, but so far all he'd landed were a few out-of-state Z-list films and car commercials.

She typed out a brief, loving message full of good lucks, breaking of legs, casting couch warnings, and signed off. She stood, stretched, and maneuvered her freshly de-glassed hair into a bun. Tammy hadn't blinked when she walked into her salon asking if she knew how to get glass out of hair. All the woman asked was, "Beer bottle or automobile?"

Chuckling, she stopped by the kitchen, grabbed milk and an apple, and paused when she saw paperwork on the bar. It sat on the dining room table all this time and now it was there. Intrigued, she flipped through it briefly, seeing Heart had recently added smart addendums, made effective language changes, and marked joint ownership and responsibility of the condo on it.

Maya's condo was worth $1.5 mil. She bought it for a little under $900K because of the divorcing couple's sudden turn around and he wanted to be a full half-owner on a cop's salary?! Did he have any notion of the mortgage and taxes on this pad? She didn't have a mortgage, of course, but still. He would take over partial ownership and put himself into debt forever, or sacrifice his retirement funds to do it. What was the point when she had plenty of money for both of them?

"Whatever. Too tired. Don't give a shit," she muttered. Eating her apple, she made her way to the bedroom. She saw him out on the deck having a ... smoke?! The hell?

"Whatever," Maya muttered. "Too tired. Don't give a shit."

Maya liked the sound of that mantra. She repeated it as she took off her clothes. "Don't give a shit," as her panties missed the hamper. "Too tired," as she put her gun on the top of the nightstand instead of in the drawer. "Don't give a shit," as she slid into bed, pulling the covers over her head.

She laid there for about thirty seconds before she decided she gave a shit. She sighed, threw back the covers, put a cotton nightie on over her naked form, and tiptoed out the sliding door onto the deck off her master bedroom.

"You are not okay," she said to his broad, shirtless back.

"No."

He blew out a puff of smoke and put out the cigarette. He had on workout shorts, his feet were bare, and his hair was still damp from the shower.

"I'll listen and won't try to fix it," she whispered. "Talk to me."

He took a deep breath; she watched the muscles in his back expand and contract. His focus never left the evening sky.

"I keep thinking about what could have happened. They could have killed you, seriously injured you, you could have lost the baby ... anything."

He was gripping the railing of the deck like his life depended on it. His body was hard, and waves of tension wafted off him. Maya moved in close and wrapped her arms around his waist, pressing herself tightly against his back.

"I'm fine, baby is fine. I've got a small ouchie and a new respect for your hand-to-hand combat skills," she said, her cheek pressed into his back. "The likelihood of a drive-by in the middle of a Rough Ridge parking lot is inconceivable. You can't plan for that."

"What if another asshole follows me home?"

"Isn't that the worry of anyone who loves a cop?" she asked. "The alternative is to be without you. Neither one of us wants that, right?"

He didn't say anything.

She gripped him harder. "Oh no. Fuck no," she said fiercely. "You get your shit together, Sheppard, and *you* get okay. No martyr shit on this one. You did your job. He did wrong. Not you. Don't even consider giving us up over that piece of shit. And if you remember, my shit could get *you* killed, too. Perhaps I should walk away to protect *you*."

He turned, breaking her hold on him, and looked down at her. His face looked a fraction less serious.

"Martyr shit?"

"Sacrificing everything because of others' wrongdoing. At times it's enchanting, other times, like now, it makes me want to scream."

He chuckled and relaxed a little.

"Your shit..."

"Is not what we're talking about right now."

"Maya—"

"Heart. My way in my time," she said, sliding her hand into his. "We need normal. Nothing has been normal since I arrived here. We can't stay in perpetual crisis mode on top of these long, hard discussions. It's wearing me out. It must wear on you too."

"I need to have your trust to protect you—"

"You protect me every day. Today you took down three men, moved through bullets to protect me. And how you can protect me now is by allowing me a few consecutive days where the drama in our lives is turned off with a remote. I need peace. You need that peace. A week of what Heart and Maya look like when there aren't bullets or tears or tables flying."

Mike looked at Maya for several long moments. He sighed a deep, harsh sigh and gave a hesitant, frustrated nod.

"Now, please kiss me and make all of this go away for a little while," she begged softly.

---

1. Creep Dubstep Remix

38
I'M THE ONLY ONE DOING THAT

DAYS LATER...

MAYA

The morning of Caine and Tori's Fourth of July party, Maya stood in the closet looking for casual and colorful. Happily she was less nauseous as she dressed, though now she had developed a craving for everything green and leafy and treated herself to Brussels sprouts for breakfast. *Weird shit, pregnancy,* she thought as she moved around the closet.

She planned to head over to Caine and Victoria's early to help set up and Heart was joining her later. He was closing in on something related to a big case he'd been working for a while. Today was about connecting with a contact. This morning she held him tight before he left, the reality of his work hitting her especially hard. Maya wished the contact had better timing, but Mike reminded her "crime didn't sleep" or stop for barbecue.

Victoria being able to convince Mike to come was a miracle. Victoria texted Mike, then cornered him at the station two days in a row. He eventually relented, and Maya suspected it was because he knew he would be gone a significant portion of the day. Tonight, she planned to lay out the whole truth of herself for him under the fireworks. The intimacy of the darkened hour might help and if not, then the fireworks would disguise his explosion. It wasn't a perfect plan. There wasn't a perfect one for this kind of thing, but it was time. Overdue.

She found an orange halter maxi dress made of t-shirt material—an impulse buy from the shopping extravaganza with the girls—and decided it was casual enough for a barbecue and had enough give in the material to fit her bump comfortably. The color highlighted her deeply melanated summer glow. She added a touch of light make-up and headed for the door. She grabbed the paperwork for the condo and decided they'd talk about that too. Get everything out under the stars.

THE COLORADO SUN was high and hot by the time Maya made it to Caine and Tori's house. The entire crew was coming through, including Caine and Victoria's friends from out of town. Victoria had bought all the food in Rough Ridge and Caine had a friend flying huge chunks of bison and elk from Montana. This friend had a ranch Caine thought was better than anything Colorado offered. Plus, the friend had a private jet and rolled like that.

Maya parked her truck and climbed out, adjusting her sunglasses against the blazing sun. She turned around and leaned in the second cab door to grasp her world-famous baked beans and potato salad. Ok, not world famous, but they tasted fantastic. She had experimented with the recipes for years and got them perfect.

"Excuse me," a deep, melodic voice said behind her, "may I carry that for you?"

Maya rolled her eyes behind her glasses at the requisite deep mountain man voice, turned around, and looked directly into eyes like deep pools of melted chocolate. Eyes she had seen before, briefly, years ago.

Xavier. Alexander.

Of all the rotten, no good, terrible, bad luck. Maya ran into one of the most successful entrepreneurs in the West in the middle of nowhere with a bunch of baked beans in her hands. This was the same man she gave her number to at a conference years ago and he had never called. Thinking on it, it did not surprise her since she called his investment group's attempt at green design cosmetic at a minimum and false advertising at most. And now she realized who her brother's friend with a private plane was - oof.

"I'm Xavier Alexander," the tall drink of water said, smiling at her warmly. "I'm a friend of Caine and Victoria's."

And he had forgotten her. Whew and dang.

She took off her sunglasses stiffly, apprehension filling her, and looked at him for a moment. When she saw no glimmer of recognition in his eyes, she introduced herself as Maya Anderson.

"Let me take those for you," he offered again, white teeth bright against mahogany-colored skin.

She took in his tall, lean, cut body and shrugged. "Sure muscles, think you can handle potato salad too?"

"I am at your service," he replied with a wink.

Smooth. Exactly what she remembered from four years ago. He was a physical reminder of her old life. The good parts. Impeccable casual wear, he wore the expensive version of average Americana - golf polo, khakis, casual rugged loafers. He had beautiful manners, if not formal, and a confident ease that comes from successfully moving through and dominating power circles.

She led the way to the house and, using her keys to let them both in, she called out their arrival.

Right after walking in, Maya got to work helping Victoria in the kitchen, and surprisingly, Xavier joined her. Over prep work of a massive amount of dead animal flesh, Maya learned a lot about the man behind the mogul.

He was witty besides being easy on the eyes with a smooth bald head, neatly trimmed beard, and beautiful smile. If she wasn't already wrapped in Michael to her core, she would make another run at Mr. Xavier. Instead, she thanked heaven above he didn't remember their fleeting moment of mild flirting disguised as an EPA standards debate.

While Maya and Xavier immersed themselves in what was the second wave of raw meat, Caine was getting more coals ready on his massive quad barrel barbecue. It appeared to be a modified grill made from those giant black metal trash barrels. It had chimneys, grates and was a monstrosity. Everyone called it 'The Beast' and it could cook a whole human if needed.[1]

Maya shared the thought to Xavier, and he laughed loudly, showing straight white perfect teeth. *Hmmm...* She made a mental note to introduce him to Shay after she came clean to Heart. She'd make Friend of the Year. Shay had a problem dating men with money like her family's or dating in general. She was an f-'em and leave 'em kinda woman, but something told Maya for Mr. X she'd change her mind. Thinking about their upcoming double dates, she caught him tasting her baked beans.

"Hey!" she protested, bumping him with her hip.

"Oh man. You put your foot in these beans," Xavier said, his eyes closing as he savored the flavor.

"Eww! Maya put her toes in the baked beans," Gabriella screeched to the house.

"Auntie, did you really put feet in the beans?" Livi asked quietly.

"Only to stir them," Maya teased.

"Yuck! Moooom!" Gabriella wailed. "Maya made feet beans and Unca X ate 'em!"

She took off down the hall in protest. Tori waddled down the hall explaining to both girls it was an expression for someone who had made fantastic food. Gabriella accepted the explanation, but Liv was still eyeing the pans of beans with distrust.

"You've ruined her now," Victoria huffed, smacking Maya on the arm on the way around the big kitchen island to answer the door.

Maya snorted and set on the last rack of ribs. It was getting hotter in the kitchen. Maya's hair was getting bigger and her already pregnancy-affected body temperature climbed. When perspiration rolled down her back, she went bananas. Elbow deep in ribs, she called out to Xavier, "Hey are your hands clean?"

"Almost," he replied quickly, "one moment, Maya." The water turned off and he was at her side. "What do you need?"

"My hair — it's driving me nuts and I'm covered in the dead." She wiggled her seasoning covered hands. "Can you tie it up for me? I have a ponytail holder in my purse over there."

"Uh ... sure."

"It doesn't have to be perfect," she said, mistaking his hesitation.

"And I don't mind you going in my purse, shoot, when you season hunks of meat to offer in sacrifice to The Beast together, you're practically family."

Xavier blinked at her, then moved to her purse. He located the elastic and moved behind her as she leaned her head back away from the food. Xavier began pulling her hair high on top of her head.

"You have an enormous amount of hair."

"Yeah, and it only gets bigger with all the cooking, heat, and humidity going on in here." She laughed.

"It's beautiful," he said, his voice low.

Maya heard him, but Victoria's excited voice took over her ears. "I've already got a plate for you to take with you to work to hold you over until you get back and..."

Maya looked from the ribs to see Mike staring at her and Xavier.

"Hey hon," Maya said, delighted to see him. "Are you headed back to the station right now or—" Maya noticed Mike's tense jaw.

"Mike," Victoria said, jumping in and correctly noting the temp of the room, "this is our good friend Xavier Alexander. X this is Detective Mike Sheppard, also our good friend and Maya's man."

Xavier immediately let go of Maya's hair and reached out a hand to Mike. Mike took it and the two men quickly and forcefully shook, giving each other a polite nod. Victoria shifted from foot to foot nervously, while Maya looked puzzled.

"Maya, can I see you for a minute?" Mike said, turning his full attention to her, green eyes meeting brown.

"Well, I'm kinda elbow deep in these ribs to sacrifice to The Beast."

"TO THE BEAST!" Caine boomed randomly as he walked from the hall to the patio.

Maya and Victoria rolled their eyes.

"Sunshine."

Maya saw the look on his face and raised her hands as Victoria moved in. "I've got it. Go ahead, sweetie."

"Okay, let me wash my hands," Maya said slowly, her eyes on Mike the whole time, understanding dawning.

After she dried her hands, she grabbed him a cold bottle of water out of the refrigerator and ventured out to the dark wood wrap-around deck where he was standing. He was on one side of the deck, Caine and Xavier were on the far side poking coals and stoking The Beast.

MIKE

Maya smiled at him, held out the water, and cocked her head slightly.

"Honey ... "

"What did I walk in on back there?"

Maya waved a hand dismissively. "Cooking, honey."

"He had his hands in your goddamn hair, Maya."

Maya rolled her eyes. "I got so hot in there and I asked him to put it up for me since his hands were clean."

"I didn't like it."

"It meant nothing."

"It did to him, and I didn't like it. You didn't see the way he was looking at you." He wanted to punch the smooth operator in the face. He hated these bouts of insecurity, but sometimes he wondered what Maya saw in him.

"Oh," Maya whispered. She bit her lip and sat the water on the deck railing and moved into him close, placing her hand on his heart, pressing her upper body against his. "Babe. I thought nothing of it. And that's what matters."

"I know," he said, looking over her face while running his hands along her arms, thinking. "Everyone loves you."

"I don't know about all of that," she said, blowing the statement off.

"Especially men."

"Pfft."

"Just because you don't see it all the time, Sunshine, doesn't mean it isn't true. It can be ... hard to watch."

Maya paused for a moment. "He's a nice guy. I was thinking of hooking him up with a friend from back home."

"Good for them," he mumbled, turning her around so her back was to him. He slipped the ponytail elastic off her wrist and slowly slid his fingertips from her wrists to her shoulders. Her eyes closed at his touch.

His hands barely skimmed her neck as they became entangled in her curly coils where he made gentle, slow movements, gathering her hair in a nice snug bun, carefully winding the elastic around. What should have been a simple act turned into delicious foreplay and her body responded as it always did. Her nipples perked up, her breasts rose and fell on shallow breaths, and she gently rocked her ass against him.

Slowly, he trailed his fingers back down her neck and soft, teasing kisses followed the path his fingers left. Her body flushed with goose bumps all over and she reached to touch his face as he slid an arm protectively around her ribcage and her softly rounded belly.

"I love it when you touch me," she murmured, her mouth pressed into the side of his neck and jaw.

"I'm the only one who will," he said with a smile playing on his lips.

He sensed when Maya's eyes opened, and she caught Xavier shifting his eyes from them back to Caine and the grill. She stiffened. "You're using me to make a point."

"Sunshine."

She turned to him swiftly. "I'm not a tree you piss on," she snapped, jabbing him in the chest with a pointed finger.

"Then darlin', don't let other dogs sniff around," he said, his lips barely hiding a grin, his eyes crinkling as he leaned his face close to hers.

She wound up ready to let him have it when her eyes widened and her hands flew to her stomach.

"Maya, baby, what's wrong?" He reached for her as worry caused his pulse to tick up.

"I felt her!" Maya said with an awestruck giggle. "I thought it was your kisses causing the fluttering, but it was the baby. It's so slight, it's like butterfly wings."

Maya's eyes sparkled, her face lit like the sun. It struck Mike just how much he loved her. How that love grew from moment to moment. Every time she smiled at him, it was a mule kick to the chest - and he liked it. He reached out and she quickly pressed his hand against her belly, holding it there.

"Do you feel it?"

He paused, holding his breath as he waited.

"No," Mike said finally, barely hiding the disappointment settling deep in his stomach.

"Oh honey, it's so slight. I guess she has to get a little bigger." She kissed him. "She's going to be kicking you in the back while you sleep before you know it."

Maya danced in place, hopping a bit.

"Holy crap, this has got to be the coolest, weirdest thing I have ever done. There's a being growing in me!" Maya yelped, giggling.

The knot of disappointment disappeared, and Mike touched his forehead to hers, smiling. "I love you, Sunshine. You're kinda crazy though, kid."

"Yo Maya," Caine yelled. "Those ribs ready?"

Maya waved a hand and motioned to the kitchen as she started moving.

Mike followed Maya back into the house and watched as she helped Victoria put slabs of meat in large, disposable aluminum containers.

"Your plate is in the fridge," Victoria smiled as she spoke to Mike.

He shook his head slightly as she waddled in that direction and pulled out a chair for her to sit. He waited and Tori flashed her megawatt smile while she sank gratefully into the chair with an 'oomph.' Mike crossed the kitchen, opened the fridge, and pulled out a to-go container heavy with holiday fixings. Warmth bloomed in his chest.

"Mmm ... This is going to be great for lunch," he said, looking at Victoria. "Thank you."

"You're family now Mike, I always take care of my family."

Mike jerked in surprise at her comment and his heart thumped heavy in his throat, but before he could say anything the patio door opened.

"YO! Maya! Sacrifice to The Beast!" Caine boomed again.

"Ok, babe, if he 'Yo Maya's' me one more time, I'm going to sacrifice him!" she complained as she leaned into him and kissed him. "I love you, see you later today. Be safe, okay?"

"Yeah darlin'," he said, smiling down at her, letting all the warmth and love shining in her eyes wash over him.

She gave him a smile, a flashing full dimple, and hustled out of the kitchen, through the family room, and out to the patio door. As soon as Caine slid the door open for her, she yelled, "I BRING SACRIFICE TO THE BEAST!"

"TO THE BEAST!" Caine and Xavier boomed.

When Mike looked away from the scene, he still had a small smile on his face when he caught Tori staring at him.

"You love her."

He studied her for a moment and looked back to the patio.

"Deeply."

"Don't waste a moment," Victoria said in a rush. "Say it. Show it. Life can ... change in an instant. It's too precious to waste. Especially holding on to the past. Mike, you can't hold yourself responsible for what he did."

"He did this to you."

His eye raked over the scars on her face and down her small, almost delicate hand to the missing finger tip. He brushed it gently with the tip of his own hand, as if to wipe it away. "My family has caused yours so much pain ... "

She placed her hand on his.

"And I ended your father's life."

"You didn't have a choice."

"Neither do you - not in what family you're born into. I haven't spoken to my family since I was ten years old," Tori confessed. "They were cruel people who should have never had kids."

Mike's head snapped back in surprise.

"I built my family," Victoria continued. "I made peace with the past so I could have a future. You must do the same. We both have to look at each other and see beyond the hurts to see the good happening right now. If not for ourselves, then for our goofy girl out there."

Tori nodded her head toward the patio, where Maya was animatedly telling a story. Xavier and Caine were laughing full out and Maya was doing jazz hands.

Mike thought about what it meant to let go of the guilt he'd lived with for so long. The burden became lighter with Tori's words as he looked at Maya. He'd give her anything, including a chance to be comfortable making a life in this town with people she connected with.

"Is she doing jazz hands?" Tori asked.

"Yep," Mike said.

Tori smiled at him, and he squeezed her hand.

"For her."

---

1. Love Train by the O'Jays

39
HE FOUND ME

MIKE

The party was in full swing when Mike arrived back at the Walters' home. He was on a high. His contact gave him critical information — a concrete link to the bigger reason behind the drive-by and increased trafficking making its way through Colorado. He connected the information to a name, and tomorrow he'd dig into everything. Tonight, however, it was all about him and his girl.

Half the town was still there. The kids old enough to still be awake were playing with sparklers in the backyard's dampened grass. The little ones were asleep in guest bedrooms, and everyone waited to watch the fireworks that could be seen from the Walters' property.

Mike stopped to say hello to Shannon and Mace, gave Paul a nod confirmed the good contact, and exchanged pleasantries with Caine's father Thomas before he spotted Maya.

She was next to a large speaker with Max - Shannon and Mace's son - holding his hand and dancing to Michael Jackson's *"Pretty Young Thing."* They were clearly smitten with each other and together they made a cute pair. As he moved through the crowd, people greeted him left and right. Everyone was friendly, and it was nice to feel a part of the town, and not worry about if someone was looking at him and thinking of his father.[1]

Maya looked over, saw him, and smiled her dimpled smile. He waited for the song to end and asked Max if he could cut in, and he thought for a moment the kid might challenge him.

"I'll take good care of her, Max, promise," he said to the little boy.

Mace came by and grabbed his son on his way back to the house. "Out of your league, kid." Mace chuckled.

"If this doesn't work out between us," Maya joked, "I've got a boyfriend in twelve years."

"Then I guess it better work," Mike rumbled back, taking Maya into his arms as Goapele's "*Closer*" came on.2

"You made it in time for the fireworks," she said as the first colorful blast shot across the sky. "And you're in a good mood, so the meet went well?"

"Yes, and yes," he said, pulling her closer, swaying with the music. She smelled like summer. Like grass and sun and sweet, sweet Maya.

"I missed you," she said, holding him close as a brilliant explosion of golden twinkling sparkles lit up the sky. "Oh! Those are my favorites. The fireworks with the mountains in the background ... I have never seen anything more beautiful in my life."

Mike watched the colored sparks light her face and knew there would never be a moment as special. "Me either," he said, his voice low as he looked at her. She met his eyes and her eyes sparkled more.

"I love you, Sunshine."

Maya swallowed and paused. "Heart, I've been wanting to say this for a while ... "

She stopped when she realized Mike was sliding something onto her hand. On her left ring finger, to be exact.

"One of the few things I wanted from my family," he started, his voice low and quiet as he held her close, his lips against her ear because what he had to say was only for her and he didn't want her to miss it.

"It was my great aunt's. She was a sweet, kind woman who lived in California. A tiny thing, delicate, but she kicked ass, was honest as hell, and could light up a room. You two have a lot in common." He gave her a squeeze. "The center stone is a yellow diamond, for my Sunshine."2

"You made it in time for the fireworks," she said as the first colorful blast shot across the sky. "And you're in a good mood, so the meet went well?"

"Yes, and yes," he said, pulling her closer, swaying with the music. She smelled like summer. Like grass and sun and sweet, sweet Maya.

"I missed you," she said, holding him close as a brilliant explosion of golden twinkling sparkles lit up the sky. "Oh! Those are my favorites. The fireworks with the mountains in the background ... I have never seen anything more beautiful in my life."

Mike watched the colored sparks light her face and knew there would never be a moment as special. "Me either," he said, his voice low as he looked at her. She met his eyes and her eyes sparkled more.

"I love you, Sunshine."

Maya swallowed and paused. "Heart, I've been wanting to say this for a while ... "

She stopped when she realized Mike was sliding something onto her hand. On her left ring finger, to be exact.

"One of the few things I wanted from my family," he started, his voice low and quiet as he held her close, his lips against her ear because what he had to say was only for her and he didn't want her to miss it.

"It was my great aunt's. She was a sweet, kind woman who lived in California. A tiny thing, delicate, but she kicked ass, was honest as hell, and could light up a room. You two have a lot in common." He gave her a squeeze. "The center stone is a yellow diamond, for my Sunshine."

MAYA

Maya's heart soared and was heavy at the same time. Her breath hitched as she took a step back out of his embrace. She looked down to see a beautiful, obviously antique, engagement ring. The European cut center diamond was surrounded by a wreath of smaller diamonds and set in a platinum Art déco setting. It was beautiful and unlike any ring she had seen before.

Her breath caught in her chest, her heartbeat thundered in her ears, and felt like it would tear through her chest. She couldn't make out any more details of the ring because it was dark out and her eyes clouded over. She shook her head, trying to clear the tears, beat back her heart-beat, and focused on what she absolutely had to tell him.

She couldn't accept his proposal, not until he knew everything. When he looked at her face, he was concerned. She found her voice and started putting more distance between them.

"Heart, I love you, but I can't let—"

"Momma look, Auntie Maya's on TV!" Gabriella yelped.

"Oh wow!" Liv yelled, running past, headed to the patio doors.

Maya looked stricken as she watched the emotions flash over Mike's face.

"Oh no. No no no no no no," Maya whispered. "God no. Not like this." Focusing on his eyes, she tried again. "Heart, I was trying to tell you, my brother, my company, no wait, I'm not—"

Her words tumbled, jumbled, her mind raced back and forth from topic to topic, unsure of where to start.

"Maya!" Caine barked from the house, his body tense. "Both phones."

Both her secure phone and regular phone were ringing. Panic seeped into her bones. The look on Heart's face froze her soul, and the ringing meant Griffin was coming. Everyone around her was in danger. The thought unfroze her body and her mouth.

"He found me."

MIKE

Mike's gut sank when she first pulled away. The look on her face filled him with dread and now ...

"Maya!" Caine called again as he walked to her. She took one last look at Mike and took off toward the house.

Mike followed quickly behind her, and when she walked into the house, all eyes turned to her. Several things happened at once. Mace walked toward her, holding out her purse. Victoria gathered the kids and took them to the game room, and Mike turned up the volume to hear the report.

If you're just joining us, the Fourth of July holiday gossip is so juicy! When the cast of the upcoming Moon Falls film was announced, internet sleuths thought they were seeing double. Hollywood newcomer Mark Anderson landed the coveted starring role as the mystical master One Soul. Fans of the comic discovered that Mark and an elusive CEO of a small, influential architecture firm in Ohio could pass for twins. Instead, we've learned the actor has been using the same skills that landed him the leading role to pose as CEO.

All evidence points to his assistant Maya Angel Walters as the green build guru behind the new Matthews building in New York, the redesigned Central City Entertainment Complex in Columbus, and the innovative Xi Chang skyrise in Shanghai...

He watched Maya Walters on the huge sixty-inch flat screen television. Her hair was stick straight, and she wore jet black designer clothing. They showed her attending events and accepting awards. It was an alternate universe, a second side he never knew. The headline on the bottom of the screen read "M.A. Wall CEO Cast in New Moon Falls Trilogy, Maya Walters Outed as Green Design Genius."

Sources say Walters has pulled off one of the greatest business coups in recent memory. For years she's played Pepper Potts to her fictional partner's Tony Stark, but turns out she's the real Iron Man, or Iron Woman. The question on everyone's lips? Why? Why would a woman who obviously has the brains to lead her own company hide behind a man? That's the $24.7 million-dollar question - Maya Walter's net worth. We'll follow this story as it develops.

"Turn it off," Caine growled.

He stood behind Mike and Victoria grabbed Mike's hand gently, slipping the remote out and hitting the button, turning the screen dark. Mike hadn't realized he still had it. Walters ... Maya was in danger, and she was Caine's ... sister?

"My brother..." His mind flashed back to moments ago, when she rejected him, and what she was telling him. The months since Maya's arrival made sense. And he realized she had played him from the beginning, and he never saw it.

Thinking with his dick, he never noticed the family resemblance, never put Caine's almost inappropriate level of protectiveness together with those same fucking eyes. Thomas's eyes.

And fuck him. As pissed as he was, he couldn't block out the fear and pain in her eyes. Her whispers of sadness and fright made it so he couldn't leave her fucking side. Even as part of him urgently wanted to get away from her and the lies.

The room was silent until Leslie called out to Maya.

"Honey are you okay?" she asked, taking a halting step toward her. Maya threw out her hand, motioning her to stop. She withdrew into herself, her arms wrapped tightly around her body as her breathing became quicker and shallower. A panic attack. She shook her head, eyes wide, and, as Mike stepped out to go to her, Caine tried to stop him with a hand on his shoulder. Mike shrugged off the hand and crossed the length of the room in long, determined strides. When he reached Maya, she threw out both hands, backing away, shaking.

"Don't touch me," she shrieked. Mike stopped short, experiencing the physical pain of being rejected again.

Maya backed to the wall, closed her eyes, and slid down it. She started reciting the names of streets out loud - the streets from her childhood home. As her breathing slowed, she seemed to get herself together.

"Maya," Mace started.

"Wait," she said forcefully, her voice rough. "Please," she finished in a quiet pleading whisper as she dumped the contents of her purse out on the floor and snatched it inside out by the lining. Mike choked back the bile in his throat as watched her unzip a hidden compartment and pull out a second phone.

Then she did something Mike had never seen her do before. She straightened tall and rotated her head from left to right and back, cracking it. She rolled her shoulders, hit a button on the phone, and waited.

"Anderson? Walters." Her voice was low, quiet, and commanding. "I know ... I understand ... No one checks email on a holiday."

Listening.

"That was the old me. I need you to release a statement. Who is your rep?" She frowned at his response. "She's good, but flighty and melodramatic. Stick to the script on this Anderson. Briefing to come in two hours."

Listening.

"He hasn't contacted you yet, but he will. You are now too famous to touch, you're safe. Expect a dummy call from the open line soon."

She hit the end button and promptly started another call.

"Selene, it's happened. It's out. I need Shay on the line with us now."

Listening.

"Shay? It's me."

Listening.

"I know," she said as her voice broke for the first time. She closed her eyes as a tear fell. Then she repeated the neck gesture and her quiet, commanding voice returned. "Time is of the essence. The longer I stay where I am, the more people I put in danger. Selene, at nine a.m. tomorrow, call a press conference at the Omni Hotel in L.A. for noon. I don't want any blowback on where I am now."

Listening.

"I'll drive into L.A., I can't fly, my alternate I.D. is compromised now and can be traced back here if he comes looking."

Listening.

"Selene, focus. We need to adjust Plan B. We expected mid-scale interest, mostly industry and local. Because of the movie, this is now far bigger. Spend this evening gathering the right press contacts who specialize in the narrative we want, plus the usual local journalists. Arrange a room where they have a live feed and I'll answer local right after the conference via satellite. Tonight, leak what we previously planned to lay the groundwork. Tomorrow's conference is a statement, five questions for national and local. No personal information. I need a bulldog for crisis management."

Listening.

"Thompson is too controversial."

Listening.

"Tagan is fantastic, but she prefers entertainment, and this is NOT entertainment."

"Jada Spencer," Xavier spoke from the side of the room.

All eyes turned to Xavier Alexander. Maya looked at him and nodded. "Call Jada Spencer. She gets all the information except the name. I want to feel her out myself before sharing. She needs to know what she's dealing with.

"Security will contact you regarding their needs. Order my uniform to be delivered to the hotel I give you later tonight."

Listening.

"No! No black. Greys, pinks, and creams." Maya paused, strengthening herself, "Selene, you'll, um, you'll have to change the sizes. I'm ... pregnant and I'm not sure what size I am anymore."

Tori leaned over and confidently relayed Maya's current sizes, and Maya related them to Selene.

"I'll need enough for at least a week. Book KG for hair and makeup at seven a.m. tomorrow and retain him and an assistant for the week.

Listening.

"No Shay, I need you and Selene both on the ground at the agency for this," Maya clipped swiftly, her voice still in professional mode.

Mike watched the woman he loved with wonder, pride, and pain as she showed a hint of the other side of herself. The side she had never allowed him to see.

"I'll record a video message for the staff tonight, en route. I've got to move before he's tipped off. The next 48 are critical, but we've got this well in hand. You're experts at what you do, and I have complete faith in you both. We work the plan, stay agile, and in communication. I love you both."

Maya clicked off and closed her eyes. When she finally opened them, there were tears in them.

"I'm sorry," she whispered to the room, but her eyes focused on him.

"Sweetheart," Thomas said as he attempted to draw her near him. His eyes locked on Mike's.

"No, I've got to say this," she said as she twisted her neck again.

Maya launched into an abbreviated version of her story quickly, showing little to no emotion. Mike tore his eyes off her and looked around at the core group of friends remaining in the home. Most of them didn't look surprised. Concerned. Sad. Worried for her, but not surprised. It was then he realized he was one of the few people who hadn't known all of this.

That. THAT killed him. She had told everyone else but him. Something in her voice brought his attention back to her.

"I've learned there are two times you can see the truth in a man's eyes." She looked at Mike, then glanced away. "When he tells you he loves you and when he tells you he is going to end your life."

"I did this all wrong," she said sadly. "I should have come clean ages ago after Caine found out about my past and our connection ... but I fell in love." She chanced a look at Mike. "I fell in love with the town, all of you, and got hypnotized by the dream of having a family, friends. I was selfish and put you all in danger, and I am so sorry."

She shook her head ruefully and inhaled deeply.

"I must go to L.A. and through the media, I'll throw people off my time here. I have no doubt he's behind this to flush me out, but you should be safe. Don't answer any media questions and it should keep the interest to a minimum. I ... I love you all."

Maya started walking toward the door. Mike met her there.

"I'll drive you home," he said without looking at her.

"Thank you," she whispered, her voice shaking.

MAYA

She decided right then to block it all out. Emotions would not keep her alive. Laila's training kicked in. Thinking about leaving all this behind would take her mind out of the game, and she couldn't afford to be distracted. Griffin wasn't. She was leaving her heart and soul behind in Rough Ridge. The pain was too great and she shut down.

She focused on the problems she could solve and left her heart out of it.

"I'll get the car. You take the time to say goodbye," he said, making sure she nodded before he walked out the door.

On autopilot, she turned and allowed Tori to pull her into a hug. Then one by one all the women there - Leslie, Shannon, Tammy - and later Mac, gathered around her, whispering words of encouragement and love.

MIKE

Outside, Mike focused on not losing his mind. She was in danger. She kept so much from him, and they all knew. He felt a hand on his shoulder. For the second time that evening, he shrugged it off and looked Paul in the eye.

"You knew."

"She wanted to tell you herself," Paul started, releasing a deep sigh. "I wanted to bring you in from the beginning. Caine ... he wanted her to decide."

"There is a sick bastard out there forcing her into and now out of hiding, and you have been keeping this shit from me," Mike growled.

"Calm down, Mike," Paul started.

"Were you calm when you almost beat the man to death who hurt your woman? Don't fucking tell me I'm supposed to be okay with this," Mike shot back, his fists clenched.

"Fine. Don't be okay with it, but get it together because she's coming out right now, and she needs you," Paul warned, standing directly in front of Mike.

"This is fucking bullshit," Mike growled low as he walked back to the house to help her down the stairs.

MAYA

Maya noticed Xavier, Jake, Mace, and Paul had grouped into a conversation while Caine stood at the door with her. Michael reached out and took her arm, and he appeared cold. She didn't let that in either.

As they headed out to the car, she was aware the men had followed them.

"Maya, wait," Jake said. "We've got a way to get you to L.A. unnoticed."

"My contacts told me the story was going live seconds before it did," Mace said.

"You know how powerful he is," she replied quietly.

"Not as much as you think. His power lies mainly in his resources and those have dried up."

"What?! That's impossible. They are worth billions!"

"Who. Are. They?" Mike growled.

Maya looked at him.

"Remembered I'm here, huh?"

"Heart, I—"

"Man, this ain't the time," Caine interjected.

"Stay out of this, Caine," Mike clipped, his whole body tight with tension.

"The fuck you mean 'stay out of it.' She's running for her life, and you want to get into your FEELINGS?" Caine roared. "This coming from the man she didn't trust with any of this shit and who already almost got her killed. YOU stay the FUCK OUT OF IT."

Maya watched as another time bomb exploded when Mike's fist connected with Caine's jaw, sending him stumbling back several feet.

---

1. Pretty Young Thing PYT by Michael Jackson
2. Closer by Goapele

40

AND STILL HE LOVED HER

MAYA

[1]To Maya, it looked like the gods of Olympus at war. Power, strength, and so much anger. Caine came back at Mike, hitting him with a two-piece body shot combination. Taking aim at Caine's face, Mike landed a blow to his nose. If Maya had been in her right mind, she would have known both men weren't going for the kill. If she remembered Mike's dispatching of the drive-by perps, she would have recognized the difference. He wasn't even blocking the shots Caine sent.

It was over quickly as all the men in attendance rushed to separate them, but it was a struggle to contain them. After Jake, Xavier and Mac had held back Caine, and Paul and Blake held back Mike, Maya's quiet, tired, feminine voice broke through.

"Are you two finished? Do your dicks measure up? Because I've got to keep a fucking monster from descending on this town and I'm short on time."

"It's always on your time, isn't it Maya? Your schedule, your rules, your control," Mike barked.

"Mike—" Paul said low.

"You have my ring on your finger, lay with me every fucking night. Your baby became mine the moment I learned about her, but you go to every other fucking man in this town for help?"

"Mike, stand down," Jake said. "Don't go there, not right now."

She walked to him, moving Paul's largeness out of the way with a touch of her hand.

"Heart, please. It's not like that. I didn't want ANYONE involved in this. They pursued this. I tried to minimize the damage. I wanted—"

"Bullshit, Maya, you manipulated me," Mike growled. "Think about someone else for one fucking minute instead of what you want. My entire life revolves around protecting people I don't fucking know, and I've tried to do that with honor. Yet the one woman in my life that I would give up everything, EVERYTHING to keep safe, kept shit from me that made protecting her and our child that much fucking harder."

"I tried to tell you, a thousand times I wanted to tell you. I wanted us to get to a good place. I was trying to tell you today—"[2]

"Today. Meanwhile, since you've been here, he could have shown up at our front door and I wouldn't have known," he said furiously. "Or if you had gotten in trouble and used that gun under an assumed name, baby, the consequences ... I couldn't have saved you from that!"

He ran his hands roughly through his hair in frustration.

"It's not the lies," he said, shaking his head. "It's the fucking epic layers of lies. I'm not an idiot. There is a file on my desk right now with everything I need to know. It's been there for weeks. And despite EVERYTHING in me telling me I should find out how fucked up your situation is, I gave you what you asked: 'Your time, your way.'"

He stood with his hand on his hip, the other at his neck. "I respect you, love you, and I trusted you. I waited for you to give me your trust and you gave that precious gift away to literally every other man you've met here, which tells me one fucking thing." He dropped his arms and stared at her, eyes blazing, the anger and pain etched across his face. "It's not just about your fear of this man. You've used your trauma as another fucking way to keep me out. And the saddest part of all this shit is you're lying to yourself. You don't let anyone in. Not all the way. You have a family, and I don't have to guess that you used me to keep them at a distance ... whatever keeps you closed off from everyone that loves you started long before that son of a bitch put his hands on you."

It was too much. His rage. Her shock. The eyes of everyone on them.

Maya was exposed, and she grasped for control. And she found it quickly, surrounding herself with bricks in a hastily built wall.

"I apologize the situation unfolded this way. It was never my intention, for you to learn the truth like this." Even to her own ears, her voice sounded cold. She held herself closed off. Her body language screamed, stay away.

"I know, baby," Mike said, breathing deep. "But it's not enough."

Four words. Four words from him and that wall blew apart, and she shattered, splintered inside. She closed her eyes to the pain.

"Even now you're shutting down." He shook his head again. "I understand there are things you must do right now to keep it together so you can save your business and all you've worked for. But to fix what's broken between us, apologies aren't enough, not for either of us."

Maya felt more pain shooting across her chest. God, was it a heart attack? A split second later, she realized exactly how acute the physical pain of a broken heart proved to be. It stung heavy and hot, radiating throughout her body until she could hardly stand. She couldn't breathe and her nerve endings sizzled. It was so intense she went further into herself, trying to find any way to keep from screaming out as it blasted through her.

She dared to glance at him again. He looked like he was wrestling with himself. His movements were agitated and stilted when he walked over to her, yet he still held on to enough control to take her face gently into his hands. There was a deep sadness combined with an almost rabid urgency in the look he gave her.

"A man has four things he can give to his family, to his woman: his love, his name, his protection, and provision," he said, low and serious. "You've always had my love. My name ain't worth shit. You won't allow my protection, and by never sending off the condo agreement, you've shown me you won't allow me to provide for you, either. You've kept the other half of yourself hidden from me, maybe more because you're afraid to let me in."

He stroked her cheek with his thumb and his jaw set in anger, eyes unflinching. "You deserve more than a quarter of a man, Maya Angel Walters, and I want more than these fragmented pieces of you. I love you too much to force you."

He kissed her gently on the forehead and let her go. As he stepped away, he looked over to the men waiting at a distance.

"Who the fuck is involved and what's the plan? She doesn't go anywhere until I know—now."

Maybe it was instinct, maybe it was a brick in the wall falling, or maybe she was being completely stupid. Maya reached out her hand and grabbed his arm.

"Griffin Levy."

Mike froze and turned slowly to her. "What did you say?"

"He's the one who hurt me," she whispered.

She looked at him and she glimpsed it before his face became a mask. A dark light glowed behind his eyes. She had never seen it before and for the first time she was frightened of him, of what he could do to another human being.

MIKE

Mike's body turned to ice. It snaked and clawed its way from his toes through his veins until all the turmoil diminished and he had one purpose. Centered determination he hadn't felt since his time on SWAT in L.A. took hold.

"Heart, don't—"

Mike closed his eyes for a moment. Turning to Maya, he said roughly, "He is no longer your problem."

"Please, oh God, please don't jeopardize your career, your life, Heart, please," she begged, holding onto his arm.

"Darlin', either trust the man I am to do what I have to do or not. Either way, he is no longer a problem for you."

She searched his face, brown eyes peering into green, and he knew all she saw was a calculating, dangerous mind. He was who he was and would always be descended from a line of dark men. She swallowed hard, closed her eyes, and willed her fingers to open. Her fingers felt reluctant, but when - without a glance at her - he stepped out away from her, they offered no resistance.

The look in Mike's eyes set the men on edge as he stalked over to them. "Shit's changed," he said. "Paul, get the Cap on the phone. We need to meet—tonight. Mace and Jake decide now - either deputize in and work with me, or protect Maya. You can't do both. If you choose Maya, then you stop anything beyond security surveillance of Griffin Levy. I can't have you fuck this case."

Mace crossed his arms and asked, "What case?"

"This is bigger than what that bastard did to Maya and more innocent people are in danger," Mike growled.

"Name the play," Jake said, his face intense.

"I need time. I almost have enough to nail him, but I need time to get to Ohio and dig. I can do that faster if I know Maya is safe. I want both of you to stay with her. I don't trust anyone outside of the men here with her. Leaving her to hired security is too risky. If it doesn't go the way it should, then there are other ways to take him down," he looked at Mace. "And you provide cleanup and recovery."

Mace jerked in surprise. "Recovery?"

"This discussion never happened," Mike said, and the men caught the briefest glimpse of the same dark glow. Solemn tension came over them all as they exchanged glances with each other.

Paul rejoined the group, and his sharp eyes zeroed in on Mike with concern. "Cap is an hour out to the station."

"Take your wife home and meet me there in two," Mike suggested to Paul. Turning to Jake, he said, "How are you getting her to L.A.?"

Xavier spoke up, "My jet out of Denver. I've also arranged for a section of rooms at the Sofitel for greater security."

Mike considered him for a moment. "Altering your passenger manifest is risky."

Xavier shrugged. "Not doing the right thing is a risk too great, Detective Sheppard."

Mike sighed and nodded. "Please bill me for expenses, including security."

"That is unnecessary, Detective."

"Rebecca at P & J Holdings will reach out for a detailed accounting of expenses," Mike said firmly, then turned and walked away. It didn't pass his notice there was a surprised look in the mogul's eyes at the mention of Mike's own company. A company that was an investor in a few of Xavier's projects.

Small world, smooth fucker.

He got to his Jeep and looked to Maya standing off a ways from the group, staring into the night as Thomas rubbed her back and spoke quietly to her. She held herself impossibly straight. She must've felt his eyes on her and turned, face visibly wet in the low light coming from the house. He had gone from joy to shock to anger and pain to mechanical in the span of an hour.

And still, he loved her.

To the very depth of his existence. More than his job, more than his own life, he'd burn it all for her. He wanted to love her completely. But she wouldn't allow it and that killed him. And pissed him off. Growling, he rubbed at the burning sensation in his chest, swung into the Jeep, and sped off into the night.

HE WATCHED from the shadows of the hangar as Jake helped her tired, ripening body climb the steps to the plane. Mace was doing a sweep behind them. *He is as good as they say.* Mace paused when he spotted Mike and gave him a brief chin lift.

Shortly after the plane taxied down the runway, Mike crushed out his cigarette. As the lux executive jet lifted, he allowed himself a single moment to appreciate the weight of her leaving. To live through her heart speeding away from his. When the plane became a distant blinking light, the ice returned. Without looking back, he headed an hour back to town to see his captain.

---

1. Bodies by Drowning Pool
2. You Give Love a Bad Name by Bailey Rushlow

41

FORT KNOX ROUTINE

MAYA

Maya woke, airborne, in plush surroundings. She yawned, taking in the polished dark wood and smooth, buttery dark brown leather of the Gulfstream G650ER as it sped through the sky. A criminally soft and warm black cashmere throw slipped from her shoulders as she slowly sat up on the couch in the back of the plane. She stared out the window into the darkness as the miles whizzed by, wishing she could stay airborne like this forever. The only thing missing was her Heart.

Blocking out the pain and the truth of the last words he said to her, she stood and folded the throw, placing it neatly on the couch. She then made her way to the front of the eighteen-seat jet. Jake, Mace, and Xavier were on their phones, working their contacts for their arrival in Los Angeles. Xavier smiled as she approached and ended his call.

"Maya, how are you?" his kind brown eyes filled with concern.

"Emotionally closed off, facing scandal at the company I built from nothing, and hours away from exposing myself to a billionaire who wants me dead," she said in a monotone voice. "But what has my attention is a desperate need to use your powder room."

"Ah, right, priorities," Xavier said as he glanced at her hand gently resting on her round little belly. Standing up, he escorted her to a discreetly located lavatory. Mid-stride, he grabbed a simple white paper shopping bag from a boutique in Denver.

"These are for you to change into before we land. We are about twenty minutes out," he said.

Maya accepted the bag and ducked her head, embarrassed. "I'm sorry you've gotten dragged into this drama. Some holiday for you - tears, secrets, fistfights, and billionaires, oh my," she shook her head. "You have been kind and remarkably well-equipped to handle an off-hours panic flight."

"Pas de souci," Xavier replied with a soft smile and a wink. "Ce n'est pas la mer à boire, Maya (It's not as if you have to drink the sea, Maya)."

"Bah," she grumbled as she rolled her eyes and headed inside the restroom.

She heard Xavier laugh as she shut the door.

A FEW HOURS LATER...

AA knock at Maya's bedroom door brought her out of a dead sleep. Her body was sore, her mind fuzzy from a mere couple hours sleep, and her bladder full as it always was lately. She dragged the covers back and waved at Jake, leaning against the doorjamb. He had slept on the couch in the living room area of the suite, loathe to leave Maya alone. This was despite Xavier renting a floor of suites at the Sofitel. The security company Mace hired installed men built like boulders at the entrances to each end of the hallway. More men patrolled the hotel that Maya hadn't seen. Yet, Jake was adamant someone stay with her always. Mace and Jake planned to alternate between sleeping in the room on one side of hers and on the couch. Xavier took the room to the other side. She was well guarded, surrounded by people, and yet she felt so alone. She swallowed those thoughts and plastered on a smile. Jake looked decidedly badass rumpled after his own short night.

"Rise and shine darlin'." Jake grinned back his usual devastatingly handsome smile. *Good grief. It's a wonder Leslie makes it out of bed in the morning.*

"I got the rise, not sure about the shine," Maya said, her voice husky with sleep. She yawned and wandered toward the bathroom, scratching the top of her backside. With her hair lopsided and flopping over her face, rounded tummy, and too big PJs with sheep on them, she felt more like a sleepy toddler than the CEO of anything.

JAKE

Maya's assistant had the hotel stock her suite with everything to keep her comfortable for the days ahead. As Jake waited for her to come out of the bathroom, he cataloged the creature comforts that made Maya tick.

A wide selection of designer clothes arranged by style, color, and item type hung on large clothing racks in an open staging area. There was an assortment of lingerie, shoes, jewelry, and other accessories on low tables between the racks. Large bowls of M&M's and bottles of water with metal straws stood in various spots around the suite. She also had a full refrigerator stocked with milk, juices, fruit, veggies, and containers of Indian food. Her bed had a homey quilt instead of the hotel standard linens and several changes of goofy-looking pajamas and overlong t-shirts laid at the foot of the bed. Fresh flowers and potted plants were on several surfaces while a selection of DVDs - romantic comedy movies, architecture and historical documentaries, and past Ohio State football games sat on the console below a large flat-screen TV.

Maya only slept on one side of the bed he noted, she left the other side turned down as if she was waiting for someone. The gun she borrowed from him sat on her nightstand, within her reach. The only other things on the stand were her prenatal vitamins and more water.

Shaking his head, Jake hoped the shit Mike had on Levy would come through and he further hoped Mike got his shit together about Maya. As far as he could tell, they both had fucked it, and neither was going to recover. Not without each other.

Jake glanced at his timepiece as Maya brushed her teeth. He pushed away from her door when Mace walked into the suite.

"She's got a bunch of people waiting for her in the lobby right now,"

Mace said as he tagged a couple of M&Ms from a bowl and popped them into his mouth.

"Press?"

"Nope," Mace said as he shook his head, amused. "A glam squad."

"The hell is that?" Jake asked, his face screwed in a grimace.

"Hair and make-up and whatever other stuff girls need," Mace replied.

Jake grunted and accepted the coffee Mace held out to him.

Maya finally emerged from the bathroom wrapped in a large bath towel that reached her knees. With her hair wet from the quick shower, she smoothed leave in conditioner into her hair and looked more awake than a few moments ago.

She took in Mace's understated crisp navy suit with a stark white shirt and navy tie and blinked. "You know you can wear the hell out of a suit."

He grinned lazily. "We blend in better this way."

"Ah."

"Yours is in the suite," Mace said to Jake.

He nodded, gave Maya one last nod, and walked through the suite and out the door to shower and change.

MAYA

Mace gave her distance as she made her way to the clothing area. She set out clothes, pairing shoes, and accessories. She selected lingerie and walked back to the bathroom.

"Your team is waiting whenever you're ready," he called out.

"Send them up," she called through the door. "Hair alone is going to take two hours."

A knock on the door brought hair and make-up, a stylist, a temp personal assistant for Maya, Xavier, Jada Spencer, and her assistant. The suite suddenly buzzed with activity. When Maya walked out to the living area of the suite - now transformed into a full-on salon - she anxiously searched the room. She relaxed slightly when she met eyes with Mace who had moved to a spot where he could scan everything mostly unnoticed.

The brief reprieve was undone when Xavier approached with a beautiful petite woman with a short pixie haircut, smooth dark skin, and power woman vibe. Power suit, Christian Louboutin power pumps, flawless make-up, and assessing eyes, she radiated energy in waves that tagged everyone in the room.

Maya wished she had already gotten dressed instead of standing there in her slate gray silk robe being sized up. She rolled her shoulders, popped her neck, and waited.

"Good morning, Maya," Xavier said, his eyes scanning her face. "This is Jada Spencer, your publicist."

"Have you eaten yet?" Jada started. Her voice was firm and crisp as she motioned to her assistant, who produced a takeout container, hot beverage cup, and a small pastry bag.

The assistant handed them to Maya and disappeared into the background again.

"Hot ginger tea and a toasted bagel with strawberry cream cheese," Jada said quickly.

"My favorite, thank you," Maya smiled, relaxing a little again as she sipped the tea that was perfectly prepared.

"Now it's my understanding you've been off the grid, yes? You're pregnant, but not discussing. You have security concerns and you've been using an actor to pose as your partner, but everything *legally* is on the up and up. Is there anything else? Arrest records, out-of-court settlements, lawsuits, child porn, sex tapes, crotch shots?"

Maya swallowed a sip of hot tea a little too quickly and coughed - the woman spoke fast, thought fast, and kept it all the way real. She held Jada's eyes for a moment, then taking a deep breath and leaning forward to keep the glam squad out of the business, she said quietly, "Griffin Levy."

Not missing a beat, Jada asked, "The father or the security concern?"

"Both."

"Yikes."

"You got that right," Maya said as she observed the woman fidget briefly with her bracelet.

"Are you still on board? And please remember, you have already signed the non-disclosure agreement."

"That explains the Fort Knox routine," Jada mumbled, glancing around at Mace. "I am on board; do we expect any issues?"

"With disclosure? Not likely, with security, possibly."

Jada nodded. "I'll leave security to the fine gentlemen surrounding you. Let's go over possible questions and your statement while you begin with hair and makeup. I've taken the liberty of creating a skeleton statement. I've also included a brief report on the buzz to this point, favorability meter, and a list of the press that will attend and their background."[1]

Maya walked toward the hair and make-up station to sit on the tall director's chair set up by the stylists, when she stopped and stared at the woman. "You've pulled the metrics already?"

"Yes, and added the same time, last year's comparison for perspective. I've also pulled the articles written thus far. And finally, I worked with your assistant in Ohio to create the virtual press box for the local press. They have a live feed of the conference, and we have camera access in a smaller room at the hotel where you can answer their questions after the initial conference."

"I wasn't sure before now, but Jada, you are the shit."

Jada smiled, clearly taken by surprise by Maya's compliment.

"I need you to speak with Mace to get the full scope of the threat against me. I will go over this,"—she raised the iPad Jada gave her—"make any notes I need and we can go from there."

Jada nodded and moved toward the back of the room where Mace stood watch. Maya quickly briefed the stylist and makeup artist on the look she was going for, and as the stylist and his assistant got to work sectioning, moisturizing and gently stretching her hair to create two-strand twists, she settled in to read Jada's report. Her hands flew over the tablet as she made edits and notes.

---

1. Bring the Pain by Method Man

42
HOES 'R US

MAYA

Maya stepped out of the bedroom into the main living area of the suite on the phone with her assistant Selene. She stood slightly turned toward the window, the late morning sun bathing her in light. As she talked to her assistant about increasing their server capacity, she had a smile on her face.

She wore a dove gray Sergio Hudson pencil skirt, a dove gray, sleeveless silk fitted turtleneck with silver accent jewelry, including a wide cuff bracelet and small silver spike earrings, and a diamond ear cuff. Her mix of edge with classic business attire came together beautifully down to her peep toe, four-inch, hot pink Christian Louboutin booties. She actually kissed the shoes when she saw them. They were sleek and gorgeous, made by a shoe god.

Her eyes on the activity many floors below, Maya wrapped up social media strategy. She clicked off the phone and rubbed her belly as she stared out of the window, tapping the edge of the phone against her chin in thought.

"Maya?" Jada called. "We need to get moving. We should leave in ten minutes."

Maya turned toward the room and noticed everyone staring.

"What's the matter?" she asked, looking down at her clothes and touching her hair. "Is there something wrong with the outfit? Something bad didn't happen, did it?" She looked to the faces in the room, her throat getting tight at the thought.

"You're stunning, and it has taken our breath away," Xavier said. Her eyes landed on him, then grew wide in surprise at the look on his face.

"Oh ... " Maya said, biting her lip, not sure what to say for once. Luckily, Jada came to the rescue.

"Don't mess the gloss, honey, we have no time for fixes," she said in a rush while tossing Xavier a look Maya couldn't read.

"Then let's be off. I hate to be tardy," Maya said, slipping into the safety of work mode. "Mr. Mace, are we ready to move out?"

Mace's eyebrows raised in surprise as she addressed him so formally, but he recovered quickly. "I am if Mr. Matthews is." He nodded toward Jake with a grin.

"Ready darlin'."

Jake handed Maya the gun he'd given her when they arrived in L.A. and checked it for fit after she strapped it into a sleek holster at the small of her back. She slid her oversized matching Sergio Hudson cream, structured jacket over top. Maya nodded to the room and walked out the door with the team following.

When she arrived in the underground garage, she took in the breadth of her security and sighed. Stepping forward to the middle SUV, in a caravan of three giant black Cadillacs, Maya introduced herself to Gunner, her driver, as she slipped into the backseat. Xavier and Jada climbed into the first SUV, and Mace rode in the front seat of Maya's SUV with Jake right next to her.

Maya closed her eyes and exhaled. Then she dug in the hot pink clutch she carried, pulling out her phone. After commandeering the AUX cord she popped two M&M's in her mouth, sat back, closed her eyes, and bobbed her head as Method Man's "Bring the Pain" and a couple other hip-hop hits banged through the speakers.

They pulled into the underground garage at the hotel where the conference was taking place. She made them wait through the end of Lady of Rage's "Afro Puffs" before signaling she was ready. Gunner turned down the music and Mace mumbled, "Thank fuck."

"Amen brother," Jake muttered. "Give me Metallica any day."

Maya laughed hard, her face breaking into a huge grin as her whole body relaxed. "That's what I needed," she said, still chuckling. "Before we're done, I'm going to make you guys into total hip hop heads."

When the car doors opened, Maya Angel Walters, CEO of M.A. Wall Designs, stepped out, fully prepared to take on the day. Mace and a hired guard walked in front of her while Jake, Xavier, and Gunner brought up the rear. Jada walked next to her and gave her the final run down before falling into companionable silence beside her. They took the service elevator to the floor where the press conference was being held.

As they stood outside of the staff entrance, Maya listened to the buzzing coming from the room.

"We have screened everyone," Jake said, looking Maya in the eyes. "If you see something that isn't right, or get uncomfortable, look to me or Mace and we'll take care of it, okay?"

"Okay." She bounced slightly on the balls of her feet and rolled her neck. Her glam squad actually did have time for a refresh and gave her one more tuck and touch of gloss before backing away. She looked to Jada and nodded.

Mace opened the service door, and Jada walked through. Maya exhaled, shook her hands loose, settled a gentle, confident smile on her face, squared her shoulders, and strode through the entrance following a few paces behind Jada.

MIKE

Mike had eyes on two things, and both were taking everything in him not to snap. He was in L.A., in the same hotel as Maya's press conference. He had one eye on the monitor streaming the press conference, and the second on the feed of men sitting in a booth also watching the press conference on one of the dozen TVs in the bar.

He was skirting the "conflict of interest" line. Once Maya revealed who harmed her, he turned over his evidence to his friends in L.A. - guys he knew and trusted. As they examined the men, Mike identified Griffin Levy, Foster Hitchens, and a couple of low-level bodyguards.

The team had tailed them to the hotel, and Mike stayed torn, alternating between the desire to take Levy out where he stood and allowing it to all play out legally. Every moment it was a toss-up whether he'd kill him. Right now, Martinez was in his ear, keeping him mindful of why he was doing what he was doing.

"You can kill him now, but then we don't find out his contact here and that's more victims lost," Mike heard his friend say low as he stood next to him in the room. "You're the coldest muthafucker I know in this kind of situation, Mike. We're almost there."

Mike grunted and kept his eyes ahead to the screen. He watched Maya walk to the clear glass podium. Her security detail fanned out of the camera shot quickly, but not before Mike saw Jake and Mace among the discretely moving men.

He saw Levy sit at attention, his demeanor alert and anger waving off him. Sam, a ten-year vet of the force, dressed casually like an average Angelino having lunch, sat close by and had gone unnoticed by Levy and his detail the whole time. This told the team a couple good things - one Levy's money was short because his hired guns were not the caliber one would expect, and two Levy was distracted beyond care, his thoughts solely focused on Maya, which meant he would make a mistake.

He'd already made several, including gaining way too much confidence in his business ventures and seeing to them personally. Shit was coming together, and Mike bet he'd have enough to shut his ass down permanently soon.

MAYA

Maya looked at the crowd of reporters and was at ease. She knew Griffin was out in the world, watching her, but he wasn't in the room. She smiled at the crowd, glanced at the script in front of her and spoke.

"Good afternoon, everyone. I appreciate so many of you coming out on a holiday weekend. I have a brief statement, then I will take a couple of questions so you can get back to your weekend."

"I am Maya Angel Walters, and I am the CEO and architect of note behind M.A. Wall Designs."

The flashbulbs were blinding.[1]

MIKE

Mike took her in — the measured speech patterns, her hair pulled back off her face, her cutting-edge business attire. She stood poised, sophisticated, commanding, and cool. Maya, the businesswoman, was as captivating as the woman who ran into him at the grocery store. *So fucking phenomenal.* The pain in his chest increased, and so did his pride. Once he took that brief "hit" of Maya, he shut his heart down and the ice returned.

GRIFFIN

The bitch was mocking him. Daring him.

BITCH!

He had to keep control, he always kept control, unless people didn't do as they were told and there she was, big as day. Pregnant, her hair not the way it was supposed to be, with those fucking whore colors on.[2]

She knew, she knew!

She knew what he liked. He had trained her well, but she thought she had beaten him. Everything about her was wrong. Disgusting. He could see her gut from behind the clear podium...

Stupid, stupid bitch. She'd pay. She'd never be free, and once he had what he needed, that bitch would wish she were dead.

Griffin looked down at his hands. They were fucking shaking, the edges of his manicured nails cutting half-moon indentations into his palms.

This operation had to go right. She put herself out in the open for her precious company and now he had her. He'd wipe that smirk off her face. His plan was brilliant, and it would work.

Griffin ran his hand through his hair and sat back, his hands clenched in his lap.

It would work.

MAYA

"Four years ago, I was a young architect with a new firm. My mother had died of cancer and outside of a few friends, I was essentially alone. Everything I had worked and sacrificed for to that point felt like it was slipping away. Proposals were ignored. My calls for meetings went unanswered. When I got meetings, I was rarely allowed to complete the presentation before questions about my age, credentials, methods, and gender became the focus. After being repeatedly turned away, I tried something else."

Maya explained how the ruse worked, then gazed out to the crowd.

"M.A. Walters was the architect. Mark Anderson fit the profile. Everything that was used as an excuse for not hiring me became an asset when Mark became M.A. I supposedly lacked the wisdom that came with age, while Mark had 'fresh eyes.' My inexperienced perspective changed to innovative vision when the same client spoke with Mark."

"Those types of assumptions led to people shaking his hand while asking me to get coffee even though they were sitting in *my* conference room. They even applauded him for his diverse hiring practices." Maya offered a brief smirk at the memory. "Every award given was for M. A. Wall Designs. I made every speech. No one bothered to check Mark's credentials, they simply loved the designs."

"I could have worked to find other avenues, or bided my time until someone noticed and let me in."

She paused for a moment, then gathered herself while leaning into the podium. Her eyes grew serious.

"I watched my mother spend the last seven years of her life battling a disease that robbed her of what she wanted most - time. I was unwilling to waste that same precious resource.

"My commercial buildings leave smaller ecological footprints than most family homes in North America. That's the change we need right now. Ideas we must utilize *now*. Instead of beating my head against the ceiling, I hacked the system. When they told me there was no room at the table, I brought my own exquisitely designed, sustainably harvested chair and made room."

Flashbulbs blinded her again. Fixing her eyes above the crowd, she allowed them to clear for a moment, letting them get their shots. Then, focusing back on the crowd, she said, "Now, let's get to the questions."

"Pierre DuVaul of the Montreal Star --"

"Oui?" Maya replied.

DuVaul blinked in surprise. "Parlez vous français Mademoiselle?"

"Oui, votre question Pierre?"

"Selon vous, quel sera l'impact sur votre entreprise?" (*What do you think the impact to your business will be?*)

"Autre que de voir Mark sur le grand écran au lieu de ma salle de conférence, je soupçonne pas grand-chose ... un intérêt élevé bien sûr, mais si vous demandez si je m'attends à voir une baisse dans les entreprises ou les entreprises retirer - je ne sais pas. Cela indiquerait qu'ils étaient mal à l'aise avec moi à la barre, ce qui est ridicule car rien n'a changé. Mais s'ils ont un problème, c'est leur problème, pas le mien. (*Other than seeing Mark on the big screen instead of in my conference room, I suspect not much ... an elevated interest, of course, but if you are asking if I expect to see a drop in business or companies pull out - I don't. That would indicate they were uncomfortable with me at the helm, which is ludicrous as nothing has changed. But if they do have an issue, that's their problem, not mine.*)"

"Next question."

"Amy Duncan of the Sun Times, what if there are companies with issues? Will your business survive?"

"To repeat myself slightly in English, it would be silly of them to pull out. It would mean they would prefer an actor pretending to be an architect because he's a white male. There are also costs involved on their end. And no, it would not kill my firm."

Maya pointed at the next reporter.

"John Walsh of the Post. Was it legal?"

"Absolutely. Clients may have assumed one thing, but I was the licensed architect. I led the projects. We've never had any issues with any of our builds, which is a big feat, simply because of the nature of the work we do."

She pointed to the next reporter.

"Mary Sims of La Prensa."

"Hola Mary, me encantó tu artículo sobre las cuarenta latinas menores de cuarenta. Mi amiga Laura Alvarado hizo la lista. ¿Tu pregunta? (*I loved your article on the forty Latinas under forty. My friend Laura Alvarado made the list. Your question?*)

"¿Puedes hablar sobre el impacto en la industria que tendrá tu revelación? (*Can you speak to the impact on the industry your revelation will have?*)"

"Espero ver un par de cosas. Lo primero sería lo que podemos hacer como industria para derribar las barreras y prejuicios que experimenté. Yo no fui el primero y ciertamente no será el último en pasar por esto. En segundo lugar, espero que esto aliente a las personas de color y a las mujeres a considerar la arquitectura como una oportunidad de carrera viable y abra los ojos de la industria a aquellos que ya están allí. (*I hope to see a couple things. The first would be what we can do as an industry to break down the barriers and biases I experienced. I wasn't the first and certainly won't be the last to go through this. Second, I hope this encourages people of color and women to look at architecture as a viable career opportunity and open the industry's eyes to those that are already there.*)"

Someone from the back shouted the next question. "How many languages do you speak?!"

Maya laughed along with a few reporters, "Six after English - French, Spanish, Arabic, Mandarin, Swahili, and Xhosa. It's my stupid human trick—that and a walking handstand."

The crowd of reporters laughed.

"Are you taking on new clients?"

"Right now, I'm on sabbatical and have been for a few months."

"Why?" another reporter called out.

Maya took a moment to think and came from around the podium, leaning against the side casually, crossing her feet.

"I've been working or studying intensely since I was fourteen years old. I've cared for my dying mother, created a business, and speaking again about time being precious, I wanted to take some of that time."

Jada leaned over and whispered in Maya's ear, "Be careful."

Maya nodded and called out, "Two more questions."

"What do you say to those who say you are doing this for publicity? And to follow up, some would say you talking about what amounts to privilege while wearing designer clothes in what is obviously a very expensive hotel is hypocritical." The reporter sat back smugly.

MIKE

If the question pissed Maya off, most couldn't tell. She stayed as relaxed in the same position as before, but Mike could tell. He tensed as he heard Griffin laugh loudly.

"Easy Mike," Martinez said in his ear. "You once spent 24 hours in one spot on a stakeout to save a 12-year-old runaway. There are dozens counting on you now. And so is she."

Mike continued to chew his toothpick and willed himself to relax.

MAYA

"My designs and firm have been featured in top architectural magazines for three of the last four years. We've run out of space on our walls to aesthetically put them all. We've won two Design of the Year awards. I don't need the press. It is my understanding someone out there in the world is both an architecture and Moon Falls fan and recognized Mark. To be honest, I wanted to simply phase Mark out of the picture. This kind of attention is disruptive. Now, to answer your second question,"— she leveled a gaze at him that should have turned him to stone— "privilege is not only socio-economic. It's gender, class, race, and more. I do not deny that because of the country of my birth, and my business success, I have a level of privilege. That does not negate what I experienced in the field, in the classroom, and in the boardroom as a double minority in a white male-dominated field."

She took her eyes off the reporter and looked around the room. "I think it's important to be careful in criticizing a woman's wardrobe and looks when she's addressing systemic issues of power and privilege. Not only does it reinforce stereotypes, but it also reduces women to objects for the male gaze and THEN makes that perception the bar on whether our concerns and experiences are valid. Finally, I have a question for you." She turned her gaze back to the reporter, who was now red with embarrassment. "What would you suggest I wear as the CEO of a design firm to a press conference that has international implications for my company? What would make you feel better? Where should I hold a press conference outside this typical setting? Where do you suggest I 'belong?' And before you answer any of those questions, don't."

The room was silent for a moment and then exploded as everyone vied for the last question and applause rang out.

Maya scanned the room and said, "Hey aren't you from *Teen Vogue*?" making eye contact with a junior reporter in the audience.

The reporter stood and cleared her throat nervously. Maya waited patiently and gave a small, encouraging smile.

"What do you say to young girls and women who don't want to put a male figurehead at the top of their company?"

"Don't." Maya said firmly without hesitation. Then she smiled.

"My choice is not for everyone, and isn't that what feminism is about? The ability and space to make choices? The responsibility of those choices should be considered," —she gestured at the press around the room as an example— "and those in a position to make choices are responsible for dismantling barriers for those coming behind them."

"Are you a feminist?" she asked.

"I am an intersectional feminist or womanist, depending on your definition." She looked around the room. "For those who don't understand, Google it. I love Franchesca Ramsey's video explanation for Decoded. And with that, I'll let you all get back to your holiday. Thanks everyone."

Maya smile, waved and turned to walk away.

"Maya! Is it true you have an IQ of 150?" "Maya, are you worth over thirty-five million?" "Maya!" "Maya!"

Jada stepped to the podium as reporters continued to lob questions, saying, "Thank you, everyone, that's it for the afternoon. Have a great holiday weekend."

"Maya, are you pregnant with Griffin Levy's baby? Is it true you two are engaged?"

Maya almost fell off the step at those questions, but Jake was right there on one side and Mace on the other.

"Keep walking Maya," Jake said quietly next to her.

"Mark that reporter," Mace barked into his mic as they moved out of the service side door.

GRIFFIN

He chuckled as he stood to leave.

"Gotcha, little Angel," Griffin said, low.

"Too much security to take her now," Hitchens warned.

They walked out into their waiting SUVs. Once inside, Hitchens turned to his boss.

"Now what?"

"We wait. We've got time. Let her get comfortable."

"WE?" Hitchens scoffed. "Your money is running out, Richie Rich. You're running through it like water. Expanding your stable of whores will not subsidize it fast enough."

"If you had done your job right, I would have gotten it all. Instead, you left the old man to live and now he's spooked." Griffin did a line of coke. "You're lucky you're still a part of this operation, Hitchens, and you'd do well to remember that."

He held Hitchens's eyes in challenge.

"We know Maya is staying at the Sofitel. You are on her from now until I say otherwise. That is your punishment. Surveillance. No women, no playing, nothing but eating, sleeping, and shitting Maya Angel Walters. I want to know everything. Where she's headed to next, where she buys her toilet paper, how often she wipes her ass, and in which direction. You fuck this up, and you're out. After I get my hands on the kid, you've got ten million more reasons not to fuck this up."

Griffin popped a few M&M's in his mouth.

"However, disappointments aside, you have been loyal, so I will give you a gift. You can have Maya after I get the kid."

At that, Hitchens relaxed and grinned.

"Can I get messy?"

"Don't care what you do, as long as no one finds her when you're through."

Griffin checked his watch.

"Let's go. Next stop, 'Hoes 'R Us.'"

MIKE

"Why aren't we hearing shit?" Mike asked in a voice that sent a chill through everyone in the room.

"Something's wrong with the equipment," the guy to the right of Martinez said. "I can't get it up."

"That's a problem for your fucking wife," Mike barked back as he walked out the room. "You've got one job. Do it or else."

"He can't fire me, can he? He doesn't even work for the department anymore," Adams asked Martinez.

Martinez turned to the kid, who was all of 25.

"You know the stories everyone tells about him? They're true. You want to fuck with that guy?"

The kid swallowed hard and went back to furiously troubleshooting.

---

1. Girl on Fire by Alicia Keys
2. Creep by Radiohead

43
I'M SUFFOCATING

"I NEED A BURGER, M&M's and a nap," she declared as she walked from the service exit to the waiting SUVs in the hotel's underground parking lot. Right away she started taking hairpins out of her faux hawk once she got into the Cadi.

"You did good, kid," Jake said.

"It was good until that last set of questions." She moaned as she rubbed her hands through her hair, working her hair loose. "Whew, that thing was squeezing my brain!"

"We're checking on that reporter now, but so far it appears they got an anonymous tip this morning after the conference was called," Mace said, looking into the back seat.

Maya nodded.

"He's such an asshole. I should have been ready for anything. I guess I was more ready for him to jump out of a closet waving an Uzi. It's always mental before physical with Griffin. Little dick fucker."

She slipped her hands behind her, unsnapping her bra. Slipping it off through the arms of her turtleneck, she tossed it across the car in frustration, sat back, and closed her eyes. "Wake me when we get back to the hotel." She yawned before promptly falling asleep.

XAVIER

When Xavier looked in the open door of the SUV, he had to bite back a laugh. Maya had her hot pink shoed feet on Jake's lap and lay stretched across the middle seat, snoring loudly.

"I guess we're done with interviews for the day," Jada said with a smile.

"She took off her bra so, I'm guessing yes," Gunner said from the front seat, tossing the bra onto Jake's lap. "It takes a bomb blast to get my wife to leave the house once that happens."

MAYA

The next morning was more of the same. Early morning shower, the glam squad, and briefs from Jada.

"You ready for headlines?" Jada asked.

"Shoot."

"Architect Whiz Kid Wows at Presser—"

"Who am I, Doogie Howser? I'm thirty years old and feel forty-five."

"You look twelve, hold on to that," Jada clipped. "*#BlackGirlMagic Puts Sustainable Design in the Forefront of Architecture*," "*Feminist Move or Cop Out? Using a Man to Get Ahead*," and "*The Complete Guide to Maya Walters' Wardrobe, Including Those Shoes!*"

Maya snorted loudly at that one.

"The shoes are badass. Totally keeping those," she muttered as she checked her phone again. Like she'd done dozens of times before. Still nothing from Heart. She swallowed her disappointment.

"Let's see, there's more like all of those, everything mostly positive, a few focused on your pregnancy, a couple racist ones from the usual suspects, and a few are digging around the Levy story, but I've got them headed in a different direction. Now they think you may have a thing with Xavier."

Maya nodded absentmindedly, then shook her head and focused on Jada. "Say what?"

Jada looked completely unapologetic. "You either get in front of the story or get run over by it."

"But Xavier? I have a fiancé. . . I think."

"Uh huh. Right. And that's as solid as air in terms of the press. If you can't produce a fiancé, you are as good as a Levy. Especially in your hometown."

"I don't like lying," Maya snapped, worrying about the latest development and Mike hearing about it.

"Says the woman who lied about her company for how long?"

Maya grumbled.

"Listen, there are unconfirmed rumors that you and Xavier are an item versus the absolute denial of a current relationship with Levy. That's all. You've been photographed with each other, unlike you and Griffin. It kills the Griffin story, and believe me, you want that story dead. If they go digging, with enough money? Your abuse photos are front page news. It's he said versus she said and it's going to hurt your company's image. Like it or not, women get the short end of the stick on this."

Maya sighed, "You're right, but..."

"Call your possible fiancé, tell him, and get back with me."

"Even when I tell him, he can't come forward."

"Because?"

"I can't say. It's literally illegal for me to say."

"Dear Lord woman, what kind of life do you live?"

"You have no idea," Maya said before excusing herself to check in with her assistant, Selene.

"MAYA, Johnson pulled out this morning. He already faxed in his canceled contract. I had the lawyers look at it and it's solid. He thinks you're making a political statement."

Maya almost jerked the pins out of her hair before she remembered she was at the start of her day, not the end.

"Grrr ... A political statement. Remind him his deposit is nonrefundable, and he still owes for any unbilled hours. And make sure he knows those designs are mine. If a single bathroom vaguely resembles what we've put together, I'll sue and expose his ass. And this time you can say ass to a client," Maya said, hitting the table with her hand. A moment later, she sounded a bit defeated. "Right, I forgot you don't swear. No ... 'butt' loses the impact... 'tuchus' is worse, Selene..." She sank down into the stylist's chair in frustration as she listened.

Maya held up her hand, and the room quieted. She jumped out of the stylist's chair and began pacing.

"How did they sound when they called? And they said 'call anytime?' What time is it in Beijing now? Shit. Shit. Shit. Shit. That contract is for three builds Selene!" Maya barked into the phone and moved to the bedroom. She paced back out. "I know. It's not your fault. My chickens, my roost. Give me three minutes and connect me directly."

Without looking at or acknowledging anyone, Maya walked back to the bedroom and quietly shut the door. Everyone in the living room waited in tense silence. After ten minutes, the bedroom door opened with Maya smiling speaking in Mandarin - *I look forward to dinner with your family soon. As long as you don't let me win at cards again.*

She gave the thumbs up sign to the room. When she disconnected the call, she passed out on the couch.

"Thank goodness!" she yelped. "This wasn't the difference between affording beautiful fourteen-hundred-dollar shoes, it was the difference between cutting back staff and selling plasma to meet payroll."

"You saved the deal?" Xavier asked.

"It wasn't in jeopardy. They wanted me to know they knew about Mark but didn't want to be impolite by bringing it up. They are sending me flowers as we speak, which is really sweet. Whew, Brad's wife has a new baby and is on our company's health insurance plan. Amanda is going back to school. We do tuition reimbursement, and we took on three paid interns because of the Beijing contract. Losing that would have been a disaster."

"Maybe you should get investors," Xavier said, bringing her a bottle of water. She reached out for the bottle while shaking her head.

"Thank you," she took a long swig. "I thought about it, especially with things going well, but I don't want to be beholden to anyone else. My ship. We sail or sink, it's on me. Money isn't the bottom line, the work we do is, and I can't imagine that's a good pitch to any investor."

"No, not most," he conceded with a smile.

Maya looked down at her phone, frowned, and gave Xavier a distracted - and fake - smile. She made moves to hit the rounds of morning show interviews from the hotel conference room. Later, they ordered lunch in, and she promptly passed out until early evening.

This was her routine for several days. Often the interviews were in the hotel, less frequently they were in a studio, but it ended the same. She had dinner with the fellas, laughed and joked with security, always bringing them dinner and treats, then she closed herself off in her room for hours with her music loud enough to cover her tears.

MAYA LOOKED at the last text she had sent to Michael.

> I miss you. Please talk to me.

She sent it three days ago. Seven days since she left Colorado. Three days since she had reached out, hoping he would respond. She knew he communicated with the fellas, keeping them "in the loop," but he never called her, never asked to speak with her.

She alternated between feeling crushed to feeling like a naughty child sat in the corner, which meant she alternated between sadness and pisstivity and her mood swings combined with pregnancy made for shitty evenings. As long as she focused on work, she was fine. Once she took off the mask, she was drifting.

She was wearing out her Heartbreak playlist, and she had to get off the rollercoaster. The interview requests were leveling out. Jada had done her job well, and it was mostly public speaking opportunities and fluff pieces at this point. The tough work was finished, and her company was in better shape now than before she left.

"Three days," she muttered to herself as she walked into the suite, quickly unfastening her heels - royal blue "Ferme Rouge" Louboutins — classics. She was back from another in-studio interview and with her mood darkening by the moment.

"Seven fucking days total," she growled to herself as she looked at her phone.

"Maya?" Jake asked, looking over at her.

"I'll be damned if I wait for it to happen." She punched the call button with her finger as she walked to the bedroom. Voicemail. Perfect. No smooth "darlin's" and "Sunshines" to distract her. When the voice-mail connected, she tried to make it brief. She made it a mess.

"Hey, it's me. I ... It's obvious this is over. You said we couldn't be fixed with 'I'm sorry' and you're right. Especially when you won't speak to me. This is something I'd wait to do in person, but honestly, I don't think I could survive it, at least not without becoming more damaged than I already am. I can't live in limbo — in this silence waiting for the other shoe to drop, so I — I wish you happiness ... Grrr ... Fuck that, no. I don't. Right now, I wish you'd slam your dick in a door. And I hope you're miserable." She sighed as tears dropped on her silk dress.

"Damn ... but not forever. But right now? I hope you're miserable as shit. I'm not mature enough to wish you better..."

She sighed again; her voice was thick.

"God, I'm losing it. I love you and I ... can't feel my heartbeat anymore ... not without you ... There's only pain where you should be ... I ... I shouldn't have called."

BEEP.

"Son of a bitch voicemail bastard!" Maya groaned, throwing the phone and pacing the length of the bedroom. "That's going to sound ridiculous. Freakin' great, Maya, and you can't call back. You'd sound like a bigger idiot ... Dammit!"

She paced out into the living area and passed the men looking at each other, clearly uncomfortable. Grumbling, she stalked to the fridge and shoved food around.

"No Brussels sprouts?! Every other damn vegetable in the world and not the one I need. I need BRUSSELS SPROUTS!"

"Maya darlin', maybe you should—" Mace started.

"No golden fuck nuggets of truth and wisdom, according to the mountains. No. No no no no no no. You hold it in," she growled, pointing at Mace who retreated in defense posture.

She stomped to the hotel phone and called room service.

"Hi. I need Brussels sprouts. A lot of them. I'm talking enough to serve eight, ten, people. Sauteed with real American, from a cow, butter. Like Midwest grandma from her larder butter. But you've got to cut them in half before you sauté them. Okay? Promise me. Promise you'll cut them in half.... Okay, then after you sauté them in more butter than anyone should use, please sprinkle Parmesan on them. But not Parmesan from the wheel, aged to perfection. I want the stuff you shake out of the bottle. I know it goes against everything you believe in as chefs and progressive Californians. But I need Brussels sprouts, okay?" she sniffed. "Thank you and I'm sorry I was gruff."

"Maya," Jake said. "You gotta calm down darlin'."

"It's been a week. I've been calm. And on task. And apologetic and humble and now I'm done. Men lie and they manipulate. People always—"

She grunted, unzipping her dress partially as she stomped back to the bedroom.

People left her. They always did, and it was time she got over being surprised. A father she never knew. Her mother. Michael. And that was the top three.[1]

She was both crawling out of her skin and being slowly suffocated. Anxiety and the weight of sadness... She couldn't hold it all back anymore. Each of them had left holes, chunks of her open, and she didn't have the strength to ignore it anymore. Her baby kicked a little harder and Maya realized her mother would never meet her child. There was so much she had missed and so much they would never share.

"Oh God! Momma," Maya whispered as the weight of everything she had dragged behind her for years, but kept at a distance, finally, horrifically, caught up to, rushed over, pressed down, and consumed her.

And it brought her to. Her. Knees.

The thump in her bedroom brought a swift-footed response from the men charged with her care and they found her on her knees, her arms wrapped around herself tightly as she wept desperately.

"It's not ... it's too much, all of it, and I can't do it any ... anymore. I'm not strong enough ... not anymore ... "

JAKE

She seemed to crawl into herself more until she wilted onto the floor on her side. Her body shook with sobs.

Jake looked at Mace and Xavier standing in the door, bewildered. They returned the look.

"Are you hurt?" Jake asked, looking her over, trying to lift her arm away from her, but she only pulled in tighter, shaking her head no.

"Let's get you into bed," Mace said quietly as he bent with Jake to pick her up.

"No."

"Ok darlin'," Jake whispered, patting her gently on the knee. He paused, then slowly rose and turned toward the bed.

"You can't leave her on the floor," Xavier growled, his eyes narrowed on Jake in disbelief.

Jake ignored him, snatched the quilt off the bed, and tried to wrap it around Maya.

"No," she grunted, wiggling out of the comforter like it was strangling her. "Too heavy. It's too heavy. Please don't…"

He exchanged a glance with Mace, who had settled on the floor sitting next to Maya with his back against the bed like it was simply another day of them hanging out.

Jake walked past Xavier with the other man following closely behind.

"We've got to call somebody, her brother. This isn't normal," Xavier said, agitated, but Jake was already on it.

With his phone to his ear, Jake stared off, unseeing.

"Brother, I wouldn't ask this with Tori being so close to her time, but you need to come see to Maya. She's … closed up tight, crying, and won't get off the floor. This is somethin' else, and I don't have the skills to deal with it. None of us do," Jake said low, holding Xavier's eyes. "Is she still seeing that therapist?"

"Tell him the plane will be ready for both of them in Denver when they arrive," Xavier said without hesitation, slipping his phone out of his pocket.

CAINE

Caine, his father Thomas, and Maya's therapist, Dr. Flemmings, arrived late in the evening. Mace nodded hello to Thomas and Dr. Flemmings as Caine strode in, his face hard as he headed straight to his sister's bedroom. When he saw Maya, his face softened. She was lying on the floor on her right side curled in a ball and still in the clothes she had on in a TV interview he watched earlier. A white dress billowing around her against the dark grey plush carpeting. She looked like a broken doll. Her eyes were open, red and swollen. His eyes connected with Jake, who was sitting on the floor, his back to the bed next to her, his arm outstretched close to her, but not touching her.

Jake rose and motioned for Caine to sit.

Caine quickly replaced Jake, but instead of sitting, he laid on his back next to her, sliding a hand out to touch her. She gripped his hand tightly.

Caine blinked in surprise at the strength in her grip, given the position she was in. They lay that way for a while in silence.

"How are you doing Maya?" Dr. Flemmings asked from her seated position in the doorway.

"You're a long way from home," Maya observed. "I'm not having a psychotic break, you know. I ... hurt."

"No. I can see you haven't left us Maya," Dr. Flemmings started. "But you do need someone to talk to and you need to keep taking good care of yourself. When was the last time you went to the bathroom?"

Maya shrugged. "It's too heavy. I can barely move."

"What's heavy?" Dr. Flemmings coaxed.

"Grief."

"It is." The doctor nodded. "It has hit you like a Mac truck," Dr. Flemmings said knowingly. "Can I help you get to the bathroom?"

Maya shook her no. She couldn't move.

"I'll take you," Caine said and rolled quickly to his side, helping Maya.

"No."

"You need me. I'm here. Shut up."

Maya didn't have it in her to fight anymore. She let her brother help her to the bathroom. He unzipped her dress the rest of the way, helped her out of it, then turned his back while she did her business. She managed to stand and walk to the sink, but her arms were too heavy to do anything else. Caine turned on the taps and washed her hands in his like he had done hundreds of times with his daughters.

He grabbed a washcloth and dipped it in the warm water, dabbing her face. The amount of makeup left behind on it and the raccoon-like marks around her eyes made him look around until he found a bottle marked "cleanser." He squeezed too much on the cloth and began massaging it into her face.

"Close your eyes," he ordered softly.

He washed all the shit off her eyelids, rinsed the rag, and started wiping the soap off. It took several attempts, and he wondered if he was doing it wrong, but she didn't say a word. It killed him to see her like this, so small and sad. Maya was energy personified and to see her stripped of it hurt and made him so damn angry.

He grabbed her pajamas off the hook behind the door and helped her slip them on. She moved like she was underwater. Slow, heavy, plodding. He flinched when a hot tear landed on his arm and he pulled her in for a hug, holding her tight as her tears soaked his shirt. How long they stayed that way, he couldn't tell, but when her weight sagged against him more, he walked, half-carrying her to the bed, where he helped her in and tried to pull the quilt over her.

"God no," she whimpered as she struggled against the blanket restlessly. "I'm suffocating." She pushed the covers off, closed her eyes, and rolled back into that protective ball. After she settled, Caine, sitting on the side of the bed, dropped his head in his hands.

Movement at the door caught his attention, and when he looked over, a red mist clouded his vision. Caine moved so swiftly Dr. Flemmings barely had time to react as he charged Mike, forcing the man out of the room and back to the living area where Jake, Mace, Xavier, and a few men from security quickly separated them before they came to blows again.

---

1. Medicine by Daughter

44
HEAR MY PRAYER

MIKE

"Get the hell out," Caine growled.

"She is my *life*," Mike said fiercely, standing completely still in the face of Caine's fury, while radiating his own big, dangerous energy.

"She hasn't heard from you for a fucking week, you son of a bitch." Caine leaned in, growling.

"We got him."

"You-—What?" Caine's head jerked and as he reared back on his heels, the room stilled.

Mike glanced at the men hired for security and clearly communicated they were not needed. As the room cleared out, Dr. Flemmings closed the door to Maya's bedroom. When just the inner circle remained, Mike ran his hands through his wild mass of hair, green eyes itching and tired. His face was covered in a week's worth of beard and his colossal body was weighed down after seven days of non-stop work, intense pressure, and travel.

"I could lose my job and, more importantly, fuck this case, by tellin' this..." Mike chewed his toothpick roughly and narrowed his eyes on Caine. "But today the Feds executed a raid on a social club in Columbus that catered to the rich and dealt in the sex trade. The last couple of months, Levy staged a silent hostile takeover and expanded its reach, recruiting and trafficking women and children from around the country, particularly the West Coast. One of those West Coast routes came through Rough Ridge. Levy was offering big money for quick shipments, which is why, when I interrupted that supply line, the retribution was so intense. Most pimps and recruiters would cut their losses and set-up a new route, but with so much money in the game, they made a play to take me out to keep the pipeline open. Our work in Colorado cost them about three mil on the front end and untold millions with us choking off that route.

"Levy was smart at first, not putting his name or face on anything. And he marketed the same way his family did with their legit brands to build his stable. But he's impatient and cocky, which makes him stupid. Instead of slowly gaining territory, earning and displaying respect, he pushed his way in, trying to squeeze out old heads who have been in the game. He didn't show proper respect, and when he started putting other traffickers out of business, he made big enemies. It didn't take long before the Feds had more than enough people willing to get on the inside to shut him down. He was here, in L.A. the day of Maya's conference. He contacted people here as well. We got them too."

"And your work?" Dr. Flemmings asked, looking at Caine.

Mike sighed and scratched his beard with both hands. "It tied him to three direct West Coast pipelines. He's facing federal and local counts for various crimes ... money laundering, human trafficking, use of interstate facilities to transmit information about a minor, and if that wasn't enough, they got him on RICO violations. Tomorrow, the District Attorney for Franklin County, along with the FBI, are announcing the charges. He's going away for a long time."

"And Maya won't have to testify," Caine said, more as a statement than a question.

"The case she has against him is too risky, according to the D.A., especially with the evidence compromised by CPD. The trafficking case has much more evidence. There is still a chance she could be called as a witness, but that's a long shot. We've got victims, records ... she should be okay."

Caine blew out a mouth full of air, placing his hands on his knees bending at the waist. Thomas clapped him on the back gently. After a moment, Caine rose to his full, impressive height and walked to Mike, his hand outstretched.

Mike grasped Caine's hand without hesitation and found himself being dragged roughly into a tight, one-armed bro hug.

"Thank you," Caine rumbled, his voice low and thick.

Stepping back out of the embrace, Mike looked Caine in the eye. "I would do anything for her."

"I see that now."

"About time."

The two men assessed each other for a long, uncomfortable moment.

"I think you both have an understanding," Thomas said from behind them, sounding both amused and impatient.

"Did you get through to IA?" Jake asked.

"Internal Affairs at the New Albany Police Department are working with Columbus' IA and three officers have been relieved of duty connected with improper conduct with the Levy family, Griffin Levy in particular. The union is looking like they will go to bat for them so it's a wait and see now." Mike growled low, shaking his head. "There is one problem: Foster Hitchens is in the wind. He skipped out right after we clocked them all meeting the L.A. contact, but with Levy going down, it's only a matter of time before he's tracked down."

"Shit. That isn't good," Mace said. "He's ex-military. He could be on the run for a long time."

"I'm wondering if Levy got shot of him," Jake said.

"Right now, he isn't talking so I don't know," Mike said, doing the full beard, two hand scratch in frustration. "I'd just landed here when I got Flem's call."

The room turned to the good doctor.

Dr. Flemmings stepped away from Maya's door.

"The three of you - Mike, Caine, and Thomas - can either help Maya get through this or damage her for a long time. Mike, she has abandonment issues brought to the surface by your ghosting. She's feeling the weight of her mother's death after avoiding it for years. She's dealing with grief, guilt, and a lot more."[1]

"What does she have to feel guilty about?" Thomas asked.

"I was glad she died. I was tired of seeing her suffer and tired of taking care of her. What kind of daughter does that make me?" Maya said softly from the bedroom door.

Everyone turned to her in surprise. She leaned heavily on the door-jamb and slowly slid down to the floor. Alarmed, Mike rushed to her. She opened her eyes wider and fiercely said, "Don't come near me. Seven days you didn't, don't come now."

"Baby, I couldn't—" Mike started.

"You could. You could have texted. Or left a message. You've done it before, and anything would have been better than being made to feel like I was being punished or worse, like you didn't ... "

Love me anymore.

She couldn't say it. They again had an audience, and she didn't have the strength in her to form the words. He heard them anyway.

Mike's head dropped. "I should have," he admitted. "I thought you were okay ... that you didn't need ... me."

"Then you don't know how much I love you."

Mike's chest burned, and he lifted his eyes to hers.

When the silence stretched, Thomas caught Caine's eye and began moving toward the door of the suite to give them privacy, with everyone following suit, but Dr. Flemmings placed her hand on Thomas's arm and called over to Caine, "Stay."

Mike kept his eyes on Maya. Caine and Thomas stayed and stared awkwardly at Dr. Flemmings.

When the door closed behind Xavier, Jake, and Mace, Dr. Flemmings addressed the room. "Maya is stubborn," Dr. Flemmings started.

Maya's eyes snapped over to the doctor and narrowed.

"It's protection. She stubbornly ran from her feelings about her mother's death for years and now the combination of her abuse trauma, the discovery of Caine and Thomas, her intense relationship with Mike, the stress of defending her professional choices has broken her protection to shit."

"I can hear you," Maya said, irritated, her voice stronger than she felt.

"You miss your mom," Dr. Flemmings continued like Maya hadn't said a word, "especially now that you are to be a mother yourself. You worry about your natural reaction to your mother's death and you're intensely worried about losing each of these gentlemen. Now's the time to examine that with each other."

And with that, Dr. Flemmings sat, whipped a notebook out of her purse, and helped herself to the bowl of M&M's sitting on the coffee table in front of her.

Caine and Thomas looked at the doctor, then at each other as if to say, "Is she serious?"

MIKE

"I was glad Rose Marie died."

After a half-hour of silence, Mike couldn't stand it anymore. Between Dr. Flemmings chomping on M&M's and unanswered prompts, the Walters men's' restless shifting, and the endless leak of tears from Maya, he thought he would go crazy. He broke the ice like Maya would, with the uncoated truth.

Maya speared Mike with a penetrating glare.

"Don't lie."

He spoke haltingly, his mouth working thoughtfully on the toothpick in his mouth. "Maybe it wasn't gladness so much as relief that she wasn't in pain anymore, and that the waiting..."

"Was over," Maya whispered.

He nodded slowly and looked over Maya's head at nothing.

"When they last longer than expected, you hope," Mike said, stepping closer. He was relieved that Maya didn't protest his approach.

Maya snorted. "The hope is the worst."

Mike sat on the floor near Maya against the wall. Close enough to smell her scent, but not to touch her. It messed with his mind to be even that far away from her.

"You feel like a monster if you don't and a fool if you do," Mike stated roughly.

"Until you don't have to anymore," Thomas said, watching Maya with kind eyes. "There's nothing wrong with feeling that way, baby girl."

"She deserved better than that," Maya said, the tears coming in a faster rush.

"She deserved to have the girl she raised take the good that comes to her with both hands, and leave the bad behind," Caine said, grabbing a chair that belonged to the desk in the room and easing himself down onto it in a straddle, his hands resting on the backrest.

"You were a kid, Maya. A smart and mature one, but a kid. It was too much to deal with and you shouldn't have had to," Thomas said. "You had to grow up too fast. It's okay to,"—he cast his eyes around to think of the words — ". . . mourn what you lost. And mourn Elise too. I have for over thirty years."

Maya's brow furrowed, and she rubbed her belly. Caine stole a glance at his father, appearing to see him in a new light.

At that thought, a giant yawn overcame her. Huge. Mike could tell the baby was zapping all her energy, and whatever she had left, the emotional rollercoaster sucked out of her. She rolled over to her knees, pulled herself up, and walked to the bed, snoring before her head hit the pillows.

"SHE'S OUT," Mike said quietly to the room as he looked in on her.

"We should go," Thomas said, standing.

When Mike came close enough, Thomas grabbed him by the back of his neck, bringing his head close. Speaking roughly, his voice was thick with emotion. "Thank you. I'm proud of you, boy."

"Sir?" Mike said, trying not to feel intensely uncomfortable at the intimacy of the gesture.

"It's Irv, kid. You two work this out? I'm happy to have you in the family. You don't... you still have a place. I can't guarantee she won't try to shoot you over the Thanksgiving table, but you're welcome, hear?"

Mike nodded the best he could with his neck in Thomas's death grip. *Shit, he was strong.* Mike realized he and Maya were going to have giant, healthy kids–at least the boys. Maya and his kids. Mike grinned a bit for the first time in a week. Well, there was the moment he watched

Levy enter lock-up. Thomas spoke again, pulling Mike out of his thoughts.

"Me and Caine will sleep across the hall. The doc's next to us," Thomas said with a yawn and a deep stretch of his long body. He rubbed his hand over his face.

Mike watched them leave and found himself in an odd position. His place was next to Maya in bed, but things were ... unsettled. He didn't want to strain things any more than they already were by crawling into bed with her. But it was all his mind and body craved. Not sleep or food, just her sweet softness pressed against his body. He ached to kiss that spot on her shoulder before burying his nose in her hair and drifting off to sleep. Yet he knew instinctively she wouldn't appreciate him taking that liberty.

God, how had they gotten here? And the better question was how were they going to get back - no - get to someplace better?

He'd struggled but succeeded in pushing thoughts of Maya and what happened to the back of his mind while, off the record, he worked the case against Levy. Now that several pieces of shit were behind bars, his mind was free to brood.

He let out a frustrated growl and washed off the cross-country travel in a hot shower. Later, smelling like cocoa butter and vanilla from Maya's shit in the shower, he climbed into the bed next to her, staying on top of the sheets. She was sleeping like she had all those weeks ago in the hospital - on her side, her hands tucked under her cheek. Her face was puffy from crying and her hair was still partially bound in one of those updos women tortured themselves with.

He reached over and started pulling out hairpins. At seven, he got indignant. At twelve, he was upset; her head had to be killing her. Running his hands through her twists, he made sure he got them all and then absentmindedly began rubbing her scalp. She let out a soft little sigh, followed by that jagged inhale that always comes after a heavy crying jag. It almost broke him.

MAYA

Maya found herself the next morning on her side, curled around her belly. Mike was curled around her, his forehead touching hers, his hand in her hair.[2]

Her eyes drank him in like she was seeing him for the first time. Delighting in how his hair curled and waved, a lock falling over his forehead. Mesmerized by those little freckles on his nose and cheeks. Fascinated by the minor bump on the bridge of his nose that spoke to rough and tumble times. Enthralled with his new beard. Charmed by how young he looked when he slept. Captivated by how his dark lashes closed, whisper soft and still against his cheek. Thrilled with watching his chest rise and fall. She loved that it didn't matter he was so achingly beautiful because his heart rendered any physical beauty superfluous.

Hesitantly, watching his face to make sure he was still asleep, she reached out. Slowly, she slid her arm from tight against herself until her fingers stroked his chest. The heat of his body and the beat of his heart stole her breath away like so many times before. The heaviness of her grief had not left, the pain of their issues had not subsided. She was still terrified of being abandoned, scared to dream of a future with happiness and love, but what they had couldn't be denied. All because of the heartbeat under her fingertips, forever connected to her own.

Flattening her hand against his heart, she closed her eyes.

"Please God, hear my prayer for him," she said, barely above a whisper. "Bring him happiness. Protect him. Please help me love him the way he deserves. We need your help to heal. I need your help to heal. Give me strength to give myself to him. I don't want to hurt him anymore ... I don't want to hurt anymore ... Please ... Amen."

After a while, a shift occurred somewhere within her. She felt ... better ... lighter. She couldn't explain it, but it wasn't long before sleep quickly claimed her again.

MIKE

When Maya relaxed, he opened his eyes. Her face, still puffy, was peaceful. She had prayed for him.

Prayed over him.

His mother was the only person who had ever done that for him. There was a shift in his own soul as he looked at her and digested the gift she'd given him. He gathered her sleeping form in his arms, tucking her in tight to him, and gave that gift right back, praying over his woman and his child before he drifted off back to sleep.

---

1. Fix You by Canyon City
2. Glitter in the Air by P!nk

45

YOU GOTTA?

MAYA

Maya woke with the suite's cool, air-conditioned air sweeping over her exposed wrist, raising goosebumps over her flesh. The rest of her was wrapped in a warm cocoon of man body. Her head rested on Mike's arm, tucked into his chest, with his other arm wrapped tightly around her. His hand lay gently on the widening curve of her belly. That same belly forced their hips away a bit, but their legs tangled together. She must have placed her hand on his face in her sleep and cupped his jaw.[1]

There was a week's worth of beard underneath her fingertips. Mike's body heat radiated through her thin silk pajamas, giving her more warmth and comfort than the expensive, crisp Egyptian cotton sheets and quilt could ever hope to provide. Simply put, he was home. His body stirred slightly, letting her know he was awake and, heart open, she started talking.

"In third grade, I stole a pencil from my teacher's desk because it sparkled," she whispered into his neck. His throat moved as he swallowed, and his heart beat faster. "I was so ashamed I went to Confession though I wasn't Catholic and lit two candles after. I didn't have the procedure all down, and Father Kirkpatrick snickered at me through the confessional. It was all pretty embarrassing. I've never stolen since ... "

"In eighth grade, I let Larry Chatham grab my booty because another girl he liked had boobs and let him get to second base ... I almost got arrested for mooning people. I forget to return library books for months at a time. I'm not a morning person, and I hate the University of Michigan. On a dare I ran around the Horseshoe naked, save for tennis shoes - there may be video. I'm worth about $21 million dollars the last time I checked, and my company is worth much more. But I don't care about money, only the good I can do with it. I'm heavy liberal in my political leanings and I fix problems. It's my way of trying to find a place to help in this crazy world. I still think fart jokes, sex jokes, and puns are hilarious. I Dutch oven unsuspecting victims."

She took a pause as she sifted through the hopes and memories in her head. She traced slow, lazy patterns on his jaw.

"I love what I do, but it's lonely sometimes. A lot of times, I have little in common with colleagues beyond work. I look around to high-five a woman or relate something to a brotha and there's just me..."

She moved closer to him, her voice dropping to a whisper, as she opened it all to him. "Someday I want to sit in front of the Taj Mahal and watch as the sun moves across the sky. Did you know it looks different depending on where the sun hits it? I know I'm going to cry ... My favorite thing to do in the winter is to blow soap bubbles and watch the ice crystals form on them. Big dogs scare me. And horses. Oh! And clowns. I fell in love with a kind heart that came with a beautiful man wrapped around it. I was scared to love, to trust, and I was afraid to be who he needed me to be, and I will never do that again. I want to marry that man and have his possibly green-eyed babies. Genetics will be out on that one ... But if you don't want that anymore ... It won't kill me, but I'm not sure I'll really live for a while."

When he said nothing, she took a big breath. "That's me. All of it."

Mike grinned into her hair, his voice rough with sleep and emotion. "You sure?"

"That's all I can think of right now." She let her fingers trace patterns on his chest as she spoke. "No wait," she stilled, taking a big gulp, "you can't ghost on me again. Get mad - because I'm going to piss you off. Yell, throw tables, but don't disappear on me. If you need time away, do it, but tell me. Tell me if you are coming back ... God," her voice broke, "please say something. I can't handle it. I wish I could, but I can't."

"Sunshine," he whispered. He took her face in his hands, sweeping his thumb over her cheek and kissing it. "Never again."

She searched his eyes, saw in them more than the brilliant green spokes that never failed to captivate her. She saw pain identical to hers. A lump in her throat prevented her from speaking, so she slowly nodded. He squeezed his hand in her hair tightly and crushed her to him.

"My sweet girl," he whispered into her hair.

Maya burrowed into him, desperate to get as close to him as possible, her hand resting flat on his chest, covering his heart. He held her that way for a long time, then out of the blue, he started talking.

"I'm not nearly as interesting. Like you, I graduated from high school at sixteen. I traveled a bit and started at UCLA when I turned 18, majoring in criminal justice and business. I was on the SWAT Team until I transferred to what became the human trafficking division. My father beat my mother until I put a stop to it. The trafficking unit lets me help women who don't have sons like me. Kids who didn't have sisters like mine."

She clenched him tighter at that revelation, her nails biting into his skin under his shirt. He swallowed and continued.

"I only speak one other language - Spanish. I wore a sock on my dick and hitchhiked on a dare, and there is video. Ask my buddy, Martinez. My political leanings were center right except for human rights issues where I've always been strongly liberal. Now with the way things are and the more I research on social and restorative justice, I'm finding myself moving very left. Fart jokes are funny. I'll Dutch oven a girl. I'm worth a couple of mill give or take a few grand thanks to investments I made in college, and my land."

"I felt up Wendy Gaines in high school one day and her mom the next ... I chew toothpicks to keep from smoking. I can still hear my father's voice when I walk into that house, so I'm having it bulldozed. Dr. Flemmings was my shrink from the time I was fourteen until I graduated high school. She helped me get into UCLA, actually. I have a darkness in me you keep at bay ... "

He took a deep breath and inhaled her, her scent, her presence, and kept talking as he held her close, squeezing her when emotion threatened to take over.

"God! I am so proud of you, Maya, and the career you've built. I want to get to know that woman. I want to watch you kicking ass in meetings. I want to walk through buildings that came from your imagination. I want to watch you wrangle three of our kids that have your dimple ... shit girl, I'd marry you today at sunset if you'd have me."

Wow!

That was a lot to take in and Maya took her time letting it seep into her pores. Mike gently stroked her back the whole time and didn't stop after he stopped talking. As moments passed, Maya watched the sun stream through the window and kiss the skin at his neck. Then she asked the most pressing question on her mind.

"You felt up Wendy one day and her mom the next?"

Mike jerked back, and she got those green eyes. "Jesus honey, that's what you got out of all that? Not that I can take care of you, that I want to marry you, just that I got to second base with someone's mom?"

"No, no, I got all that," she said, waving her hand dismissively, "but that was the only thing I found especially unusual. I've always known that you would take care of me, even if you had to work yourself to the bone to do it. I'm done crying, at least for the next hour, I hope. Now all I want to do is laugh with you as I bust your balls. And Wendy and her trampy mom are worth having your balls busted."

"Wendy's mom was hot."

"Maybe, but she was still a tramp, violating girl code with her daughter's man."

"Hmm."

"Now I know why Tank Ass Snyder thinks she's got a shot."

Mike stilled, going rock solid for about half a second before his body shook as he roared with laughter. His laughter rolled from deep in his gut and through his whole body. The vibrations from his body washed over them both and he still held onto her tight. She tipped her head back to watch his face glow, and it was better than she remembered.

"So much goodness and light in one man."

Mike's smile died as she spoke, and she regretted saying anything.

"Please keep laughing," she pleaded quietly, touching her fingertips to his lips. "I love watching you laugh."

"You believe that?" He looked at her with intensity as his breath stopped. As if everything hinged on her reply.

"Of course. As sure as you are that you love me, I am that sure you're a good man."

"Shit," he said, shifting and taking her with him. "Now I gotta fuck you."

She laughed loudly, squirming in his arms.

"Wait, what?! You 'gotta?'"

He stopped unbuttoning her pajama shirt and looked at her with a slightly disgruntled and exasperated grin.

"Babe, it's been a week since I've held you in my arms. We've had a big blowout. We're supposed to talk, connect, build trust, and go slow. Then after you're feelin' good about where we are, I can get back to fillin' that sweet, tight little pussy like we both like. But you said what you said, so I've gotta skip all that and bury myself in you until I need to come up for air in about a week. It'll earn me extra sessions on Flem's couch, but it's worth it."

"Wait, you said a lot there." She sat forward, forcing him to sit back on his haunches. "Who said that's how it's supposed to go? Why can't it go 'It's been a week, we've talked, we keep talking and meanwhile we gettin' it like we like to get it?'"

She threw out her arms in frustration, the long pajama sleeves flapping.

"Why do we have to stand on ceremony? Since when have we ever done anything remotely like we're 'supposed' to do? And why have you stopped taking off my clothes?!"

Mike reached out and grabbed her by her pajama top, pulling her roughly to him. She softened against him on impact as he kissed her hard, releasing her top long enough to slide his hand down, slipping out buttons along the way.

"You're crazy as hell you know that?" he said against her lips.
"So are you," she whispered back. "It works for us."
"Damn right."

---

1. He Loves Me (Lyzel in E Flat) by Jill Scott

46

THANK YOU

MIKE

"Ride me, Sunshine, like that, baby, yeah." Mike groaned as she dropped her head to his neck, sucking it as she continued to grind down on him, her body tightening around him and releasing with every stroke.[1]

"Let me see those beautiful eyes, baby."

She lifted, bracing a palm by his head, her hair falling in a curtain of long twists around them. She focused on him, connecting with his brilliant green eyes made dark with desire as he moved to hold her face, his other hand gripping tight to her hip as he thrust to meet her grind. When her moans reached a fevered pitch and she was close, he slid out and grabbed her hips, sliding her against his body until she centered over his mouth. She shrieked as his lips formed a tight seal around her clit and his tongue stroked her.

She soon overcame her shock and rode his face with wild, wanton abandon. His moans vibrated against her clit as she screamed out his name and came so hard she got a cramp in her left ass cheek.

"Cramp!" she yelped. "My ass, oh shit ... cramp!"

Mike slid her down his body, groaning as her wetness coated him from face to belly. He gently rolled her on her side and kneaded her ass cheek to relax it.

"You need more bananas, baby."

"A banana made my ass cramp!"

"You can take it baby ... As a matter of fact," he slid back into her from behind, hoisting her leg over his. "Take my dick."

"Ooooo," she groaned as he fully filled her. "Fuck ... I missed you."

He pumped slowly from behind as he held her in an iron grip with one arm across her chest.

"I missed you. I love you. I'm sorry," he whispered into her neck.

"Heart." She grabbed onto his arms as he thrust harder.

"Love you," she gasped with each thrust.

Those words became her mantra and his undoing. The more she said it, the harder he thrust until they shattered together. They stayed coupled - him inside of her, Maya wrapped tight around him, her sex still quivering and gripping him - well after they reached climax. Mike jerked with a groan every time she clenched until, finally, he begged her to stop.

"You're going to kill me," he groaned against her chest.

"Good way to go. I think my heart stopped for a minute there." She panted against him. "La petite mort."

"Little death," he rumbled. He turned her over and promptly stuck his face between her soft breasts, inhaling the intoxicating scent of her with each breath he drew in.

"You so get me." She sighed happily, spent.

He tugged her hair back, exposing her neck to him. "I definitely get you."

He placed unhurried kisses from her collarbone to her chin, causing her to pant all over again.

"Wait," she said, holding on to his shoulders, stilling him. "Hey Siri?" she yelled.

Beep Beep.

"What time is sunset tomorrow?"

Mike's arms tightened around her painfully before quickly releasing.

"Sunset tomorrow in Los Angeles, California, is at 8:08 p.m."

Siri's voice rang out across the room.

She looked at him with a big grin, radiant, flashing that dimple he loved so much. "It's Sunday. No licenses on Sunday, plus I need a dress. But I'll marry you tomorrow."

His eyes grew wide with hope. "Are you serious?"

"You're mine and I'm yours. Everything else we figure out along the way," she said with a bold smile.

"Damn, now that's earned you coming so many times you beg me to stop," he said, quickly and gently flipping her on her back.

"La Petite Mort," she said with a fake sigh. "A damn good way to go."

MAYA

Maya was sleeping the rest of the morning away when her phone started ringing off the hook. Mike's phone buzzed like crazy. There were the knocks at the door. Maya woke to a cacophony of sounds from all angles and the noise sent her heart to her throat.

"Shit, what's happening now?" she said, throwing off the covers and slipping out of bed, looking around in confusion about what to do first.

Mike's face was like granite as he looked at his text messages. He had one eye on the phone and one on the pregnant, naked woman standing in front of him. "Don't answer that," he commanded. His tone shook her, and she steeled herself.

"Damn," she said in a low voice. She took a deep breath and shook her head. Her brain kicked in and she figured she better greet whatever was going on in clothes, so she snatched on the first pair of pajamas she saw. Pink PJs covered with skulls wearing glittery neck chokers. They were ridiculous pajamas, which was why she liked them, and they made Mike's face twitch a bit before his eyes returned their steely gaze to hers.

"You're going to be okay," he said as he yanked his jeans over his naked body and walked to the door. She followed him out of the bedroom and watched as he let in the guys, her dad, and a watchful Dr. Flemmings.

"Damn it, seriously, what now?!" Maya said, one hand nervously clutching her belly, her other hand drawing small, random, frantic patterns on a side table she was standing next to.

"Maya honey, come sit over here with me," Thomas called as he sank his long body onto the couch and absentmindedly reached for M&M's.

"Either tell me what's going on now or … " she said, inching over to Thomas and sitting close. She looked over as Mike was pulling on a shirt and moving to sit opposite her on the coffee table. When he sat, cautious green eyes met wary brown ones.

"Today they charged Griffin Levy with multiple counts of human trafficking, racketeering, corruption of a minor, child sex trafficking, and more. He's currently in jail and the District Attorney has made the announcement."

Boy, he said it. Ripped off the bandage. He watched as she blinked rapidly, her face in a bewildered frown. She shook her head slightly as if to shake sense into the words Mike had said. He reached out and tucked a twist behind her ear and waited. She looked slowly around the room and back at him.

Then she reached out to Caine, who was standing near her behind the couch, and pinched him. Hard.

"Ow! The hell Maya?!"

"Ok, so I'm awake," she said, taking a deep breath, and then she popped her neck. "Tell me what you know and how you know it and what it all means."

Mike patiently relayed the entire case, while Dr. Flemmings moved to turn off Maya's phone, which was going crazy in the other room. In the silence, the vibrations coming from multiple phones around her in the room added to the tension. After about ten minutes of Mike speaking in straight facts and some police jargon, he realized her breath was coming fast and shallow.

"Maya, Sunshine, I need you to stay with me, okay? Take deeper breaths or you might faint. Do you need your inhaler?"

She nodded her head jerkily, a long halting wheeze dragging from her chest. Her shoulders tightened closer to her ears.

Caine was on the move before she finished nodding, with Mike barking out the medicine's location. Maya briefly squeezed her eyes shut and tried to take in a few deeper breaths until Mike pressed the inhaler into her palm.

"He's behind bars baby, the case is solid as hell and no judge in his right mind is going to give 'im bail."

She exhaled slowly, taking her time to let the medication work. When she looked up, her haunted eyes brimmed with tears.

"He sold ... he sold people. Ch-children?" Maya asked, her voice breaking, the horror hitting her like Griffin's fists all over again.

MIKE

Mike nodded, his eyes getting cloudy as he watched the love of his life, an African American woman, a descendant of America's ugly legacy; feel the impact, the deepness of Levy's crimes - people used as chattel.

Maya reached beside her and clasped Thomas's hand, then reached across the back of the luxurious linen sofa to intertwine her fingers with her brother's. The room's air grew heavier under the weight of the moment.

Blinking back tears, she swallowed slowly, squeezed her family's hands tight, and asked, "Were the victims recovered?"

Mike wanted to lie. He desperately did. Instead, he told the truth and broke her heart. "Not all, honey. And there's a chance not all of them will be."

"I should have..." She struggled with her thoughts. Her quick tongue moved like it was heavy and foreign to her, her bright mind foggy and dulled. "Anything. I should have stopped it."

"What do you think you could have done, Maya?" Dr. Flemmings asked patiently.

"I ... told more police, different ones, maybe?"

"No one believed you, and you had no guarantee anyone else would have. Instead, you would have exposed yourself and your baby to more abuse or worse," she said in a no-nonsense voice. "You did not know what he was up to, and it's not likely assault charges would have been enough to stop him."

Maya looked at Heart. "If I had told you sooner?"

"I didn't have a name behind what was happening, or all the dots connected in Rough Ridge until the Fourth of July. I would have been pushing your assault case instead of figuring out his wider operation."

Maya took that in and nodded. She stood and paced. "There has got to be something we can do," she said. "What stops people from being found?"

"Time. Leads go cold, manpower. Sometimes there aren't enough skilled personnel, and there are times they sell victims out of the country or they die," Mike said gently, never taking his eyes off her. "There are still people working on this, with the victims. It's going to take time to track down as many players in this as possible."

She stopped mid-stride. "Money, influence, or both? Which one is going to get this pushed to priority?"

"It's already a big fuckin' deal. The press interest in this is off the charts. That's pressure enough," Jake said.

"Is it enough to recover the victims, or will they only be interested in exposing the wealthy sex slave owners?" she asked, her voice hard.

"You have a point," Jake agreed.

His expression reflected Mike's cautious one.

She started pacing again, mumbling to herself. Then, snatching her phone, she dialed a number.

"Selene, I already know. I need Ethan right now," Maya said, stopping the woman in mid-speech. Maya paced more, snatched the remote off the side table and click on the news. Never taking her eyes off the screen, she watched the talking heads express their surprise and analyze the small amount of information the DA put forth to the public.

"Ethan. I need your help, but I have something to tell you first and when I do, you're going to be pissed at me for not telling you sooner, but you're going to have to get over it pretty quick, or table it for later ... " she said in a rush.

She wandered into the bedroom, speaking in a soothing voice. Ten minutes later, she came back.

"He wants to talk to whoever was in charge of the investigation about how he can help," she said. "Do you have their contact info?"

"I don't think you get it, sis. Mike led the investigation until he discovered Levy's connection to you. He had to pass it off, officially, but it was his work that got 'im," Caine rumbled. "He's been in Columbus since you left Rough Ridge."

"Why didn't you tell me?" The phone dropped from her ear.

"Because you'd ask a lot of questions, and I didn't want to admit how often I had to resist killin' the fucker."

She nodded. "This was hell for you."

"Yes."

"And you wouldn't leave it to anyone else."

"Only way to make sure it was done right."

"He's no longer a problem for me," she said, mainly to herself, repeating his words to her.

"No."

"Because of what you did."

He only looked at her.

She lifted the phone back to her ear. "Ethan, I gotta go."

Without listening for a response, she dropped the phone on the side table with a thunk and asked the room for privacy. She waited until the door shut behind them before she walked over to him. He sat stone still on the coffee table, watching her sink to her knees in front of him. Taking his hands in hers she kissed them. Scooting closer between his knees, without breaking eye contact, she said, "I know what you're thinking. You're not a monster."

"I wanted to kill him, baby, 80 different ways, I wanted to kill him."

"But you didn't."

"But I wanted to."

"It doesn't matter to me. I trust the man you are," she whispered. "Completely."

When he said nothing, she closed her eyes, brought his hand to her heart, and said, "Thank you."

"For not killing him?"

"For saving us, all of us that could be saved."

She leaned forward and placed her forehead against his chest. "Thank you."

---

1. Dangerously in Love 2 by Beyonce

47
SAY YES TO THE DRESS

MAYA

"This is going to be a bit of a shock, especially after everything that came out today, but I'm getting married tomorrow here in L.A.," Maya said into the phone as she laid across Mike's chest on the couch. Chinese take-out littered every surface. The fellas sat around watching one of Maya's Ohio State DVDs, and the room's mood relaxed.

"I can run the business from anywhere with the right team in place. Plus, I wanted to open a West Coast office, so this would work. I know you want to say a lot, Shay with Selene, backing you with logic, but this is happening. My tasks today are to find a wedding dress and wedding band because I'm marrying a real-life superhero tomorrow. Then I plan on spending the rest of the day making his toes curl, and the rest of my life making sure he never doubts how much I love him. That's going to have to be enough for you."

"Well, that was direct," Mike said quietly, rubbing her back. She swatted him gently on his side in response as she listened.

"He *is* amazing. Now, focus with Ethan on putting the pressure on getting those people found."

MAYA WAS DETERMINED NOT to let Griffin take away any more happiness than he already had. There was a lot to process. She felt grief, guilt, but she would face it head-on this time and with her husband by her side. Telling the room at large to find something beachy cool to wear for the event was her last missive before she took her Heart into the bedroom.

They took what she thought of as a Colorado shower - getting clean and getting dirty at the same time - then she went dress and ring shopping with her driver, Gunner. None of the other men wanted to go, and Dr. Flemmings had a massage scheduled, so it was just Maya and Gunner out on the town. Technically, she wasn't shopping *with* him, he was her escort, but he insisted on being right by her side the whole time. The big man definitely enjoyed the process more than she thought he would.

"My wife watches 'Say Yes to the Dress' so much she has her favorite episodes memorized," the big man said without a hint of embarrassment or derision in his dark brown eyes. He looked completely out of place in the temple to all things bride with his all-black ensemble, big muscular frame, dark glasses, and military cropped hair. But as he settled in, he looked as relaxed as if he was in a sports bar. You could have knocked her over with a feather when Maya came out in the second dress she tried on and he declared it was the one. When she waffled, wondering if it was too much with her bump and all, he requested the attendants "jack her up." The saleswoman looked at Maya's shocked face and laughed.

"It means add accessories," she said with a snicker at Maya's relief that he wasn't suggesting they beat her up to comply. "It's from that dress show."

And jack her up they did. Maya turned in the three-way mirror and got a funny, tingly vibe that started in her belly and spread out to the bottom of her toes and the top of her head. Even the baby did a double kick in agreement.

"It's perfect," she said with a huge grin.

"Told you," Gunner said, a cocky grin playing on his lips as he nodded approvingly. "Half-hour shopping trip and BOOM. I should hire out my services."

Maya and the sales attendant fell out laughing.

. . .

Twenty minutes later, Maya had Mike's wedding band and she and Gunner were eating burgers on the outside patio of a little restaurant he loved.

"This has got to be the easiest wedding ever," Maya said, happily dipping a group of shoestring fries in ketchup and chomping them down in two bites.

"Not big on weddings, huh?"

She considered him for a moment. "I never thought about it, but the longer you've gotta plan, the more upset people seem to get. This is him, me, and the beach. Hard to mess that shit up."

Gunner laughed and nodded. "Me and the wife almost didn't make it. She wanted my opinion on invitations. Didn't have one. Shared that. Found myself on her mother's lawn at three in the morning, begging her to show me all 10 books as long as she married me."

Maya laughed until she had tears in her eyes. "Bring her tomorrow. Please. I'd love to meet her and swap belly stories."

"You cool people, Maya," Gunner said appreciatively. "Most people we're hired to protect don't see us as anything but shields at best or errand boys at worst. You always ask about how she's doing or make sure we are taken care of. 'Preciate that."

Maya attempted to shrug off the compliment when her skin crawled. She slowly scanned the surrounding area, sensing she was being watched. That prickly sensation Laila awoke in her was now activated by someone else.

Gunner took in Maya's change in demeanor and followed her eyes.

"You feel that?" she asked, her voice shaky.

Gunner, in one smooth movement, slipped from his chair shielding her from the street and curving his body slightly around hers as he helped her from her seat. "Time to go."

A few moments later, Maya had a to-go bag in one hand and Gunner's spare gun at the ready in the pocket of her maxi-length circle skirt. Gunner made a thorough scan of the street, called for backup, and stood at the door of the restaurant, waiting.

Once the second vehicle arrived with Mace and Jake in tow, they all walked out, flanking Maya on every side, scanning the area as they moved, bodies poised and ready for anything. The sensation she had was gone, and she felt silly for causing all the drama. Griffin was in jail. Hitchens had disappeared, but with his money guy locked up, he surely had slid into the anonymous underbelly of the world. Once she was in the SUV, it took off quickly, heading back to the hotel.

"I'm sorry, I don't know what came over me."

"Don't apologize for those instincts," Jake said. "It could've been paparazzi, but nothing wrong with being sure, darlin'."

"Oh shoot, I've got one more stop," she cried. "I've got to get Mike a wedding gift."

"Mike wants you back at the hotel," Mace said from the front. "No buts."

Thinking quickly, she called Gunner in the other SUV and explained what she needed. After she was sure he got it, she settled back and grinned.

"That was some list," Jake said.

"Yep, but I've learned Gunner is a man of many talents. It's as good as done." She yawned and promptly fell asleep.

When they rolled into the underground garage, Gunner drove past the entrance, setting out on Maya's errand. Driving as close as possible to the service elevator entrance, they barely had the car stopped before Mike snatched open the door to check on Maya with his own eyes. The scene that greeted him made him laugh out loud: Maya sprawled out on the seat snoring; her gold sandaled feet laid across Jake's lap.

HITCHENS WATCHED from his car as the tracker on the SUV drove to the hotel and kept going. He took up a spot across from the hotel and settled in for the night.

MAYA

Maya woke at dawn the next morning, smiling as her eyes watched the sun play favorites with the hard edges and fluid lines of Mike's body. It was beautiful the way it rippled over the striations of muscle and glanced off the waves of his hair. She got to wake up to this for the rest of her life. *Not a bad deal.* She rolled from her side to her back, giving her hip a rest. Glancing down at her belly, she let out a loud, unexpected "Whoa!"

Maya's belly had grown overnight. Or at least, it seemed to have. Mike stirred next to her, opening his eyes and then training them in the direction Maya was staring.

"Is it me or—"

"Heart honey, did you read anything about this in your book? Because I've worked through over two dozen pregnancy books and, while there is a myriad of contradictory messaging and theory, overnight growth wasn't covered. I've focused on the medical aspect. Perhaps I need to read more colloquial accounts designed for laymen."

Mike smiled at her studious assessment and added a shrug to the conversation.

"It said something about you popping, but I didn't think it was like this. That's somethin,'" he said in a mixture of awe and confusion. He slid down the bed until he was nose to belly button with Maya. She held her breath a moment as he slid his hand softly, reverently, across the firm, round mound poking at her belly button.

"Good morning baby," he said in a low rumble, his lips pressed close. "I love you so much."

Maya watched him bond with the little bean inside her. She let out a slow, steadying breath when the baby kicked. Hard. Her eyes flew to Mike and his face ... *Dear heaven, his face looked like Christmas.*1

"I felt her!"

He stilled, waiting for another bump and ... nothing.

"At least I got to—"

More bumps and kicks. On the outside, it was slight to Mike, but he felt it as he pressed his lips against Maya's belly. It was almost like wings underneath his skin.

It turned out the baby was highly responsive to Michael's voice. For the next few months, Maya would alternately get misty eyed or supremely annoyed that Michael's voice sent the baby on a kicking spree. The annoyance mainly came from Mike lifting Maya's shirt like she was a parlor trick to anyone and everyone in town or when the baby practiced her daddy induced high kicks on Maya's bladder. But right then, the first time, it was heaven.

"Welp, no time to waste. I'm going to take my hair down before we get our license," she said, sliding out of bed and skipping to the bathroom. When she had finished with her morning duties, she wandered back into the bedroom, intent on getting dressed. Instead, Mike swung her in the air from behind.

Yelping and giggling like a kid, Maya wrapped her hands around his forearms, bending slightly at her neck to kiss the skin closest to her.

"Eight oh eight tonight," he rumbled against the back of her neck.

"Yeah," she sighed. "I wish a couple of folks could be here…"

"We can do something at home … a reception of sorts. Or we can wait."

"Getting cold feet on me, detective?"

"I want you to be happy."

She turned in his arms and stared into those startling green eyes. "I am happy. We'll record ourselves and bore people by playing it at every holiday."

He searched her face and then grinned. "Let me do your hair."

"Honey—"

"Come on," Mike said, settling back on the bed.

Maya looked at him for a second, grinned, and scooted over the bed to sit between his legs, and settled in. On her wedding day, her husband spent the morning lovingly taking out her twists, then they both got dressed in jeans, flip-flops, and t-shirts to get their private marriage license before it got crowded.

When they got back to the hotel, they parted ways. Maya journeyed to her suite to relax and Mike went to finish whatever he was pulling together for their sunset nuptials. He told Maya to leave the planning to him. It was sweet, and as long as he showed, and they had witnesses; she was golden. When she opened the door to her suite, her heart leapt up into her throat and she let out a scream that brought a half dozen grown men scrambling.

Two others joined her scream because her girls, Shay and Selene, were standing in her suite. Shay clapped, dancing in place like a loon. Selene, a bit more on the chill side, simply grinned and threw open her arms for a hug as she yelled. Before Maya could hug her friends, Mike scared them out of their minds when he hit the door, gun drawn, while Mace yelled, "Stand down, Mike!"

Mike's eyes blazed as he looked past Maya around the suite and back to her again quickly. Mike rolled his eyes, holstered his gun, and ran his hands through his hair as he took long strides across the room to the women. "Sunshine baby, you scream like that, I shoot somebody." He stopped next to her and placed a rough kiss on her forehead as he pulled her close to him.

"Heart, these are my friends Shay and Selene."

"Girls, this is my fiancé, Michael Andrew Sheppard."

"Ladies, it's nice to meet you," he said, holding his hand out.

Selene took his hand first, her eyes as big as saucers, and asked in a squeaky, un-Selene-like voice, "How do you do?"

Shay took his hand next and while shaking it, she looked him over long and then passed her gaze through the men crowding the room. "Holy shit Maya, this is like a lottery jackpot, but with penises. Which one can I have?"

48
BIGGEST MISTAKE OF MY LIFE

MAYA

"Okay, I'll be the bitch with no home training and ask the obvious question," Shay started. "Are you sure about this? You're ready to get married? This is the first dick you've had since Griffin a few months ago, right? I mean ... "

Selene sucked in a quiet breath, looking intently at Maya like she was waiting for ... something. Like angry tossing of things or a line of expletives that would make a Navy Seal blush. Instead, Maya smiled.

They made the introductions, exchanged pleasantries, and shared a few shocked gasps when Maya introduced her dad and brother. Eventually, Dr. Flemmings and the men left the ladies to catch up. Maya figured it would be an interrogation.

"I'm positive. It makes little sense to anyone on the outside. Hell, it didn't make sense to me for a good while. It's so fast, and drama and heat have punctuated our relationship. We all have this idea of the proper way things are supposed to go, right? Meet, date, get the friends' approval, live the Instagram life, wed, and breed. But..."

"But you feel an emotional connection. Sweetie, that may be hormones. Pregnancy heightens the need to establish normalized family units - a protector for you and the child. And as an officer, he appears safe," Selene said in her direct way. "A member of the 'pack' selects you as a mate. The pack accepts and protects you. I can see the appeal. They are a classically handsome, typical alpha male group. But you don't know these people."

"Selene, you put logic over everything. You thoroughly researched your argument to prepare for coming here today. Here I thought you all were coming to be bridesmaids."

The girls didn't laugh. Instead, Shay pulled Maya to sit next to her on the couch.

"We still don't understand all that has happened ... I mean, we're your friends Maya, doll. We would be the worst kind of friends if we didn't ask if you were rushing it a bit, shit - a lot. He's fine. Those eyes and that body. And I checked, he's packing in the pants, but you don't have to get married. Life partnering is chic *and* an easy out - at least legally."

Maya crossed her feet under her on the couch and looked at both her friends.[1]

"I'm sure you've noticed I don't exactly open up all that much," she said. "Not even to y'all. In Colorado, I met another side of myself. A side I forgot was there. I have fun with these guys. I have a family, I season racks of meat to sacrifice to a grill called The Beast, I have nieces who demand pancakes first thing in the morning, I have my father and brother and Tammy who can get glass out of my hair—"

"You're home there," Shay said quietly.

"Yes."

"Pardon me, I don't understand," Selene said. "She tripped and fell into Hot Guy Mayberry and now she's getting married and we're all going to be okay with this? Maya, before you left, the running assumption was you were in love with Griffin."

Maya shook her head softly. "I was in love with the idea of someone safe, who didn't ask for too much. Let me rephrase," she said when Selene shook her head. "He didn't ask for anything that was hard to give. He didn't ask for my heart, he didn't require me to take care of his, I didn't have to grow and stretch to meet him where he needed me. His demands were, like our relationship, superficial. I think that is how I can so easily separate Michael from everything Griffin was. Griffin was power, control, obedience, ego. Michael is love, faith, partnership, and, yes, passion. He's generous with his love and fierce in his protection. He believes in me. "

"I watched you," Shay said quietly. "I watched you lose yourself to Griffin, submitting to his whims with barely a fight. I can't let you do that again — and I bet you don't have a prenup! Cops make little to nothing, especially those in little podunk towns."

"Shay."

"He got you, Maya!" Shay yelled. "And neither one of us did anything to stop it. It's my fault. I'd heard rumors, but you are so ... you... I blew them off. You know all the crazy shit people say about my family, or anybody with money. I didn't want to believe it. Then you were gone!"

Shay dissolved into tears and Maya put her arm around her, making soothing noises. Shay's outburst shocked her.

"I missed you by a half-hour," Selene said quietly from where she was standing, her eyes downcast. "I went to your apartment and your neighbors caught me before I left. We couldn't track you."

Maya held her other arm out for Selene to join them on the couch. Selene hesitated a moment, then finally walked to them and sat.

"I'm going to tell you both what happened to me prior to leaving and most of what has happened since. There are things I can't say because it affects the case against Griffin. Other things are private between Michael and I, like his bank account. In the end, I hope you'll stay and come to the wedding, but regardless, know that none of this is your fault and you will have to trust me to learn, recover from, but not be defined by one of the biggest mistakes of my life... "

---

1. My Life by Mary J Blige

49

MOMENTS

MAYA

The wedding of Maya Angel Walters and Michael Andrew Sheppard was beautiful and perfect, and ... normal. It lacked the drive-bys, drama, and tears that had punctuated their courtship. And while some guests held their breath until "I do," Maya and Mike were the picture of calm.

The day, when they both looked back, would be a day of moments. The quiet ones and a few loud ones made the day special.

Maya could have afforded, and used glam squads to the stars, but let her husband do her hair as she sat nestled quietly against his body. Selene did her make-up, and Shay helped her get dressed. Their time together - spent belly rubbing and giggling in quiet, excited whispers - marked a turning point in their friendship. Maya embraced the barrier lifting. She allowed her vulnerability and joy to show. She understood they still had reservations. In fact, Selene took a moment to slip out and Maya was certain it was to assess Mike on her own. She came back cautiously optimistic.

The moment her father came into her room and the way he said her name in that deep, rumbly voice of his brought tears to her eyes. "You're so happy," he said, his eyes never leaving hers, and they sparkled when she smiled big, and nodded.

MIKE

When Mike opened the door to one of the spare suites he was staying in, he didn't expect to see Dr. Flemmings standing there looking pretty in a sky blue sundress. Her hair was out of the professional chignon she'd worn ever since he'd known her.

"You clean up well, Doc." He stepped back and let her into the room.

"I can say the same thing about you. The man bun — it looks good on you," she said with a smile as she patted him on the arm and swept into the room. "Mike, I'm here on behalf of your mother," she announced.

"Is that so?" Mike crossed the room and leaned a hip against the couch, looking at Dr. Flemmings, his thoughts hidden. The toothpick in his mouth stilled, giving no tell to his emotions.

"Your mom and I grew up together, and I loved her to pieces," Dr. Flemmings began. "She got married, I moved away, and we only talked occasionally after, but one thing we always talked about is how much she loved you and your sister. She would have liked Maya for you. It would have warmed her heart how that girl over there loves you."

Mike dropped his eyes and nodded, clearing his throat roughly.

"She would have worried too," she continued. "You've been through a lot. Both of you have. But you are tough, and you didn't inherit that from Mary. She was ... fragile." She leveled a stern gaze at him, and it was like she could read his thoughts. He long suspected she could. "He was a weak bully, so you didn't inherit it from him either. You got nothing from that man."

She walked over to Mike and placed her hand on his, forcing his eyes to hers. "You've always been a good kid. From your looks to your heart, you've always been all Mary. Maya helps you see the good in yourself. Hold tight to that."

She waited until Mike nodded. "Now show me what you're giving your bride for your wedding day."

"THIS IS BECOMING A REGULAR HABIT," Mike said out loud. He was on his knees, hands clasped in prayer. His soon-to-be wife's gift to him sat on the glass coffee table, glinting in the sun. His eyes roamed over the handsome mahogany box with black velvet lining. He took in the sophisticated, contemporary carvings in the wood. It was pure class and all Maya. Then his eyes rested, for the hundredth time that morning, on the contents. A pristine brick, a modern, corked glass jar filled with what he figured out was mortar and a battered, well-worn trowel with an elegant cream ribbon tied around the handle. Green eyes caressed the simple cream linen notecard and the neat, pretty handwriting:

I don't need these anymore. No more walls.

He waited for a sign as he crossed himself and sat back on his haunches. He didn't see a burning bush, but he did hear a knock.

"Heart, it's me. Don't open the door," Maya said through the door.

He chuckled, rose smoothly, and moved to the door. He resisted the urge to open it. Instead, he placed his head against it. "I didn't know you were superstitious."

"The last few months have made me cautious about tempting things," she said with a smile in her voice. "I missed you. I needed to hear your voice."

He swallowed hard. "Missed you too, darlin'."

"I can't wait to marry you."

"I'm opening the door, Sunshine," he warned.

"No! You can't see me, please Heart!"

"Hold your panties woman, I'm just gonna put my hand out. I want to touch you."

"Ok, but if you look, I'm gonna be so mad," she snapped. "And I'm not wearing any."

"Still a pain in my ass woman — wait. Seriously?"

"Seriously. But if you look, I'm going to go find the biggest, wrinkliest, elephant gray drawers in L.A. and wear them for the next year!"

The door opened, and her warm, soft, small hand reached out for him. He closed his own around hers and heard her sigh.

"That's better."

"Yeah, it is," she said, squeezing his hand, her head against the door like his, on the opposite side.

Click.

"THAT was a moment," Shay whispered quietly to Selene as she lowered her camera.

MAYA

"I just got you and now I'm giving you away," Thomas said as he adjusted the orchid in her hair. The warm sea air lifted her twist out hair, creating a moving halo around her.

"I'm not going anywhere, not now," she smiled at him. "They'll have to drag me away from my family kicking and screaming."

Maya looped her arm in his and let him set the pace as they walked down the steps that led to the beach. "We've got all the time in the world to walk down there. They can't start without us."

She was eager to marry Heart, yet hesitant to leave this quiet space with Thomas. Maya tried to memorize the movement of his gait, the rhythm in his stride ... the sound of his shoes on the wooden steps as sand crunched softly underneath them. She wanted to always remember the strength in his arm as he supported her as they walked, the soft brush of his cream linen shirt against her shoulder, the quiet words he spoke to her as they walked, and his chuckle when she kicked off her shoes to walk in the sand. And she would never forget how he held her close when they rounded the corner and she saw everyone standing in a semi-circle waiting for her.

The number of people in attendance shocked her so much she almost lost her footing, but Thomas held her firm. Most of her friends from Rough Ridge were there in their own versions of badass beachwear, and their wives had made the trip over the mountains to join them. Leslie blew her a kiss, Mac and his husband Duke grinned big, and then her gaze settled on a heavily pregnant, seriously-about-to-pop-how-did-she-get-on-a-plane Tori! Maya did a little hop and pointed to her, waving her bouquet like a maniac.

Shay and Selene stood smiling, Shay clicking away with her camera. Ethan looked fresh off a plane from Washington, his arm around Vivian. Jada waved and mouthed, "go girl!" Xavier stood off to the side watching. Amid all her drama, Maya forgot about him the last few days. The realization embarrassed her - she'd been so selfish. She mouthed, "Hey," and he inclined his head slightly.

There were also several people Maya assumed were Mike's friends from L.A. - most of them had a cop look about them. Their eyes scanned her, then the surrounding area. Yep, those were cops. She spotted Gunner and his wife and then her eyes finally landed on Michael in the center of the circle and her heart nearly burst out of her chest.

The sun moved low in the sky, bathing him in gorgeous golden and pink rays highlighting his sun-bronzed skin. He wore a crisp linen shirt and slacks that moved in the breeze. His hair was swept back in a simple elastic, and he had shaved, leaving a dark goatee that rimmed his bright white smile. His sparkling emerald eyes were laser-focused on her face. Her hand flew to her mouth, covering most of her face with her simple bouquet of perfect red roses.

Moments.

Suddenly the musicians began playing Rotimi's "*I Do*" and Maya heard a familiar voice. Turning to her right, she looked past Thomas to the small group of musicians and saw Laila in a dress, hair loose and smiling - in a non-maniacal way - as she sang.[1]

As Laila sang the words about prayer and marrying an angel, Maya and Thomas met her Heart at the center of the semi-circle. Thomas placed her hand in Mike's outstretched one, then paused for a moment to kiss her cheek, whispering, "Kicking and screaming."

Moments.

The ceremony was simple, officiated by a rough-looking reverend dressed in a black tee and jeans. There were the usual vows of love and fidelity, but to Mike and Maya, the words were brand new. She was so loved. She marveled in and was humbled by the glimmer of wet in Heart's eyes. Humbled by the friends and family who dropped every-thing and trekked to the West Coast on a Monday evening. She hadn't spent her life alone. Today proved it, and now she was promising herself to the wonderful man in front of her.

MIKE

Maya made him believe he was fifty feet tall. He would fight lions and walk through bullets for her daily. She made him feel like he could do all that and more. The way the breeze lifted her hair, the way she looked at him ... like he had all of her love and trust. It was so good it hurt.

Each little moment.

MAYA

Maya's favorite moment was the last moment of the ceremony. Not the dancing by torchlight, or the impromptu cop-led karaoke by the bonfire. Not the to-die-for chocolate cake covered in buttercream frosting and off-white pearlized M&Ms... it wasn't even meeting Mike's friends and Tina's Mom - who she loved immediately. Her favorite moment was when Mike placed her hand on his heart and covered it with his own, then put his second hand on her belly and touched his lips fully to hers as the sun slipped past the horizon. It was THE moment that would always stay in her mind. Whenever the world became too much, Maya would go to this moment of peace and love for the rest of her life.

MIKE

For Mike, his favorite moment was when she looked at him and said, "Oh yeah, I totally do."

When his friend Martinez, who was an ordained reverend in addition to being a cop, asked Maya if she promised to love, honor, and all of that, she took a deep breath. The wind gently lifted her hair, the setting sun hit her with a diffused glow highlighting the warm undertones of her skin. It glimmered off her blinding white silk, off-the-shoulder dress that clung to her baby bump and draped gracefully to the ground into a small train. She was so beautiful and ripe, an angel sent straight from heaven into his arms. She parted those fantastic lips of hers to speak, broke out into a huge smile and said the first thing that came to her mind - "Oh yeah, I totally do."

He loved it. He reached for her right then, but Martinez stopped him, clearly enjoying torturing his friend, to the delight of their friends and family.

It was that exact moment he revisited in tough times.

He loved the time Maya spent embracing each one of his friends like she had known them forever, and when she gamely took on the ill-advised karaoke challenge and warbled/wailed her way through a Celine Dion song in his honor. He cherished the many times she exclaimed in delight over a detail of their hastily put-together wedding. He felt Tina with him when Maya met and hugged her mother. He remembered when Caine officially welcomed him to the family, at which point Tori and Maya fell into each other's arms crying happy, pregnant lady tears. Each of those moments mattered, but the most precious moment was hearing, "Oh yeah, I totally do."

---

1. I Do by Rotimi

50
I WANT HIM TO SUFFER

MIKE

Mike woke the morning after his wedding, sore, dirty, and happy as hell. The party lasted well past any party on a Monday night should. By the time he and Maya drug themselves into the room, they were wet, smelled like smoke and seawater from the bonfire and beach, had sand in places they shouldn't, and were all over each other. They had done things Mike was sure were illegal in a few Bible Belt states and only retired to sleep after the sun came up. When he looked over, he saw Maya watching him, smiling.[1]

She looked adorably mussed. Her twist out smooshed on one side, bonnet forgotten in their lusty haze. There was makeup smeared around her eyes, but God, her smile.

"The baby and I want to go home."

"Home?"

"Home. With you. To our town. I'm ready for our life together to start."

Home. A little town most didn't know existed became heaven on Earth at that moment.

After what looked like a Three Stooges routine of packing and dressing, they notified the Rough Ridge contingent of the wedding group, who were leaving within the hour. They surprised them all with their decision to fly back right away.

Maya signed off for her L.A. assistant to pack and ship the things she had amassed since being in L.A. and shuddered at the price tag of the total trip.

"The jet, rooms, wardrobe, glam squad, Jada's fee, my assistant, security ... Shit, room service alone is insane. Who knew Brussels sprouts cost so much? This is more than many families make in a year or three! Griffin is a rat bastard ... " As the hustle and bustle moved around her, he saw Maya sit for a moment.

MAYA

He had sold people, children, into a fate from which they might never recover. And for what? Money? Power? Cruelty? When was it ever enough? The weight of the knowledge never left her since she found out. It was always there on the outside edges of her mind. She had incredible guilt about being happy and getting married after finding out what he'd done. It would be a long time before she could go a day without thinking about it. Staring absentmindedly at the coffee table, her hand traced patterns on the seat cushion. Warmth at her back stilled her hand. Heart's face was a little blurry as she turned to face him.

"He sold kids," she whispered.

"Sweetheart." He kissed her shoulder, wrapped his arms around her, and pulled her snug to him.

"How do you ... how do you cope with what you see out there every day; what you saw working here?"

"You don't get used to it or let it consume you. It's doing the best you can to ease what burdens you can for people, and you find an outlet when your best ain't good enough. I'm not gonna lie Sunshine. Shit cuts deep, but it makes people - the smart ones - appreciate what the fuck they have and hold on to it."

"I'm stressing about the cost of this entire week and angry about having to do it all because of him. I got a grip and remembered so many people have lost so much more."

He squeezed her again, kissing the top of her head.

"I want him to suffer," she said, her voice hard. "Life in prison isn't good enough. A bullet to the head is too quick. I want him to die of exposure in a desert with fire ants peeling the flesh off his body, or worse."

"Worse, huh?"

"I've got an active imagination."

"Baby, that's normal. As long as you keep letting that shit out, talkin' it out. It's all good."

"Hmm..."

"Baby?" he said, shaking her gently. "Let's get my family home."

MIKE

Maya took a moment with each of her friends from Columbus individually, pressing a small linen card into each of their hands as they hugged. She gave their security team bonuses and gave Gunner a well-deserved bear hug and plane tickets to visit Colorado after his wife Theresa had their baby.

As the Xavier-owned jet taxied down the runway, Maya yawned and pulled her hair into a bun. The next two hours in the sky was one of the most fun flights Mike had ever had. He was taking his pregnant wife home. Griffin was behind bars, and Mike was a part of a family for the first time in a long time. Foster's disappearance worried him — a lot — but on his own, it wouldn't take long to find him. Military training or not, the Feds were scouring the country for his ass. Mace's question to Maya roused him from his thoughts.

"How did who break-in where?" Mike asked, his face looking bemused, weary, and a tad irritated.

Maya gave Mace a wide-eyed, "really?" look and then looked at him with a placating smile. "No walls, right?"

Mike looked at his wife, rolled his eyes to the ceiling, then back to her, releasing an exasperated sigh. "Killing me."

"I broke into Jake and Mace's houses and took things, and from Caine's safe too," Maya said in a rush. "But it's all good. It was to prove a point to them, and they are cool with it now. I thought no one would bring it up again ... and also, I kinda forgot."

"You forgot you broke into the homes of men, two of whom I am certain have firearms, to steal. What the fuck was the point in that Maya?"

Maya quickly laid it all out, answering Mace's question, assuring alarms would be on all day in the men's homes, regardless of who was there.

"And the dogs didn't do a thing?" Mace asked, his curiosity getting the better of him.

"I'm pregnant, friendly, and I had treats." Maya shrugged. "I figured they'd either let me in or not. The lab took the treats and because the rotty is trained I contacted my security people and told them I was dropping off flowers to a friend and their dog had me cornered. After trying a few words in a couple different languages, she let me pat her and get in. I wasn't there as a threat. But speaking of pets..."

Maya relayed to Jake what happened to his cat. Despite Mike's severe frustration that Maya had put herself in that kind of danger, he chuckled with everyone else as she described her panic over the cat getting out.

"Spent 15 minutes in the woods bawling my eyes out trying to find her." Maya laughed as she shook her head. "Horrified I'd allowed that cute little cat to get eaten by a mountain lion, I came back to face your wrath. There she was on the fucking deck, staring at me with an attitude. I've never been so happy to see a damn animal in all my life!" Tears streamed down her face as she laughed. "I almost punted her prissy behind through the window! I was so done with her."

Before long, the plane landed. As the passengers departed, each thanking Xavier, Maya hung back. A wordless exchange passed between her and Mike. He gripped the man who'd embraced the challenge of protecting his wife. While he didn't appreciate the way Xavier looked at her; he didn't begrudge the man. Maya completely devastated *him* with one little dimpled smile, and he was married to her. Mike made his way out into the hot Colorado sunshine and waited at the bottom of the steps for her.

––––––––

MAYA

Maya looked at Xavier and smiled. He smiled back.

"Thank you, X. For everything—"

"I remembered you. From the moment I saw your face, I remembered you. That day with your beans," he said as he cocked his head a little. "You're not the type of woman a man forgets easily."

"Why—"

"You needed discretion."

Maya nodded and looked at him appreciatively, "You're an amazing man, X. I don't know what to say, except whenever you need me, if you need me, I'll be there."

"Rarely do I miss winning opportunities, but I missed a big one with you," he said, reaching out to take her hand.

Maya let out an embarrassed chuckle. "I'm a winning opportunity?"

"For the right man. Detective Sheppard is the one for you. You both deserve all the happiness you can handle and more. Someday ... I'd like to have something close to that. I haven't thought about it before now, so thank you."

He kissed her hand lightly and then let her go. Maya bit her lower lip and suddenly hugged him. "You are going to find a love so amazing; I can feel it in my bones," she whispered before she released him and walked to the steps of the plane.

Mike helped her down the few stairs, and they walked across the tarmac through the glass doors of a private hangar at the Denver International Airport.

––––––––

XAVIER

Xavier stood watching them walk away - Maya's white cotton skirt swirling around her, Mike's head bent toward her as she spoke, his eyes never leaving her face, a smile on his lips - and smiled himself. If ever there was a perfect couple... "I never had a chance," he chuckled to himself as he rapped on the door of the cockpit to talk to his pilot.

---

1. Funny How Time Flies by Janet Jackson

51

SURPRISE

MIKE

Mike looked at his new wife. The breeze aided her curls in escaping her loose bun, blowing them around her face. The hot summer sun warmed them both and created magic as it kissed her shoulders. A slight smile danced on her lips, her hand stroking his as they drove the hour home to Rough Ridge. She looked ... content.

"Sunshine honey—"

"Hmm?" Her head lazily turned to him, her smile wider.

"You happy?"

"Happier than a Buckeye in the Horseshoe on a fall afternoon."

His chuckle was light in his chest. Everything felt lighter. Her thighs were warm as he leaned across her, never taking his eyes off the road. He yanked open the glove compartment with a clang, grimacing as it stuck, another reminder of the drive-by. He'd have to get a new Jeep soon. The quick repairs weren't good enough for his bride and their baby. He pulled out a long, thin jewelry box and set it in her lap.

MAYA

Her hands were shaking as she lifted the lid on the velvet box. On a bed of satin lay an exquisite rose gold necklace with an unusual heart pendant formed from unique pieces, each treated with a different technique. Small dents on one section, tiny overlapping pieces of gold with rough edges forming what looked like scars and other sections had no covering at all. They were just open spaces.

It was stunning. And unique. It was everything.

The box blurred as her eyes filled with tears. She quickly tried to blink them away.

"It's beautiful," she said, her voice thick. She gently traced it with one finger. "It's you."

Mike nodded. "Got rough parts, scars, but what I have left is filled with you."

"Shit, you're making me cry. I'm already so happy and then you up the ante. I never allowed myself to dream this big, let alone hope for a life like this."

She looked to her side shyly and saw his jaw had gone rigid. Then she noticed the trees whizzing by and glanced at the speedometer.

"Public servant! You're twenty miles over the limit!"

"Gotta get you home."

"But—"

"Gotta get you in our bed," he rumbled lower.

"Oh."

Damp heat sprang between her thighs and radiated through her.

"Let me see if I can speed things up for when we get there." She lifted in her seat, slid her skirt up to her waist, and hooked her thumbs into the waistband of her panties. With a whisper, they dropped to her ankles.

Mike glanced over at her, his grip tightening on the steering wheel. He tried to keep his eyes on the road, but then a black scrap of lace landed on the dashboard.

"Oops, I was aiming for somewhere else, but that'll work."

"Sunshine, quit playin' around."

"Mmm..." was her only reply as she slid her fingers through her slick folds, her head falling back against the seat.

"Babe, are you?" Michael rasped, his voice husky with want.

"Oh yeah."

"Shit," he mumbled. "You better not come without me."

"Wha-mmm, what are you going to do about it? Spank me?" she dared, her breath coming out in a low moan as she worked herself.

"Is that ... something you'd like?" he asked hesitantly.

"You're trying to distract me. You know I have to answer questions. I'm an excellent student," she giggled. "But ... it's a ... curiosity."

"Even after what happened to you?"

She stopped her slow torture of him and herself to think about what he was saying.

"Is that something you're into?" she asked quietly.

"Yes."

She examined his response in her head for a moment, trying to decide what she thought about it.

"Does it ... hurt a lot or ... why do you like it?"

"I like control and I like to please. My reward is your trust and pleasure and to know I give that to you. It is a different pain, but in a good way. But ... I don't have to have it. It's a different game to play, but if you aren't into it, it's absolutely fine. You don't have to be a shrink to figure me out, darlin'. I like what I like and I love you. Any way I can be with you."

She nodded, taking it in. "What if I don't like it?"

"We stop."

"What if it reminds me of..."

"We. Stop. Safe space, remember?"

"... I want to try it."

She saw his throat move as he swallowed.

"You sure?"

She slipped her hand back between her legs. "Positive."

He switched hands on the wheel and reached across her seat, trying to still her hand. Instead, she ground against both their hands.

Mike tried to jerk his hand away. Maya caught it and brought his fingers to her mouth, sucking in the tips of each of his fingers achingly slow, one at a time. She tasted herself on his hand and it drove her crazy, but it was his response that almost had her coming right then. He fidgeted like his ass was on fire.

"Fuck." Snatching his hand away, he slowed the Jeep and made a U-turn speeding back the way they had come.

Now Maya was unsure. Maybe she had pushed him too far. Suddenly, they slowed down again, turned onto an old logging road, and sped down for a mile until he reached a clearing in the middle of a field. Stopping short, he threw the car in park.

"Michael—"

He pressed the button to undo her seatbelt, hopped out, and stalked around the hood of the Jeep, his eyes never leaving her as he made it to her side in a few strides of his long legs.

Oh boy. She was tense and excited and ...

He opened the door, reached in, and snatched off her halter top, tossing it to the ground. Pulling her toward him, he promptly latched onto her exposed breast.

It all happened so quickly her mouth was open with no sound. He teased, licked, and tormented her sensitive bud until she found her voice and begged him to take her. Ignoring her words, he switched to the other breast, giving it the same exquisite torture. Then suddenly, he let go and softly turned her and pressed against her back.

"You like to tease, so do I," he whispered in her ear as he slowly skimmed his fingertips lightly down her arms, giving her goosebumps under the blazing hot summer sun. When he reached her fingertips, he gripped them and gently lifted her arms, placing her hands flat against the doorway of the Jeep.

"You don't like what I'm doing say 'Skip.' It stops right then and we do something else you enjoy. Understand?"

She nodded.

"Say the words darlin'," he whispered.

"I—boy, do I understand."

"Don't move."

A request. A demand, and Maya damn near fell out. Her legs were weak with desire. She couldn't let go if she wanted to without collapsing to the ground, half-naked in the middle of nowhere, so she held on. And tried not to move as Mike slowly kissed, licked, and gently nibbled his way down her neck, across her shoulder blades, down the center of her back to the top of her skirt at her waist.

Shivering, she moaned as he slowly slid the zipper down, kissing and licking at each inch of skin revealed. Disbelief warred with desire. They were out in the open, creating one of the most erotic experiences she'd ever had. She felt earthy and free. The embodiment of life and sexuality.

With her skirt around her ankles, Mike smacked her ass. It jolted her and before she could move, his mouth covered the spot he hit. He licked away the sting and followed by blowing gently across her moist skin. The sensations - tingling and heat, whispers of breath and sooth- ing, moist tongue, the softness of his lips, the scratchy brushes of his goatee, the whisper-light brushes of his hair - it was mind-blowing. She wasn't sure how much more she could take, but she didn't want it to end, so she stood there, gripping the Jeep as he played with her body in a whole new way.

Again and again, he slapped an open hand to her round backside, always in a unique spot as to never make her too sore. Never too hard, but there was a bite to it each time his hand landed against her. Then he was there to lick, stroke, and blow.

"Are you okay?" he asked, pausing while his voice left breathy bursts on her ass cheek. He was gently sliding his fingertips up and down her thighs over the old injuries, kissing them. The mental roadmap he made was unbelievably accurate. Her heart expanded.

He would always keep her, care for her. She looked deep to assess how she felt. Nothing Michael did reminded her of that basement. She had no fear. The part of her brain not screaming "Oh God yes!" or concentrating on holding on to the car understood that, while she was getting spanked, he was the one on his knees on a dirt road somewhere in the middle of the Colorado forest giving her pleasure.

She arched her back more. "Please, don't stop."

He kissed her hip softly and went back to the ministry of pleasure, she being his chief convert.

When she was close to finding it, finding that peak he worked her toward, he stopped again. She couldn't believe she was about to come and he stopped.

"No, no no no," she moaned, out of breath, "please don't stop."

"Don't come."

"Please," she begged.

"Don't. Come." he said sternly. "Tell me when you're close. You can't come until I tell you."

"That's mean." She panted, trying to get her body under control.

"That's the game. You want to play while I'm driving, there are consequences. But you have all the power here," he reminded her.

Oh, hell yeah! Who would've thought she'd be into this?

"Sunshine."

"Don't come until you tell me." She moaned, doing a little hop in anticipation and when her ass jiggled, he groaned deep.

"Damn beautiful," his voice sounded like gravel against her ear.

He stepped back and she heard the zip swish of clothing. He was now butt-ass naked too, standing behind her, watching her. The thought sent fresh tingles zinging around her body and the anticipation was its own foreplay. When she couldn't take the waiting much more, he was there, pressed against her back, his raging hard-on positioned at her warm, wet core as he rocked her slow along his shaft, but not entering her.

The pads of his fingers were rough as he spread her open more so that he could rub his shaft along her clit. Her moisture coated him as she wiggled to get where he would enter her, but he held her back. Her whimper lifted on the breeze as he smacked her ass again. This time when he smacked, he rubbed against her, creating a novel sensation. Smack, then gliding his heavy, swollen member over her clit. When she signaled she was close, he would stop and resume the spanks. It was so ... Intense.

It reduced her to mainly speaking gibberish and when she was close a fourth time, she expected to him to stop. Instead, Mike rewarded her by thrusting into her, filling her completely. And she came fast and hard. Sensing her weakness, Mike placed his hands over the top of hers, holding her upright as he claimed her. And before her first orgasm subsided, Mike slid her hands lower on the side of the Jeep, tipped her hips up, and increased his powerful thrusts as the second one built or was it a continuation of the first? Maya didn't give a flying fuck about the distinction.

Women wax poetic about rainbows and stars, but Maya came so hard she saw nothing but blackness, her body vibrating like a tuning fork, then stiffening as it rolled through her. She was vaguely aware of Mike's shouted curse as he spilled into her. Nearby, birds' rustled as the echo of her cries filled the area. She welcomed the weight of him against her back. With his heart beating against her, an absurd thought floated through her head before she opened her eyes: *I think he fucked me blind.*

Clarity came to her as she opened her eyes with a giggle, taking in the blinding Colorado sunlight reflecting off the hot Jeep. Nope, she could see. She had long since abandoned her hold on the Jeep. One of Mike's broad, powerful arms kept her clamped tight to his sweaty, hard body as his other hand held on to the car and he panted like he'd sprinted ten miles.

"That was—"

"The hottest shit ever. You are my dream, Maya."

"Ditto. Wow … Where the hell are we?"

"Who cares?"

"You've got a point."

He kissed her neck and shoulders, then stood, keeping her snug to him. "I love the smell of you," he whispered against her. "Even your sweat smells great."

"That should be a greeting card," she laughed, reaching behind her to stroke his hair. "Babe."

"Hmm," he answered, gently rocking her from side to side in a slow dance while caressing her stomach and holding her close.

"I'm hungry."

His laugh boomed out around them, and he placed a quick peck on her head before he reached down and pulled her crumpled skirt off the ground, sliding it over her hips. Without letting go of her he reached into the Jeep and snagged the jewelry box. The necklace glimmered in the sunlight as he dropped it over her head, quickly fastening the clasp.

He turned her in his arms and brushed her cheek with the back of his knuckles.

"My wife," he whispered, his face intensely focused on hers.

"My naked husband." She grinned back, dimple on full blast.

"The way God intended." He chuckled as he kissed her. After a while, she broke their kiss.

"Maybe we could stay here and continue to scare the wildlife - if you have snacks." She laughed, stepping back and taking him all in as the sun bathed him in warm light. *Damn, he is fine. My husband.* She did a little dance in place. When he looked at her questioning she shrugged.

"I'm happy. Can't help but dance."

Her admission won her a full-on bright Michael Sheppard smile.

"Wait right there," he said.

Still naked, he looked completely comfortable and in command of his environment. He reached in the back of the Jeep, pulled out a blanket, and then dug around in his duffle for a moment.

"I have these for you from Columbus, but you can't eat them all," he warned.

Maya screamed and ran and snatched the bag out of his hands. "Grippos! How did you know? These are the BEST potato chips on the planet," she yelped. "Aww, and you bought the double bag!" She ripped open the first bag and popped one in her mouth, rolling her eyes back in her head. "Oh, that's good!"

Laughing, Mike grabbed her hand, his clothes, and led her into the trees.

"Are you going to screw my brains out?"

"Yep."

"Sex and potato chips! The second best day evah."

It was early evening when Maya woke to the gentle hum of the garage door opening. She was wearing her skirt as a dress because her halter top had disappeared somewhere in the woods. Her bun was lopsided. She was sticky from ... well ... and she had drops of barbecue sauce on her belly from the diner they stopped at on the way home. For the second time in the two days since she'd gotten married, she looked a hot damn mess. All she wanted to do was take a shower, spend the next two hours detangling her hair, and put on something appealing for her husband and herself. A girl has to have standards.

Mike looked adorably rumpled. *Dammit men always do that. No matter what, they look good. Bah.*

As she reached back to get her bag, Mike stilled her hand.

"Leave it." He swept her in his arms and carried her upstairs from the garage.

"You already carried me over the threshold at the hotel."

"Does it matter?"

"Nope." She giggled as she laid her head on his shoulder. "Can we do that again?"

"What?"

"Sex and food!" she exclaimed. "You and me, snacks and screwing our brains out."

"Sunshine."

"No seriously, babe, think about it," she said, getting into the idea. "Me eating Fruity Pebbles, riding your big, beautiful—"

"Sunshine!" Mike said louder.

"What?! We can call it Cookies and Kegels."

"SURPRISE!"

A room full of folks.

Maya prayed they were all deaf.

She buried her face in Mike's shirt, mumbling, "Oh dear lord."

She looked at him accusingly. "You knew about this."

"I tried to stop you pretty woman." He grinned back at her.

"They heard about my Kegels and Fruity Pebbles, Michael!" she said, smacking him in the arm.

"And I'm going to shove a hot poker through my ears later," Caine's deep voice rumbled.

Michael set her on her feet and turned her to the crowd in their living room. The half of Rough Ridge who didn't make the wedding were there grinning at them.

"Oh dear," Maya said, looking around at the decorations, food and smiling faces. "This is so beautiful and ... I'm so embarrassed," she wailed, covering her face in her hands.

"It's okay, darlin'," Regina said loudly as everyone laughed. "He's supposed to have ya' comin' and goin'."

"Check please!" Maya yelped as she turned and tried to make a break for the garage.

Mike laughed as he caught her, wrapping his arms around her and tucking her into him. "Y'all open the beer and dig in. We'll be right back. We're gonna take a shower and wash off the travel."

"That's what they callin' it now?" Paul crowed.

"Shoot me," Maya mumbled as she shielded her face and took the stairs two at a time to the bedroom and master bath.

Fifteen minutes later, Maya was in leggings and two of her wedding presents from Mike - a genuine Queen UK Hot Space Tour t-shirt in better condition than the one that was cut off her when she arrived in Rough Ridge months ago. And her heart necklace that winked as it caught the overhead light. Her hair was loaded with leave-in conditioner. She pulled it back, popped on a shower cap and wrapped it all in a stylish scarf so she could get the tangles out later. She slipped on large hoop earrings and left her feet bare. Mike walked out of the closet and spotted her t-shirt and grinned.

MIKE

"That's not the signed one, is it?"

He found two tour tees, the one she wore, and one actually signed by Freddie Mercury, the lead singer of Queen. He spent weeks in bidding wars on eBay. Ever since the morning after he met Maya. He'd lost a lot of bids, but finally, he stopped being stupid and put his detective skills to use tracking one down in a little town on the outskirts of London. It took a fair bit of convincing, and Mike thought he would have to fly there personally, but when he finally told the collector why he needed the shirt, the older gentleman immediately agreed to sell it. Turned out the grizzled rock and roller was a romantic at heart.

Mike had planned to give them to Maya at Christmas, but when everything went crazy, he carried the shirts everywhere on the chance he could bribe his way back into her life. Turns out he didn't need them as a bribe, but as a wedding gift.

"As if I would expose a signed Freddie Mercury t-shirt to the elements." She grinned, gave him a kiss, grabbed his hand, and drug him out to the party.

For the next two hours, no one talked about the press conference or the media surrounding Maya. They were simply happy for two of their friends and celebrating them. It felt good.

During the party, Paul slipped out and came back with more food and six boxes of Fruity Pebbles, plopping them in front of Maya with a naughty grin.

"I will never eat that cereal again," Caine grumbled.

Maya's gaze whipped over to him, her eyes big and on Caine, "I have NEVER seen you eat cereal. You drink protein shakes with granite and nails for breakfast."

Jake chuckled. "She's got you there, brother."

Turning to Tori, Maya asked, "Has he ever eaten cereal?"

"Victoria? Hon, what's wrong?"

"My water just broke." She looked at Maya, a shocked giggle escaping from her lips.

52
YES IT IS

MIKE

The room stilled for about point five seconds and then everyone sprang into action. Leslie ran to get towels, Regina started tossing keys to Mike, Caine, and others. The rest of the folks cleared the food and drinks.

"In your chair, oh honey." Tori looked at Maya, embarrassed.

"Fuck the chair," Maya and Caine said in unison, sparking startled laughter from Tori.

"Ok," Tori said as Caine helped her up, "I'm ready. Let's go."

"I'll drive you guys. You sit in the back with Tori," Mike said, talking to Caine.

"Shotgun!" Maya yelled as she slipped on ballet flats.

"I'll get the girls from the sitter and bring them back here," Thomas said reassuringly.

AFTER FOUR HOURS OF WAITING, with Maya intermittently covering her ears whispering, "happy place, happy place," Caine came out with a huge grin.

"Thomas David Walters, ten pounds eight ounces, twenty-two inches. Tori is doing great!"

The waiting room erupted in cheers as Maya whispered, "Ouchie."

Mike looked down at her wide eyes and grinned his reassurance.

"You heard him, babe. Everyone's fine."

"Said like someone without a vagina," she shot back. "I think this birth thing is a cruel joke. I don't wanna do it. Did you listen to her? She was in agony."

"You'll be fine, sweetheart, like she is." Mike said as he kissed her on the nose, yet Maya remained unconvinced.

"Her poor vag." Maya walked over to her brother, hugged him tight, and pinched him. "That's for her vagina," she whispered fiercely as she walked back to the room to see Tori and the baby.

MAYA

Jake carefully and reluctantly passed his godson to Maya. He was soft and warm and gorgeous. He smelled like baby, and his little lips pursed a smidge like he was dreaming something good. Maya cradled him close, sweeping a soft finger over his cheek and taking him all in.

"You're a natural," Mike rumbled in her ear.

"And you're out of luck. I'm never having this kid. I'll stay pregnant forever. And I'm never having any of your genetically predisposed gigantic ass babies either. No way." Her voice dropped to a whisper. "She's wearing a maxi pad the size of Texas and it's ice cold to soothe everything down there. Naw man, fuck that." She covered the baby's ear with her free hand and shook her head vigorously.

Mike's body shook with laughter behind her. "The fearless Maya is scared sh — scared," he said, adjusting his language for the sleeping babe. "You'll have more of my babies, darlin' - all six."

"Six?!" she whisper-screamed. "You said three. Three is a long way from six!"

Baby T began rooting around sleepily, and she reluctantly passed the baby back to Caine's outstretched arms and rose on tiptoes to kiss her brother on his cheek. She leaned in close and whispered, "Save me, big bro. He wants six kids. They are going to be huge!"

"Oh no, you wanted that lunatic, you got 'im." He gave her a quick peck.

Maya was still whisper protesting as the couple made their way to the door with Maya looking panicked and Mike looking completely amused.

LATER THAT NIGHT...

Mike and Maya drug themselves into the house at close to three in the morning. It was another full, exciting day.

"I'm happy we came home." Maya sighed happily. "My very first nephew!" She rubbed her lower back sleepily.

Mike took one look at his bride, at the circles under her eyes, and barked, "Bed. Now." She was pushing too hard, trying to drink in life, happiness, and family in big gulps, but nothing was more important than her health and rest. And for once, his wife didn't give him sass as she threw up the peace sign and shuffled down the hall.

"She has to be tired. She didn't say shit," Mike mumbled to himself.

"I heard that," came a sleepy call from down the hallway.

Chuckling, Mike turned and checked on the girls in their guest bedroom. Thomas had tucked them under the covers and stretched out next to them, riding the edge of the queen bed with his long body. Mike quietly walked to the closet and pulled out extra pillows, placing them on the floor on the side of the bed where the girls slept. Smiling, he rearranged Gabriella - the spread-eagled wild child, taking up two-thirds of the bed - and grabbed a thin summer throw, laying it over his father-in-law. His smile was softer as Livi snuggled closer to her grandfather, snuffling gently. He held his breath as he watched baby Simone shift in her Pack and Play. Shoving two fingers in her mouth, she settled back down with her tush in the air. *Whew.*

The door made a soft snick behind him while he made his way through the condo, checking the locks, setting the alarm, and breathing a deep sigh of satisfaction at a house filled with a happy family - something he hadn't dared to dream of in a long time.

When he got to his bedroom, his beautiful bride was still awake, wearing one of his t-shirts, and sitting cross-legged in bed yawning deep.

"Baby, go to sleep."

"I wanted to wait on you. Is this from you?" She gestured to a wrapped box on the bed.

"Nope, Jake." Mike stripped off his clothes as Maya unwrapped the package. He put on a loose pair of pajama bottoms, keeping in mind the little ones were visiting.

Maya let out a small yelp and read the card out loud as he peered into the box.

M, NOW YOU'RE LEGAL.
-J

"Nothing says love like a Glock." He watched as she took out the piece to examine it, loading and unloading the clip with ease. "That is hot as hell." Kissing her shoulder, he slid the gun out of her hand as she let out another enormous yawn, mumbling about how her back hurt. Mike rose, punched in 332459 — the safe room code — and stored the gun in a lockbox on a top shelf near his own equipment.

He found Maya stretched across the bed snoring. He carefully maneuvered her to her side and began rubbing a tennis ball across the muscles of her lower back. After a few moments, she sighed deeply, letting out a long, loud snore. Mike flicked off the light on his nightstand and, after briefly saying his prayers, joined Maya in a deep sleep.

AT WAY too early in the morning, a little girl with serious little kid morning breath was nose to nose with Mike.

He opened one eye and smiled. "Hey darlin'.'"

"Grandpop said you're my new unca," Gabriella whispered.

"I am. What do you think of that?"

She blinked.

Hmm. She might need persuading.

"Do you know how to make pancakes?"

"Yep."

"Oh, good," she said, looking unsure.

"You hungry?"

"Um..." She fidgeted, looking more uncertain. "Can you help?"

"You want to help me make pancakes for your auntie? She's gonna be hungry soon, especially since she's growing a baby."

She thought for a moment and nodded slightly. "Pregnant people eat a lot."

A deep chuckle rumbled from Mike, and Gabriella smiled a small, shy smile.

Rising, Mike grabbed a shirt off the edge of the bed and, after dragging it on, he held out his hand. "I heard Maya showed you how to crack an egg. Is that right?"

Gabriella beamed with pride. Slipping her little hand in his, she marched them out of the room and spoke barely above a whisper, "I already started! They're a lot of slippery."

Aw damn. He braced for the craziness in the kitchen.

MAYA

The smell of pancakes brought Maya out of her sleep coma. And she needed to pee. She tried to ignore them both, but no such luck.

As she handled her morning duties, giggles and the rumble of low voices came from the kitchen. Sliding on a pair of pajama pants and stretching deeply, the baby thumped as she quietly padded her way toward the comforting sounds of morning. And when she reached the bottom of the steps, the scene before her made her heart swell and her breath catch in her throat.

Mike sat on the couch with Gabriella on his lap as he put twists in her hair. She ate pancakes and hummed while Liv chatted to Thomas, who manned the stove. Baby Simone played with toys on the floor. A special joy moved through her. Her father, her husband, her nieces ... her family.

When Mike looked at Maya, his face grew soft. "Good mornin', Sunshine."

She smiled big. "Yes it is."[1]

FOUR WEEKS LATER...

Maya walked into the garage with a big fluffy robe tied tight and hit the button to make the garage door open. She waved at Caine backing up the driveway. He pulled all the way into the mostly empty two-car garage.

"Judging by the shoes, I am certain I want you to keep that robe shut." His mouth formed a half-grin.

She laughed as he swept her into a hug. "Yeah. You'd be right. Though I need your help to get up here. Oh! And putting the bow on."

"The hood's still hot. How long before Mike gets in?"

"Paul said he would make sure he left by 5:30, so we have about a half-hour. I figured I'd lay in my robe until he arrives, then wiggle out of it."

After Caine boosted Maya onto the hood of Mike's present, he synced her phone with the radio and raised the volume.

"You good?" he asked, taking in the bow on top of the car and Maya eating apple slices from a baggie.

She gave him a thumbs up while chewing and patting her other robe pocket, looking for matches. He laughed at her and hit the garage button, lifting a long leg over the sensor, and ducking under the door.

It was hard to resist swiping her finger through the icing of the cake she'd made, so she pulled her phone out to play a word game while she waited. After a bit, she heard what sounded like footsteps outside the garage door.

She listened closely, certain she'd heard something, but the door didn't open. *Maybe Caine was back.* Her tummy did a roll that wasn't the baby. Taking the risk she'd have to use a stepladder to get back on the hood, she slid off and walked to the door quietly. There was definitely movement, but when she shifted, her phone fell out of her pocket and the sound stopped.

Backing away from the garage door, she wished it was one with windows. Instead, she ran up the stairs to look at the door from the kitchen window. Her heart in her throat, she saw nothing there, but that didn't make her feel any better. She walked through the condo, looking out all the windows, not seeing anything. She paused for a minute and then texted Bishop.

> MAYA: ADDITIONAL CAMERAS. CAN WE DO THAT ASAP?
>
> BISHOP: FINALLY. WHY NOW?
>
> MAYA: GOT A FUNNY FEELING TODAY.
>
> BISHOP: SENDING A GUY OUT NOW.
>
> MAYA: NO. MIKE WILL BE HOME SOON. BUT CAN WE GET ON THIS
>
> BISHOP: I'LL SEND OUT MY BROTHER FIRST THING TOMORROW. GUNNER WILL BE THERE IN SIX MINUTES. HE'LL DRIVE THROUGH AND CHECK IT ALL OUT.
>
> MAYA: OK. THANKS, BISHOP.
>
> BISHOP: KEEP YOUR PHONE AND PIECE CLOSE.

Maya saw Mike's car at the corner and, after one last glance, she dismissed going to get her gun. Instead, she scampered down the stairs, tossing the robe as she moved. She lit the matches and held the cake as she leaned her hip against the car in what she hoped was a sexy way, considering she now looked like a Who from Whoville with her tummy.

As the garage door opened, something was off still, and she scanned the wood across the street from their house. Their condo sat on a pretty, secluded, wooded lot. She thought it would help maintain privacy. Now she realized it could also easily hide someone. Her thoughts returned to Mike when he suddenly stepped on the brakes. His mouth hung open as he stared at her.

MIKE

Mike was dreaming. A wet one, judging by the uncomfortable tightness in his jeans. Maya stood in the garage, the sunlight highlighting her from top to bottom as it made its move from behind the clouds. She wore a big red bow around her bare breasts, kick-ass red heels with bows on the sides of her ankles and nothing else. In her hands, she gripped a lopsided cake with candles. *God, her smile.* He must have stared too long because she laughed, jerking him out of his trance. He managed to put his Jeep in park and climb out, never losing sight of her.

"You make a girl feel good about herself. Honey, you didn't even look at your gift." She quirked a brow and popped her hip.

"I'm looking at her."

"Besides me."

"I like cake well enough."

"Detective. You're missing all the clues."

He frowned a little and peeled his eyes away from her as she threw her arm out in exasperation. He finally took in the entire picture. A brand new, jet-black Jeep Wrangler Unlimited 4x4 sat in the garage topped with a bow. He froze.

When he didn't say anything, her face dropped. "Oh ... You don't like it. I ruined your birthday then 'cause that and this cake was it—"

She stopped when a hunger came over him. He quickly closed the distance between them and pulled the cake out of her hands, setting it on the hood. He covered her mouth with his, kissing her deep and long until her heart galloped.

"I love it," he said in between kissing her jaw and moving to her neck. "I love you. It's the best gift I've ever gotten beside God giftin' me with you. I am just real surprised darlin'. No one's ever ... We didn't grow up doin' a lot of celebrating occasions. It's never been a big deal."

"But it's your birthday," Maya said softly, holding him tight. "We celebrated everything because you never knew if mom would see another one ... Did I overstep?"

"No baby, overwhelmed me," he whispered. "In a good way. Your family had the right idea."

"Happy Birthday," she whispered softly.

SIX WEEKS LATER

MAYA

"They said newlywed life is an adjustment," Maya said, "but he's being ridiculous, right?" She looked at her midwife, Lilith Moon, for confirmation that Mike had lost his marbles.

Maya sat back in a huff, rolling her eyes heavily as Mike watched her with a closed expression on his face, his muscles bunching as he crossed his arms across his broad chest, the toothpick in his mouth working.

"Well, honestly?" Lilith started with hesitation. "You shouldn't seek things that make you upset. Stress can cause early labor. Not that you are showing any indications of that happening," she finished in a rush as she caught Mike's expression sour.

"But he cut Downton Abbey off in the middle of the episode!" Maya yelped, tossing her long twists over her shoulder, giving her husband a side glare.

"I walked in from work and found her pacing. Tears in her eyes, staring at the TV talking about, 'Oh God, the baby!' I freaked out, and she's talking about some old damn British show."

"But did you have to rip out the wires?" she questioned as she threw up her hands, her yellow diamond ring catching all the Colorado sun streaming through the window.

"How else am I going to keep you from watching that, and the other show about midwives where it's hit or miss whether the kid or mom survive, and all the other fuck crazy shows you have saved?"

He looked at Lilith. She visibly braced.

"Every night it's the same thing. She watches, gets upset, paces and it drives me crazy."

"I'm learning about birth!" Maya yelled, ripping, balling up, and throwing the thin paper sheeting from the exam table at Mike.

"You're scaring yourself half to death and me too!" he yelled back as he batted the paper ball aside with a small flick of his hand.

The room got quiet, though there was a frightened squeak in the hallway.

"Oh." Maya replied quietly, her eyes big and round. "Oh Heart, I'm so sorry. I wanted to prepare for every potential outcome. I've read every medical book and layperson pregnancy guide, but I thought popular dramatizations might lend more of a bird's-eye view on.... nevermind all that. You always seem so chill as long as I use the peephole. I didn't think ... " She took his hand and kissed his palm, placing it against her cheek as she whispered, "I'm sorry."

"Listen, it's normal to feel anxious about giving birth," Lilith said gently. "And after what you've been through, Maya, I can understand wanting to feel a certain amount of control. And as her partner, you want to protect her."

Mike grunted.

"Both of you need to talk to each other and bring any concerns to me so we can go through them together."

Looking back and forth between the two she continued, "Yes, a lot of things can go wrong during pregnancy or labor and delivery, BUT in a healthy mom like Maya, those are rare and certainly not to the level of danger you'd find in nineteenth to early twentieth century Britain. And Maya, you can't control everything. You have a birth plan, but it's a series of suggestions and desires that depend on the conditions on the ground. We do what's best for you and the baby. Period. And you need to accept that. Let go ... and stop watching those shows until you deliver."

"Thank fuck," Mike muttered, dipping his head to kiss Maya on top of hers.

"Okay. I will try to pull back," she said as she closed her birth plan binder on the latest set of questions (thirty-four) and the ten-point amendment to her plan, "but can you tell him sex swings are fine during pregnancy?"

"I cannot believe you asked her that," his hands moved to his waist, and he looked toward the ceiling, a hint of blush shaded his corded throat.

"It's going to waste, honey."

"If it's properly installed," Lilith said, speaking over them and trying not to laugh, "and you have help to get in and out of it and aren't too strenuous or put pressure on your tummy, you're good to go."

"Still think I shouldn't have asked?"

"Pain in my ass, you know that?" he grumbled, helping her off the table gently and rubbing a hand over her belly.

"Yeah, well, this pain in the ass has swing clearance and a fresh delivery of panties, so..." She smiled wickedly.

"Gotta go doc," he rumbled.

LATER THAT WEEK

Della Reese waxed poetic about one of her talented courtesans on the Sheppards' new TV screen.

Maya and Mike cuddled in bed with snacks watching "Harlem Nights." When they got to why she thought he had nicknamed her Sunshine, she watched him.

He turned to her, taking in her mischievous grin. "No argument there."

She dissolved in a fit of giggles, and he clicked off the TV, turning her giggles into moans of passion for the third time that night.

That's how life was for Mike and Maya. Some salty, but a lot of sweet. They argued and fussed, but often, it was easy. They fell into a rhythm. Mike almost always made breakfast. They took turns bringing each other lunch, and whomever made it home first made dinner. They couldn't keep their hands off each other and they spent weekends in bed watching movies, babysitting their nieces, and making quiet plans. It was a good life, and both recognized it.

---

1. Like You'll Never See Me Again by Alicia Keys

53

PREDICTABLE

WHEN THE FIRST BULLET HIT, the sound differed slightly from what she expected, maybe owing to the acoustics of the room.

The splatter, however, was predictable. As was the heavy sound of the first body hitting the floor.

With the second, her brain adjusted its expectations, and by the third, it sounded "normal."

What her brain refused to register was the splatter hitting the back of *her* living room wall, streaking it with brain matter.

Her mind also didn't register the mad scramble taking place around her.

The hiss of a door sealing...The sound a bullet made when it tore through her own flesh was different indeed...Her brain chose not to process the burning heat of pain...And, as darkness pressed in from the corners of her eyes, she had one last thought:

She's safe.

And one last vision:

He placed her hand on his heart and covered it with his own. He put his second hand on her belly and touched his lips fully to hers as the sun slipped past the horizon.

She could almost smell the ocean.

And then - darkness.

54

PATIENT

MIKE

Mike arrived home to Maya clad in a fluffy navy sweater, leggings, and thick woolen socks. She sat at the kitchen island in deep thought.

She looked at him and blurted, "Ethan called. The judge handling Griffin's case is dead. And Griffin is asking for a new bail hearing."

"The fuck? How?" Shock froze him where he stood.

"Car accident." Her voice was hollow. "Black ice on the road and a tractor-trailer or something." She ran her shaking fingers through her hair, pulling it back in frustration. "I don't know. After that bombshell, I lost a lot of information. He had twin girls starting college and his wife died last year."

"Jesus. That's terrible news, but there's not a judge alive that will grant that nutbag bail." Though from experience, Mike knew judges were human and did all kinds of stupid shit.

Maya looked equally unconvinced. And scared.

"I-I called Bishop. He'll be out first thing in the morning to introduce us to the team that will take over 24-hour protection and to go over options. They expect a hearing set within the week if it happens," she said.

He walked to her and gathered her in his arms, hugging her tight as he could with her baby belly between them. "You're going to be safe. You and Butterfly will be fine."

"Okay."

He looked into her eyes. She was putting on a brave face.

"Fuck baby, I am so sorry. I should have taken care of this permanently."

She jerked in his arms. "All I care about is you, the baby, and my family being safe. Anything that takes you away from me isn't worth it."

They stood like that for a while until Maya finally pulled away, muttering about being tired.

"You hungry, Sunshine?"

"No, I—I'm tired." She kissed his jaw and slowly waddled up the stairs to the bedroom.

Mike was seething. Poised to punch in numbers on his phone, it started ringing in his hand. He spent the next few hours talking to everyone from his chief, to the joint task force leads, and the D.A. in Columbus. When he finally came to bed, Maya was asleep on her side. He undressed, slid in beside her and curled her close. He laid there for hours listening to her breathe.

FRIDAY

Maya sat at the dining room table making notes in the margins of a contract with Selene on speaker. The TV, tuned to the 24-hour news channel, stayed on mute. The bail hearing for Griffin was on, but with no cameras allowed in the courtroom, the talking heads just argued in circles about the case. She already knew what would happen after receiving Ethan's call. Her gut told her believing in a tidy happily ever after was a mistake. Sweeping her hand over her belly that was firmly in place, she toyed with the idea of being induced to get the baby to safety, but both her research and Mike were against the idea.

She'd vetoed his idea of staying in a safe house until the trial was over. It could take months, years even, and she didn't want to leave her family or have him leave his job. They'd argued about it all week and this morning they had another round. She was irritable, thirty-nine weeks pregnant, and constantly on alert. Lost in her thoughts, she had missed the flurry of activity on the TV screen.

"Oh Maya," Selene said suddenly.

GRIFFIN

"Thank you, dad for believing in me," Griffin said as they drove away from the courthouse.[1]

"Close to a billion dollars for bail. The company stock is in the tank. Your mother—" Marion collected himself. "Your mother made me promise if I could save you to save you. Don't make her last request a faulty one."

"I take responsibility for everything," Griffin said, looking down at his hands. "I thought a club would be a good way to show you I was ready to lead on my own terms. Sex was a perk. It wouldn't be the first club to allow adults to do what they like. I don't know how it went so wrong. I trusted Hitchens to recruit beautiful models for eye candy ... I wish I'd known sooner they were being trafficked."

Marion grunted, taking in the man in front of him. Though Griffin said all the right things, his father was barely buying into his humble act. Ever since his mother died, his father was undone. It was... odd. Silly even.

Griffin reached down and scratched at the unseemly reminder of his misstep. It took him months to convince his father to see him, and weeks to play the role of the chastised, repentant child. It was exhausting. His hand clenched in anger. This was all Maya's fault. Her disobedience had nearly cost him everything.

In prison filthy beasts and dim-witted guards surrounded him for months while she played house. Money made the experience better, of course. While his father wouldn't see him, Griffin never doubted his father would make sure his "baby boy" wasn't being mistreated. He smiled to himself when he thought of Hitchens' plans. The man was obsessed with Maya. Griffin didn't understand why Hitchens thought he wanted all the gory details of what he had planned for her, but his ideas cheered him a bit.

"What in God's name do you have to smile about?" Marion snapped from across the limo.

"Earth's bounty. I never noticed it before," Griffin lied smoothly. "I was so wrong about so many things," he paused for dramatic effect. When he sensed his father's rapt attention, he continued. "I was also thinking about mom. She loved days like this ... I miss her."

"When we find Hitchens, he'll pay for what he did." Marion clenched his fist on his knee and fidgeted. "He'll pay for all the pain he's caused this family."

Of course he will. Hitchens taking the fall for his mother's death and Maya's disappearance was the plan all along. He became a convenient scapegoat for the club as well. The man might know his way around a mountain, but he had no clue how power truly operated.

FOSTER HITCHENS WAS NOT a patient man, but he recognized good things came to those who waited. He had waited, faithfully, for his reward. He watched her daily, knowing her better than she knew herself. Today was Friday. The dickhead that followed behind her like a lost puppy would take out the trash. She would head over to the one place he couldn't watch her - the gun range. She was likely doing the same stupid shit women did to make themselves feel better about living in a world of wolves - bat at somebody in a padded suit and shoot a little pink gun at paper targets.

He adjusted his dick as he saw her pass by the window.

TWO WEEKS LATER

MAYA

Snow gently fell outside of the condo's big deck windows as Maya looked at the scene. It was like she was living inside of a snow globe.

The sun kept winking out through the clouds, casting a brilliant sparkle over everything, the snowflakes refracting light like airy diamonds.

As the snow piles grew on the deck, Maya zoned out. Her phone in one hand connected to Tori chattering away and a warm mug of tea in the other. Maya was now a week overdue, and while her midwife wasn't worried, Maya was anxious. She looked down over the report she received every morning following Griffin Levy's release. Still confined to the family mansion, he made no moves to leave.

She swallowed slowly, willing herself to relax. Two weeks they watched his ankle monitor via Bishop's team and nothing had happened. Surveillance would capture him briefly on the grounds. It was difficult without someone on the inside and the Levy home had been on lockdown since Griffin returned. *Today it is okay, we are okay.*

Focusing on Tori's voice, she caught the tail end of the conversation.

"...So, if she doesn't have a fever, ugh this is so gross, by now, I mean it smells so bad. I think we're in the clear." Tori said as she talked and cleaned sick from what sounded like vomit-geddon at her house.

"Liv is fine," Maya said with a slight smile. "No fever, no sniffles, not a thing but a healthy little pixie leaving glitter everywhere."

"Oh good," Tori said. "If I can keep her from catching this, I'll count it as an early Christmas present. Promise me, at the first sign of sick, you'll let me know."

Maya laughed as she glanced over at where Liv was playing with blocks. "She's fine, she lucked out. Or I guess you did. Both ends are free of explosions."

"Both ends of three kids," Tori lamented. "Caine and I are playing zone defense, and we're going to have to burn the couch. Maybe I'll ask Santa for one for Christmas."

"I'd be happy with signs of labor. Anything, an email, a knock on my cervix, something. This kid is so settled in she's ordering magazine subscriptions."

Tori hooted loudly. "She's dropped low so she may be filling out her mail forwarding card."

"I'm so unwieldy. I feel great, but there is no place to put my energy. Laila and I practiced hitting yesterday, but I've still got energy to burn.

I've washed everything, sorted everything, rechecked everything. I even wore out Liv. She asked if she could go play by herself for a while."

Tori cracked up. "How's Mike doing?"

"He's afraid of me. They say sex helps bring on labor and I've been on him constantly. I think he was happy Liv came to stay with us so I couldn't drag him by his hair back to the bedroom."

Now Tori was howling.

"Honey, I understand. I think I made Caine cry when I was pregnant with Liv. He won't admit to it, of course."

Now it was Maya's turn to snort.

"Damn, Maya I gotta call you back. I've got another diaper blowout."

Tori clicked off while Maya let out a long, unsettled sigh.

DENVER, COLORADO

BISHOP

Bishop had a knotty vibe in his gut that had helped him make it through the war and never-ending special ops missions. Something was wrong. He looked at Mace. He took in his agitated demeanor - a marked change from the man Bishop had known since they both spent time recovering from injuries in the same rehab facility ten years ago.

"And you say the lawyer's daughter still hasn't turned up?"

"No. But the guy is still working for the family. They found his oldest daughter at the club so high she didn't know who she was. The official story is the younger sister is studying overseas. Suddenly. But there's no passport hit, no credit card use, nothing."

"And Levy's girlfriend is off the grid too."

"And I don't think she's in Fed custody. We moved from being able to get updates to radio silence on her," Mace said.

"You already have an idea," Bishop said.

"I think they're with Hitchens."

Bishop's eyebrows shot to the top of his head.

"On the run, heavy two civilians? No one's seen them. That's almost impossible."

Mace's eyes narrowed. "My gut tells me there's something we've all missed, and I can't shake the feeling Maya's running out of time."

Bishop sat back in his chair. "Say your gut's right. What's the play? Why keep two women on the hook?"

"The girlfriend's obvious," Mace said, pacing back and forth, his brain flipping through everything it had already cataloged again. "She's seen something, knows where the bodies are, something damaging. He'd want that info locked up. The kid ... If she's not bait, she's leverage. The lawyer isn't a criminal attorney, he handles estates. Levy's mother died and we have no record of increase or change in assets for Levy."

"It's the baby," Bishop said, sitting forward in his chair, a shadow falling over his face. "Either Maya or the baby inherits it all. That type of shit is usually held in a trust–"

"And the lawyer acts as trustee."

"If he gets his hands on Maya's baby, none of them stand a chance." Bishop ran his hand over his smooth bald head in frustration. He reached out and punched a button on his desk phone. "Full staff in five," he barked out.

IN ROUGH RIDGE...

"Time's up," the voice said over the line before it disconnected.

MAYA

Maya wasn't sure what woke her from her nap, but her belly hurt. She laid there a moment and waited for the tight sensation to pass. It was harder than the Braxton-Hicks contractions she'd been having for weeks. Excited, she checked on Liv lying next to her and the little girl stirred.

"Hey sweetie, are you ready for lunch?"

After a sleepy nod from Liv, Maya picked a few sparkling pieces of glitter off the little girl with a grin. Then they took turns on the potty and washing hands. Maya, out of habit, slipped her gun lock off and slid her Glock into the holster at her back. She adjusted her thick, soft cream sweater over top and took Liv's hand as they both walked down to the kitchen singing the theme song to *The Wiz*. As they slowly walked, both shaking off sleep, Maya checked her text from Michael:

I love you.

She tried to send a heart emoji back but didn't have a signal. Halfway down the steps, the phone fell out of her hand with a thunk as she froze in place.

"Good afternoon, my darling Angel," Griffin said.

---

1. Creep (Metal Mix) by Leo

55

DISOBEDIENCE

MAYA

All thoughts left her mind, all plans, action, bravery, skill gone in an instant. Her brain screamed incoherent words, her heart threatened to jump out of her chest, her feet were lead. She was trapped, not only by Griffin and the six men with him, but by absolute fear.

"Cat got your tongue?" Griffin chuckled. "You'd be cute right now if you weren't so fat." He paused; his head cocked to the side in an assessing manner. He flicked his eyes to the side of her. "Are you sure you want that? She's gross now that she's let herself go."

Foster Hitchens stepped out of the shadows of the Christmas tree and looked Maya over slowly. The feral, unseemly hunger bloomed on his face. "It's Friday," Foster said, his voice like ice-covered gravel - abrasive, cold, and stinging. "Your panty delivery is late."

Maya whimpered.

BISHOP

"We still have a lock on his monitor?" Bishop barked, looking around the room at the men assembled there. Maya was a favorite client. She sent monthly care packages full of gag gifts and candy. He hadn't seen a cap gun since he was eight until Maya sent the team a box full of toy guns, caps, bubble gum cigarettes, toy sheriff badges, and tiny ass cowboy hats.

"Yeah boss, everything is normal besides the party preparations," Monk, Bishop's brother and right-hand man responded.

"Party?" Mace asked disgusted.

"The annual Levy Christmas party. Despite the death of his wife and his son charged for a variety of crimes, the show will go on," Bishop muttered. "Sick fucks..."

Mace checked his watch. "The chopper will be here in ten. We gotta move before the storm comes in."

THE AREA EXPECTED a slow-moving storm to dump a ton of snow and ice all around the state. Movement would be nearly impossible, which meant they had a few scant hours to get Maya out and replace her with a lookalike. Bishop slid his phone out and placed a call. Frowning, he pulled his phone from his ear.

"Straight to voicemail. I can't get in touch with Gunner either. He's on her until 5 ... "

The chopper fell into stony silence.

Mace's voice broke the quiet. "I'd like to report a bail violation. Yes, they have guns and are smoking meth." He listened for a moment, then gave an address. "Yes, that's correct. Griffin Levy is high as we speak. I'm Bart Smith, I work in the kitchen. Yeah, thanks."

"We'll have a visual ID within an hour."

Bishop raised his finger as he listened to his assistant. "Grant, are you hearing what's happening? Yeah, scan the last three hours of footage on Maya. Then get ready to activate our reserves."

MAYA

Maya was shaking so hard it was a wonder she was still standing, and both Griffin and Foster Hitchens seemed to feed off her panic. They were clearly enjoying themselves.

Her brain couldn't compute what was happening. *How was he here? How could everyone be wrong? I wanted to see my baby before I died.* As soon as the thought popped into her head, Griffin's next words pushed it out.

"What a beautiful little girl. She'll fetch a small fortune. And she'll have you to thank for her new life." He smiled at Maya and winked. "My thriving business is right in your niche, Maya. Cunt is a sustainable resource, more than half the world available for sale. And more born, every minute. Local harvest, recycled, it's even organic!"

Hitchens snickered.

Absolute rage replaced absolute fear. Maya's blood super-heated while a calm fell over her.

"You will NEVER touch her."

Griffin blinked for a moment, taken aback by Maya's swift change in demeanor. She slid herself in front of Liv, keeping her hand connected to the little girl. She squeezed it and Liv squeezed it back.

Maya glanced around the room, her mind clicking through where everyone was, wondering where her friend and guard Gunner was and checking her body to see if she could run fast enough to give her and Liv a chance to get to the safe room. She glanced down at the phone.

"Don't get any ideas, sweetheart," Hitchens barked from the corner, causing Liv to jump behind her.

"No cell signal, no alarms, no *living* guards. Now make it easy on that little treat and do as you're told. Or not ... I'll enjoy it either way."

When Maya's eyes grew large, Griffin laughed cruelly as he watched her closely. "I won't lay a hand on you, my golden goose, so *she* will pay for *your* disobedience."

"God, you're such an asshole! I have nothing you want. Why couldn't you leave me alone? I'll never stop trying to get away from you. I will fight you until the day I die." Flicking her eyes toward Hitchens, "Both of you."

Hitchens swiped his lip as his eyes twinkled. "I'm counting on it."

Maya backed away slowly. "Liv sweetie, remember my snack closet?

There was movement at her legs, and she prayed it was her niece nodding. "Go baby, now!"

Liv paused for a split second, then took off, her little feet thundering on the stairs. Maya whipped her gun from her holster and aimed it at the room as she retreated.

"Disrespectful," Griffin said, sounding bored as he flicked a piece of lint off from his black slacks. "Go get her. We're low on time."

The first thug moved in on Maya and, as she aimed, she thought his eyes reminded her of the ocean. Squeezing the trigger came easy and automatic, like Laila predicted.

When the first bullet hit, the sound differed slightly from what she expected, maybe owing to the acoustics of the room.

The splatter, however, was predictable. As was the heavy sound of the first body hitting the floor.

With the second, her brain adjusted its expectations, and by the third, it sounded "normal."

What her brain refused to register was the splatter hitting the back of *her* living room wall, streaking it with brain matter.

Her mind also didn't register the mad scramble taking place around her.

The hiss of a door sealing...

The sound a bullet made when it tore through her own flesh was different indeed...

Her brain chose not to process the burning heat of pain...

And, as darkness pressed in from the corners of her eyes, she had one last thought:

She's safe.

And one last vision:

He placed her hand on his heart and covered it with his own. He put his second hand on her belly and touched his lips fully to hers as the sun slipped past the horizon.

She smelled the ocean.

And then - darkness.

GRIFFIN

"WHAT! THE! FUCK!" Griffin screamed as he pulled himself from the floor behind Maya's heavy wood coffee table. He checked his own body for bullets and looked around him. "YOU SHOT HER? YOU FUCKING..."

Another shot rang out. Griffin ducked again, before realizing it was Hitchens putting a bullet in the head of the person who shot Maya. Hitchens coolly stepped past the man's body and headed to the pregnant woman collapsed on the steps. Bending down, he checked the pulse in her neck and hastened down to her wound, tearing open her white sweater.

"Lucky bitch, it's straight through." He turned toward Griffin, snatched the scarf from around his neck and began wrapping it around the wound.

"That's cashmere," Griffin said in a pout as blood seeped through the fine white material.

Hitchens silenced him with a look. He looked at the dent in the wall. "She smacked her head when she was hit. She'll live for now."

"And she's ANNIE FUCKING OAKLEY," Griffin yelled. "You've been watching her for weeks and didn't know we'd need a fucking SWAT team before coming in here? She took out three fucking men! Have you been jacking off and writing out your little torture plays instead of doing YOUR ONE FUCKING JOB?!"

Hitchens snapped at Griffin. "Watch it. I've been running this shit better than you could hope to."

The last remaining goons stood there, guns drawn, looking back and forth between the two arguing men, unsure of what to do.

Hitchens looked down at his hands, at Maya's blood on them, and sniffed them. Then he slowly sucked the blood off each finger like it was honey. Closing his eyes, he seemed to gather himself and stood. He bent down, lifted the unconscious woman in his arms, and stalked toward the door.

Griffin watched Hitchens looking more interested than disturbed. He stood, straightened his $400 shirt, and ordered the closest bodyguard to go get the little girl. After waiting a moment, Griffin's blood pressure flew off the charts when the guard, Griffin couldn't remember his name, came back empty-handed.

"She's in a safe room, Mr. Levy. No way to get in before someone shows up."

Griffin had a full-blown meltdown.

"That FUCKING CUNT! I'm going to KILL HER MYSELF!"

He paced forward two steps and back another two.

"This does not look like she took off. It's a fucking bloodbath. FUCK. The kid's seen us!"

He stopped when Hitchens came back in.

"Time's up," Hitchens said, not bothering to conceal his hard on.

"None of this works, *Hitchens,* if they can place us at the scene. Get your mind off your dick. You don't get to get 'messy' with that bitch if we go to jail and I am NOT going back."

Griffin glanced at his watch. "FUCK it. Torch the place. The kid can't ID us if she no longer exists." Griffin stomped out of the house, running his hand through his hair and pulling his suit jacket together against the cold.

Turning to Hitchens, the shorter, stockier bodyguard of the two remaining threw his hands up. "I didn't sign on to kill kids."

Without hesitation, another gunshot rang out and the stocky guard dropped. Hitchens turned his gun to the last remaining bodyguard they had at that location.

"Do you have a conscious Nowakowski?"

"No sir, I don't," Nowakowski replied. He headed to the garage to look for a gas can.

Three minutes later they were driving away - a UPS truck and a FedEx truck - as smoke poured out the side of the condo. Exactly one block away, they pulled into another home, transported Maya to the basement, and then sent the two trucks out of the county as the snow continued to fall.

56

332459

MIKE

Mike hummed "*This Christmas*" by Donny Hathaway — the latest Christmas song Maya had stuck in his head — as he stepped through the police station door. Shaking off the cold snow, he grinned as he took in the scene before him. Ladies from town had decorated both the police and fire station with Christmas and Hanukkah decorations. They spared no ornament. It looked like a holiday store exploded everywhere except Laila's desk. She had a single golden angel and the rest of her desk, hyper-neat as usual.

He confiscated all the mistletoe the decorators left after Laila almost got a reprimand for flipping, pinning down, and twisting the nipples of the last three men that tried to kiss her. Mike's grin grew wider as he thought about the look on the mayor's face — and the photo that landed on the front page of the paper. Of all people to try and kiss for a photo op.

Patting the pockets of his thick down coat, Mike groaned as he realized he left his phone in the Jeep. Further punishment for the mistake of not bringing a lunch. The weather was the first punishment. Freezing and windy with stinging ice and snow added to the torture. Days like this he missed California.

Shoving his grey knit cap back on his head with a grumble, he turned around to head back out into the cold when he walked by the 9-1-1 operator station and froze.

"Hi Olivia, what does your auntie need help with sweetheart? You said her name is Maya?"

Mike's gut dropped, and he leaned over the desk, motioning to Janine. Startled by his sudden appearance and the look of alarm on his face, she handed him the headset.

"Liv?"

"Unca Mike?"

His heart clenched painfully at hearing her little voice. She was terrified.

"Baby, where are you?"

"In your closet. With the snacks. I-I peed Unca Mike," she whispered.

"Honey, that's okay, where's Maya?"

"With those men. She told me to run Unca Mike, and I did. I ran fast, but the noises scared me and I couldn't hold it."

"Honey don't worry about the pee. How many men? What did they look like?" His voice was sharp as he tried to get more information, and he instantly regretted it.

"I-I don't kn-kn-know," she said as she cried.

"Baby don't cry. I'm sorry for barkin' darlin'," Mike said gently as he signaled Laila and Paul. Mike snatched a pen and piece of paper off Janine's desk, wrote quickly, and pushed it into Laila's hands:

332459#Safe Room

She committed it to memory and bolted out of the station. Focusing on Liv, Mike cleared his mind to see the safe room as he remembered it.

"I'm on my way honey, but I need you to do me a favor. Do you see the TVs in the closet?"

"Uh huh."

"There's a red switch. Can you flip that switch on?"

"Okaaay," she said through her tears, snuffling.

Janine was calling officers in and sending them to his house. To his. Fucking. House.

Goddamit! Focus!

"Is anyone still there? Do you see anyone on the TV?"

"Yes?"

"You're not sure? What do you see?"

"People on the floor ... Aaaand ... It's smoky, maybe?"

On the floor ... knocked out or dead.... the smoke ... why... Panic tried to take over once he realized what she was saying.

"Liv honey, are any of the people on the floor Maya?"

"Uh un. Auntie Maya's sweater is white. She said she looks like a snowman."

"She told me the same thing, sugar." He forced out the fear and focused on keeping the little girl calm. "Ok honey, turn the knob right below the TV button. Turn it all the way and hold the phone out so I can hear, yeah?"

"'Kay..."

The unmistakable crackle and roar of fire came through the headset. But no smoke detector.

He signaled to Janine, mouthing *fire!*

"Liv honey, listen. I need you to do one more thing: there is a silver blanket on the bottom shelf right behind you. It's shiny. Do you see it?"

"It looks like glitter." *Sniffles.*

"Yes, it does darlin'. It's a blanket that'll help keep you safe."

He looked at Janine and horror drew slowly across her usually stoic face. *Jesus, God* ... he swallowed and closed his eyes. *Focus, Sheppard.*

"Ok Liv, I want you to wrap the glitter blanket around you and lay on the floor, okay, sweetie? Watch the monitors and you'll see firefighters come. Stay away from the door. Don't open it. They'll get it. I'm on my way. I love you, sweetheart."

"O-o-k-kay, love you." She started crying again.

Mike snatched off the headset, tossed it to Janine, who promptly put it on, and tried to keep Liv talking about glitter. Laila and Paul had gone ahead. Mike dug into his pockets, hitting the remote engine starter as he ran across the parking lot to his truck. Snow crunched under his heavy feet. He snatched the car door open and floored it out of the parking lot.

His phone rang as he turned toward home, his brain firing off a million miles a minute. He jabbed the button to connect over the car speaker and gripped the steering wheel as he navigated a hairpin turn.

"Ten minutes out," Bishop's deep, aggravated voice boomed over the speakers. "Can't get through to Maya. Levy—"

"My niece is at my house alone in the safe room. She called into the station. Maya told her to run. The house ... my house is on fire. He got Maya. I know it. Somehow, he got ... "

"Fuck," Bishop clipped. He relayed the information to his team.

"Maya..." Mike whispered. His mind worked overtime as he thought about his wife and baby in the hands of a lunatic.

12:40 P.M.

"Does anyone have a visual on Levy and not his damn monitor? The chief is trying to get through to Columbus PD," Paul barked into his phone to Mace as he followed behind Laila.

"New Albany and CPD are closing on the Levy estate in a few minutes according to the P.O.," Mace said. "Landing soon. Out."

Dropping his phone in the cup holder, Paul floored it as fast as he dared, with the weather getting shittier every minute. Keeping Laila's taillights in his sights, he did the only thing that came to mind. He prayed.

12:41 P.M.

"Mike, I need you to keep your shit," Bishop said bracingly over the phone. "You can't help Maya if you lose it."

"The tracker on her necklace? Turn it on."

"I thought she didn't want to be tracked?"

"I put it on anyway. Fucking find my wife!"

Mike heard Bishop barking out orders to the people with him. "Connecting now... it says she's at the house."

"The house?" Mike echoed. *The people on the floor? What if Maya was in the house somewhere?*

"Don't lose it Mike, we are almost there."

Mike veered over for a fire truck to pass him, heading in the same direction. He pressed his foot further to the floor. Damn the snow.

12:45 P.M.

Mike was out of his Jeep as soon as he threw it in park, the door left open and keys in the ignition. He ran to the first fire truck that was beating back flames that reached high into the gray winter sky. One group focused on the front of the condo, and a second group had already broken down the garage door and foamed down the garage and Maya's truck. He nearly lost the contents of his stomach seeing the blackened truck, the flames consuming everything, including the baby's car seat.[1]

A second rig arrived, and the crews jumped in to join the already busy teams. Fire consumed the front of their condo and threatened the empty attached condo on the left. It burst forth out the windows, licking the front of its face. Crews trooped around back to gain access. The snow began coming down heavier, and with temps below freezing, water from the fire hoses froze on everything. He shoved his way, slipping over ice to the nearest firefighter. Before he said a word, detective-turned-fireman Joshua Greatt stepped in front of him. He held his hands in a calming gesture.

"We've got a crew searching for them now, Mike. Let us do our jobs. We'll get to them faster and safer than you—" The fire chief came up, interrupting.

"Detective the door—"

"3324—," Mike barked.

"Got the code. The instrument panel is damaged. Gotta cut through.

It's a steel-reinforced door, but we'll get through. The ventilation system appears to be holding," he said, trying to get through to Mike. "It went up quick, too quick for a condo of that build, those materials hold for some time against wildfires ... don't call it official, but this was deliberate. We're keeping foam on the truck in the garage to keep it from blowing and are looking at about twenty-five percent containment right now. We're getting there, son."

The chief clapped his hand on Mike's shoulder twice and traveled back to the line of firefighters. Mike never looked at him. Instead, he focused on his home as malicious orange and red devil-fingered flames continued to snake along the side of the condo, licking the roof. The wind sent stinging, tiny shards of ice across his face. Water was dumped on the same place Maya kissed him goodbye that morning. It blew back on him in a mist that froze his hat, hair, his face, even his heavy winter coat. He felt none of it.

12:55 P.M.

LAILA

Laila watched Mike pace back and forth along the police line for what seemed like years. She was getting soaked and cold. They all were, and they hadn't been out there long. The wind whipped the water around the area like a demented arctic water park. Freezing water formed gruesome, thick, opaque icicles on every surface. Ice covered the firefighters from their hats down to their coats. Their faces already looked raw from the elements.

She made mental notes of the scene as she waited for clearance to get into the house. She knew from experience that it took time to cut through metal specifically designed to withstand being breached. Evidence was being destroyed in the battle to extinguish the flames and the longer it took for her and the detectives to get inside the building, the harder it would be to figure out exactly what happened.

Paul instructed teams of patrolmen to canvas the neighborhood. More officers called in from surrounding counties to volunteer their help. Others created checkpoints between Rough Ridge and the surrounding areas within minutes of the call going out.

Stepping toward the fire chief, Laila got his attention and spoke in his ear. The chief nodded. He radioed in while Laila turned her attention back to the surrounding scene. She looked for anyone or anything out of place. And she was also being a coward. She couldn't watch the flames anymore. When she did, the nagging sensation that things would not end well sat on her soul. She sucked in a shuddering breath, flopped her mop of sagging, wet, bunned hair back, tucked it under her cap, and moved along the perimeter of the scene, taking in the spectators and trying to find clues in the snow.

1:04 P.M.

MIKE

Mike itched, literally itched, on the inside of his skin, to go in there himself. While he paced, he looked for clues around his home. He noticed a package discarded on the side of the steps, crushed by the hoses. As he looked for the best route to it, Caine arrived, raising a thousand dollars' worth of holy hell.

Caine attempted to pass the firefighters.

They attempted to stop him.

That was a mistake.

Mike didn't see who all went crashing down, but he saw Laila leap over them and get to Caine, trying to calm him. Firefighters and officers from all sides wrestled with the big man and Mike ran to his aid.

"Get the fuck off me! Liv! Maya!" Caine was in a full-blown panic. "Move out of my fucking way!"

"Stop! That's my brother! His daughter's in there!"

Mike's voice distracted Caine long enough for him to focus.

"She *is* in there?" Caine said as shock caused his body to slump, his eyes revealing anguish no parent wanted to experience, and it looked like his knees would give out. The firefighters went from holding him back to holding him up.

"They are working to get everyone out. She's in the safe room. It's fire resistant."

"But not fireproof. FUCK! Where's my ... where's my sister?"

Mike couldn't swallow or say anything. He opened his mouth, but nothing came out. *They got her. Fuck, how did I let this happen?*

"We don't know yet, Caine," Laila said, filling in for Mike. "We are pretty sure someone attacked them."

Caine's body went rigid with fury and he stood, unaided, his muscles bunching and releasing, his jaw locked tight as he listened to Laila explain. As she spoke, he focused on the door like he could extinguish the flames and make his sister and daughter appear by sheer will.

After a lifetime, movement at the back of the condo drew their attention. Josh Greatt came around through the trees, carefully picking his way over the slick, frozen landscape, his face streaked with soot. He carried a small bundle in his arms, close to his chest, a pink blanket flashing from underneath his open coat.

Caine shrugged off the men who half-heartedly tried to hold him back and shot to the fireman. Mike and Laila followed with Paul bringing up the rear. The group formed a circle around Joshua.

"Caine, wait!" Laila said low and fierce.

Caine's eyes snapped to her when she put her hand on his arm and spoke quickly, "They wanted her dead and don't know she made it. We need to let everyone think she died to keep her safe." She waited for her words to sink in. "Do. You. Understand?"

Caine's head jerked before he cautiously slipped his hand into Josh's coat. His hand touched his baby's warm, soft cheek, and a relieved sob tore through his throat. He bent low at the waist to touch his forehead to hers tenderly. Mike and Paul both closed in, shielding him and Liv from public view and to be there if he needed them. The photographers and news van that arrived were far enough away that they couldn't get a clear shot or overhear.

Josh shifted Liv and whispered in the closed circle of their bodies, "Olivia honey, I'm going to give you to your dad. Keep your eyes closed and don't move like we practiced 'kay?"

"'Kay," a small voice whispered back. It was barely audible, but it was strong and healthy.

"Pickle," Caine whispered to her.

"Hi daddy," she whispered back.

Reaching out, he accepted her into his arms and tried to not crush her as he held on so tight. Laila slipped the blanket over her sooty face and draped it over her dirty clothes. She shifted her arm around Caine's broad back as best she could and led him to the waiting ambulance. Shortly after, the vehicle started moving with no siren or lights, further promoting the idea that the child was beyond saving.

A deep shiver coursed down Mike's spine as he watched it leave.

---

1. The Air that I Breathe vs Creep by The Moon Loungers

57
REPLACEMENT

1:55 P.M., TWO BLOCKS AWAY...

"No response from Maya's guard, Gunner. Tracking on his truck shows it is still at the condo," Mace said angrily. "How the hell is everyone 'there' but not?"[1]

We've been compromised," Bishop said, not seeing the snow and passing landscape before him.

"Got past your guy, bypassed the security system, and knew where the cameras were. Any idea on who?" Mace asked, his voice tight.

"We're a family. I never thought..."

"Maybe they haven't," Mace said. "Think about it. It's not so hard. Any of us or the team could do that in our sleep, so a decent tracker or someone with a small amount of training could..."

"They knew we were on our way. They got her out before we could get here. The timing is too much of a coincidence," Bishop said.

"You've got a point. Until you figure it out, you need to ground your entire team and investigate."

"That'll take time Maya doesn't have. I need to call Wolf."

"THE Wolf?" Mace asked.

"I don't have a choice."

"Wait. Wait. Wait." Mace said as he gritted his teeth, pulling out of a slide in the truck. "Not that guy. There's nothing left but bodies when he comes through. He needs to stay in his little world, pretending to be a good ol' singing boy."

"A lot of the rumors are just that." Bishop reached into his pocket, pulling out a second secure phone.

4:07 P.M.

Maya woke for the second or third time. She wasn't sure which, as each time was a blurry mess, with brief snatches of voices and pain. She didn't move as she checked herself physically. Her baby chose that time to make herself known by running a foot across the top of Maya's belly. Maya's head pounded and her arm strangely felt both numb-ish and sorta painful. Like a pain more powerful than her current experience waited beneath the surface. She was still dressed, her undergarments in place.

Why is that important and what happened?

Her mind stayed foggy for a moment, then suddenly it all rushed back. *Griffin and Hitchens, and Liv ...*

She stayed still, listening for anything to tell her where she was and if she was alone. Her heart pounded in her chest. That pounding translated to greater throbbing in her head and muted thumping in her arm and back. She had the distinct feeling of being watched. Suddenly, in her mind's eye, she saw bright red spray across her living room wall and remembered the metallic smell of blood, and she gasped involuntarily.

"I thought I hated you," a woman's voice said.

All pretense gone, Maya blinked open her eyes against the bright light. She was in a large, blank room. She was on a bed, but the room was too quiet to be a hospital. Her eyes scanned around further and rested on a woman close to her age, a few years younger. She had long, straight dark hair and light brown eyes that looked ... weird on her. She was pale, especially against her black clothes...

"You're his, aren't you?" Maya asked.

"He says so."

Maya blinked at her words. They belied the fierce look on her face. She weighed her next words, pushing through the fuzziness as her brain slowly kick to life. *Keep her talking.*

"Hated. Past tense. What have I done to earn favor now?"

"Nothing."

Okaaay...

Maya rose slowly, winced, and hissed a slow breath against the pain. Her arm and head throbbed when she moved. Her movements were slow, like her body was separate from her mind. Had they had drugged her? Then she remembered they shot her. Like actually shot! Her arm didn't cooperate when she tried to move it. Unfortunately for her, she wasn't ambidextrous. The list of disadvantages was getting long.

Her mouth and throat were dry. Trying to swallow, she looked around the room further, got sick to her stomach and had to gulp back the acid burning her throat. The other half of the room was a makeshift staging area for labor and delivery. Surgical instruments, including a baby warmer/bassinet, sat waiting.

"They want my baby," she whispered, agonized. The full extent of her situation caused her eyes to fill with horror. Out of the corner of her eye, she saw the woman back away quickly and focus on the floor.

"Being a sole heir to billions makes one popular, Angel."

Maya blinked, trying to steady her heart rate and clear the red mist threatening to cloud her vision as he stepped through the door.

"Greedy, crazy bastard," Maya said, her voice vibrating with anger.

He moved swiftly to her and leaned in close. His pupils were blown and darted over her face, erratic in their movements. He was high as a fucking kite.

He smiled and placed his lips near her ear. She instantly shirked away. Snatching her bunned hair, he yanked her face back to his. His face swam in front of her eyes. She was having trouble keeping her head straight and being jerked around didn't fucking help.

"I take what belongs to me. If I want it." He shrugged. "Then it belongs to me. So, the kid? The money? Xenia Lux Corp? Mine. You?"

He grinned like he knew a secret. "Mine ... at least you were. Now, I've got a new Angel. You're a dime a dozen, darling."

He tugged hard again on Maya's hair and straightened, swiping at his nose with a telltale cocaine sniff.

"She's not as pretty. Or smart. *But,*" — he clapped his hands loudly, making them both jump, — "she is obedient. You should get to know her. She'll take care of it—"

"It? *It* is a baby," Maya said quietly, holding her head against his yammering, trying to blot out the pain. Her head was killing her, and her words slurred a little. "I cannot believe you are monologuing. Blah, blah, blah ... "

BAM!

For the second time that day, Maya watched blood spray. It was her own.

Her head whipped around with the force of the slap and the blood droplets sprayed across the white sheets. The pain in her head exploded, and she saw white blobs. Listing to the side, she retched as the room spun and her skull blazed. A half-moan, half-sob escaped her lips as she collapsed back on the bed, clutching her head.

"You'll hurt the baby, dearest," came a quiet whisper from the woman as Maya watched two Griffins draw back a fist. "Stress can make a woman go into labor too fast and the baby can die," she said, her eyes still on the floor.

Slowly nodding, he believed her. He clenched and unclenched his fist in jerky movements as his face twisted further in anger. "Any sign of this cow calving, I want to know."

Through squinted, watering eyes, Maya saw the woman nod and watched Griffin's back as he rushed away. When the door slammed, she moaned again, feeling the sound like another blow to her brain. *Fuck-face bastard.*

After a moment, the woman neared her again, this time close enough to whisper. "I can't believe he bought that ... How hurt are you? Can you walk? "

"Why?" Maya asked in a moan, suspicious of her "replacement."

"Because if you don't leave before the storm lifts, he's going to kill you as soon as you have the baby. That's if he doesn't let Hitchens have you. And he has been planning for you a long time..." Her voice grew thick. "It would be better to die than endure what he wants to do to you."

"Get me a weapon, maybe I can ... "

"Not with that arm. Hitchens gave you a local, but it's going to wear off soon enough. He wants you to ... feel everything. I can't leave, but I can get you out."

"You can't be serious, you can't stay here," Maya said, squinting against the bright lights of the room. She had never had a concussion before but suspected she had one now. What she knew for sure was that she was in a shitload of trouble and her brain acted like it was riding the Witch's Wheel at Cedar Point.

"I have a tracker on me ... like a dog. Wherever I go, he'll find me."

Maya stopped focusing on her head long enough to focus on the woman's words. The situation was getting worse and worse.

"Shit. Shit. Shit. Shit," she said as she cradled her belly with her good arm absentmindedly to relax the tightening she was experiencing. Everything hurt. Her head, her back, her stomach, arm ... "We've got to get you out of here. Where is it? Maybe we can..."

"I already thought of that. I don't know and there's no time ... Leave us here."

"Us? Wait. How many of you are here?! Who are you and why are you helping me?"

"Two, Callista, and because you're Mandy's best hope right now, besides, I can't blame you anymore."

"Blame..." Maya let out a deep sigh, her next words slurred. "You're right ... It is my fault. I should've—"

Callista snapped her fingers. "Hey, focus. You don't have time for this. Get out and send someone back for Mandy. She's only fifteen. They've had her for months. She won't last much longer here. You owe her to get out."

Maya tried to digest her words. Her head was throbbing, and she prayed for clarity. She watched as Callista popped open a bottle of Tylenol, giving her two that she quickly swallowed.

"It'll take twenty minutes, I guess, to take the edge off, but then you've got to get out."

"God. Okay," was Maya's hesitant reply. She laid back, willing the medication to work. She ... needed ... a few minutes...

CALLISTA SHOOK MAYA AWAKE.

"You need to go. Now," she whispered. "Something is going on. You need to get out of here."

Rising slowly, Maya clung onto Callista for a moment, panting. She wiped the dried blood off her lips and grimaced when she touched the part Griffin split. "What's ... What's the plan?"

"Easy, I walk you to the bathroom on the first floor, you leave out the deck door off the bathroom and run for it. I'll stall as long as I can, which should be easy as long as they think you're in labor. The entire police force is looking for you and we are near your house."

"They won't stop you? We need a weapon."

Callista shuffled Maya toward the door and lowered her voice.

"The only place I can't go is Mandy's room. Not since one of the animals they hired tried to get to her. Hitchens has her under lock and key now. Her room is the only one inside with a camera, the dumb asses. The rest are only around the perimeter. More to watch who's out there versus in here. And no, they won't stop me. I'm obedient, remember?"

Callista stopped at the door and took a deep breath. Then she slowly opened the door.

MIKE

"Talk," Mike spat as he stood in the interrogation room of the station. The station was the last place he needed to be. He methodically tracked how long it had been since anyone heard from Maya and it had been hours. Barely keeping it together, he knew Cap was looking for any excuse to pull him. On the outside he was ice, on the inside ... he would not allow himself time to examine. They were testing his patience with everyone gathered in this tight-ass room when they should be out looking for Maya.

"He paid a man on staff. Paid him to roam the grounds of that giant mansion for the last two days and pretend to be him. Stayed out of sight, wore the ankle monitor," the Captain said. "We all know it ain't hard to tamper with them."

"The dad claims he has hidden exits in case of attack or kidnapping attempt," Mace chimed in. "There are three different ways to get off the property without being seen by anyone, including security."

"We know all of this shit already," Mike ground out. "You got dick, and you got me in here when I should be out there looking for my wife."

He sensed a shift in the room, and Paul closed in on his flank.

"I don't need to be handled," Mike said, his voice deadly quiet.

"Hold on to that thought, brother, because we found the trucks they took her in," Paul said, his face a shuttered mask. "Neighbors reported both FedEx and UPS trucks in the area around the time little Liv called in - not unusual for this time of the year. Thing is, FedEx and UPS had no more trucks left in the area. They finished well before noon."

"The package at the condo confirms a delivery at ten a.m.," Laila volunteered. "Colorado State Patrol called in about two abandoned trucks with the markings of both companies ... Mike ... we found Gunner's body and a second pool of blood, but no sign of Maya. We're waiting on forensics to ID the source of the second pool."

Mike sucked in a deep breath through his nose and focused on the wall above Laila's head, unwilling to make eye contact with Maya's friend, his friend, as he asked the obvious question.

"How much blood?"

"Not fatal. Any loss is a concern given Maya's condition," Laila said in a clipped tone.

"There's no evidence around the truck which leads us to believe they transferred Maya before dumping the trucks about fifty miles outside of Rough Ridge."

"My wife could be somewhere between our burned-out house and fifty miles from town or on the road in this fucking weather with killers, and we're all in here chatting about shit you should have shared on the phone. Why?" Mike slid his eyes to his captain in expectation.

The man looked everywhere but at Mike for a few seconds, then heaved a heavy sigh. "The Feds have taken over the investigation and we are now in support capacity only. They want you off the hunt."

Mike's roar of "WHAT THE FUCK?!" shot through the building.

"Detective Sheppard, we understand this is a tough time," Agent Fitzgerald said as he challenged the big man in front of him with barely concealed irritation.

The sentiment was mutual. Mike developed a dislike of Fitzgerald when they worked together on the Levy case. He was lazy and sloppy. Quick to throw his weight around and claim credit after the heavy lifting was done. It seemed none of the other key people in that inter-agency case liked him much either, but you do what you have to do to get the job done. Now he was back in front of him, stopping him from finding his wife.

"We don't need a loose cannon out there with a federal witness that needs to be recovered."

"Recovered?" Mike's face passed from confused to stunned to double his previous anger in seconds as reality hit him. The room seemed to contract as his rage-filled it. Hardened officers of the law appeared to shrink a little as he spoke.

"Jesus Christ! Callista's gone. How the FUCK did you manage that, Fitzgerald? And that's why he got bail..." Mike said, putting it all together and slamming a hand down on the table. "You guys fucked up, didn't tell anyone, and you hung a pregnant woman, my wife, out as bait to cover your ass?!"

"That information is above your paygrade. YOU screwed this investigation when you fucked his baby momma," Fitzgerald shot back.

The roar from all the Colorado officers in the room was instant, and before Mike could do something that would land him behind bars, Paul grabbed him. Laila hopped across the table light as air and had Fitzgerald face down on the table, leaning her weight into him as he sputtered and turned beet red. Agents rushed in from outside the room while Laila leaned into the hold more. "Tell your friends to relax."

"Are you fucking crazy? Do you—AH!"

"Tell your friends to relax, Agent Fitzgerald," Laila said calmly.

He grimaced in pain, then spoke.

"Guys, get the fuck out of here," Fitzgerald mumbled. The agents looked from Laila to Fitzgerald and backed off, but they didn't leave.

"Now, you owe Detective Sheppard an apology for insulting his wife. She is not a baby momma as per your derogative use. You've attempted to trigger Mike into abusing you," Laila continued without the slightest irony that it triggered her into abusing the federal agent.

"I'll have your badge—grr—ah!"

Laila leaned in more, increasing the pressure on the joint.

"This arm belongs to me now. And I will take it with me unless you apologize, Agent. I have the better end of the deal. I can always use an extra hand." She giggled.

"You're fucking crazy!" came his muffled reply.

Laila leaned further and he screamed.

"Laila," Mike clipped.

Laila frowned at Mike, then stepped back, as cool as ever, releasing Agent Fitzgerald. He shrugged his jacket back into place, unable to cover a wince, and got nose to nose with Laila. Without blinking or any emotion, Laila called to the Captain who massaged his left temple.

"Suspended, Cap? Badge and gun, right?" She continued to stare at Fitzgerald as she removed both and leaned into Fitzgerald to place them on the table behind him, but not before she saw Fitzgerald flinch. Hard. Only then did she show emotion and it was mild disgust.

"Yeah, Laila, I gotta put you on the bench." The captain sighed like he should've retired years ago.

"And Agent, rein it in," the Captain barked. "It's been well established everything Mike did was on the up and up and we put precautions in place once Detective Sheppard realized the connection between Ms. Walters-Sheppard and Levy."

Turning toward Mike, "Sheppard, go ho—go grab some coffee, call your niece. We'll find Maya. I promise, son."

Mike tried to ignore the Captain's trip over the word home, but it was impossible. His home was a partially burned-out shell and a missing heartbeat. The building didn't matter. Without Maya, he'd never be ... He swallowed back that thought and willed himself to focus. Something in Laila's eyes made him think there was more to what was happening.

The room full of cops cleared a path and Mike stalked through, staring Fitzgerald down as he left. The agent's eyes were full of shame and defiance.

Bastard.

MIKE AND LAILA moved in silence through the precinct until they made their way to the locker rooms. When he got there, Bishop stood by Mike's locker. Paul, who followed them at a distance, backed out of the room, closed the door behind him and stood guard in the hallway.

"My team's been compromised," Bishop said, without preamble. "The only people that know it are those in this room and Mace. It's my fault they got to your wife and I am going to get. Her. Back."

Bishop was battling his own rage and Mike resolved he would trust him still. He didn't think about who betrayed them or that Gunner, a man who had shared their dinner table regularly, who was a new father, was dead. He kept a singular focus on finding Maya.

"Mace has the rest of the team on a wild goose chase. Until I can figure out who the backstabbing bastard is, they'll be out of our way."

"The Feds are involved now, and their first concern isn't Maya, it's covering their own asses," Mike growled.

"They must think the Amanda kid is still alive," Bishop said, nodding unsurprised. "And maybe Griffin's girlfriend."

Mike scrutinized Bishop and glanced at Laila. "This room isn't secure."

Laila pulled out a small signal jammer from her pocket. "Of course it is."

"Callista turned a long time ago. We had witnesses to what was happening, but not as good as we wanted. We needed proof of organization for RICO and tracking the money proved to be harder.

"When I arrived in Columbus, I worked my way through his crew, eliminating possibilities, and it came down to either Hitchens, his father, or her. The father was clueless. Hitchens doesn't like him much, acts as his beta with designs to take over. But they have their shared love of pain and humiliation to bond them. That left Callista."

"She went nowhere without a heavy escort. The only places she was ever alone were the inner rooms of a spa she would frequent after bad beatings from Levy ... and Hitchens." Mike paused with a grimace. Shaking his head as if warding off a terrible memory, he continued.

"I wanted to get her to wear a wire or try to find information. Turns out Callista memorized details of account information, locations, and times of money transfers and wrote them down during her time at the spa. She didn't know who to trust, so she kept all that information hidden there. When I cornered her, she could recite several transactions, conversations, and account numbers from memory. Until Levy snatched her, she was one of the top students in her law school. When I recovered her notes, we knew we had more than enough, especially with her testimony. I mean, she had hand-drawn maps to where Levy kept his records with passwords. Levy has a habit of underestimating his prey, so he did everything in the open in front of her. The plan was for marshals to get her and the kid right before Levy went down, send them to separate safe houses until trial. Something must've gone wrong after the bust."

"You knew he'd come after her for the baby," Bishop said.

"Callista spelled it out ... though I had some idea when I looked into his mother's death. He had no inheritance. I thought ... I thought I could keep my family safe," Mike said bitterly. "I didn't want her to worry more than she already was ... I failed them."

"Not yet," Laila said from the side. "You get all morose and lose your focus and you will."

"I'm headed back to the house, see if we missed something," Mike said, turning.

"No. Wait. We're going to get you out of here without you being followed," Bishop said, slipping him a bit of paper.

"Laila, I told Jake to get Wolf."

Laila prided herself on her poker face. However, the twitch in her eye was obvious this time.

"You sure know how to fuck up a situation, don't you?" she said, her voice tight.

"Maya doesn't have time for dicking around, it's done, and we need to go," Bishop said, his voice brokered no argument.

---

1. Artic by Sleeping at Last

58

PAIN

MAYA

Maya and Callista met with no resistance, only watchful stares as they made their way down the hall to the stairs that would lead to the bathroom and Maya's freedom.

Until they encountered Hitchens.

"You look in pain." Hitchens grinned.

Maya said nothing.

"Nothing to say now." He chuckled. "You'll scream soon enough."[1]

Snatching her away from Callista, he pulled her stumbling, woozy form through the door right before the stairs.

"I've had time to get it ready and I think you'll like what I've done," Hitchens said conversationally. He threw open the door, flicked on the light, and turned to watch Maya's reaction.

It was an unfinished laundry room, but instead of a washer and dryer, there was an x-shaped table with restraints for wrists and ankles positioned near a downward sloping drain in the floor. Next to the table was a smaller, wheeled steel table like the one in the room she was in before, with another set of surgical instruments and a third table with a variety of sex paraphernalia. Photos of her covered the walls. He'd watched her for months and he'd been everywhere, including her home. Horror and rage filled her as she peered at the photos of her and

Gunner eating lunch that one day in L.A. and her wearing nothing but a bow on Michael's birthday ... photos of her and her family ... with her nieces ... walking into her doctor's appointments ... he'd violated every part of her life.

He was watching her, rubbing himself, waiting for her reaction. She steeled herself to not give him one. He let her go, and he unzipped his pants. She readied herself to fight. Instead, she had to try to block out the sounds of him pleasuring himself. It could have been a minute or twenty. She didn't know. It seemed endless and she couldn't turn her mind's eye to her favorite moment, and she couldn't conjure Heart's eyes. She could not escape this moment. His grunts, the way he moaned her name. It was all in HD with surround sound. Suddenly, he reached out and grabbed her injured arm in a vice-like twisting grip, and the dull throbbing pain exploded into waves of excruciating agony throughout her entire body. His low, guttural grunts of climax accompanied her high-pitched scream.

Her screams of pain tapered off into whimpers as she slumped into the nearest wall for support. He let go of her arm and pressed against her, trapping her against the wall. She tried to still her breathing, become like steel, but it was no use. She flinched when he breathed on her skin. Her mind screamed, *Fight back, dummy! Fight!*

"Get used to the smell of me."

And when he attempted to rub his wet, semen-soaked hands against her face, Maya, bless her, lost it. She rejected the instinct to shut her eyes and instead zeroed in on his exposed neck. With one arm, weak as she was, she moved for his throat. Surprised by her sudden attack, he fell back against the wall, gasping and turning red. Maya quickly brought her shin to his exposed genitals four times in rapid succession. She thought she heard something pop, but she focused on her attack. Instead of screaming in pain, he only made muted, forced exhalations of breath. Worried he would pin her with his weight, she backed away as he fell forward. His open mouth made ghastly hollow grunts and his face contorted in rage and pain.

"Get used to the feel of me," she whispered as she looked him in his beady eyes and kicked him in the balls again with all of her strength before stomping on his face with the heel of her foot twice. When he stopped moving, she darted toward the door, half-expecting to be met by men with guns, but she saw Callista hovering. Looking skittish, Callista rushed Maya and looked over her shoulder into the room. Taking in Hitchens passed out form. She yanked on Maya's sweater, ripping it.

"Take off your leggings," she hissed. When Maya hesitated, Callista fussed quickly, "No one will look twice if you come out of this room mauled. They *will* pay attention if you appear fine and he doesn't show up at all."

The lightbulb finally illuminated in Maya's injured brain, and she wiggled out of her leggings. As Callista grabbed them, Maya pulled more hair out of her bun. With a wince, she squeezed her cut lip and rubbed the resulting blood around her nose, smearing it across her cheek. She let the tears from her watering eyes flow and looked askance to Callista. A ghost of a smile passed the young woman's lips before her face became blank again.

Callista came to Maya's side and began "helping" her to the bathroom on the main floor. Maya clutched her leggings to her chest and avoided eye contact. She didn't have to fake the trembling. The terror for herself and for Callista was real.

JAKE, Bishop, and Laila stood in front of the TV in a small cabin, watching Griffin's father in disgust.

"*My son is missing. So is the architect Maya Walters, and I believe this man,*" he said, pointing to a huge photo of Hitchens next to him on a monitor. "*Foster Hitchens is responsible. We also believe he is behind the car accident that killed my beloved wife, Sharon. Sweet little Maya is, as you know, pregnant, and was last seen here, in this little town. I believe my son courageously, out of concern for her, left house arrest to see if he could talk some sense into this monster. I have letters, you have all seen them, letters that Hitchens sent my son in prison detailing the horrible things he intends to do to this woman. Let me be clear, my son never initiated contact with Foster Hitchens in prison and never replied. Hitchens has manipulated and hurt this family long enough - creating a sex trafficking ring with my son's business, murdering my*" *wife, and now likely orchestrating the disappearance of my son and his friend. I am offering a ten million dollar reward for any information leading to the whereabouts and capture of Foster Hitchens. That's all I have to say for now."*

The press exploded on the screen as Jake hit mute.

"Tell me I didn't see what I saw," Jake ranted. "Did he call a press conference to make sure he set it up so his son gets off? Who the fuck allowed this?"

"And he sold Hitchens out in public, giving the press evidence the cops don't have and now Hitchens knows Griffin is a rat bastard," Laila said, shaking her head. "They'll turn on each other with Maya and the others caught in the middle."

"Hitchens still beatin' his meat?" Griffin asked, thinking hard and snorting more coke.

"He's been in there the whole time, sir," Nowakowski said. "He must've done something to the woman. She went to the bathroom looking freaked."

"Heh good. She should be ... Hitchens hasn't seen the shit my father pulled ... Ok ... Then kill Foster, Angel #2, and Maya after she has the kid. I say he did it and we killed him trying to get out. I make sure Helman gets his kid back on the condition he advises Father to change his will again. After all, I have a child now and I risked life and freedom to rescue it. The Feds have a dead bad guy, I have control of mom's money, and next year, Dad'll have a heart attack or something unfortunate, and the year after that the kid'll meet with a nasty accident..." Griffin took another hit of coke. "And Dad says I don't plan ahead ... "

LAILA CLICKED OFF HER PHONE. "Paul said the agents are getting ready to move out. Doppler shows a break in the storm soon and he thinks they have a lead, but they ain't sharing. We don't have time to wait. We need to go now."

MAYA WAS SO COLD. The clothes Callista smuggled into the bathroom did little, by the way of warmth, and she'd been out here too long. It was dark and so hard to see. The snow kept swirling, changing directions, but she should have come across a house by now. She was only a block away from her own. There were big lots between houses and units, but it didn't feel like it should be this far...

"I THINK I FOUND HER," Wolf spoke from his perch. "I've got two guards in the yard. Something must be going on for them to be out in the open in this weather."

Bishop put the phone on speaker and opened his laptop as they moved out of their location, taking an old logging road back to Maya's neighborhood. Mike leaned over to look at the map Wolf sent.

"Y'all already searched recent property purchases and rentals, so I dug into my resources, and two places caught my eye. Both spots are using an above average amount of electricity for the area. I'm sending you the info now."

"This one," a circle appeared on the map, "is one block away from Maya's home. If I had to pull a long-term job and get off the streets, I'd pick a location close like this one. No one would expect we'd be there after the initial public search, and it would allow me to closely monitor the search. Then, when it was clear, I'd head through the forest to one of the three paths and bug out from there. Drone confirms ten heat signals above ground, one below. No visuals, but I detect ballistic glass and cameras."

"Agreed," Bishop said. "No police, Wolf. We're going in soft, two blocks away."

"Place has been under renovations for months now," Mike spoke, his eyes burning a hole in the laptop, his voice a cold monotone. "It began weeks after the wedding. Under our noses."

"He's had months to get the lay of the land and secure it," Laila spoke up. "All right, here's how it's going to go down..."

---

1. Tourniquet by Evanescence

59

MONSTER

"Power cut to the house. Team A move in," Mace whispered into the comm.

"Roger that," Laila replied.

"Movement three clicks south and closing," Mace alerted. From his perch, he could see most of the property, including a black SUV, slowing to a roll at the bottom of the street. Focusing his scope on the occupant, Mace almost couldn't believe his eyes. The wind picked up, snow blew down on him from the higher branches in the trees where he perched, but his scope and his eyes were true.

"It's Levy, the elder. Mike, you're closest. Move in on Levy."

Mike responded, "Fuck that. I'm getting my wife out of there."

"Mike, the Feds are going to be close behind Levy. They get here and fuck this up. Maya could die. Get. Levy."

"Fuck. On it."

"I've got movement in the woods behind the house," Bishop said into his own headset. "That explains the yard guards."

Before Marion Levy got the nerve to get out of his rented SUV, he found himself snatched out and tossed against the side of the car like a rag doll.

"You knew where he was the whole time," Mike said, inches away from his face. His hands crumpled the man's coat and shirt like paper.

"Who—you're that girl's husband," Levy's eyes widened as he sputtered. "My family. I've had them chipped," he rambled. "Griffin's was somehow damaged, it took longer to locate, but my son's trying to help, he's—"

Mike silenced the man with a look.

"Your *monster* has been planning to kill her, take our baby and the inheritance for months, you blind, stupid, selfish son of a bitch." Mike looked down at him as he struggled to keep control. "If anything happens to my girls, I'm killing him, then I'm killing you."

Mike slipped a set of cuffs on the older man and tossed him into the back of the man's own rented SUV. He took the man's car keys and tossed them several feet into a snowdrift along with Levy's phone. Mike's eyes narrowed as Laila spoke in his ear.

"She's not here. We've got the little girl. No sign of Callista either."

"You're an officer of the law," Levy pleaded and grunted as he struggled to right himself.

Mike snatched off his badge and tossed it on top of Levy.

"Not tonight."

His head snapped around as he heard Maya's scream coming from the woods behind the house.

SHE COULDN'T BELIEVE IT. She had walked in a circle. A little girl was depending on her and she was lost a block from her fucking house. Callista might die because of her. Maya stopped to orient herself. She was nauseous and couldn't stop shaking. Her head throbbed, everything hurt, and she was having trouble focusing. Feet that were once in pain from the cold were warm again. Which was a good thing, right? Or was she freezing to death? *Shit ... If I turn right, then that should take me to the closest house ... Right? Wait ... maybe that wasn't the house.* She was so tired and so cold. She had to keep moving. *Or maybe I should sit down for a minute ...* Maya leaned against a tree when she heard movement in the woods.

She screamed, but it was too late. A large beefy hand covered her mouth and a vaguely familiar voice whispered in her ear.

"I can get you outta here."

Maya looked over her shoulder, readying herself to fight again, and peered into a pair of brown eyes she didn't know as she backed up.

The mystery man unwrapped the scarf covering the lower half of his face, and she gasped. Biscuit.

He gave a half-hearted shrug. "I thought I'd come back out here and look. My daddy used to take me huntin' in these woods before they built all these houses and condos and shit," he explained in a hurried whisper. "Figured I'd check the old loggin' road back here."

He hurriedly wrapped the scarf around her head and face. When he finished, he took off his coat and put it around her shivering shoulders. Biscuit froze in mid-step and made a horrific gurgling noise in his throat as his eyes grew wide. He stumbled forward, gasping.

Maya stumbled back as she watched his body sink into the snow.

When she looked past the body, she saw a man slipping a big ass knife back in his waistband sheath. She kept moving back in shock as he advanced when a hand landed on her shoulder.

"Boo," Griffin whispered in her ear.[1]

Maya screamed and took off running. Her nightmare had come to life. He was behind her, and it was only a matter of time before his teeth sunk into her flesh. Her body shot with adrenaline. She moved as fast as her belly and balance would allow toward the house, spotting a branch a few feet away.

LAILA MOVED her head to the right—the last room in the basement. She pushed the door open when a frightened squeak made the hairs on the back of her arms stand up. The rescued girl dropped to the floor, clutching her side as ghastly pale Hitchens launched himself at Laila with a frenzied yell. She fired once before he fell on her.

Laila used his momentum to flip him onto his back. She tripped over the little girl and slipped in a thick, dark pool of liquid spreading out around the teenager. *Shit!*

Laila slipped into autopilot as she got a glimpse into Hitchens' eyes. He was gone. Crazy gone. His pupils were so dilated his eyes were black. Soldiers, spies, security etc., she handled, no problem. When they crossed over to bloodlust, almost nothing short of death stopped them. That had to be the only way to explain why he was still standing. Clearly, someone had already kicked his ass before they arrived.

Laila slipped out her knife and sprung from a crouch just as Hitchens lurched himself at her again. She switched swings in mid-direction, slashing him from his neck down across his already blood-soaked middle as she moved, throwing herself out of his reach.

He dropped to his knees before falling face-down on the cold concrete floor with a heavy crack as his head hit. She watched briefly as his blood began making the slow trek to the drain.

Laila turned her attention back to Amanda on the floor and shoved a rapid release sponge packet into the gaping wound in the teen's side.

"Hitchens is down," Mace heard Laila say over the com in his ear.

"Merry fucking Christmas," he muttered to himself. "Anyone got an eye on Mike?"

"No, that big bastard is fast as fuck," Bishop swore. "I have to move to a different spot - you stay on extraction."

"Roger that." Mace's gut continued to burn as he listened and waited for Laila, his scope trained on his area.

"Sub and first floor clear, targets neutralized, Baby Bird secured, but injured," Laila said.

Wolf moved through the house, eliminating the last of the second-floor targets as he positioned the drone's feed. There was a heat signal above him in what looked like a crawl space. It wasn't moving and Wolf was unsure if the person was lying in wait or something else. Carefully he slid back the panel, pointing his gun, ready for any movement, when a small, bloody hand fell out the opening.

"Shit ... found Callista," he said into the headset. "We need medics."

MIKE STOPPED and held his breath, listening. Light, quick footfalls were coming toward him. The snow began again, and the wind increased. He trained his eyes on the dark woods for the slightest movement.

"Mike 11 o'clock, two figures, no three, one looks like it could be Maya," Bishop warned into his communication device.

Mike turned toward crashing sounds as two forms came barreling out of the woods. The smaller of the two cracked the other upside the head with a broken branch she held with one hand as her right arm hung limply at her side. A third figure appeared at the edge of the wood and spotted Mike. Mike saw the reflection of the assailant's gun barrel as he swung in Mike's direction. Mike fired, dropping him.

Two more guards came into the yard opposite Mike. Two shots from long distance dropped them. Throughout, Mike never stopped running.

It was like he moved in slow motion as he tried to get to her. The harder Mike ran, the slower he seemed to move. He raised his gun again and swore, unable to get a clear shot.

"Shoot him," Mike barked frantically. "Somebody—"

His heart stopped as Griffin rushed Maya, knocking her off her feet. He was living a slow nightmare as he watched her instinctively curl around her belly before she crashed to the ground with a sickening thud. Griffin fell to the side of her and began brutally tightening and yanking the thick scarf around her throat. Maya's muted choking gasps rang out, and mixed with Griffin's furious yell, as her nails raked down his face. He yanked at the fabric harder, choking off all sound from her.

With the roar of his pulse in his ears, and his vision turning red around the edges, he finally reached them and pulled Griffin off Maya. Maya's body jerked as Griffin clutched the scarf, but he released it when Mike wrapped his large hands around Griffin's throat, determined to kill him.

With his knee in Griffin's chest, Mike continued to squeeze. Not too hard and not too quick. He wanted to watch the bastard die, slowly. As he watched, Griffin - wild-eyed with the strength of drugs coursing through his veins - fought, losing consciousness, batting uselessly against his arms.

"I want him to suffer."

Maya's words from months ago drifted to the front of his mind and his eyes scanned the surrounding area, landing on the shed in front of him off to the side of the house. He got a new idea. He released Griffin and quickly rose as Laila slid to a stop next to Maya. She gently took Maya's face in her hands, began assessing and calling out her injuries to the team. Listening to her report his wife's list of injuries made him more determined.

Mike snatched up the pile of filth next to him and drug Griffin like trash to the edge of the shed by the cliff. Grabbing a can of kerosene by the shed's door, Mike doused Griffin with the pungent liquid. After pulling a flare out of a pocket in his gear, he hammered it against his leg, sparking it to life.

"Oh shit," Bishop said to the team. "He's 'bout to set the fucker on fire."

"Ambulances are still five minutes out, roads are shit," Wolf said. "The kid's bleeding has stopped, but she's lost a lot of blood. Wait, who's setting who on fire?"

"Fuck, he kills him and he'll only see that baby from behind glass and bars," Bishop swore as he ran with his rifle flat out down from his perch to the scene below.

"Mike, don't do it." Laila said as she kept a hand on Maya's scalp, holding a profusely bleeding cut closed. Her other hand on Maya's belly, she kept willing the child to move as she continued to speak.

"Mike ... Mike!"

MAYA WAS SO COLD, and in so much pain. There was so much noise around her. Lifting her eyelids took all of her concentration, but when she did, she saw an angel. An archangel with a flaming sword standing over a demon on the edge of a cliff. The angel's face was fiercely beautiful and filled with righteous anger as he stood over a demon ready to vanquish it. Diamonds swirled on air around the angel, glittering in the red glow of his sword. The angel paused and turned to her. She couldn't see them, but knew his green eyes were on her. With the last of her remaining strength, she reached out for him.

MIKE SAW Maya reach for him and froze. He stared at her bruised, swelling face and felt rage, but when he looked into her eyes, he saw her trust.

She trusted him to be there for her and their Butterfly. She trusted there was goodness in him... He drew in a deep, brutally frigid breath, his arm still raised as it shook. His whole body shook.

It would be so easy to drop the flare and fry the bastard before him. To watch him writhe and scream in pain, to smell his flesh as his evil purged from the Earth...

He agonized over it for what seemed like an eternity.

His heart raced and the need to kill Griffin was so strong. *God, help me...*

With a roar from his very soul, he chose a life with Maya's love over the darkness. He swung his arm wide and with all the anger and anguish he had in him; he threw the flare over the side of the cliff at the edge of the property.

Barely righting himself on the slippery stone underneath the snow, he turned when he heard the snow crunch of a person approaching. He was slightly surprised to see Marion Levy. Only slightly because the day had been fucked all to shit.

"I will always own her," Griffin rasped on a sinister laugh.

"DROP THE GUN, LEVY!" Laila yelled, and assumed a position over top of Maya, clear with her intentions of protecting her at all costs.

Griffin's eyes swung to his left and saw his father with his own gun raised.

"Perfect.... timing ... da—dad..."

"Gun down, Levy!" Laila barked.

"Mr. Levy, what are you doing?" Agent Fitzgerald squawked.

Griffin made a show of discarding his kerosene-soaked, heavy cashmere coat. Climbing to his feet, he swayed as he grinned a bloody, crazed grin at his father.

"I failed you, son," Marion Levy said, his voice carrying on the wind swirling around them.

Griffin's eyes grew large with surprise when the heat of the bullet ripped through his belly. He staggered toward Mike unseeing, his mouth gaping.

Mike's first thought was to stop Marion Levy from making a worse mistake. One he wouldn't be able to live with, "Not like this—" he managed to say before it was over.[2]

MACE KNEW, and he was powerless to stop it. Mike would be dead even if he survived the hail of bullets Marion Levy meant for his son. The drop off the side of the cliff was at least two hundred feet.

Later, he would hate himself for not getting in his new position in time to get a bead on Marion.

BISHOP WAS ALMOST THERE. Mike had a baby on the way. Bishop had to—

His strength and agility were no match for the icy patches that coated the ornamental stone surrounding the shed. As he landed with a teeth-chattering crunch, Bishop scrambled to the edge only to see darkness.

He would later swear he only needed an inch more.

The mind can be cruel and memories lie.

He needed a full twelve to reach Mike in time. Too much to expect of any man.

LAILA MADE no move from where she crouched, protecting Maya. The anguish in her heart almost climbed out of her throat as her gun jammed. She reached for her second as she decided not to restrain Levy. She didn't allow herself to second guess her choice to protect Maya over an attempt to save Mike. But she steeled herself for the day when her friend asked her why.

THE MOMENT MARION LEVY pulled the trigger, he was a hollow shell. With a heart shattered like worthless glass, there was nothing keeping his soul tied to his body. When his only child disappeared into the darkness, taking that officer with him, Marion Levy was beyond grief. He never felt the bullet that tore through his torso from Laila's first shot.

It is said that in death, all things are revealed. Perhaps it was because he was so close to death that Marion saw it all for what it was ... the lies, the monster in plain sight, his part in it all...

He dropped to his knees, holding his gun to his chest. Chest heaving, Levy called over his shoulder, "Tell her—"

"Levy no!" Agent Fitzgerald yelled.

"—Frankenstein apologized for his monster." Shoving the gun into his mouth, he thought of his wife one last time.

BANG!

---

1. Creep by Scala & Kolacny Brothers
2. Fallen into Darkness by Hirotaka Izumi

60

SHOCK

DR. KENT AND LILITH, Maya's nurse-midwife, walked into the waiting room where a significant crowd waited for them. The storm raged on outside, guaranteeing everyone would be there most of the night. Dr. Kent scanned the crowd, looking for Mike.

"We should wait until Mike arrives," she started. "He's not stuck at the station, is he?"

Bishop and Paul glanced at each other while Tori burst into tears. Little Liv was on the pediatric floor asleep, and this was the first time Tori and Caine had left their daughter's side since they brought her in.[1]

"Doc ... ," Paul started. "Mike was killed tonight during Maya's rescue. He passed over the side of the canyon by the Ridgeview condos. The storm's..." Paul cleared his throat roughly. "The storm's keeping us from recovering his body."

Dr. Kent stepped back, stunned. Her hand flew to her throat in horror as she tried to absorb the information. Taking off her scrub cap, she clenched it to keep it together. Lilith's hands balled into tight fists.

Nodding finally, Dr. Kent swallowed deeply. "I'm so, so sorry ... Caine, Thomas, as Maya's next of kin, you will need to decide on her care."

"Go ahead doc, we're all family here, spell it out," Thomas said, his eyes rimmed with red.

Taking another deep breath and finding purchase, Dr. Kent's voice grew stronger. "Maya's stable for now, but her poor body has been through a lot. She has a concussion and a deep scalp wound that required twenty stitches. She was shot through her right arm and while we've repaired much, there's nerve damage and we won't know for a while if it's permanent. We are also watching for infection from the wound. We've given her blood to replace what she's lost. She also has a bruised trachea and ribs, and multiple bruises and lacerations to her face and body."

"Doc, the baby ... " Caine asked.

Lilith spoke up, "Baby is doing amazing. I was with Maya during her C-section, so she wasn't alone. During her ordeal, Maya must have gone into labor. She was about eighty percent effaced and dilated about five centimeters when she arrived. With her injuries, elevated blood pressure, the risks involved with letting her labor progress were too great. For Maya, the next couple of days are crucial. For baby, we are going to keep her under observation, but she'll be ready to go home well before Maya is and until Maya can care for her, it needs to be decided who will care for her."

"They gave up everything, both of them, for their baby," Caine said. "My sister ... Mike..." Caine dropped his head back to stare at the ceiling. "We will take care of her, that's what Maya asked. Maya will be out before we know it. She's strong."

"Caine, you saw her when she came in," Laila said. "She saw everything. Covered in Marion's Levy's blood. We both were ... she was awake and not responding to anything. Not pain, questions..."

"Acute stress reaction," Dr. Kent offered. "Mental shock. We don't know what she will remember or how she's going to be when she wakes up. This is not something you can will yourself through."

"Fine. She's going to be fucked up!" Caine yelled, unable to keep calm anymore. "Her husband is dead, she's had to kill people, run for her life through a fucking snowstorm, who knows what they did to her when they had her ... she's ... God, she..." His hands dropped in defeat, followed quickly by his head.

Dr. Kent reached out and placed a soothing hand on his arm and after a while, she spoke softly.

"When a body, a mind, goes through what she experienced, the residual effects can slow the healing process. She's going to need all the support and love she can get. She's stable. Let's start there."

"Can I see my daughter, my granddaughter?"

"Of course, only two at a time, however. Maya will be in the ICU until she wakes and is off the ventilator," Dr. Kent said.

Deep sadness settled over the waiting room. It penetrated the floors and walls, soaking into the bones of everyone there. All they thought of was the beautiful young couple, bright and wild, living in the sun and how the light had gone out.

Their hearts broke for the young wife whose heart was so big it swallowed the demons of Mike's past. She had wrapped her arms around the entire town with that same big heart ... now she had lost hers. They mourned the wild, young man who won the fight every man feared - the fight over the darkness in his heart.

The snow continued to fall hard and swift around Rough Ridge that night and would continue through the next several days, preventing any recovery attempt for the body of Michael Andrew Sheppard. As the hours wore on, the men grew restless, eager to begin the search. Their wives provided some comfort, but they too were consumed with grief and anxiety of what was to come. Maya had become, in a short time, a big part of their lives. Mike was a native son. A native son done good, despite every obstacle, every stroke of bad luck, every pain. He deserved to come home. To rest beside his mother and sister. His wife and child deserved a place to lay flowers.

IN HIS DENVER OFFICE, Xavier held strong at the news coming out of Rough Ridge. He flew in from Paris as soon as he heard Maya was missing, stopping in Columbus to grab Selene and Shay. When engine trouble grounded them in Chicago, they hopped in a car and drove the rest of the way. The biggest storm to hit Colorado in years slowed their progress and after finally reaching his office they got the latest, connecting with Caine, who told them everything.

Selene was subdued and stoic, as usual. Shay wept openly as Caine described how Mike died and Maya's injuries. When they got off the phone, he made a call to his contacts at the FBI.

THE WOLF SAT in a chair watching over the two young women a long way from home, going through their own version of hell. Dr. Kent spoke when she walked in.

"You shouldn't be here," she said.

"They don't have anyone else with them. They've only had each other in all this. Seems only right they have someone else now."

Dr. Kent considered him for a moment, then finally nodded as she relented.

"I think everyone needs someone to care for them right now. Stay, but you should take some of that off," she said, gesturing to his bullet-proof vest and gear. "You might scare them when they wake."

Wolf shrugged and took off his gear down to his long-sleeved, tight athletic tee. He kept his holster and gun. Catching Dr. Kent looking at it, he simply said, "I'm not taking any chances."

After checking on her patients, Dr. Kent left to check on the rest of the critically injured. The storm had swamped the hospital and the high-risk rescue had filled the hospital morgue and many of the beds. The sound of the door closing woke 15-year-old Amanda with a start. Seeing the large man with a gun in the room with her sent her into a panic. She wanted to run, but her body wouldn't cooperate.

"Whoa there, it's okay," Wolf said, his hands up in a soothing gesture. "You're safe in a hospital. Your family is on their way. You're safe, it's over."

Her panicked eyes darted around the room as if looking for proof. She eyed the medical equipment, the door, and only relaxed when she saw Callista in the next bed. Then she cried.

Wolf, barely standing as to not frighten her by looming over her, grabbed the box of tissues off the table next to her and sat them by her hand. "Let it all out, darlin'. You've been a brave kid; you can let it all out now. I'll be here to make sure no one bothers you two again."

She looked wary of his offer. Her eyes darted to Callista's sleeping form.

"Who are you?"

"My name is Wolf, though my friends call me Logan," he said with his slight New Zealand accent. "I help find lost people. I'm glad I wasn't too rusty..." He looked around awkwardly for something else to tell the girl to help her relax. "I sing in dive bars. I heard you sing too."

Amanda looked unsure, still. "Will I really go back ho-home?"

Logan's grin was genuine. "Absolutely love. As soon as you heal up a bit, you'll be back home with your family. Would it make you feel better if I sat outside your door? Or ... Do you want a female officer to watch over you two."

Amanda nodded, appearing afraid of his response.

"No problem." He smiled kindly. "I'll get my friend Laila. She's a cop and can kick my ass if she really tried. No one is going to get past her."

***

THOMAS SAT by his daughter's side, only leaving to check periodically on his granddaughter. He sat pouring over every inch of her face, grateful even in its bruised and abused state. He shifted his eyes to her hands, memorizing every inch of visible skin. She had long, elegant fingers similar to her mother. Artist hands. Thomas took time to clip her nails even, removing the broken and chipped evidence from her fight for life. Then he painstakingly removed bits of Marion Levy's blood and tissue from her hair. It had been cleaned, but he still discovered things that he never wanted his daughter to deal with. The nurses, moved by his dedication, helped. His fingers ached, arthritis flared up, but he kept working until she was completely clean.

He talked to her while he worked. He told her about what her mother meant to him. He told her how much he loved her. He talked about everything and nothing, keeping his voice and tone positive and hopeful. The sadness threatened to overtake his heart, and he tried to shut it down, but when they brought in Maya's wedding rings, it happened. Holding them in his hands, Thomas broke down.

HEARTBEAT

1. Issa Albeniz, Opus 165, Prelude

61

LOSS

THROUGHOUT THE FIRST days after the rescue, the fellas and Maya's girlfriends took turns sitting with her and Thomas. None of them were prepared for what they saw when they entered her room the first time. Her face, usually lit from within, was ashen, bruised, and swollen. The medical staff parted and clipped her hair back, revealing a deep, sutured gash in her scalp. There were tubes and machines. Her right arm heavily bandaged. Worst of all, she was so still. For a woman that radiated determined energy, her absolute stillness was scary.

Logan, looking very much like his Wolf codename - angry and dangerous - conferenced with Jake on the fifth day.

"There's a break in the storm tomorrow," he grumbled to Jake. "We are clear to climb. I'll get the drones out this afternoon and we can get the chopper up tomorrow."

Jake nodded. "The search and recovery team from Denver is heading over now. The boys from Montana are coming, too."

Tori continued to stare at a spot on the floor as she spoke. "It's been days with this storm. Do you think you will find his ... him?"

"We have to," Logan said.

Caine appeared in the doorway of Maya's room and looked past them in the hallway to where Xavier, Shay, and Selene were walking up quickly. "She's awake and talking."

Shay and Selene ran toward the room and only slowed when they reached the door. Each greeting Caine.

"She doesn't seem to remember much from after they took her," he warned in a whisper.

The women filed in nodding, followed by Maya's "fellas." Tori rounded out the line, motioning for Xavier to follow. "You're family too," she whispered, taking his hand.

As they filed in, Maya connected eyes to each of them. Her father sat at the head of her bed, Caine on the other side, both in chairs too small for them. Selene and Shay were crouched next to Caine, their eyes warm and overbright.

Jake, Mace, Logan, Xavier, Bishop, Blake, and Paul stood shoulder to shoulder with Tori at the foot of her bed. Maya shifted her weight and grimaced.

"They said you guys found me," Maya said, her voice hoarse, and her throat sore from Levy's abuse and the ventilator.

"We were clean up, doll," Mace said quietly. "You were rescuing yourself."

"Livy and my baby—"

"Are fine sweetheart, remember?" Thomas spoke patiently, assuming she was having trouble remembering.

"Biscuit?"

"He's down a kidney, but he'll live," Blake volunteered.

She frowned angrily. She passed her eyes through the room; her face growing more troubled. "Then why..." Her hand traveled to her throat and rubbed. "Why ... do you all look like that?"

"Sis, what else do you remember?" Caine rumbled, patting her head, careful of ugly black crisscrossed lines of the stitches in her scalp.

She closed her eyes, trying to search her mind. "Bits of dreams," she whispered.

"Callista," she croaked, her eyes popping open. " ... Mandy?"

"They're ok, just up the hall," Logan said.

"Hurt." She clenched her hand tightly.

"They'll heal," he answered vaguely.1

"Need. Heart," she whispered, her movements becoming restless.

Her hand moved to where her necklace normally sat. She turned her head slightly to her brother, grunting with the effort. "Need ... him."

Caine looked into his sister's pleading eyes and did what he thought was right. He placed a gentle hand on her side and placed his forehead against hers. "Sis. I'm so sorry. Mike didn't make it."

Maya's body stilled and her eyes squeezed shut tightly. "No," she croaked. "Not ... possible."

Caine spoke so quietly to her; the machines were almost louder than him.

"He fell, honey," Caine said.

"Fell?" She whimpered. "No... no. I can ... still feel ... him."

Her eyes drifted closed, and she remembered. It was like a horrific collage of single framed images.

Michael and Griffin.

The wind.

A glowing red flame.

His eyes were on her.

Gunshots.

Heart's body jerking with impact.

Griffin flailing into Heart.

Their backward tumble.

Their forms suspended in the darkness. Then gone.

Another gunshot blasted loudly in her mind. A body dropped, and she remembered the sound of it hitting the snow. A large, gaping hole where a face should have been. And so much blood... It landed warm and wet on her skin.

Her hand kept grasping for the necklace he gave her, reaching for his heart. Her movement became frenzied as the pictures flashed through her mind until she was practically clawing at her chest. Thomas quickly reached across her and placed a hand over the top of hers, stilling it against her. When her hand stopped, her body shook. She took in an involuntary breath, and it was like she sucked all the air out of the room. She gasped in shallow breaths, holding it in until she couldn't hold on anymore. She screamed.

SHE SCREAMED PAIN.

She screamed out loss so acute, so full of anguish, it had its own register.

She screamed unrealized promise.

She screamed the violent sound of a dying dream, of murdered hope.

It was a loud, long, single scream of a soul torn in two that sent shock waves through the room, out the door, and down the hall. It shredded hearts, stopped people in the hallway in their tracks, brought nurses running, and echoed forever.

Maya's already damaged throat gave out. Her body writhed with sobs and pain and she, unable to do anything more, made the most pitiful, raspy grunts of despair. She took in desperate, wheezing gasps and exhaled pain. Monitors flashed and blared as Maya writhed on the bed.

The door burst open, with Dr. Kent and several other doctors and nurses rushed in.

"Everyone out," Dr. Kent barked.

"Heart rate spiking."

"Check her airway. We don't want her swelling shut ... "

The door closed on the doctors as they did their work.

"What have I done?" Caine moaned as he collapsed to his knees in the hallway.

62

GET CLOSER

CAINE

The sun rose over the mountains overlooking Rough Ridge. The high wind that had accompanied the snowstorm finally blew out. Caine and his friends gathered at the police station along with most of the police force, Denver search and rescue, a search team from Montana, volunteers from town, and a shitload of news trucks.

Logan detailed the area and where the drone had searched unsuccessfully, pointing out where teams would have to cover by foot. He laid out his plan for Mace, Caine, Blake, and himself to rappel down from where Mike and Griffin had fallen to scan in case the bodies caught somewhere along the jagged face. When the teams broke out to their assignments, one rookie on the Denver team asked his captain about Logan.

"Who is that guy?"

"Ex-military. He's the best damn tracker we've had around here in years. He's more comfortable in these mountains than wolves, and they say more deadly and as rare. I don't know about all that. My wife says he has a lovely singing voice. Regardless, if he says go left, I'm following him. After all, he designed our search software."

Janine walked around the station, topping off everyone's travel mug of coffee as they were leaving. She held her hand out to stop Caine.

"How is she, honey?"

"Heartbroken," was his gruff reply.

Janine dropped her hand and her eyes lowered, full, as Caine, Mace and Logan walked past.

WHEN THEY REACHED THE PROPERTY, the teams silently passed small patches of onlookers who began leaving candles and stuffed animals in front of the home where Mike died. They passed more news vans and worked carefully to avoid crime scene tape and evidence tents. Walking by the FBI agents still working the scene, Logan's eyes narrowed.

"No sense getting pissed at them," Mace muttered. "Fitzgerald is the one that let Levy out of that car. Xavier has some connections, and now Fitzgerald is toast."

Logan grunted his response.

When they arrived at the spot where Mike fell, they found Bishop standing there. His jaw clenched tight. He stood with his arms crossed. Rappel gear already set up, he peered over the edge. Several members of his team were operating drones.

Without taking his eyes off the drop below, Bishop said in a monotonous tone, "My brother is on his way to one of our black sites where he will stay until the team can pursue all leads into his counter activity. Maya may not have been the only client he sold out."

Logan walked past and clapped Bishop on the shoulder. "And you're sure?"

"That my brother betrayed me, his family, and Maya's? Fuck yeah, I'm sure, but that story can wait. I'm also sure I need to take Caine's place on this."

Mace nodded in agreement as Caine protested.

"You've been awake for days man, you look dead on your feet. One slip out there and your family has two funerals."

"Be our eyes," Logan said, agreeing. "Monitor the drone and watch our backs."

"That's my brother out there," Caine growled, pointing to the cliff. "I've got to bring my sister his body back. I couldn't keep her safe, I broke her myself. I broke that girl's heart! I've got ... I've got to bring him home."

"We all failed her. We won't again," Mace said firmly.

Caine's jaw worked. He looked through the men, and after a tense moment, he jerked his head once in agreement.

MAYA DRIFTED in and out of sleep and fogs after learning of her husband's death. When awake, she still didn't believe it, even though she'd seen it with her own eyes. *She still felt him.*

The facts turned over in her head - freezing conditions, days exposed, a two-hundred-foot drop, shot. But her heart, what was left of it, couldn't let go. When she wasn't trying to make sense of it, she was reliving their wedding day. An endless loop of their kiss played in her mind. It allowed her to block out everything and everyone else. Her eyes were open, unseeing, as the world tiptoed around her.

TEAMS CHECKING in were reporting no sign of either man. After searching for hours, frustration set in. Caine peered into the monitor and saw something giving off a glint moving in the slight breeze. On a hunch that was more whispered prayer than anything solid, he turned on the heat signature. He saw four men on lines and something smaller, barely registering on the screen.

"Go in closer there, by Mace," Caine said. "What's that sticking out there?"

"The signature's too small to be a human," one man from search and rescue said as he examined what caught Caine's attention.

"Get closer..."

Logan moved closer to Mace, with Caine guiding his location.

"Looks like a tree growing out of a break in the rock, Caine, and some kind of reflective piece of something—" Logan examined the area above and around them, zeroing his focus back to the area.

"You see that?" he asked Mace. The snow mounded differently than the other snow around the area. Like someone packed it. He and Mace started moving the snow from around the tree when a bit of heat release into the frozen air around them.

"GET THE CHOPPER OVER HERE NOW!"

63

SUNSHINE

MIKE

Mike heard scraping around him and voices before sunlight blinded him.

"It's a tree pit!" Mace yelped. He slowed his digging in order to make sure the walls of the rudimentary survival shelter didn't collapse.

"Mike! It's gotta be Mike, right?" Mace babbled to himself. "No way Levy survived ... I'll kill him my damn self ... Mike!"

"Yeah," he rasped. His voice sounded strange to himself. "Here! I'm here."

"Holy shit! Shit, shit shit shit shit! He's here! Thank fuck, you lucky son of a bitch!"

Mike was weaker than ever. He tried to pull himself to a sitting position but slid back down. Exhausted from the fall, the exertion of creating the shelter, blood loss from his wounds, maintaining the fire, and no nutrients except snow for days, he regretted several things as he lay there thinking about getting help and dreaming of Maya. One biggy - turning down food after she disappeared. That alone should have killed him.

"A tree pit and a big ass crevice for shelter." Mace laughed in relief and disbelief as he dropped to where Mike was. "You should play the lottery."

"Sure," Mike mumbled. "How's ... my ... Maya..."

"She's in hell, so you have to get back to her," Logan clipped as he checked Mike over. He lifted his eyelids and peered in, using a small flashlight. "She thought you died. We all did. Are you dizzy mate? Can you move?"

Mike moved his arms and legs briefly before petering out again, partially in relief at hearing she had made it through.

"Exhaustion, blood loss," Logan said to Mace and those listening in. Ripping open Mike's heavily damaged black jacket and thermal shirt, he opened his bulletproof vest. "Two stopped, two in, one superficial ... Fuck, he cauterized his own wounds ... Hold his head and neck steady while I turn him ... Shit, no exit wounds, no wait ... got it. How the fuck did you reach this one?!"

"I'm not dead," Mike muttered.

"We know man, we know."

"Tell her ... tell her so she doesn't worry." He groaned as Logan pressed on his ribs.

"You're going to tell her yourself in a few minutes, man," Logan replied seriously. A frown marred his face.

Logan continued his methodical assessment of Mike, barking his findings into the base of operations as the chopper moved into place. Caine's eyes were glued to their location. His phone vibrated in his pocket.

Victoria: We're going to bring in the baby to see if she'll respond.

Caine sighed. *Come on, come on, come on...*

DR. KENT STARTED to head up to see Maya when she was almost run over by a gurney flying through her E.R. to an elevator.

"What the?!" She started toward the elevator when a giant pair of hands moved her out of the way. "Watch out, doc."

She watched with shock as Caine breezed past her, followed by Paul, Bishop, and Blake as they hopped on the elevator. "Wait, who is that?! They have to be seen! Shit!" she yelled as the doors slid closed.

Calling out to a few nurses, she took the stairs, happy she religiously adhered to her gym routine as she double-timed it to Maya's floor. She rounded the door as the elevator doors opened.

"He's stable lady, move," Logan barked.

Dr. Kent's eyes snapped down to a pair of slow blinking, brilliant green ones and she gasped. Throwing herself against the wall, she allowed the team - two female EMTs and Mike's friends - to fly past.

When they finally reached Maya's room, they paused, with Caine and Mace hoisting Mike as he groaned deeply. Paul stood at his back while Logan held an IV bag, and together they helped Mike walk back into his wife's life.

LILITH CAREFULLY PLACED the chubby little one on Maya's bare chest, covering them both with a blanket.[1]

How was it possible for her heart to be shattered yet love her so much? Maya clenched her working hand against her baby's back as tears streamed down her face. "He was right," she hoarsed out. "You are the most beautiful ... he was right ... he loved you before he even knew you, Puddin'."

Lilith continued to check Maya's stitches and check her uterus by pressing on it as she tried to cover her emotional sniffs.

Focused on her work, the noises in the hallway didn't register until they were right outside the door. She glared at the door when whoever knocked.

"Honestly people, wait a—HOLY FUCK!" Lilith swore as she clutched her chest.

Maya jerked her eyes up, clutching her daughter with her good hand tighter, afraid someone else was coming for her. Instead, Caine entered first, gingerly with his arms around her Heart.

Time froze.

Suddenly, Maya felt her heartbeat banging painfully in her chest. It clanged, searching out its mirror as he slowly shuffled into the room. She couldn't believe it, but those green eyes told her it was true. He looked like shit - gaunt, pale, with bruising all around his face, his clothes ragged ... he had never been more handsome. Because he was alive. With her. Them.

"Heart," she whispered. Her lip trembled, followed by her body as she reached for him, too weak to sit up.

"Sunshine," he whispered back as his forehead touched hers. He grabbed her hand in his and slowly slid it to his heart.

They stayed together like that for a long moment until the little baby on her chest wailed.

"You're a dad." She croaked the words past the raw pain in her throat and her emotion. Pulling the blanket down with her good hand, she used the last bit of energy she had to say, "Michaela Andrea Sheppard, meet your beautiful daddy." The last thing she saw before she drifted off to sleep was her husband gently kissing their daughter, his lips cracked and rough, a small sign of his ordeal.

As soon as Maya's eyes closed, the last of Mike's energy left him and his knees buckled.

MIKE

"Falling off a mountain, five days in the wilderness, a pint of donated blood, surgery for gunshot wounds, three broken ribs, a broken collarbone, lacerations, a concussion, and a host of bumps and bruises," Dr. Kent said. "And you still think you can get out of bed?"

"Sunshine," Mike grumbled, coming out of anesthesia.

"I'm here Heart," she whispered, placing her warm hand in his.

He turned his head toward her voice and fought his eyes open. When they did open, he saw her in a hospital bed side-by-side with his.

She looked like shit.

The setting sun highlighted what was left of what must have been one hell of a shiner. She grinned lopsidedly because of a healing split lip. He saw the deep cut on her scalp - the stitches striking a jagged contrast with the skin of her scalp. She had on an ugly ass hospital gown. She looked exhausted. But she was alive. Beautifully alive. And so was he. A little squawk announced Michaela's entry into the conversation he was having with himself about how grateful he was.

He watched with heavy-lidded eyes as Lilith placed Michaela on his chest, where she snuffled close to his neck, warm and soft. The top of her head, covered with a thin little cap, smelled so sweet he took as deep of a breath as he could with three cracked ribs and filled his soul with her. He took the hand not holding Maya's and slowly, with achy stiffness, placed his hand on his daughter's back as she fussed a little. She stilled with the sweetest little sigh.

They were alive, together, and it was all he'd ever need. He closed his eyes, squeezed Maya's hand, and began. "Our Father who art in heaven..."

---

1. Hold Back the River by James Bay

64

EPILOGUE I

THE STINK of smoke and burnt things; the metallic smell of blood, and the stench of death met his nose. Bishop had memorized the crime scene photos, and after doing a quick sweep, he noted the police tape showing the bodies' positions. They determined which bodies Maya tagged and others they suspected Foster Hitchens killed in what was once Maya's living room.

Bishop stopped and knelt at a final dark, dried stain on the steps. Gritting his teeth, thinking of Maya, he began searching around the area. Carefully moving burnt debris from one of Maya's Christmas trees, his eyes caught on a gold glint. Carefully digging through melted plastic and broken glass, his hands closed around something precious. Placing it carefully in a white handkerchief, he slid both back into his pocket.

MAYA WOKE TO A WHISPERED ARGUMENT. She neared the end of her hospital stay, and while she hated being cooped up, she couldn't complain because she was still so tired.

"It's poop, not a bomb," Jake grumble-whispered.

"Then you change it," Bishop bark-whispered back.

"Paul is the one with kids," Logan accused.

"One kid and he's a boy, girls you gotta get all the stuff from all her places," Paul said, horrified.

"Maybe we should wait," Logan whispered.

"Who wants to sit in shit all day?" Bishop groused.

"Maybe you guys should grow a pair — of ovaries." Maya laughed hoarsely from the bed.

"Aaaand ... you woke her up," Jake said, glowering at Bishop.

"Relax fellas, I'd like to change Michaela, if you don't mind. I haven't had a chance to yet."

Bringing her baby - who squirmed in indignation - Bishop stooped low to place her in Maya's lap as she rose with a grimace to a better sitting position.

"She's so soft and warm," Maya whispered as she traced her facial features. Across her delicate brows, around her round cheeks, down her round little nose and perfect lips, she landed at her daughter's small little chin and smiled, grimacing a bit as it pulled on her healing lip.

Taking the changing supplies from Paul, she unwrapped Michaela's swaddle. Her eyes feasted on her baby's every movement, down to her little socks, as her tiny feet kicked and stretched. Changing her carefully and slowly, Maya whispered little coos to her baby. Her friends watched with gentle grins on their faces.

"You did good with one hand," Logan said. "You're a natural."

"I'm clumsy with my left hand, but I guess it'll take practice," she mumbled.

"Do they think it's going to be permanent?" Bishop asked, his voice gruff as he nodded to her limp right arm.

She smiled a small, sad smile that didn't reach her eyes. "They don't know. Either way, we'll figure it out."

She slid her good hand underneath her baby, bent low with a small groan because of her C-section incision and sore body, and scooped Baby Mikki against her chest.

"How are Callista and Amanda doing, Logan? I'd like to see them. I'm supposed to move around more today."

Logan looked uncomfortable for a moment. "They are healin' ...

Callista has a long road ahead and a couple more surgeries. Both of their families have been with them since the storm blew out, but..."

"But what?"

"Amanda's family shrink advises that she not meet you until she has had time to process, and Callista, or her family ... they don't want to see you," Logan said with an apologetic shrug.

Maya looked taken aback for a moment before her shoulders sagged. "I can understand that I guess. I mean, of course. It's not about me at all. They need every peace and comfort."

She looked down at her lap to hide the wet in her eyes. "Can you find out ... if there's anything they need? Their bills or someplace for the family to stay that's close or travel, specialists ... I don't know... make sure they don't have to worry about a thing and please don't say it's from me. Selene, my assistant, can take care of all of it."

"Sure darlin'," he said.

Bishop glanced at the fellas and they took the hint and shifted out quietly. Turning back to Maya, he waited a moment, then sat next to her.

"I need to apologize. For all of this. I—"

"Bishop. I don't want to hear it," Maya said curtly.

Bishop stopped short, his face a mask. "I understand."

"No." She sighed and grimaced. "I don't think you do ... You didn't kidnap me, kill Gunner, sell me out, shoot me ... you didn't do any of this. You worked to save me, and you worked to bring my husband home. Don't borrow guilt."

"It was my brother, under my nose..." His face revealed his private agony - a mixture of rage and heartbreak.

"And it hurts my heart that you have to deal with and live with it. That's hard enough. I don't blame you and Heart doesn't either. Promise ... promise me you'll find out everything you can so he can't hurt anyone else."

Bishop nodded, his face a mask again. Maya figured she was the last person he wanted to talk to about it, so they sat in silence for several long moments, his hand on her immobile one. Finally, Bishop cleared his throat and reached into his pocket.

"I found this ... I wanted to make sure you had everything I could get you back."

He shoved a pristine white handkerchief at her. She cocked her head briefly at a guy like him with handkerchiefs, but she figured it was for chloroforming people and moved on. She looked down at it and then at him with an apologetic shrug. Her one good hand held Mikki to her. He gave an embarrassed look at forgetting her injury and slowly peeled open the soft white material until he came to a pool of gold. Her necklace.

"Oh," she whispered. "Oh. Wow. Thank you, Bishop, thank you."

He nodded, re-wrapped it, and pulled her to him as she quietly wept. They sat there like that for a while until Mike came back from physical therapy.

Bishop was the first in a line of tough conversations. Next, Maya had to relive everything that happened that day for her statement to the police and FBI.

Michael had to relive that, too. Not that he stopped. He had difficulty with processing it. She had difficulty with what she had done to survive. Did she have to shoot those men? She was accurate with nearly every shot she took. She should've aimed lower. She should've done more for Amanda and Callista. If she hadn't gotten lost....

Questions and guilt plagued her for months. Her injuries did too. It took four weeks of physical therapy to get movement back into her arm and six months for it to return to normal. There were days that her bullet wound burned like it was fresh.

Mike struggled with nightmares. The house burning, Maya bleeding, their baby dying. He could never reach them in time because he was always falling into darkness. When that dream didn't come, he had the endless loop of video from Foster Hitchens' torture room. Hitchens wanted to keep memories of what happened there, and with a motion-activated camera, evidence of Hitchens' crimes was irrefutable.

They dealt with the outstanding issues surrounding Michaela's parentage and unfortunate inheritance. Mike adopted Michaela officially and privately as soon as they could get the paperwork through, with no objection from Griffin's grandfather Eli. While they had every intention of Michaela knowing the truth, the private adoption helped keep Michaela safe from both the press and anyone else curious about the girl's connection to the Levys.

In fact, Eli had already met his great-granddaughter.

After an unlucky climber stumbled across Griffin's frozen, broken body, Eli called Maya, requesting a moment to meet.

Mike was more reluctant than Maya and completely against bringing Michaela at all. They compromised and met him in Denver at Xavier's building while keeping the baby in a separate room.

When Eli entered the room, he looked like a man who had once been energetic but who had aged several years in a short time. Still, he carried himself with great grace, though he appeared to be nervous.

Maya and Eli sat awkwardly on the couch in Xavier's office, with Mike standing behind her, his unease apparent.

"Thank you for meeting with me," Eli started taking in the woman before him, who traced nervous patterns with a hand that still didn't work too well. He sighed a deep sigh of a heavy burden. "I won't keep you long, dear ... I am so sorry. About everything, from before you had to go into hiding. I—" his voice faltered. "I am aware of what happened to you and your husband, of what happened to little Amanda and Callista, and all those victims ... " He cleared his throat and patted his pockets.

When he reached into his pocket and withdrew a gleaming white, embroidered handkerchief, she covered his shaking hand with her own. They sat like that for a moment while Eli found his composure. She could tell he was a man who didn't lose it often, but his reserve had been pushed to the point of breaking over the last months.

"We all failed to protect you and your family," Eli said, his back straight as he looked Maya solidly in her eyes, then made direct eye contact with Mike. "My son, his wife, myself, we all failed you when it mattered. But I won't fail my great–ahem–*your* daughter. I would like to provide security for your family for the entirety of your lives, in addition—" he started as he flipped open a leather portfolio and began shifting around papers.

"Michaela truly is the sole heir to Marion and Sharon's estate, and she's my closest surviving relative," he said it like an apology. "She will inherit everything save some funds earmarked for charity, mental health research, and the like. We have relatives that will also receive an inheritance, but essentially, when you bravely fought for her life, she became entitled to—"

"No." Maya had removed her hand from Eli's and shook her head vigorously. "We don't want it. That money is part of why he came after us. It's why I wake up screaming at night, why my husband dreams of us burning ... I cannot allow something else to make Michaela a target. We don't have your kind of money, but we are not poor by any stretch. I ... no. Absolutely not." She shook her head, creating distance between her and the older gentleman.

"We have already decided for you, my dear. Her grandparents willed everything to her irrevocably. She has a trust with a monthly stipend and, provided she's continuing her education, she will receive a certain amount when she turns eighteen, a second amount at twenty-five, and the entirety of her inheritance at thirty-five. The only stipulation is her mental health, to prevent someone like—"

"—like Griffin ... oh fuck me." Maya sighed, dropping her face in her hands.

"Sunshine, we'll figure something out," Michael said, as he crouched beside her and rubbed her back.

"How do you raise a billionaire heiress?" Maya said, her voice full of horror. "What kind of life is she going to have with guards around her and the world at her fingertips to buy whatever she can imagine on a whim?"

"I obviously don't know the answer to how to raise a child well," Eli said sadly. "But ... your reaction tells me you will do a good job, both of you will. She can live as normally as you allow, I'd wager. I think that is partly where I went wrong, and believe me, I've been trying to figure it out..."

"And there's no way you'll do a Buffet and give it all away?" Maya asked from behind her hands.

"Warren is a dear friend and I'll seriously consider your request ... But Maya, I've heard you speak about responsibility and privilege. The daughter you are raising will understand what that means from her first moments and her birthright comes with the economic power and influence to make an incredible impact."

Maya still looked unsure, and Mike spoke up. "This is nothing that will get solved today. We need to talk about it as a family."

"Of course, of course ... could I ... no I'm sorry I have no right," Eli said as he stood and his face flushed red.

Mike looked at Maya and communicated silently, he knew her heart like he knew his own. Mike looked back to Eli as he shuffled papers back into his portfolio nervously.

"Would you like to meet Michaela?" Mike asked.

Eli's head shot up and his face lit with hope. "I would love to."

Mike nodded, left Maya's side to go to the next room, and came back with a little bundle that Eli couldn't take his eyes off of, until she was right in front of him. Mike peeled back her wrappings to reveal more of her face, and Eli inhaled an amazed breath.

"She's beautiful. What a perfect little butterfly," he whispered, to which Mike looked at Maya in surprise at Eli's unwitting use of her nickname. "You can hold her," Mike offered. Eli immediately sat and reached out his arms.

"Wait!" Maya started digging around in her purse and produced hand sanitizer in front of the polished billionaire and - without asking - began squirting it on his hands. As she watched him carefully rubbed them together, she asked, "When was your last flu shot?"

Eli smiled wide, making eye contact with Mike before answering the concerned new mother, who was squeezing a second helping of sanitizer onto his hands.

"At the beginning of October. I've always been in perfect health, until recently," he said.

Maya's brow furrowed with concern. "Are you okay?"

"A broken heart can actually be a physical thing," Eli said, his voice wavering slightly as he looked down and continued to rub the already evaporated liquid further to distract himself.

"Baby cuddles, help with that," Maya said softly as Mike laid the sweet-smelling baby into Eli's arms. He promptly began singing to and rocking the sleeping babe, tracing her features with a soft finger.

After a little while Michaela's eyes slowly blinked open, and she calmly looked at the unfamiliar face and yawned.

"Say hi to your great zayde," Maya said softly, using the Yiddish word for grandfather.

Eli looked at Maya with a mixture of surprise and gratitude, his eyes going moist, then at Mike, who was kissing the top of his wife's head. He looked back down at Michaela, who gave a lopsided smile as she passed gas.

"Is that a dimple?!" Eli asked, laughing as he felt the little rumble from her bottom. It was the first time he had laughed in a long time.

65

EPILOGUE 2

ONE YEAR LATER

IT HAD BEEN a full year for Mike and Maya. The little family recently settled into their beautiful new home, built from the ground up, and were having an early Christmas party to celebrate. It also helped to combat the anxiety of the anniversary of the final run-in with Griffin. Mike and Maya didn't avoid it, but they didn't want it to consume them.

Shay helped decorate Maya and Mike's home and Mike's heart now swelled every time he drove up the mountain to the home his wife had imagined for them to live out their lives. News of the beauty, design and advanced tech of the house was out in the architecture community, but Maya had, so far, refused to share it with the world. She was fiercely protective of their privacy and saw the home as their sanctuary. He watched while she flitted around the sunken living room, making sure each detail was right.

"It's perfect, Sunshine, relax," he said. "It looks like a holiday fairytale."

She looked over at him and smiled as he walked past carrying Michaela, who was trying her darnedest to get down and roam. She had begun walking and was determined to perfect her stride ... and investigate the gifts under the tree. Instead, Mike held her upside down by her ankles. She rewarded him by giggling and squealing that little toddler squeal - all high pitched and wild.

The bell rang and in walked Jake and Leslie.

"Hey, baby girl," he said as he leaned in to kiss Maya on the cheek, tickling her with his beard. Maya was less star stuck now, but still ... she giggled.

"How are you doing?" Leslie asked Maya, looking into her eyes.

"Good."

"Good good?"

"Yeah ... pretty good," Maya said, smiling as Leslie's face grew soft. Leslie knew Maya still had nightmares and while they were much less frequent, they did still happen.

"You look fabulous as always," Leslie said, turning Maya around so she could see the full outfit.

Maya wore a creamy, winter white, cropped sweater with bishop sleeves and a neckline that was high in the front and dipped in a low drape in the back. She paired it with high waist, wide-leg cream slacks with a generous cuff at the bottom. She wore, as always, her heart necklace, but had turned it around so that it hung down her exposed back. That move earned her a good, hard, soul-filling, and ornament-breaking quickie with her bent over the back of the couch not even an hour ago Mike remembered fondly.

Maya and Leslie continued into the living room as Mike and Jake hung back.

"How's our girl doin', comin' off the anniversary?" Jake asked, his eyes watchful on Maya and Leslie.

"She has her days, but she's working through it. We both are, and we're doing it together."

Jake nodded, clapping Mike on the back.

Soon, the rest of the crew began pouring into the house. Tori and Caine and their four kids were first. The kids promptly demanded their Auntie Maya show them a walking handstand again.

The kids were all over the living room in various attempts at handstands or, in Michaela's case, scooting across the floor on her two afro puffs of dark curls with her ruffled pantied bottom high in the air as her deep green holiday dress pooled around her elbows.

When their core group of friends were all present and settled, Maya and Mike stood by the enormous tree Mike and Caine had spent an afternoon cutting and lugging from further up the mountain. Their friendship and brotherhood survived the tree trip, and Maya coined the arguing, grunting, and begrudging appreciation once the work was complete, a new tradition. They stood smiling with their arms around each other and looked out over their friends at a scene that was much happier than the previous year. Maya called everyone's attention by clinking her sparkling cider glass with her wedding ring.

"We asked you here early because we wanted to make new, much happier holiday memories. And to thank you for being there for us when we needed you the most." Maya took a deep breath and swallowed hard. "A year ago ... a year ago..."

Mike caught Caine's reaction as a single tear dropped from his sister's eye and looked over to Thomas who still looked at Maya like a man who had missed out on thirty years of his daughter's life - in awe, like he couldn't drink her in enough.

He squeezed his wife when she faltered. "A year ago, my wife was fightin' for her life. I was fallin' off a mountain, and everything was going to hell. Right, Sunshine?"

Maya laughed despite herself. "Yeah, that sums it up."

"Each of you worked desperately to keep it from falling completely apart, even when there was little reason to hope," she continued. "You saved two other young women; you brought my husband back to me ... you even donated blood."

"And after a tough recovery, no place to live and a brand new baby, you all did everything from opening your homes, to babysitting, to being a sounding board when things got dark ... you never let us feel like we had our asses hangin' out there alone," Mike said. "There's no way to repay you, but I now know I have a host of brothers and sisters in a place I wasn't sure I'd even have a friend."

"We have these for you as a small way to say thank you," Maya said handing out stacks of boxes to Jake and Leslie, Caine and Tori, Paul and Tammy, her dad, Logan, Bishop, Mace and his wife Shannon and Blake.

"Aww! I thought we said no gifts," Tori said as she tore open hers.

"The Foundation," Thomas read out loud, reading the front of the jet-black t-shirt. He flipped it over and saw his old road name on the back. "Smooth Operator," he said with a deep chuckle. The group checked out their own shirts, chuckling at the nicknames.

"This is a kick-ass logo!" Tammy said appreciatively.

The logo was a strong font that combined the 'T" and "F" together and had a grunge look to it. It was completely modern and cool, giving off a badass vibe.

"The Foundation is a new non-profit organization whose charge is simply to make a difference in people's lives. It has seventeen board members, fourteen of whom are in this room right now. Its current operating budget is $14.5 million dollars. Seventy-five percent of which was donated by Eli Levy, fifteen percent donated by Xavier Alexander Enterprises, and the rest by anonymous supporters. Everyone here has an equal vote in what we do. In that portfolio is a list of viable projects and fundraisers," Mike said.

"You changed our lives. The only way we could think to show our appreciation is to help you change more," Maya said, grinning.

As the group excitedly talked about the different project ideas with each other, Mike and Maya beamed.

"I think they like it," she whispered to him.

"Yeah, even Bishop."

Maya looked over at the big fella, conversing with Logan and Jake about a motorcycle rally that collected toys for foster kids.

"Laila's not coming?" Mike asked.

"She said, and I quote, 'I don't do that kind of stuff, cupcake,'" Maya said with a shrug. "I took that to mean she keeps the holidays simple. She also won't wear the shirt unless it's an official uniform of the group." Laughing, she excused herself and slipped out to go to the restroom.

After a few moments, Maya made her way back to the living room, where she got a case of déjà vu. The room was quiet, and Mike sat on the coffee table, staring down at something in his hands.

It was his present.

"Maya, I'm so sorry," Tori whispered close to tears. "I thought it had fallen behind the couch. I didn't know you were hiding it … "

Maya just smiled reassuringly at her as relief slipped over her. Her last secret was out. A bit earlier than she planned, but whatever. She looked at her Heart frozen, staring at a double frame in his hand.

"Baby A and Baby B," she whispered, pointing to each photo.

The room was so quiet you could hear a feather drop.

"You're pregnant."

"Yeah."

"With twins."

"Fraternal. Yep." She giggled.

Long pause...

"He's in shock," Jake said, amused, to Leslie.

"Honey? ... Heart?"

"Officer Asshole!" She snapped her fingers loudly and giggling.

His head snapped up, his expression unreadable, and her heart dropped into stomach. *Oh no, what if...*

"Babe, are you okay? I know it's sooner than we planned..." she said. She bent down and kissed his head.

"Thank you," he said, his voice reverent, barely above a whisper, and rough with emotion.

He grabbed her waist as he slipped off the side of the table to his knees and placed a gentle kiss on her stomach. He placed his hand over her belly and prayed quietly as Maya stroked his hair and bit her lip to keep from crying. When he finished, he lifted her as he stood, holding her high above his head.

A rustle at the door brought Selene and Shay into the living room.

"Ok, what's the weird vibe?" Shay asked.

"We're having babies." Mike grinned up at Maya.

Maya giggled as she gripped his shoulders and nodded.

"Butterfly is going to be a big sister!" Shay screeched.

Maya laughed louder.

"WE'RE HAVING BABIES!" Mike yelled and kids came crashing in from the playroom.

"WE'RE HAVING BABIES!" Maya yelled, throwing jazz hands high in the air.

THE END.

Want even more Mike and Maya?

SIGN up for my newsletter and get an exclusive THIRD epilogue where we see Mike and Maya in the future.

Leave a Review!

Help another reader fall in love with Mike and Maya. Please leave a review on your favorite review site - Amazon, BookBub, GoodReads, Barnes & Noble or social media using #heartbeatnovel!

DON'T FORGET to follow Terreece on your favorite platforms, check her *"About the Author"* for more info.

ALSO BY TERREECE M. CLARKE

Contemporary Romance

Love Never

Elise and Thomas' Novella

Available Now

Chaser

The love story of Shay and Xavier.

Pre-Sale Available Now

Release: December 2022

Fingertips

The love story of Selene and Fox.

Pre-Sale Available Now

Release June 2023

Breath

The love story of Juliette and Logan.

Pre-Sale Available Now

Release December 2023

Adult Coloring Books

Available on Amazon

Black Girl Magic Mandala

Book Boyfriend Adult Coloring Book

Join my mailing list so you never miss a single release AND get behind the scenes looks and bonus scenes!

Acknowledgments

Authors often describe the creation of a novel as a lonely process. The image of the disheveled writer, typing away in the throes of distress or mania, often at night and unsupported, is a popular trope. True writers know reality is more crowded and less dramatic.

I first want to thank my family. My husband, David, never wavered from his belief in me, even though my belief in myself was less steadfast. He is my biggest cheerleader and greatest champion. He gets me. And that means everything. My babies - each one of you have uttered the phrases "You can do it Mom" and "I'm proud of you" multiple times and to know that I've made you proud gives me such joy.

Now here is where I thank people, but allow them their privacy in case they don't want their names in books with a bit of naughtiness:

I want to thank my wider family - from my mom to my sister, and sister-in-law, brothers and brother-in-laws, my aunts, uncles cousins, nieces and nephews, and all my relatives who especially came together to support my family this past year - you know why and know why I'm grateful.

To my dear Shenanigan Sistahs J. J., S. J., J. A.

My homies and voices of calm K.S. & MNOT, S. L.

The Beta Reader Team - it's been a long time coming!

ARC readers - thank you for seeing my vision and extending grace on that last chapter situation. LOL!

Super Duper Advice: V. A. S.

Translators: G. A. Jr., C. A. S.

Tech Aspects: A. W., A. H.

It takes a village to raise a child and an entire crew to raise an author. Love you all to life!

About the Author

A native of Columbus, Ohio by way of Toledo, international bestselling author Terreece M. Clarke is a storyteller whose work as an author, digital marketing consultant, journalist, and plus model dovetails into advocacy for those whose voices are often ignored.

She has written for a variety of websites, magazines, newspapers, and organizations. Her work has garnered the attention of the New York Times, Disney.com, and Jezebel.com.

Heartbeat is her first adult romance novel and became a #1 Amazon international bestseller in two categories. Her first book - "Olivia's Potty Adventures" - spent 16 weeks as a #1 Amazon New Release in two categories.

When she's not juggling family activities, she's writing naughty scenes in coffee shops or she's on Zoom cosplaying as an adult. It's also not unheard of to find her busting a move, killing plants, roller skating, or reading in her bubble. Be sure to follow her on all the socials.

a amazon.com/Terreece-M-Clarke/e/B07746K4WN

BB bookbub.com/authors/terreece-m-clarke

g goodreads.com/terreececlarke

d tiktok.com/@terreece

f facebook.com/terreecemclarke

instagram.com/terreece

twitter.com/terreece

Made in the USA
Monee, IL
20 February 2023

28288053R00319